STAY
WITH
ME

Also by Mila Gray

Come Back to Me

Run Away with Me

STAY WITH ME

MILA GRAY

SIMON PULSE

New York   London   Toronto   Sydney   New Delhi

This book is a work of fiction. Any references to historical events, real people, or real places are used fictitiously. Other names, characters, places, and events are products of the author's imagination, and any resemblance to actual events or places or persons, living or dead, is entirely coincidental.

SIMON PULSE

An imprint of Simon & Schuster Children's Publishing Division
1230 Avenue of the Americas, New York, New York 10020
First Simon Pulse paperback edition November 2017
Text copyright © 2015 by Mila Gray
Originally published in Great Britain in 2015 by Macmillan Publishers
International Limited as *This Is One Moment*
Published by arrangement with Macmillan Publishers International Limited
Cover photograph copyright © 2016 by Brand X Pictures/Corbis
Also available in a Simon Pulse hardcover edition.

SIMON PULSE and colophon are registered trademarks of Simon & Schuster, Inc.
For information about special discounts for bulk purchases, please
contact Simon & Schuster Special Sales at 1-866-506-1949 or
business@simonandschuster.com.
The Simon & Schuster Speakers Bureau can bring authors to your live event. For
more information or to book an event contact the Simon & Schuster Speakers
Bureau at 1-866-248-3049 or visit our website at www.simonspeakers.com.
Cover designed by Karina Granda
Interior designed by Tom Daly
The text of this book was set in Chaparral Pro.
Manufactured in the United States of America
10 9 8 7 6 5 4 3 2 1
This book has been cataloged with the the Library of Congress.
ISBN 978-1-4814-8847-1 (hc)
ISBN 978-1-4814-8848-8 (pbk)
ISBN 978-1-4814-8849-5 (eBook)

For John

Prologue

*D*eath is the one great certainty in life. *That's what my dad used to say.*

Nothing else is certain. Not love. Not happiness. Not your health. If you're lucky enough to be gifted with these things, which isn't a sure thing by any shot, they can all be taken from you in an instant, like toys snatched by a jealous child.

Or maybe that's not true. Maybe sometimes the signs are there and you just miss them. Maybe it's actually your fault if things are taken from you. Maybe love slipped through your fingers because you didn't seize it with both hands when you had the chance. Maybe happiness was stolen from you because you thought you didn't deserve it so you pushed it away. Maybe you lost your health because you ignored the glint of sunlight on a windshield.

The hallway echoes with my footsteps—a hollow sound that matches my heartbeat. The ward is dark but for the emergency exit lights on the far door and the soft glow of a reading lamp at the empty nurse's station.

I walk past his room and my step falters. The door is ajar. The bed stripped bare. I stop and stare at it. The ground tips beneath me, and the world upends briefly before righting itself once again. I lean against the wall, breathing hard, staring at the plastic-covered mattress. How can he be dead?

My brain can't compute. Everything hurts so much, as if my ribs have been ripped open and my insides are being torn out and shredded in front of me. I can't stop screaming. Though no noise makes it past my lips.

He's dead. And it's my fault.

A noise startles me just then and I spin around. The hallway is empty. But then I hear it again: a low sobbing noise, like someone is crying and trying to muffle the sound.

I take a few steps down the hall and notice a light seeping out from beneath a door. I draw in a breath. I had thought the ward was deserted. For one delirious, exquisite moment the thought crosses my mind that it's him. And my heart lifts, swells, almost bursts at the idea but then reason kicks in, tells me it can't possibly be, that he's gone, that he won't ever be coming back. Still, I reach for the handle and push open the door.

What I see is this: skin, a solid wall of muscle. Then I see her; her head thrown back in abandon, her lips parted and her eyes squeezed shut as though in pain. His hands are on her hips, gripping them tight, possessively, and she's straddling him, her arms around his neck, hands knotted in his hair.

For a moment I can't reconcile what it is I'm seeing, and then, when the pieces finally fit together, I stumble backward in shock, banging into the door.

They startle at the noise and her eyes flash open. She sees

me. He turns to look over his shoulder. I stare at him, mouth open. He stares back at me, his expression as horrified as mine.

I turn and run.

Nothing is certain.

Everything can change in a heartbeat.

Didi

G rumpy, Moody, Sleepy," José says, pointing to each of
the doors in turn.

I swallow. My first day isn't going so well. I've
already had to run the gauntlet of a dozen half-dressed marines
catcalling me when I walked through the wrong door and into
the male locker rooms. That sounds like a porn fantasy, and normally Jessa and I would fall about laughing at something like
that happening, but in reality it wasn't in the least bit funny.

I knew that it was going to be a tough assignment and that
being the boss's daughter wasn't going to buy me any favors,
but . . . I wasn't expecting this either.

Just then an alarm sounds, startling me. José takes off. "I'll
be back in a minute. Don't move," he yells over his shoulder.

I stand there in the middle of the hallway, staring at the post-
ers on the walls of marines in triumphant poses with words like
"*Inspire,*" "*Overcome,*" and "*Thrive*" boldly printed across them.
The center is new and shiny and full of platitudes like this.
Personally I'm not sure I'd want to see a picture of a grinning
marine running to victory if I'd just had my leg shot off, but I'm

not an interior decorator, only a trainee psychologist.

Everything is state of the art (apart from the art, it would seem), including the swimming pool that's used for therapy. Currently two hundred wounded marines and other army personnel are being treated at the center for a range of issues, from physical injuries right through to mental illness.

This is the first day of my summer internship and I'm being given a tour. The pool was the first stop, the locker room the second. I saw more in those few startled seconds than I think a tour of the entire facilities will give me—an array of limbless bodies, men missing legs and arms. But clearly not their sense of humor. My cheeks are still burning at some of the comments and suggestions made by the guys back in the changing room.

"Damn it!" someone yells, making me jump.

I scan the corridor. The cursing came from the room on my right.

"Damn!"

I inch toward the door and peer around it. There's a guy on the bed with a bandage wrapped around his eyes. One arm is in a sling. A tray of food sits on the table in front of him and he's struggling with one arm and no sight to open what looks like a carton of yogurt. Frustration seems to be getting the better of him.

I take a step inside the room. He reaches for a spoon, fumbling on the tray and knocking off a dish that clatters to the ground, spraying cereal all over the floor and his sheets.

"Here—" I start to say, but he lets out a roar, stabs the spoon through the lid of the carton, and next thing I know I'm splattered head to foot in a cold shower of strawberry yogurt.

"Oh," I say, feeling it drip from my hair onto my blouse.

"Who's there?" he growls, raising his head.

"Um," I say, blinking yogurt out of my eyes. "My name's Didi. Didi Monroe."

"What are you doing?" he snaps.

"Getting a yogurt facial, it would seem," I mumble, wiping my face with the back of my arm. Great, I just blow-dried my hair. I'm going to need to go and take a shower now and find some new clothes to wear.

"Are you a nurse?" the guy asks, scowling in my direction.

I shake my head and then, realizing he can't see me, say, "No."

"Well, what are you doing in here, then?"

I blink at him in astonishment. "I heard you shouting. I came to see if I could help."

"I don't need your help. I don't need *any* help," he shouts. "Just get out!"

I'm speechless. Totally speechless. What an asshole. "Fine," I stammer. "I'll leave you to it. Enjoy your breakfast."

I walk out into the corridor, cursing under my breath, still dripping yogurt. This day can't get any worse. And then I look up and see a poster of a gurgling baby with the words "*Laugh and the world laughs with you*" written across it in Comic Sans.

José jogs back along the corridor just then and, taking one look at me standing in a puddle of pink yogurt, his eyes widen. "Oh shit," he says, trying not to laugh and failing. "You met Grumpy, I take it."

Half an hour later I exit the bathroom wearing a very unflattering pair of green scrubs that are one size too big. I spent a good ten minutes trying to style them into something that doesn't make me look like a swamp monster, and failed. The pants are so long I've had to roll them up at the ankle, and the top is long in the arms but strains against my boobs. I've put on lashings of lipstick, hoping to divert attention away from my chest, but I can tell by the look on José's face that it isn't working. I may as well wave good-bye to my dignity for the day.

"You're wearing the shit out of those scrubs," José tells me, laughing. "You're going to make a lot of wounded warriors very happy today."

I shoot him a dark look, but the grin has now taken over his face and I find myself laughing too.

José is twenty-nine, an army medic who's already done three tours in Iraq and has now transferred to the center, where he's in charge of this ward. He's trained in physical therapy and he also seems to have been trained in positive mental attitude. Either that or he's been around all these posters for far too long. He's been given the dubious responsibility of showing me around.

"So," he says, "you want to continue with the tour?"

"Sure," I say. "I'm sure there's some ritual humiliation I'm missing out on. We'd better hurry up and find it."

José nods his head in the direction of the doors. "Right, let's go." He checks the time. "We've got half an hour before I take you to your first patient."

I get a buzz in my stomach followed by a swirl of nausea when he says the word patient. I've never had a patient before. I'm not entirely sure I'm ready to have patients. What if they see right through me? What if they figure out I have no clue what I'm doing? No, I remind myself. I have a degree in psychology. I'm studying for a doctorate. I'm smart. I'm capable. I can do this.

"Don't be nervous," José says as he holds the door open for

me. "They're big teddy bears underneath." We pass Grumpy's room. José hesitates. "Well, most of them."

I glance quickly inside. An orderly is clearing up the cereal on the floor while the guy in the bed with the bandages sits facing the window, his jaw pulsing angrily. Teddy bear wouldn't be the term I'd use to describe that one. Grizzly bear, maybe.

"What happened to him?" I whisper as soon as we're past the open door.

"That's Walker," José says, still walking. "He was with Alpha team. Youngest lieutenant in the marines, I hear. Nearly everyone in his unit was killed in an ambush."

I come to a standstill. "Oh my God."

José glances back over his shoulder at me. "Yeah, five men died. Only him and one other guy survived."

Guilt sweeps over me that I thought he was an asshole.

"Welcome to the realities of war," José says before striding off toward the elevator.

Walker

They say it's normal for your other senses to heighten when you lose your sight. I don't know if that's true, but I do know the smell of burning flesh clings to me. It's there all the time, every breath I take acrid with it, making me want to gag. Even now, with the chemical stench of floor cleaner in my nostrils, I can still smell it.

They took the remains of my breakfast tray away and asked if I wanted another, but I shook my head. I don't want breakfast. I want my fucking eyesight back. I want my life back the way it was.

I lean against the pillows and turn to what I guess is the window, but it could just as well be a wall I'm staring at. I've given up trying to picture things. What's the point? The only images that fill my mind are the ones from that day. They play on a loop in my head. There's no pause button. No way to record over it. That's all I see. That's all I think I'll ever see . . .

. . . A blue sky unmarred by a single cloud. A broken-down, rusting car on the side of the road. Jonas glancing over his shoulder, nineteen years old—too young, too nervous—looking at me for reassurance. Me yelling at him to stay frosty. We're on foot patrol in Helmand province. The most dangerous territory in Afghanistan. We cannot afford to be less than one hundred percent focused.

The tension crackles between us like radio static. My breathing's shallow, my attention on the surrounding countryside, dry and dead as a mummified corpse. There's silence all around, gravelike silence, rent only by the cry of a bird of prey riding the currents far above us. Something's not right. I can sense it. My intuition's riding off the scale. Something about the car and the way it's sitting on the side of the road with all its doors flung open bothers me. Sunlight glints off the windshield and for a moment I'm blinded, both by the light and by the realization of what it means. It's not the sunlight blinding me, it's the reflection from a rifle sight.

I open my mouth to yell out, call my men back, but Lutter has reached the car and my command is obliterated by the roar of an AK-47. Bullets start to pock the car. The windshield shatters. We're under attack. My men hit the ground, dive for cover, Sanders behind a rock, Sanchez and Lutter behind the car.

While half my brain struggles to compute—*This can't be happening. This is happening*—the other half of my brain is already pinpointing the location of the shooters, estimating wind direction, taking aim. I start firing back, lying flat on the ground, bullets whipping past my shoulder, smacking into the dirt all around me. There's more than one shooter. We're being attacked from several directions. It's an ambush. I call in our position. Yell for backup. I can't hear anything—no *roger that*—over the noise of machine-gun fire. Did they hear? Are they coming? How long do we have to hold them off for?

Beside me Harrison goes down, pitching face-first into the dirt. Bailey—loudmouthed, twenty years old, on his second tour—is lying in the center of the road, clutching his leg, screaming a high-pitched scream that cuts out in the next second as a bullet slices through his windpipe.

Heart on fire, adrenaline scoring acid through my veins, blood drumming in my ears, I ignore the dancing bullets and sprint toward him, lace my arm beneath his shoulders and drag him back off the road, down into a ditch. His eyes roll in his head, big with fear, bright with pain. He makes a choking, gurgling sound and blood foams over his lips. My hands are hot with it, slippery with it. I fumble for the tourniquet on my belt.

Taylor, the unit medic, is at my side. He jabs a morphine shot into Bailey's thigh and snatches the tourniquet from my hand. I roll onto my stomach, poke my head above the ditch, and do a head count.

Sanchez and Lutter are still sheltering behind the car, taking turns to spot and return fire. Sanders, barely concealed behind a boulder, makes a mad dash for it, out into the open, before throwing himself down in the dirt beside Sanchez. He's opting to ride out the ambush with them, behind the solid wall of metal. Oh shit. With a burst of clarity, I see the plan.

The car. They're trying to get us all to shelter behind the car. I scan the hillside where the gunmen are sheltering and catch a glimmer of sunlight bouncing off metal. Rocket launcher.

I stand up, my knee jolts out, a hot eruption of pain behind my kneecap. "Sanchez!" I holler. "Get back!"

I hit my radio button.

Sanchez turns to look at me.

"The car!" I yell.

I see the flare of understanding cross his face, and then it's gone, obliterated by a wall of white light that opens up the sky, rips apart the earth beneath my feet, and sends me hurtling headfirst into an abyss.

I'm still falling.

"Hey, Lieutenant!"

It's Sanchez. He always bangs his wheelchair into the door to announce his arrival. I hear the electric whir of the chair as he maneuvers his way into the room uninvited, and grit my teeth. It's not that I don't appreciate his company—it's better than listening to Fox News all day and the endless bullshit from the stream of neurologists, orthopedic surgeons, and trauma counselors that flow through my room; it's just that Sanchez is relentlessly positive. The guy lost a leg and an arm and you'd think he'd won a season ticket to see the Lakers. I don't know what to do with that.

"You seen the hot new intern?" he starts before stopping abruptly. "Oh shit. Sorry, dude."

Maybe if I ignore him he'll go away.

"She's Doctor Monroe's daughter, I hear. You should check out the bazungas on . . . shit. Sorry."

I grimace at him.

"She's hot, that's all," he goes on.

Hot. Right. That's a pointless descriptor for me these days.

"She looks like Vanessa Hudgens, only with bigger—you know . . ."

I have no idea who Vanessa Hudgens is, and even if I did I couldn't care less.

"I don't know what Doctor Monroe's thinking, letting her into this zoo. It's like throwing fresh meat to hungry raptors."

Someone clears their throat in the doorway. I turn my head. "Sanchez?"

It's José, the medic guy who's in charge on this floor. "You got an appointment over in prosthetics. You're late."

"All right, all right. I gotta go," Sanchez says to me. "They're fitting me for my bionic arm. I'm going to make Robert Downey Junior in his Iron Man suit weep with envy. See you later."

José is still in the room, and now Sanchez is gone I can tell that there's someone else alongside him. Maybe it's the heightened senses thing, but I can tell it's a woman. She's wearing perfume— something that reminds me of spring: fresh-cut flowers, dew on grass—and for a moment it overrides the stink of singed hair and crisply burning flesh. I draw it in deeply, fill my lungs with it, but then an image of Miranda pops into my head. Unbidden. Unwelcome. I shove it hastily away. I'd rather suffer the images of bloody limbs and flying bullets than think about my ex-girlfriend.

"Walker, I've got someone with me. Her name's Didi Monroe. You got a few minutes?"

"Well," I say drily, "I was about to go run a three-minute mile and then maybe do some paragliding. Let me see if I can clear my schedule."

"Nice to see your sense of humor returning," José says.

"Who says I was being funny?"

"So, you got a few minutes?" José asks.

"No," I say.

"Come on, you haven't had a visitor in a month. Play nice."

I take a deep breath. With the loss of mobility comes a total loss of privacy. Just another thing I'm expected to suck up without complaint.

"Fine, whatever," I say, knowing that I don't have a choice.

They might call this place a "Center of Hope and Care," but that's just a fancy term for "cripple prison." The only difference between this place and Guantanamo is that here they drive you crazy with positivity, and there they do it by blasting Barry Manilow and Christina Aguilera at you twenty-four-seven.

"Okay, I'll leave you to it. I'll be back in half an hour," José says. I roll my eyes beneath the bandage. Half an hour? I have to make small talk for half an hour?

If I had a choice I'd take the orange overalls and Manilow's greatest hits.

Didi

I take a deep breath before entering the lion's den. I'm just grateful that José didn't introduce me as a psychology intern, because I think Walker might be the kind of patient who rips up psychology interns with his bare hands and eats them for breakfast. Coated in strawberry yogurt.

He looks about as willing to spend this half an hour with me as I would be to take a stroll naked through the canteen downstairs.

I tug down my too-tight scrub shirt, self-conscious after overhearing Sanchez's comment about my boobs, but then remember that Walker can't see what I look like.

"Hi," I say in an overly bright voice. "I'm Didi." I hold out my hand, then snatch it quickly back when I realize how dumb that is. I glance at his free hand, the one not in a sling. It's resting on the bed. I could take it and shake it, but intuition tells me that wouldn't be a good idea. He might be injured, but I have no doubt that his instincts are still razor sharp. I've had a quick look over his notes. José was right. He was the youngest ever marine to make lieutenant, and even prior to his injury he had been cited twice for bravery.

"We met earlier, actually," I say, taking a step closer to the bed. "I came to see if you needed any help."

He doesn't say anything in reply, and even though I can't see his eyes I can tell he's glowering. Oh man, this is going to be hard work.

It's hard to tell what he looks like because the bandage obscures a lot of his face, but there's no mistaking he's a good-looking guy—in a gruff, stubbly kind of way. He has thick dark hair, pale olive-colored skin, and a slight cleft in a solidly square jaw, which at the moment is covered in at least four or five days' worth of beard.

He's wearing a white T-shirt that stretches across his shoulders and emphasizes an impressive build. If this is how he looks after who knows how many weeks lying in a hospital bed, I'd like to see what he looked like before he was injured.

"What should I call you?" I ask. "Lieutenant?" I know how important it is to maintain respect for wounded soldiers' ranks, especially at a time when it might feel like they've lost everything else.

"Walker's fine," he answers in a flat voice.

"I'm interning here for the summer," I say. "I'm just meeting people today. Getting to know the lay of the land—"

"Which department?" he interrupts.

"Sorry?"

"Which department?"

"Um, clinical psychology. I'm studying for my doctorate."

"You're a head doctor." Not a question.

"No," I say.

"I don't need one of those."

"Okay," I say. "That's good. Because I'm not one."

He turns his head away from me as though not interested in what I have to say.

"How long have you been here?" I ask after a moment.

"Six weeks," he answers with a barely disguised sigh.

"And how would you say it's going?"

He turns slowly back to face me. There's a slight smile twitching on his lips. "And you say you're not a head doctor?" he says. "That's a classic therapist question."

I press my lips together. He's right. My dad uses it all the time on me.

"Okay, on a scale of one to ten, how much does this place suck?" I ask him, deciding to switch gears.

He smiles now, but ruefully. "Eleven."

"You know they spent twenty-seven million dollars on this place trying to make it as non-sucky as possible?"

"Yeah? Well, they failed. At the very least they could have put locks on the doors."

"I see your point. If there were locks on the doors you wouldn't have people wandering in offering to help you and getting covered in yogurt for their pains."

His brow creases with a frown.

"And you could lock yourself away and ignore everyone who tries to talk to you and just suffer in silence instead. Oh wait," I say, "you don't need a lock for that. You're doing pretty well without one."

His cheeks start to flush. His free hand balls into a fist. Crap. I think I might have overstepped the mark. I didn't mean to needle him, I just wanted to gauge his reaction, find out where on the grief scale he is. José told me he's been depressed since they brought him in.

I've had my own brush with grief via Jessa, so I have some idea of the different stages involved. First comes denial, then anger, then bargaining, before depression hits and finally, sometimes days after, sometimes years, comes acceptance. It's obvious that though he's depressed he's also still really angry.

Walker doesn't speak for a few moments. I think we're a long way off acceptance here.

"You should leave," he says quietly, almost under his breath.

I flinch a little, my cheeks flaring. "I—"

"You know nothing about what I need or what I've been through," he says in a voice that shakes with anger. "No one does."

"What about Sanchez?" I ask. I know Sanchez was the only other survivor besides Walker. And it seems to me that Sanchez has lost just as much as Walker.

Walker's jaw knots, unknots. His fist stays clenched, the knuckles blanching white.

"Sanchez wasn't responsible for them," he says, and I notice the way his voice is straining, almost cracking. "It was my team. They're dead because of me."

I take a step toward him, my stomach cinching tight and a wave of empathy rising up inside me at the grief etched on his face. "That's not true," I start to say, but he turns abruptly away, his expression hardening to stone.

"Just go," he barks.

I open my mouth to argue but find I have nothing to say. The rage and the pain bouncing off him are palpable, as powerful as a shock wave. It spins me around and sends me straight to the door, which I close quietly behind me as though I'm scared of setting off a bomb.

I stand in the corridor, breathing hard and cursing myself silently. I was just supposed to be getting to know him, not trying out what I learned in Psychology 101. I'm such an idiot. My first day and I'm already messing up.

"Your negativity is your only hurdle."

"They really like their motivational posters, don't they?" I whisper to the person sitting beside me.

He looks up and I notice his eye and his mouth are sagging on one side. He glances at the poster on the opposite wall, of clouds scattered across a neon-blue sky with a Photoshopped rainbow bursting out of them.

He smirks. "Yeah," he says with a strong Southern drawl. "They spend millions of dollars of taxpayers' money turning you into a lethal killing machine, you get some sergeant major yelling in your face every day for months, calling you every name under the sun, *son of a bitch* being the least of them, and then, the minute you're injured, they surround you with pictures of rainbows and clouds and smiling babies. All I need is a fucking unicorn."

I laugh under my breath.

"It's like the Care Bears designed this place." He sighs.

Seeing me smile, he offers his hand. I take it.

"Callum Dodds," he says.

"Didi Monroe."

His handshake is solid, his grip firm. Before I can stop myself, I glance down at his legs. Or rather at the space where his legs used to be.

"Fallujah," he says, noticing me looking. "Roadside bomb."

"I'm sorry," I say, looking up, flushing.

He smiles grimly and taps his head. "I got a metal plate in my head too. Walk me through airport security and the X-ray machine'll light up like a Fourth of July firework."

I notice now that he has a deep scar running down the left side of his face. The muscle is slack underneath it, and that's what's causing the downturn to his mouth and eye. He's barely twenty-five years old but he looks twice that.

We're sitting in the physical therapy center—a large room with lots of ropes, pulleys, and machines. Three guys in T-shirts and sweatpants are being put through their paces and I'm observing to see how it works. One guy is being taught to walk on a prosthetic leg, another is bench-pressing weights, grunting with determination as sweat rolls down his arms.

Sanchez is over in one corner being fitted with a prosthetic arm. He's grinning and making the physical therapist laugh. I wonder at the difference in how people deal with their injuries and what it is that makes Sanchez so upbeat in the face of everything that lies ahead of him. I wonder how I would cope in his situation.

"So, you some kind of doctor?" Callum asks me, nodding at my scrubs.

"No," I say, turning back to him. "I just had an accident this morning."

He raises his eyebrows.

"No! Not that kind of accident! A run-in with an exploding yogurt carton."

He nods. I wince. Bad choice of word. "Where are you from?" I ask quickly, trying to cover it up.

"Alabama originally."

"Do you have family here? On the base?" I ask.

He shakes his head. "No. No family. I grew up in foster care. Never met my mom. Don't know who my father is."

"I'm sorry," I say again. God, that word seems so painfully inadequate in this place.

He shrugs. "The marines is my family. It's my whole life. *Was* my whole life." He takes a deep breath. "Don't know what the hell I'm supposed to do now."

One of the physical therapists comes over just then and drops a hand on Callum's shoulder. "Get back on your feet, Corporal, that's what you're supposed to do now."

I glance sideways at the physical therapist, frowning. Is he trying to be funny? Dodds raises his eyebrows and smiles at me. But it's not a real smile. It wouldn't fool a child.

"You ready for your session?" the physical therapist asks.

"As I'll ever be, I guess," Dodds says.

The physical therapist stands aside and lets Dodds wheel himself over to the far corner of the room. I watch for a few minutes before standing up and heading to the door, appreciating my body in a whole new way and vowing never again to complain about having short legs.

Walker

The first time I saw Miranda she was diving into the water off the pier at her parents' house in Hyannis. She was blond, whippet thin, beautiful in a way that few people outside the pages of a fashion magazine are—and she knew it. She was my friend Brad's little sister. A true East Coast princess whose parents had given her everything she ever wanted, including a brand-new Mercedes for her sixteenth birthday, a nose job, and an unshakeable belief in her own position at the center of the universe. A belief that was cemented by the actions of every boy within a fifty-mile radius for whom Miranda Scholes *was* the center of the universe.

There was an unofficial contest among us all to see who could get her to notice them. And she chose me. I won. For four years I got to call her my girlfriend. I thought she was the love of my life: the girl who stood by my side at my graduation from the Naval Academy, holding on to my uniformed arm, beaming with pride. The girl the rest of the boys would make lewd comments about when they were trying to get to me. Her photo was stolen so many times from my bunk during basic training and returned to me so many times with stains on it that I hid it away and instead made do with the photos of her on my phone, which I kept password protected.

I thought I would marry Miranda. I'd spent three years saving every dollar of my wages so one day I could afford the kind of engagement ring a girl like Miranda Scholes would say yes to. Three carats, and she did. The wedding date was set for November, when my tour was due to end.

She came to visit me in the hospital the week they shipped me back to base in pieces. She came with my parents, but she waited until they'd left before she told me she was breaking things off.

"Things are different now," she said in a faraway voice. She wouldn't even come and stand by me when she gave me the news. She stood over by the door, eyeing her escape, no doubt, and delivered her speech with cool perfection, as though she'd rehearsed it for hours in front of the mirror, which, knowing her, she probably had. She hadn't touched me the whole time she was there, other than for a brief cold sweep of the lips across my forehead when she first entered the room. I think I knew from that moment, when she avoided my lips and wouldn't take my hand, that she was no longer mine. It made me wonder, though, if she ever had been. How else was it possible that she could be so cold?

"I don't think I can be there for you or give you what you need," she explained with the clinical detachment of a doctor.

"I just need *you*!" I yelled at her. "I just need to know you're there for me. That's all."

She didn't say anything. No, that's a lie. She did. She said, "Sorry."

I hate that word. I can't count the number of times I've heard it in the last six weeks. Enough times to last me a lifetime.

So that was it. She said "sorry" as if that one word was enough to wipe the slate clean. Then she walked over to the bed and I heard the clink of something metal being dropped on my nightstand.

I heard her sobbing as she ran down the hall, and I reached over, fumbling blind, to find out what it was she'd left behind, knowing before my fingers closed around it that it was her engagement ring, but not ready to believe it.

I roll my head back against the pillows and take a deep breath in, then out. Fuck this day. Fuck this life.

Didi

A dozen red roses sit blazing on the table by the door. I notice them as soon as I walk into the house and smile to myself while simultaneously rolling my eyes. My parents are the most loved-up couple since Anthony clapped eyes on Cleopatra.

They've been married twenty-eight years and they still go on dates and they still make out like sex-crazed teenagers at any and every opportunity, including when there are other people in the room. In fact, an audience seems to spur them on. When I was a kid I was crucified by the embarrassment of it, especially when I had friends over. One time my parents gave an impromptu sex-ed lecture to a group of my friends using a condom and a banana as props. My mom is a famous sex therapist with her own radio show and several books that have made the *New York Times* best-seller list. She thought she was doing us all a favor because the sex education at our school had seemingly been written by the Pope, but my friends went home and told their parents, who weren't that happy that their eleven-year-old daughters were being taught how to roll condoms onto pieces of fruit.

Now, though, I'm no longer embarrassed. I'm thrilled that my parents are still together while most of my friends' parents are long-divorced. But at the same time, though I'd never admit it out loud (partly because it would be an open invitation for them to sit me down on the couch and delve into my psyche), I also blame them for my own relationship issues. Well, them and one particular ex-boyfriend.

They say that a girl's relationship with her father colors all the future relationships she will ever have with men. If you have a good dad, it raises the bar—you'll have high expectations of men and how they should treat you. Well, I not only have the highest expectations of men, but I also have the highest expectations of love. I've spent my life staring it in the face. I know it's real and not just a fiction. I know it's attainable.

I just don't know if it exists for me.

"Did you see the flowers?" my mom asks as I walk through into the kitchen where she's busy cooking up a storm.

"Yeah, what's the occasion?" I ask, dumping the bag full of my yogurt-stained clothes on the floor. "The anniversary of the first time you and dad peed in front of each other?"

"Ha-ha," my mom answers as she expertly dices an onion, pausing to brush her wild red curls out of the way with her forearm. "They're actually for you."

"For me?" I ask in surprise. "Who are they from?"

My mom raises an eyebrow at me. She wouldn't know, is what she's saying. In our house privacy is sacrosanct. When I was a kid, my parents used to encourage me to shut my door and "experiment with self-love."

My mom frowns at the sight of my green scrubs. "Why are you wearing surgical scrubs?"

I don't answer as I'm already walking back into the hallway. Spying the little card buried in the bouquet, I fish it out and tear it open.

Didi,

Thinking of you,

Zac x

My heart does a little splutter and I stare at the card for several seconds, dumbstruck. Zac? Why on earth is he sending me flowers? I haven't heard from him in close to three months.

"Hi, darling," my dad says, coming up behind me and startling me. He's wearing his glasses halfway up his forehead and carrying an armful of files. "Who's the lucky man?" he asks, nodding at the flowers.

"They're from Zac," I say, turning to him, shock making me feel a little faint.

"I thought you two weren't a thing anymore," my dad says.

"We never were a thing exactly," I say, shaking my head in confusion and following my dad in a daze back into the kitchen.

"Our daughter has an A-list admirer," my dad informs my mom.

"Well, of course she does," my mom says, smiling.

I watch my dad dump his files on the table and then walk over to my mom. They're roughly the same height, but while my dad is a pencil-drawn straight line, my mom is a curve drawn with a highlighter pen. My dad puts his arm around her waist and kisses her full on the lips. I turn away and ignore the wet smacking sounds.

"Are they from Zac or is another Hollywood star trying to

court you?" my mom asks once she has disengaged from my dad and come up for air.

"No. They're from him. I just don't know why. And *courting*? We're not living in the eighteenth century, Mom."

I grab my bag of dirty clothes and head through to the laundry room, my heart still doing a wild skittering dance.

Zac Ridgemont, recently voted into the top ten actors under thirty, just sent me roses. There are armies of teenage girls and probably a sizeable cohort of middle-aged women who would kill to be me right now. As I empty my dirty clothes into the washer, I ponder what these flowers, sent out of the blue, might mean. . . .

"Excuse me."

I turn and almost spit out my mouthful of champagne.

Zac Ridgemont. It's Zac Ridgemont. *The* Zac Ridgemont. Standing in front of me.

"I was just trying to get something to eat."

"Oh," I say, as my face flames red hot. *Of course he didn't come over here to talk to you, Didi. You're just blocking the cheese table.*

I move out the way and Zac starts perusing the cheese.

"No one ever eats at these things, have you noticed that?"

Is he talking to me? I glance around but we are the only people in this corner of the room. Everyone else is networking as though their lives depend on it, including Jessa, my "date" for the night.

"Um . . . ," I stammer, my mouth as dry as sand. "Uh, no. This is my first time at one of these things." These things being Hollywood industry parties.

Zac turns around, holding a cracker laden with Brie. His skin is so smooth and so perfect that I have an urge to stroke his cheek and check if he's real. He looks like he could be made out of plastic and fairy dust.

"But if they have cheese tables like this at all of them, it won't be my last," I blurt. "I'm going to become a more regular attendee than Lindsay Lohan at rehab."

Zac flashes me a grin that reveals his dimples and makes my stomach twist into a fisherman's knot. "You're funny," he says.

"Thanks," I answer, because I'm not sure what else to say.

"Are you an actress?" he asks next.

I shake my head. "God, no. Though I did play the role of a manservant in a school production of *Hamlet* once."

Zac cocks an eyebrow.

"I went to an all-girls' school," I explain.

"No," he says, "I was just wondering how you managed to convince anyone you were a manservant." His gaze falls briefly to my chest and I feel momentarily self-conscious before I realize that Zac Ridgemont—*the Zac Ridgemont*—is checking me out!

"I was a late developer," I answer, feeling my skin start to warm under his gaze.

"Who are you here with?" he asks.

"Um, Jessa Kingsley," I say. "She's my best friend," I add, then mentally slap myself for sounding like a five-year-old.

Zac nods and takes a bite of his cracker. I might be mistaken, but his gaze seems to flit over my body again. I throw back my shoulders and suck in my stomach.

"Awesome," Zac says. "You want some cheese?"

I nod, words temporarily deserting me.

"Let's try the Camembert," he says.

"Didi!"

My mom appears in the doorway. "What are you doing? I've been calling you. Dinner's on the table."

I start. I'm standing over the washer, staring into space, remembering that first night with Zac.

"Coming!" I say, and in my fluster hit the on button before remembering I've forgotten to add detergent.

We talked for most of the night, standing beside the cheese table, and then, when I left, Zac asked for my number. He called two weeks later, after I'd given up on ever hearing from him and had resolved that that night would just be filed away as a story to tell the grandchildren.

He took me to dinner the following night, and the week after that we went to the movies together and kissed in the back row while on the big screen Channing Tatum saved the world. I felt as giddy as a teenager—couldn't eat, kept checking my phone every three seconds to see if he'd texted, bored Jessa senseless debating every single look and word that we'd exchanged and what they might mean, even let my imagination leap ahead to red carpets and the moment he'd introduce me to his parents.

On our third date he invited me to his place for dinner—Chinese take-out—and I slept with him. I never heard from him again.

I gave myself a stern talking-to about not allowing myself to fall either for a guy or into bed with a guy ever again, not until I knew beforehand whether I could one hundred percent trust him. Because the fact is I don't want one-night stands. I want something more meaningful than that. I want a relationship, but you'd think that I was asking for the moon. Most guys I meet just want sex with no strings.

I've pored over every detail of the last night Zac and I spent together, wondering where it all went wrong. I've worn the memories thin examining them, from the moment he opened the door—barefoot and holding a bottle of champagne—to the moment he took me by the hand and led me down the hallway to his bedroom, to the moment I stood in front of him in my underwear, shaking with nerves and buzzing from the champagne, and he pulled me down onto the bed, to the actual deed, which was good but not mind-blowingly, headboard-breakingly good or anything. And, if I'm being totally honest, over a little fast and less than satisfactory on my part. But it's never like it is in the movies, and it also was our first time together, and what percentage of women have an orgasm with a partner the first time anyway?

I actually know the answer to that. It's in one of my mom's sex books. It's eleven percent.

"What are you thinking about?" my mom asks as I sit down at the table.

"Oh, nothing," I say quickly, reaching for the bread.

"How did it go today?" she asks.

I shake away the image of Zac smiling up at me from his bed.

"Not so good," I sigh, the images of Zac bursting like bubbles as they're replaced by images of Walker yelling at me to get the hell out of his room. "I don't know," I say, stuffing a hunk of bread into my mouth. "I just feel like I kept putting my foot in it all the time. By saying things like that to people with no feet, for example."

My mom and dad nod their heads thoughtfully in unison but don't say a word. They remind me of those nodding dogs you sometimes see on car dashboards.

"In fact," I say, "I think I really messed up with one patient."

"Which one?" my dad asks.

"His name's Walker."

My dad reaches for his wine and takes a sip. "Ahhh yes, Lieutenant Walker."

I wait a few moments but he doesn't continue.

"What's his deal?" I ask, taking a sip of my wine.

My dad looks up and gives me a wry smile. "You know I can't discuss my patients with you."

"So he *is* your patient," I say. I'd been curious to know. My dad only deals with the most serious cases at the center: those on suicide watch or who are dealing with psychosis or other extreme symptoms of post-traumatic stress disorder.

"I assess everyone when they're brought in," my dad says. "You know that. But yes, I'm still seeing him a few times a week."

"Does he talk about it? About what happened?"

My dad shakes his head. "No. Not so far. He's what you might call a recalcitrant patient."

I nod. That's an understatement. Does he yell at my dad too, I wonder?

"What's his story?" my mom asks.

"He was in an ambush," my dad answers. "Helmand Province, I think. His whole unit was caught up in a gunfight. It was on the news about six weeks ago, do you remember? Five marines were killed."

"Oh yes, I remember that," my mom says, shaking her head. "So terrible."

I chew my food. I hadn't put two and two together, but now I remember the story: the photographs of the five dead marines, all in their Dress Blues, the shots of the funerals, the flag-draped coffins, a still image of the charred and twisted metal ruins of the car, a photograph of the heroic survivor who dragged his team member to safety. That was Walker. It's hard to reconcile that image with the man in the hospital bed.

"How do you even start to help someone heal from that?" I ask, shaking my head in bewilderment.

My mom reaches across the table and takes my hand. "By listening, darling. By being kind. And patient."

"Every mistake is a chance to learn and improve," my dad says—something he's been saying to me since I was a kid and accidentally burned down the kitchen trying to make my parents breakfast in bed on their anniversary.

I look between my mom and dad, feeling overwhelmed by all the advice but also grateful. I'd forgotten how much I enjoyed their company. Being away in LA at college I don't get to see them that often anymore.

I exhale loudly. "It's just so much harder than I thought it was going to be."

My dad smiles at me. "Darling, you're not there to fix them. You're just an intern. It's my job to help them get better. You're just there to observe and learn."

I open my mouth to protest. I don't want to just observe and learn, I want to help—but I remember my mom advising me just now on the need for patience and shut my mouth.

"How's Zac?" my mom cuts in. "Did you speak to him yet?"

Though she tries to keep her tone and expression neutral, I know there's a judgment behind it. She's wary of Zac because she doesn't think he behaved in a gentlemanly way. Respect and honesty are big buzzwords with her.

I reach for my wine.

"What? Why are you rolling your eyes?" my mom asks.

I take an exasperated breath and pull a face at her. "I haven't called him yet."

"Well, if you need to talk about sex, or anything else, you know my door is always open," she reminds me.

Walker

Sex. I miss it. Or rather, I miss closeness. I miss touch. I don't miss Miranda per se, but I miss making love. Was it ever that, though, with her? I don't know. Maybe it was just sex and I was kidding myself all along.

I think back to the last time with Miranda, six months ago, even though dredging the memory up is like necking a bottle of tequila: an exhilarating rush of fire flows instantly through my veins, making me feel alert and alive, but I know that if I keep going—keep remembering—I'm going to regret it in the morning. Like an alcoholic, though, I can't stop myself from reaching for the bottle.

She flew out to California to see me before I shipped out. We spent the whole weekend locked in a hotel room.

I push the memory away. I don't want to think about Miranda. When I think about her, about sex, I remember that I'm never going to be with a woman ever again. Who's going to want a blind cripple?

I remind myself what Doctor Monroe said about not allowing negative thoughts to take hold, but trying to stop them is like trying to stop an avalanche with a feather duster. The fact is as obvious to me as the darkness I'm shrouded in. No one is ever going to want me again. I'm on my own from here on in.

I take a deep, shuddering breath and slam my fist into the mattress. The goddamn darkness. I can't get away from it. It's like being slowly buried alive. Every day another shovelful of dirt gets thrown on top of me.

The corridors are silent, apart from the odd echoing footstep when the medic on duty does his rounds and the muffled sound of a radio playing at the nurse's station down the hall. It's night-time. The only difference for me between night and day is that at night I hear the sobs coming from the room at the end of the hallway—a guy called Dodds who had his legs blown off in Fallujah. He gets nightmares, too, apparently. No shit.

I think about fumbling for the button on the bed that summons the nurse and begging a sleeping pill, but the pills seem to amplify the dreams, so I don't. I can't deal with the dreams right now.

So instead I zone out to the sound of the radio—it's José on duty, pulling a night shift for the extra money—and for something to focus on, other than the images in my head, I start counting down the number of times I've been touched in the last six months.

After Miranda, there was my mom and my dad, both hugging me good-bye at the unit's send-off. There's a picture my dad took of me with my arm around my mom. I shook the hand of Colonel Kingsley that day too. My mom probably has a photo of the occasion framed on the wall at home. There won't be any more photos like that.

Then there were the four months in Afghanistan living in a

tent with twelve guys passing wind and jerking off all around me, no physical contact with anything except my rifle and body armor. After that it was Sanchez. I can still remember the dead weight of him in my arms, the stabbing pain in my shoulder and the sheering agony in my knee as I stumbled blindly for what felt like miles, trying to get away from the blast zone and the flames and the bullets. I needed to save one person. At least one. That was all that was going through my mind.

I did, I remind myself angrily. I saved Sanchez. But does he thank me for it? Would he rather I'd just left him to bleed out in the dirt? I haven't asked him. But I know that if it was me, I'd rather have been left to die.

The memories are muddled after that—jumbled and in pieces. I remember the doctors and the nurses at the combat hospital at Camp Dwyer holding me down, forcing needles into my arms; the reassuringly deft touch of a nurse who squeezed my hand as the anesthetic crept like ice through my veins; the chaplain visiting me as I lay recovering in my bed, taking my hand for a brief moment before I snatched it away and told him where to stick his prayers; Major Foster patting me on the shoulder after coming to my room to tell me about the medal for bravery they were awarding me, not a scratch of sarcasm in his voice; the C130 pilot strapping me into my seat for the journey back to base; the orthopedic surgeons here at Pendleton examining my leg; the opthalmologist peeling the bandage off my eyes and running a battery of tests; José helping me to the bathroom and off with my clothes so I could shower that first week when I was little more than a zombie; my mom, smelling of breath mints and perfume, hugging me when they came to visit; my father's contrasting dry, formal handshake.

A scream jolts me suddenly upright in the bed. My heart rams into my ribs with the force of a pickax slamming into rock, and in an instant I'm back there. Back in Helmand on that dusty road, bullets flying overhead, staring at Bailey clutching his leg, writhing in agony and screaming, the sound piercing straight through metal, straight through bone, rattling around my head like a dummy bullet.

The scream cuts out and becomes a hacking sob—and I flop backward against the pillows, breathing hard, remembering where I am.

It's just Dodds. I'm in the hospital. Or rather, "The Center for Hope and Care." An ironic name if ever there was one. There should be a sign over the door saying *Abandon all hope, ye who enter here.*

My heart rate takes a few minutes to settle back to normal. I listen to the sound of José's voice stretching along the corridor. He's talking gently to Dodds, sounding like a father soothing an upset toddler back to sleep.

I fumble blindly on the nightstand until my hand closes around the TV remote and I smack a few buttons on it until the TV blasts on. Fox News. I can't figure out how to change the channel, so I'm stuck with it. A story is playing about an eleven-year-old girl who's fighting her school over a Chapstick ban. I settle back and listen. Anything to keep the nightmares at bay.

Didi

I press my lips together and blot my lipstick before stepping back to check my reflection in the mirror. This morning I'm wearing a pencil skirt and a white silk shirt, buttoned high. I've also borrowed a pair of my mom's heels. I look the part of a professional. I just wish I felt like one. In reality I feel like an actress in a movie, wearing a costume and rehearsing my lines in the bathroom before the cameras roll into action.

I'm ready to go out into the corridor when my phone rings. I pull it out. The number is undisclosed.

"Hello?" I say, putting the phone to my ear.

"Hi, beautiful."

It's Zac. My heart rate doubles and I have to lean against the sink to steady myself. "Hi," I say.

"How are you doing?" he asks.

"I'm great." I glance up and catch sight of my reflection in the mirror. Two bright spots of color have appeared on my cheeks.

"You got the flowers, then?" he asks.

"Yes, they're beautiful. Thanks. Did you get my text? I would have called but I wasn't sure if it was the middle of the night where you were." I pause. "Where exactly are you?"

"Vietnam," Zac answers.

"What are you doing there? I thought you were in Hawaii?"

"No. That film wrapped. I'm doing reshoots for *Dogs of War*."

"The Vietnam War movie?" I ask, frowning. I think I remember him telling me that film was already in postproduction.

"Yep, that's the one," he says. "The ending didn't play well to test audiences so they're reshooting the final scenes. In this version my character gets to live."

"Oh, great," I say, wishing there was an option for reshoots in real life. I'm sure the real soldiers here at the center would appreciate that. "How's it going?" I ask.

"It's hotter than hell," Zac says. "But the food is amazing."

I smile. Zac and I share an obsession for good food, though I like to cook, and not a single one of the multitude of shiny appliances in Zac's kitchen other than the bottle opener has ever been used. His cutlery drawer is dedicated to take-out menus.

"I'm back a week next Thursday," he says. "I was hoping we might catch up."

My stomach flip-flops like a fish out of water. "Um, sure," I stammer.

"How does that Thursday sound? Do you want to come to my place? I'll cook."

I raise an eyebrow. I want to see him, but is this a bootie call? I'm not sure how I feel about a bootie call. What if I go and then he never contacts me again? I don't think I can handle rejection a second time. Then again, it's Zac Ridgemont asking. I think about the girls who hang out outside his apartment building in LA screaming hysterically. They would probably give their right arm to be in my shoes.

"Sure," I say. "I'll bring cheese."

Still riding a wave of happiness and excitement, I exit the bathroom and head down the hallway, an imaginary soundtrack playing in my head.

José, who's sitting at the nursing station, looks up from his paperwork as I pass. "Someone's in a good mood," he observes with amusement.

I grin at him and stride into Walker's room. Straightaway the grin dies and the soundtrack playing in my head screeches to an abrupt halt.

Walker's sitting up in bed. He's no longer wearing a sling. He's facing the window and I wonder if he's imagining the view or thinking about something else entirely. Judging by the downturn of his mouth, I'm guessing he's not visualizing rolling green hills or sparkling ocean.

"Hi," I say, and then remember to add, "It's Didi."

He turns his head my way. Because his eyes are covered I can't tell what his expression is, but I do notice the way his lips purse ever so slightly. He still hasn't shaved. That's what strikes me now. It's odd, because in the military the grooming standard means most men are clean-shaven, except for Navy Seals or Special Forces soldiers who have a get-out clause. I wonder if it's because Walker's refusing all help and can't manage to shave on his own.

"Can I come in?" I ask.

Walker shrugs. "There's no lock on the door."

I bite back my smile and enter the room.

"I brought you something," I say.

He turns toward me as I approach, a deep furrow creasing his forehead. He's wearing a marl-gray T-shirt and I notice the Naval Academy logo on it.

I take a step closer to the bed.

"What is it?" he asks.

"It's my iPod," I say, pulling it out of my bag.

"I've got an iPod," he says, nodding his head at the night-stand drawer.

"I know," I say. I saw it the last time I was in his room and noticed the cracked screen. "I just thought you might like some audio books. I have hundreds. I listen to them in the car. When I'm driving. I drive a lot. Back and forth to classes. And back here to see my parents," I add when he doesn't say anything. "Do you read?" I ask, my voice taking on a disconcertingly high pitch. It's usually the therapist who's supposed to say nothing and the patient who's supposed to babble on.

A smirk pulls up one corner of his mouth. "Yes. I might be a jarhead but I can read."

"I mean do you *like* books?"

"Yes," he says with a sardonic voice. "I like books."

I choose to ignore his tone. "I've got a mix of fiction and nonfiction on there. Hopefully there's something you might like." I set the iPod down on his nightstand. This close to him I also get a hit of his deodorant (it can't be aftershave) or maybe his shampoo, and find myself inhaling again before I can stop myself.

"Right. Um," I say, backing away from him. "Well, it's there on the side, all set up to go. José can help you if you need it."

"I don't need help," he growls.

I wince. "Okay. Well, it's there if you want it," I say and glance over my shoulder at the open door. Half of me desperately wants to escape and the other half of me wants to stay—to talk, to get him to open up. I'm not sure why I'm so focused on him when there are two hundred other people I could focus on and Walker seems like the one who's least interested. But, then again, a psychologist would probably tell me that's exactly why I'm focused on him.

Didi, you are not here to fix him! I remind myself. I take one last look at him—he's chewing the inside of his lip—and then turn to go, resolving to leave this one to my dad.

"Is there any music on there?"

I spin back around. "Um, yeah," I say, frantically trying to remember what music is on it. It's my old iPod and I'm sure it contains some very questionable choices.

"What have you got?" he asks, feeling for the iPod and picking it up.

Oh God. I'm guessing that One Direction isn't what he wants to hear.

"What do you like?" I ask, turning the question around and wondering how I can prise the iPod out of his hand and delete all the dud music before he presses shuffle.

"A mix," he says, and I catch the first hint of a smile from him, a relaxing of the jaw. "Classical, jazz, blues."

My eyebrows lift. I hadn't pegged him for a classical guy. "So no Justin Bieber, then?" I ask, mock hopefully.

He raises an eyebrow. I can just see it poking out of the bandage.

"I'll bring my computer tomorrow and load some new music on there for you, okay?"

"Okay," he says after a small pause. "Thanks."

"No worries," I say. "See you later."

I walk out grinning. José cocks an eyebrow at me as I stroll past. "You're not covered in yogurt," he says, leaning back in his chair. "I'd call that progress."

Walker

I turn the iPod over in my hands, feeling for the buttons. It takes me about five minutes before I manage to hit the right ones in the right sequence and find the audio books. Five minutes during which I have to listen to what sounds like a group of prepubescent boys sing about what they want to do to me sexually.

I'm about to rip my own ears off—happy to be both blind and deaf if it means making the hell that is this music stop—when I find the right button and on comes an audio book. It's a Stephen King novel. I make a mental note of it for later and keep scrolling through the list, making a few wrong moves that take me back to the music and what sounds disturbingly like a Disney soundtrack.

Thankfully the books are a lot better than the music. Like Didi said, there's a real mix, from fantasy and sci-fi through to philosophy and biographies, mainly of people like Freud and Jung but also of the Dalai Lama. I keep pressing buttons, not interested in either psychoanalysis or Buddhism. I don't want to learn about the interpretation of dreams; there's nothing to interpret in mine, and

I already know that life is suffering. I've got that one down pat.

The next book is *The Psychology of Sex*, which makes me pause. Interesting. There's no point listening to that one, though, unless it has a chapter in it on how to erase memories of your ex-girlfriend. The next one is called *Sex, Love and Relationships*. I might as well listen to a book teaching me Martian for all the use that one's going to be. I notice, though, that the author is someone called Doctor Laurie Monroe. Coincidence? Or is she related to Didi? Maybe it's her mother? That would be intense, having a sex therapist and a clinical psychologist for parents. I wonder what the dinner conversation would be like.

My mom's a homemaker and a proud former Miss Virginia. My dad works in military intelligence. There were no conversations happening around our dinner table except for the odd gruff comment from my father if I didn't make the top percentile in tests and an undercurrent of nervous chatter from my mother about the weather and where the neighbors were going on vacation that I learned early on to tune out. If anyone had ever mentioned their dreams or sex at the dinner table, the sky would have fallen in, heralding the end of days.

I think back to Didi. Her perfume still hangs in the air, except I'm not sure it's perfume. Maybe it's just shampoo. She's on edge around me. That's one of the things you get good at when you can't see. You pick up on verbal clues you'd normally miss. My ability to tell when people are lying is way better these days, like when the surgeon said my leg would be good as new after the operation. I know my knee's busted and the likelihood is that I'll never be able to walk straight again or serve as a marine on deployment, not that that last one is high on my wish list anyway. The docs just don't want to tell me because they're scared the diagnosis will push me over the edge.

I know they're worried about my mental state. That's why Doctor Monroe has upped our sessions to three a week. I'm like a nut he wants to crack. Literally. He wants me to open up to him and start talking about what happened.

The first three weeks I answered him with silence. The fourth week I threw my iPod at him, missing him, of course, and hitting the wall instead. It's smashed and won't work now. My own stupid fault. When Didi came by with her iPod just now I wondered if her dad had told her about what happened to mine. The thought irritates me because that would mean they've talked about me.

Idly, I start to wonder what Didi looks like. I remember Sanchez said she was hot, but I have no idea whether she's short or tall, dark-haired or blond. I don't even know how old she is, though guessing by the music on the iPod and the fact that she's an intern, I'm guessing she's about twenty-one, maybe a little older.

The whir of Sanchez's wheelchair interrupts my thoughts.

"Yo, Lieutenant," he says, bashing through the door. "How you doing?"

He doesn't let me answer.

"Saw you had a visitor. Hot damn, dude, you should have seen what she was wearing today." He makes a satisfied sound; the same noise I've heard him make when they serve jello and ice cream at dinnertime. "What did she want?"

For some reason I don't feel like telling Sanchez about the iPod so I just shrug. "Not much."

"She hasn't been to see me yet. You reckon if I throw some yogurt at her that all might change?"

I ignore the comment about the yogurt incident. Sanchez and José both told me how she had to change into scrubs after that. I still need to apologize to her. "She's just being friendly," I tell Sanchez. "She's going to be doing the rounds with her dad later this week. That's what José said. So I'm sure you'll get a chance to meet her then."

"You think she could be convinced to swap places with José when it's time for my bed bath?"

"I thought you liked José," I say. "Those soft hands. That gentle touch."

Sanchez laughs—a full-on belly laugh—and I picture him throwing back his head. "First joke I've heard you make in a while, Lieutenant," he says. "Keep 'em coming. I've missed them."

I frown. I used to be known for my sense of humor. Not for the kind of jokes that Lutter used to make—ones at the toilet end of the scale, usually involving some kind of sexual scenario featuring goats and somebody's mother—but for my dry asides, usually delivered when tension was high or when morale was low. Sanchez is right, though. It's been a while since I've cracked a joke, or even a smile.

"Jesús?"

"Oh man," Sanchez mutters under his breath.

"*Jesús!*" A woman with a thick Spanish accent calls him again. It's Sanchez's wife, Valentina.

Sanchez is one of the toughest marines I've ever come across, all muscle and brawn. I never once heard him complain, not even on twelve-mile treks across desert carrying one-hundred-pound packs. I've never heard him utter a word of dissent when given stupid orders by fools in command further up the chain, have never seen him flinch in the face of battle. But in the face of his hurricane of a wife, the man is flattened and turns into a cowering mess.

"Shit," he mumbles now. "I forgot." He starts cursing in Spanish under his breath.

"Forgot what?" I ask. Valentina visits most days, often bringing their two small kids with her. Sanchez can often be heard tearing down the hallways in his wheelchair, pushing the engine to the max as his kids hold on to the back and scream with delight, urging him to go faster.

I don't mind Valentina. For one thing she doesn't say sorry. She doesn't pat me on the arm and tell me things will be okay. The first thing she said when she came to the hospital just after we were flown back to base was, *"You bring my husband home to me with one leg and one arm?!"* Then she slapped me hard across the face, the sound of it an explosion that made my head ring.

I was relieved that someone had finally said it, and I sat there, ready to take more, whatever she could throw at me—welcoming it, in fact. But then, much to my surprise, she threw herself on top of me and hugged me, sobbing and planting wet kisses all over my head and face. *"Gracias, gracias,"* she murmured over and over until Sanchez dragged her off me.

Now, every time she comes to visit Sanchez she stops by my room too, usually with something to eat (she doesn't trust the food here) or some flowers, once even a rosary, which I politely took and then hid in the drawer.

I hear Sanchez drawing his wheelchair closer to the bed, out of the way of the door. "We're supposed to be going to some stupid counseling appointment," he whispers as we hear Valentina stalk up the hallway, yelling out his name. "Something to do with our relationship." He lowers his voice further. "Valentina wants to know when we can start at it again, whether I'll be normal in the bedroom department. I keep telling her it's my leg that got shot off, not my dick."

"There you are!" Valentina bursts into the room and I hear her plant a kiss on Sanchez.

"*Vien aqui, nena,*" Sanchez murmurs. Valentina murmurs something back and I hear them kiss.

"You guys need a room?" I ask. "Because his is down the hall."

They both giggle and the kissing sounds amplify, so wet and loud it sounds like someone squelching through mud.

"I might be blind, but that's not an invitation to make out in my room," I tell them.

Valentina laughs and comes over and hugs me.

"How are you?" she asks. "You looking after yourself? When's your operation?"

"Tomorrow," I say. They're trying to fix my knee again. The last operation, done in the field, hasn't done the job and the surgeon here wants another go.

"What about that girlfriend of yours? She see sense yet?"

I shake my head.

"*Putana,*" Valentina spits under her breath.

"I speak Spanish," I tell her, but only halfheartedly. I secretly like it that someone is taking my side on this one. When I told my mother over the phone, she exclaimed in disappointment over the breakup, but only because she'd bought her wedding outfit and was already breaking out the crochet needles for the firstborn.

"*Sí.* I know," Valentina says. I can hear her bustling around my room, plumping cushions and drawing the drapes. "I'm just telling it like it is. That girl doesn't deserve you." She comes over to me and rubs my shoulder. "You just wait. Once you're out of here I'm going to set you up with my cousin Angela."

"You can't set him up with Angela," Sanchez argues. "She looks like Shrek."

"Shhh," Valentina hisses. "What do looks matter? And who are you to talk anyway? You're not exactly Zac Ridgemont. And besides, Angela has a great personality. A beautiful heart." She pats my shoulder. "She'll make him very happy."

"And if he ever gets his sight back," Sanchez laughs, "he'll be struck blind again when he sees what he's been sleeping with."

I hear the sound of a slap and Sanchez lets out a cry, followed by a string of curses. "What? I'm just telling it like it is," he protests, but Valentina cuts him off.

"We have to go, baby, or we're going to miss our appointment with Doctor Monroe."

"Doctor Monroe?" I ask, confused. I didn't know sex therapy and couples counseling was part of his repertoire.

"No. Not him. It's his wife," Sanchez explains. "She volunteers at the center once a week."

"You know, she was on *Oprah* once," Valentina says. "Talking about sex and the female orgasm. Maybe she can teach you a few things, baby."

I hear Sanchez starting to reverse out the room. "I don't need anyone to teach me about the female orgasm," he argues, banging the wheels into the door.

Valentina responds, her Spanish sounding like the rat-a-tat-tat of machine-gun fire, and I feel my way over to the door and shut it before shuffling back to the bed and sticking in my headphones.

Didi

Need some company?" I ask, poking my head around the door.

Dodds looks over his shoulder. He's parked in his wheelchair over by the window and is staring out at the lake. "Sure," he says, giving me a weak smile.

I walk into his room and pull up a chair beside him.

"What have you been up to?" I ask.

"Not much," he says. "Just physical therapy. What about you?" he asks.

"Well, I just spent the morning observing an art therapy class."

He snorts through his nose. "Man, those classes. I did one once. The teacher told me to paint whatever I was feeling."

"What did you paint?" I ask.

"I just colored the whole piece of paper black. Seemed like a good idea at the time."

I nod.

"The teacher said it was 'interesting' or some other bullshit. What was she expecting me to paint? Flowers? A pretty sunset?"

"A unicorn?"

Dodds smiles—a real smile this time.

"Who's that?" I ask, pointing at a picture of a stunning blond girl on his bedside table.

"Just a girl," he mumbles.

I get up for a closer look. The photo is faded and a little crumpled, but there's no disguising how beautiful the girl is. She's wearing a sundress and the light is behind her, so the outline of her body is silhouetted against the sun. She has a slyly knowing expression on her face as if she knew when the photo was being taken that her dress was see-through.

"Is she your girlfriend?" I ask.

Dodds shakes his head. "No. She's just a girl."

I put the photograph down, taking the hint that he doesn't want to talk about her. Beside the photo is a pack of cards.

"You want to play cards?" I ask.

"Yeah, sure," he says. "You know poker?"

I nod. "My best friend's brother was a marine. He taught me," I say.

"Yeah?" Dodds asks as I hand him the cards to shuffle.

"Yeah. You better get your wallet out and be prepared to pay up."

Dodds snickers under his breath and wheels himself over to me. "We'll see about that," he says.

I smile to myself, shuffle, and deal. Dodds takes his cards and I search his face for any sign of a tell. He's good. His face stays blank but his fingers start tapping on the arm of the wheelchair, which is a dead giveaway. I make a note of it and play my first hand.

"This don't feel right without a bottle of tequila," he mutters as he tosses some quarters onto the bed.

I glance up at him.

"I'd kill for something to drink. It's been way too long since

I had a beer. You'd think the least they could do after I gave my legs to the war on terror would be to provide me with a refrigerator stocked with ice-cold Buds."

I smile. I get where he's coming from, but it seems to me that drinking is the worst thing he could do right now. Alcohol makes you depressed. And on top of that, the alcoholism rate among wounded veterans is sky-high.

"Have you thought about what you're going to do when you get out of this place?" I ask, wanting to deflect him.

Dodds sits staring at his cards. He shakes his head. "No idea."

We play on for a few minutes. "What about going back to college?" I say.

"Back?" he asks me with a wry smile. "I never started in the first place."

"It's not too late," I say, showing him my hand.

He grimaces and shoves the pile of quarters at me. "I was never much good at learning," he says as I deal a second hand.

"What about a vocational course?"

He picks up his cards and shrugs. "What's the point?"

I frown. Is this about his legs? Plenty of people with disabilities lead busy and fulfilling lives. I think he's probably heard that pep talk already, though, so I refrain from saying anything. Instead, I tip my head at the poster on the wall outside in the hallway. It's a silhouetted man standing in front of a setting sun. *The future's what you make it.*

"Well, that's bullshit," Dodds says. "I want to marry Kate Upton and become a stuntman in Hollywood. Think I can make that happen?"

"*You* marry Kate Upton? You got more chance of growing a new pair of legs."

I look up. Sanchez is in the doorway, not in his wheelchair but on crutches. He has his new prosthesis attached, but I'm guessing he's still getting used to walking on it.

"You playing poker?" he asks us, swinging into the room on his crutches.

"Yeah," Dodds says. "She's whipping my ass."

Sanchez hobbles toward us. "Sounds like fun. You wanna whip mine too?" he asks me, grinning.

I arch my eyebrows. He leans on one crutch and offers me his hand to shake. Though I know who he is, we haven't yet met formally.

"Corporal Sanchez," he says. "But Jesús to my friends."

"As in, Jesus Christ, who is this loser?" Dodds says, smiling, and I see that the two of them have a good rapport going.

Sanchez drops down onto the bed beside me. "Right, deal me in," he says.

I do. He fans out his cards. "You know I met with your mom the other day?" he says to me as we start playing.

"Oh yeah?" I ask, feeling my back stiffen. Here we go . . .

"Yeah. I got a bone to pick with her, actually."

I raise an eyebrow as I throw in a few quarters. My hand is almost unbeatable. Dodds's fingers are tapping out a beat again. I think that means he has a bad hand. Sanchez has the worst poker face ever. He grimaced at the sight of his cards. I toss in a couple more quarters.

"She told my wife she needed to learn to express her needs better."

"What's wrong with that?" I say.

"You haven't met my wife," Sanchez says. "If that woman learns to express her needs any clearer, I may as well cut off my balls now and put them in her handbag under lock and key."

I pull a face at the image.

"There's a lady present," Dodds says, tipping his head in my direction.

"Don't mind me," I say, laughing.

"So, if it's okay to ask," Sanchez says, "what are you supposed to be doing here?"

"I'm a psychology intern. I'm just observing my dad and a few of the other therapists, sitting in on consults, seeing how the center works. I'm also supposed to be thinking of a topic for my thesis."

"What's that? Like an essay or something?" Dodds asks.

"Yeah, something like that."

"So you're going to be a doc, then, like your parents?"

I nod. "That's the plan. Though it's still a ways off."

"A sex doc?" Sanchez asks, his eyes lighting up.

"No, I don't think so," I say, shaking my head. I'm not sure how I'd ever give good relationship or sex advice to anyone when I can't manage to get it right myself. "I'm not sure what I want to specialize in yet," I tell him.

"Fucked-up vets?" Dodds asks. "You'd never be out of a job, that's for sure."

I give him an awkward smile. "Maybe, yeah. Or maybe something with kids."

Sanchez and Dodds both nod their heads, studying their cards.

"Well, I'm sure you'll get there," Dodds says, throwing down his cards and calling fold. He turns to me with a half-mocking smile. "The future's what you make it, right?"

Walker

can hear Sanchez and Dodds down the hall, laughing and joking around. They're in Dodds's room and Didi's with them. I can hear her voice cutting through theirs, and then more laughter. I sit up in bed, trying to hear what they're saying. What's so funny?

A lightning bolt of pain rockets through my knee when I try to move, and I grimace. Damn, it hurts. The painkillers are wearing off post-op.

Before I can struggle fully to sitting, someone knocks on my door.

"Hey."

It's Didi. Even if she hadn't said hi I would have sensed it was her.

"Hi," I say back, running a hand through my hair.

Shit. I must look a mess. I still haven't shaved and I'm wearing the hospital gown that they made me put on for the operation this morning.

"How are you doing today?" she asks.

I shrug, wincing as pain flares hot in my knee again. What the hell did the surgeon do? Blowtorch the inside of my kneecap? It was only keyhole surgery, so why the hell does it hurt so much?

"How was the operation?"

"I don't know. The surgeon hasn't been around yet to speak to me."

"Do you want me to find out when he's coming?" she asks.

I shake my head. I'm happy to put that off as long as possible.

"You feel like a visitor?" she asks. "I brought my laptop so I could add some music to the iPod."

I do a weird shrug-nod thing that probably makes me look like I'm having a fit.

I hear her walk around to the nightstand beside the bed and there's that familiar smell again—it does something to me, makes the tension in my body ease up. I relax back against the pillows. My senses were already heightened after months on deployment, every moment chasing death, feeling death stalking you right back, breathing down your neck at every turn—it sharpens your senses to a knifepoint. But now my senses are riding off the scale. She's making my head spin.

"Did you listen to any of the books?" she asks.

"I started the Stephen King," I tell her.

I can hear her unzipping her bag, pulling something out, then the sound of a computer switching on.

"What did you think?"

I smile. "It's not as good as *The Psychology of Sex*."

There's a pause, then, "Oh my God, did I leave that on there?"

"Yeah."

"It's one of my set texts."

"I figured."

I hear her fingers tapping on the laptop, and after a few more seconds the sound of her unplugging the iPod and placing it back on the table. "There you go," she says.

"I hope you put some Justin Bieber on there," I say.

"Every album he's ever made."

I smile some more.

"Actually, I had to raid my dad's music collection," she says, "and I downloaded some things too. I'm not sure it's stuff you'll like. I don't know much about jazz and blues. That's kind of my granddad's arena."

"Ha-ha. Thanks," I say. She downloaded some for me? "You didn't need to do that."

"It's fine. My pleasure," she adds.

There's a few seconds during which neither of us speaks. I wonder if she's about to leave and realize that I don't want her to.

"What were you doing with Dodds and Sanchez?" I ask quickly, trying to stretch out the time.

"Oh," she says lightly, "I was teaching them how to play poker."

I grin.

"I totally whipped them."

"That I would like to have seen," I say.

Another pause. What is she doing? Is she looking at me, thinking how pathetic I am? It's so hard to know what the other person is thinking when you can't see their expression.

"You want to play twenty questions?" Didi suddenly asks.

"What?"

"Twenty questions," she says.

"Uh, okay," I say.

"Where did you grow up?" she asks.

"That's not twenty questions. Twenty questions is when

you think of an animal, vegetable, or mineral and then the other person has to guess what it is."

"Oh yeah," Didi says. "Well, I meant you ask twenty questions about me and I ask twenty questions about you. I thought it could be a good way of getting to know each other."

I pull a wry face. "It sounds like something you'd do at speed-dating."

"I wouldn't know," she answers quickly, and something about the way she says it tells me she's lying. Maybe speed-dating's where she got the idea in the first place. I wonder if she met her boyfriend that way? I'm assuming she does have a boyfriend, because according to every guy in here, not just Sanchez, Didi is officially hot, and in my experience hot girls in their early twenties normally have boyfriends.

"Anyway," I say to her now, "I thought good therapists never divulged anything personal about themselves. Isn't that the golden rule? You do the asking, and then nod occasionally and say things like, 'That's interesting,' and, 'Tell me, how do you feel about that?' At least if your dad's anything to go by."

Didi doesn't say anything for a beat, and I wonder if maybe I've upset her, but then she speaks up. "Yeah, you're right," she says, "but I'm not a therapist yet."

There's a pause.

"So," Didi says. "What do you say?"

"Virginia."

"Sorry?"

"That's where I grew up. You asked."

"Oh, right. Virginia, huh? I've never been." She takes a breath. "Brothers or sisters?"

"One. A brother. Older. Isaac. He's an artist."

"Do you get along?"

I think about that for a moment. "We used to. Until I was about fifteen. But not so much anymore."

"Why?"

"Now we're getting into therapist territory."

Didi laughs and I get the sense that laughter comes readily to her, that she's got what my mom would call "a naturally sunny disposition." She starts asking another question, but I cut her off. "Wait, when do I get a turn?"

"Oh yeah," she says. "Sorry. Shoot."

"Brothers or sisters?" I ask her.

"No. Just me."

"Did you grow up around here?"

"Yep," she says. "San Diego. Born and bred. But I'm studying at UCLA so I'm living in LA at the moment. That's where I think I'll move after college."

LA. I wonder when she'll be heading back there. I feel a slight disappointment settle in, but I quickly bat it away.

"Okay," she says. "My turn. Why'd you join the military?"

I exhale loudly. I'm not sure I want to get into it. But before I realize what I'm doing, I find myself telling her.

"My dad's in military intelligence." I shake my head. "God, that sounds so stupid," I say. "It's not like I wanted to be my dad or follow in his footsteps. In fact, I never wanted to join the military. It just happened." I take a deep breath. "My brother was always the one who was going to go into the military. He was the athletic one." I break off. "Not that I wasn't good at sports, but Isaac . . . he was really good. Captain of the football team in senior year, All-Star Athlete, you know the deal. And I guess because he was the eldest he had all the pressure on him. I got to coast a bit more, you know, because all the focus was on Isaac. Then one day he got busted for weed. Failed a drugs test. Got banned. He was expelled from school and just like that, my dad's interest in him was over. He's been the black sheep ever since."

I shrug.

"So your dad started putting all his focus and interest on you instead? Is that what happened?" Didi asks. "And you felt the pressure doubly because now you were the only son in his eyes and you felt like you couldn't let him down?

I shrug and frown at the same time. For all her claims otherwise, this is starting to feel like psychoanalysis.

"What did you want to be?" she asks, her tone softer.

I shrug again. What's the point in thinking about it now? It's not like it's ever going to be a possibility.

"Okay. Favorite food," Didi says, sensing correctly that I don't want to talk about it.

"My grandma's apple cobbler. She makes it with cinnamon. Old family recipe."

"Mmmm, sounds yum."

"Yours?"

"Sushi," she says. "Followed closely by chocolate in any form."

"Favorite movie?"

She laughs. It's a sound I could get used to, like the feeling of early morning sunshine spilling onto your pillow. "No. I'm not telling you. You'll laugh at me."

"Why?" I say, unable to stop myself from smiling.

"Because."

"Tell me," I say, laughing now.

"No."

"I'll tell you mine."

"Wait," she says. "Let me guess. *Sex and the City*, part two?"

"You got me," I say.

She laughs and I lap the sound up.

"Okay. Place you most want to visit in the world?"

I take a second to think. "Probably Brazil. I'd like to sail down there from Florida one day." As soon as I say it I feel the wind drop out of my sails, so to speak. I feel my smile fading. "I miss the water." I snap my mouth shut. I didn't mean to say that out loud.

"I've always wanted to go to South America," Didi says, a wistful note creeping into her voice.

"Yeah," I say. "Me too."

"Okay," Didi says, "back to the questions. I think it's your turn."

I think about saying I don't want to play anymore. I'm tired and the pain in my knee is starting to bug me, but I don't want her to leave. Somehow she's making the darkness a little lighter. I grab quickly for a question. "If this was a speed-dating event, what kind of question would I ask next?"

"Hmmm," Didi says. "Probably something about what my idea of a perfect date was."

"Okay, what's your idea of a perfect date?"

There's a pause. "Being whisked off to Paris?" She laughs as though realizing what a cliché that sounds like. "Probably just dinner somewhere amazing—maybe under the stars somewhere, on a tropical beach. There would definitely be sushi. And chocolate cake for dessert. And of course champagne." She pauses.

"And Justin Bieber accompanied by a string quartet?"

"Ha-ha," she answers back.

"So you're a romantic, then?" I ask, unable to keep the mocking tone out of my question.

Immediately I sense Didi's defensiveness. She bristles. "No. Maybe. Okay, yes. Probably."

I laugh under my breath.

"What?" she asks.

I shrug. "I guess I'm just not a romantic." Anymore, I should add. I used to be. I suppose I'm a skeptic now, given how Miranda demanded all those things that I complied to so readily—and how that turned out.

"So you're a cynic about love?"

I shrug again. You could call me a cynic about a lot of things these days.

"I don't want to be cynical," Didi says in a wistful tone. "I want to believe in lobsters."

"Lobsters?" I ask, confused.

"Yeah, you know, lobsters. They mate for life."

I pull a face at her. "I don't think that's true. How would a lobster even recognize another lobster? Do they have eyes? Would they have to feel the other lobster? Recognize it by the shape of its claws or something?"

"Oh," she says, sounding disheartened, then bursts out laughing. "Don't ruin my fantasy. I just mean," she goes on, "that I like the idea of there being one person that you're meant to be with."

"Like a soul mate?" I ask, cynicism dripping off my words. Miranda once told me that we were soul mates.

"I guess so," Didi admits. "Like my parents. They're still so in love after almost thirty years."

"So I guess from the way you're talking you haven't yet found your lobster?"

She pauses. "No, not yet."

"No boyfriend?" I ask, surprised.

She pauses again. Shit. Why did I ask her that? It just came out. Now it looks like I'm trying to chat her up, or that I'm interested in her.

"No. Not really," she says, as though she's choosing her words carefully.

"Not really?" I press.

"I'm sort of seeing someone," she says, then adds, "I think."

"You think?"

"It's complicated."

When isn't it? I think to myself, simultaneously noting the stab of disappointment in my gut. So she has a boyfriend. Well, who cares?

Just then, and probably for the best, there's a knock on the door.

"Hi, Lieutenant."

I recognize my surgeon by his Texan drawl. "Ahh," he says. "I didn't know you had a visitor. Should I come back later?"

"Oh no, it's fine," I hear Didi say. "I need to get going." I hear her gathering up her things. Then suddenly I feel her hand come to rest on top of mine. She leaves it there for just a moment. "Bye, Walker," she says.

After she's left, all I can feel is my hand. Even when the doc comes right in and pulls up a chair beside me and starts talking about the success of the operation and the full recovery he's expecting, my focus is split between what he's saying and the lingering pressure of her fingers against mine.

Didi

'll get a ride home with Dad," my mom tells me as she finishes putting on her lipstick in the rearview mirror.

She's come with me into work today for some appointments. The soldiers at the center have nicknamed her Doctor Sex, which I think she secretly quite likes. She's styled to the nines as usual, looking like she's dressed to appear on *Oprah* rather than to host therapy sessions with wounded vets, but that's part of my mom's whole persona as the glamorous yet still approachable sex doctor. We look alike, my mom and I, both of us with heart-shaped faces and untamable hair, though hers is red and mine dark brown. I have her narrow chin and wide mouth too, but thankfully my dad's straight nose.

When she's done, she offers me the lipstick but I shake my head. Over the last two weeks I've stopped wearing as much makeup as I used to. I felt like it was drawing too much attention to me. And I was already drawing enough of that, thanks to being the daughter of Doctor Sex and for wearing too-tight scrubs on my first day. I still get a lot of looks, and I see the nudges and winks the soldiers give each other when I walk by, but the comments have lessened and I'm definitely being treated with more respect.

My mom says that when people see a good-looking woman, they naturally assume she can't be intelligent so you have to fight that bit harder to prove you have a brain. This I have found to be disconcertingly true. Though on the upside, it also means people tend to underestimate you.

We get out of the car and start walking toward the entrance of the building.

"How are things with Zac?" my mom asks.

I can feel my cheeks start to flush. Even the mention of his name makes my heart beat faster.

"You like him," my mom states, smiling in amusement at my blushing.

I shrug, but can't help smiling back. "I don't know," I admit. "Well, yes, of course I like him." I think about the texts he keeps sending, always signed off with "xox," and my stomach does another quick flutter.

"Just be careful," she says. "He's an actor, remember."

I frown. What is she suggesting? That he's not genuine? Or that I'm shallow enough to fall for fame over substance?

She links her arm through mine and squeezes my elbow. "Sweetheart," my mom says, "I just want you to be happy. You have a tendency to see only the good in people, and that's a beautiful thing, but as your mom it makes me worry. He hurt you last time."

"He told me he never got my texts. He was away shooting."

Even as I say it I realize how lame it sounds. My mom says nothing and we reach the door to the center, but my mood is dampened. As I pull it open, I spot Walker sitting on a bench

Mila Gray

on the lawn, wearing sweatpants and a T-shirt. He's on his own, and I wonder what he's doing outside, all alone.

I hesitate, and my mom notices me staring at him. "Who's that?" she asks.

"That's Lieutenant Walker, the guy I told you about last week."

My mom nods. "He looks lonely," she says, looking at me out the corner of her eye.

She's right. He does look lonely. And about as approachable as a tornado. He seems wound tight, slouched low on the bench with his hands dug deep into his pockets, and though he's wearing his bandages he looks like he's glowering hard beneath them.

"I'm going to go and see if he's okay," I tell my mom.

She nods. "I'll see you at home later."

"Bye," I say over my shoulder, already heading toward Walker.

I feel the need to tiptoe as I get close. "Hi," I say softly when I'm standing in front of him.

His head tilts up at the sound of my voice.

"It's Didi," I say, echoing his body language and shoving my hands deep into my pockets. Even though he can't see me, I feel self-conscious around him, awkward and on edge.

"Yeah, I know," he answers.

I frown. His tone is off. I thought I'd had a breakthrough with him the other day—that he'd let down some of his barriers—but now they seem to be back up. His voice is flat, as heavy as winter rain.

"How are you doing?" I ask.

He turns his head away from me as though he's staring off into the distance, and doesn't answer.

I bite my lip, unsure how to continue. He's giving off clear signals that he wants me to go away, but something deep inside is telling me not to go anywhere. I sit down, tentatively, watching him closely for his reaction and instantly notice the way his body tenses. His jaw is locked and his nostrils are flaring. The muscles in his forearms are as taut as tripwires, as though his hands are clenched inside his pockets. I want to put my hand on his arm, wishing there was some way I could melt away the tension, but I don't. It would be tantamount to trying to pet a growling Rottweiler.

He turns toward me briefly and then goes back to staring straight ahead. What can he see? Just endless blackness?

I don't say anything, and the silence stretches out and wraps around us. At first I can see he's agitated by it—his lips purse and he frowns; but then, after a minute or two, his body starts to slowly relax, the muscles in his arms unknot, and his shoulders slump inch by inch until he finally lets out a sigh. I let one of my own out, though a quieter one, and feel my own body relax alongside his. How is it that I pick up on his mood so much?

After five minutes of us sitting together in silence, me staring at the lake ahead of us and occasionally snatching glances his way, he speaks.

"What's in front of me?" he asks.

I turn to look at him, not understanding the question.

He nods his chin at the view in front of us. *Oh.*

"Here I am sitting on a bench, could be staring at a brick wall for all I know. Or a parking lot."

"You're not. There's a path to your left that leads into the building in one direction, and in the other direction it heads down to the lake."

"A lake?"

"Yeah. There's a lawn that goes for about a hundred meters, and then there's a lake. It's not a big lake. Maybe two hundred meters across. I guess it's more a pond than a lake."

He nods. There's another pause before he asks, "What color's the sky?"

I smile, but at the same time I feel a sharp tug in my heart. What must it be like to know you might never see the sky again, or colors?

I look upward. "It's blistering blue. Swimming-pool blue. Like someone's poured chlorine into it."

"Is chlorine blue?" he asks.

I laugh. "Actually, I have no idea. But the sky is very blue today. And there's not a single cloud."

He tilts his face up to the sun and I find myself staring at him, at the hard line of his jaw and the soft curve of his mouth. I look quickly away.

A loud bang from the side of the building makes me jump. Glancing over my shoulder, I see a couple of maintenance guys throwing sacks of garbage into a dumpster. I turn back to Walker and see that he's sitting bolt upright on the bench, his hands white-knuckled, gripping the edge of the seat. He's breathing hard, almost hyperventilating, and his face has turned ghostly white.

Without thinking, I put my hand on his arm. "Are you okay?" I ask.

He throws my hand off and leans forward, resting his elbows on his knees and sinking his head into his hands. "I'm fine," he mumbles, but clearly he isn't fine. The noise must have thrown him. It's a classic post-traumatic stress response— hyperreactivity to noises or smells, anything that triggers a memory of the event, in Walker's case probably the explosion.

I scowl over my shoulder at the maintenance men and then, before I can stop myself, I put my hand on Walker's back, between his shoulder blades. He doesn't throw me off this time. Instead I feel his muscles harden, then relax, slowly. I stroke his back until his breathing calms and he sits up straight.

He takes a deep breath in and I let my hand drop from his back.

He nods a little as if to himself, a nod that I take to mean thank you, even though he hasn't said a word. And even though he can't see me, I nod back.

"Yo."

I look up. It's José jogging toward us in his white scrubs. "Sorry," he says, "I got caught up in something. You ready to come back inside? You get enough vitamin D?"

He nods at me. "Hey, how you doing, Didi?"

I smile. "I'm good."

Walker gets slowly to his feet. I stand too. He looks so vulnerable with the bandages on, and all I want to do, what I have to fight against doing, is hug him.

"Bye," Walker says, turning his head briefly in my direction.

"Bye," I say as José starts leading him back inside the building. They stop a few feet away from me and Walker turns and looks back toward me.

"Thanks," he says, and I hear the note of embarrassment in his voice.

A lump rises up my throat. "You're welcome," I answer.

Walker

Some days are worse than others. Some days I'm not just lying in a coffin hearing someone shoveling dirt on top of the lid, some days I'm buried miles underground and nothing reaches me, not even sound, just the terrifying roar of silence.

I keep having nightmares that wake me, ones where I'm screaming louder even than Dodds, ones that stay painted on the backs of my eyelids for the rest of the day so it feels as if there's no divide whatsoever between day and night. Everything blends into one. I'm back there, in Helmand, hearing the scream of a bird of prey—a solitary note that hangs in the air and that acts as a catalyst, a starter whistle, for the beginning of the end, for the tearing apart of machine-gun fire.

And then the images fly thick and fast like bullets and there's no way to dodge a path through them. All I can do is stand there and let them slam into me: a boot lying in the road containing a foot, shorn-off bone gleaming white, a smoldering fragment of twisted-up metal, a bloodied tourniquet . . .

José forced me up out of bed and outside this morning, telling me if I didn't get some fresh air and some exercise he would have to get the doc to pay me another visit. They've already prescribed me antidepressants, but I'm not taking them, and the last thing I wanted was another visit from the doctor.

José parked me on the bench, and that's where Didi found me.

"You feeling better?" José asks as he leads me back to my room.

"Yeah," I say to him. And for once it isn't a lie.

My first reaction when Didi sat down next to me was to ask her to leave me the hell alone, but I bit it back, not wanting to be rude to her again. I didn't feel like talking at all, but she seemed to sense that.

I wonder how many other people I could sit in silence with. My mother calls me every other day or so and never stops talking, never waits to hear my answers to her questions, just rattles on and on. Maybe it's nervousness, not being sure what to say to the blind guy. Or maybe it's the fact that silence is anathema to most people.

I'm constantly surrounded by noise here, by people asking me how I'm doing or handing out diagnoses or trying to get me to open up; by television and radio and the constant chatter of visitors and doctors; by the screams and explosions in my head. And what I mostly crave and can never find is silence. What I don't want, however, is the savage loneliness that usually accompanies it. It's good to know you can have company in silence—that you don't have to be in it alone.

I just wish I hadn't reacted to that bang. Jesus, Didi must think I'm pathetic. I wish I could explain to her that with the sun on my face and her description of the sky I was already back there on that mountain road, and the bang—whatever might

73

have caused it—to me was the sound of a car exploding.

I wish I could tell her, but how would I find the words? How would I ever describe to her what happened? Why would I want her or anyone else for that matter to have those images in their head? And mostly, why would I ever want her to know how I failed, how all those deaths are my fault?

José takes me to the chair in my room and leaves me. I sit in a slump. I know by now that it's in front of the window. At least now I can picture the view. I think about the last session I had with Doctor Monroe when he tried to encourage me to think of the future and start planning for it, but I push his words away. What future? What life?

I still haven't moved from my place when a few hours later I hear a familiar footstep out in the hallway. My heart rate speeds up and I catch myself holding my breath. There's a quiet knock on my door.

"Hi," Didi says.

"Hi," I say, turning my head in her direction.

"I just wanted to see you," she says. "I mean, see how you were doing."

"I'm okay," I say. Better for hearing her voice, but I can't tell her that.

"I just wanted to put something on the iPod," she says. "It's something I thought you might like to listen to."

I nod, but can't summon the energy to ask what it is. I'm tired. Everything today seems to take monumental amounts of energy.

I hear her crossing to the bed and then opening her laptop and switching it on. A minute or so later I hear her snap the lid shut and I start trying to think of things to say to make her stay, but I can't think of anything. My conversation skills are limited, my brain too foggy to come up with anything.

"Okay," she says. "I'll see you tomorrow then."

I nod. *Stay. Please stay.*

She doesn't move, and for a moment I think that maybe she's heard my silent plea and is going to come over and put her hand on my arm or on my back like she did earlier. She takes a step closer, and my whole body is suddenly tuned to her, to her presence in the room.

Her hand falls on my shoulder. Beneath the bandages I squeeze my eyes tightly shut. I will her to stay like that. Her hand feels like an anchor, something holding me, pulling me away from the hard, narrow edge.

I sit there, lips pressed together, words gathering behind them, all jumbled, nonsense, the essence of which is *thank you, please stay, please don't go.*

But she doesn't hear them, can't hear them, and after thirty seconds her hand drops away and she's gone.

Didi

'm halfway home when I realize I've left my laptop back at the center. Damn. I need it. I have a paper to finish. I turn the car around and head back to the base, checking the time. It's close on eleven p.m. I stayed late because I wanted to observe a cognitive behavioral therapy session, and then I helped the art therapist pack up her materials.

The parking lot is empty when I pull in and I hope it's not too late. I think I left the computer in my dad's office, which might be locked—he went home hours ago as he had a date with my mom—but it's open and the laptop isn't there. I scour my memory, and finally remember that I left it in Walker's room.

I head down in the elevator to his floor, hoping he isn't asleep. As soon as the doors open, I hear the soft murmur of a radio at the nurse's station, and then the sound of talking and what sounds like crying coming from Dodds's room. I pause for a moment, holding my breath and listening, before hurrying off. I don't want them to think I'm eavesdropping.

The light is off in Walker's room, but the TV is on and an eerie blue light is escaping out of the door, which is ajar. I peek inside. Walker looks to be asleep. He's lying on his side with his back to me. I can see my iPod on the nightstand and my laptop still on the floor, leaning against the chair leg.

I step inside the room quietly, heart pounding, and start tip-toeing toward it.

"No!"

I spin around, my heart slamming into my ribs.

Walker has rolled onto his back and is thrashing his head back and forth. "No!" he shouts again. "Get down!" He mumbles something I can't make out and then a howling sob bursts out of him. "Sorry . . . Sorry," he sobs. Tears start soaking his band-age. His hands are fisted tightly in the sheets. Before I can stop myself, I cross to the bed and take one of his hands in mine.

"Shhh," I say, stroking his hair back off his forehead with my other hand. "It's okay."

He draws in a shuddering breath, his whole body wracked with heaving sobs as if he's drowning and struggling to breathe, and then suddenly he curls into a tight ball on his side, facing away from me. I sit down on the edge of the bed and keep strok-ing his hair as the sobs ease into gentle crying. Is he awake? I have no idea. I can't tell.

"It's okay," I whisper to him. "I'm here. You're okay."

Finally, when his breathing has settled into a calmer rhythm and I'm sure that he's asleep, I ease myself off the bed and let go of his hand. I should go. I tell myself to leave. But I can't seem to drag myself away from his side. I don't want to leave him.

Walker

can feel her standing by the bed. I'm not sure what she's doing or why she's even in my room. It must be the middle of the night. I pretend I'm asleep. I don't want her to know that I know she's there.

What did she see? What did she hear? Was I yelling in my sleep? Or worse, screaming? I know she's seen me crying. That's bad enough. I don't want her to see me like this. I don't want anyone to.

But at the same time I register somewhere deep down inside me that same feeling I had this afternoon, that I don't want her to go anywhere. She doesn't even have to touch me. I just want her here. In the room. With me. So I wait, trying not to hold my breath, every one of my still working senses primed—acutely tuned—to her presence in the room.

When I woke up from my nightmare—heart thundering, feeling like a thousand pieces of white-hot shrapnel were thudding into my body, Lutter's screams still echoing around my skull—I thought at first that it was Miranda in the room with me. But then it all came rushing back: the blistering road in Helmand, the scouring blindness, the scorching pain in my knee, the engagement ring lying discarded in the drawer of my nightstand.

But instead of being sucked into a maelstrom, as usually happens when I come round and am hit by the reality that's worse than the actual nightmare—*they're dead . . . it's my fault . . . there's nothing left*—there was Didi, taking my hand and whispering to me that everything was okay.

And for a moment, just a brief one, I believed it. I want that now. I want that tiny moment of respite again. A split second outside of time where everything—both reality and dreams—is suspended.

Is it possible to crave something you've barely experienced, and only for such a short amount of time? I guess I'm just starved of affection and touch and closeness. Because right now, that's what I want. That's what I'm holding my breath for, even though I'm trying so hard not to.

But it's not going to happen. I hear Didi take a shallow breath in and then back away toward the door. I almost say something—the words are there, on the very tip of my tongue—but I clamp my mouth shut and force myself to stay silent.

I hear the shush of the door being pulled to and wait a few minutes before I roll over onto my back. I stare into the void and let the sounds of the ward filter in: the radio buzzing, the water cooler humming, nothing from Dodds.

I think about reaching for the TV remote but I don't. Instead I replay what just happened over and over in my head, trying to put a picture to it.

* * *

"Wakey wakey, rise and shine, Lieutenant, you got an appointment in half an hour with the doc."

I groan and roll over. I must have fallen asleep after Didi left. I don't normally do that after I've had a nightmare. There's usually no chance of sleeping again—the images in my head are too vivid, the adrenaline pumping too hard around my body. It's like trying to sleep after drinking a vat of coffee while watching a horror movie.

I struggle into a sitting position. For a second, as José bustles around me, setting down a breakfast tray and pouring my pain meds and happy pills into my palm, I wonder if I imagined the whole thing. Was Didi really in my room last night? Did I dream that too? But then I remember the feeling of her hand on mine, the sound of her voice—I couldn't have imagined that. She was here. She was definitely here.

"So, are you going to let me shave that beard off?" José asks.

"No," I answer, dry-swallowing my pills.

"You're starting to look like a bum."

"Yeah?" I say. "Well, it's not like I have to see it."

"The rest of us do, though," José jokes.

"I don't want to shave, okay?" It comes out angrier than I mean it to. For the first five weeks of being here José helped me shave every few days, but only because I was a total zombie and didn't have the energy or will to say no. Now I do.

José mutters something under his breath. I ignore him and start stabbing at the plate, unsure what it is I'm even stabbing at. Probably some rubbery reconstituted egg. That's usually what they serve up at breakfast.

"You got toast today," José points out helpfully. "Want some help buttering it?"

"No," I tell him. "I got it."

I put down the fork and reach for the knife, but manage to knock over a glass of something as I fumble to find the butter.

"Shit," I growl as water drips off the tray table and onto the bed, soaking my sheets.

"It's okay, I got it," José says, and I hear him whip away the breakfast tray and put it down on the side. "Why don't you get dressed and I'll change the sheets? I'll order up another breakfast for you."

"It's okay," I tell him. "I'm not hungry."

I get out of the bed, stubbing my foot on the nightstand and cursing again as I reach for the crutches they gave me yesterday after my knee op. I hobble my way to the bathroom, shut the door, and then sit down heavily on the toilet seat, realizing too late that it's up. I toss the crutches to the ground and put my head in my hands, then toss the pills I'm still clutching in my palm into the bowl.

The pain in my knee is just a dull throb today, but I wish it were worse. I want it to be worse. It's a reminder of why I'm here in the first place. It's a constant reminder of how I failed.

Why should I be the one who gets to live? Why should I be the one who gets to walk around on two legs, pain free? Why the fuck should I be the one getting a medal for bravery when five men—*my* men—are dead in the ground?

The nightmares every night? The pain? That's my punishment. A pathetic punishment, sure, but it's all I'm going to get.

Sanchez bangs on the bathroom door ten minutes later.

"What are you doing in there? Beating off?"

I ignore him.

"Want me to come back? How long do you need? Twenty seconds? Longer?"

I open the door.

"Oh, hey," he says. "You're done. Awesome."

I swing my way toward the bed on my crutches, feel for it and sit down.

"You want that toast?" Sanchez asks.

José must have brought my second tray up.

"Go for it," I tell Sanchez and hear him head toward the bed. He's not in his wheelchair and I don't hear the creak and swish of crutches either, so he must be walking on his prosthetic leg.

"How you doing?" he asks, and I hear him ripping open the butter packet.

"Okay," I say, and as I say it I remember Didi murmuring the exact same thing to me last night. *Everything's okay. I'm here.* My gut clenches.

"So listen," Sanchez says. "There's this triathlon coming up. And I want to take part."

"A triathlon?" I ask, unable to keep the smile out of my voice despite everything I'm feeling.

"Yeah. Like, you have to swim a mile and run ten miles and then cycle, like, fifty miles or something."

"Yeah, I know what a triathlon is," I tell him.

"Well," Sanchez goes on, "I figure I got a chance at winning."

I start laughing.

"What?" Sanchez asks.

I shake my head. "You only have one leg. What you going to do? Hop for ten miles? Swim in a circle?"

"That's cruel," he says, but he's laughing too. "It's a special triathlon. Only vets. It's a triathlon for wounded marines in rehab.

Everyone's gonna be injured. There are guys doing it who got no legs. I figure I got the advantage, seeing how I've got one, at least. And you should check out my prosthetic. It's made of titanium or something. I'm like the freaking Terminator."

How the hell is he so positive? Are they mashing Prozac into his scrambled egg every morning? If that's the case, I might have to start eating breakfast, or maybe swallow the pills I've been flushing.

"It's in two months' time," he says. "So I got to start training now." I hear him take a bite out of the toast. "Damn," he mutters with his mouth full, "this bread is drier than a nun's—"

A knock on the door interrupts him.

"Lieutenant Walker?"

It's my ophthalmologist.

"Sir," I say, standing up and saluting. Old habits die hard. He's a major. My knee flares; if I wasn't already blind I'm pretty sure the pain would do a good job of blinding me. I suck in a breath but don't sit.

"Oh, I didn't realize you had an appointment," Sanchez says. "I gotta go anyway. Valentina's coming in and I want to show her what I can do with my new arm."

I hear him heading for the door. "Sir," he says, saluting the doc.

"Corporal," the doc answers.

"I'll talk to you about our training schedule later," Sanchez calls on his way out the door.

"Wait, what?" I call after him.

"Our training schedule," he shouts back, already halfway down the hallway. "For the triathlon. You're doing it with me."

"What?" I yell, but I can hear the doors already slamming behind him.

"You're doing the rehab triathlon?"

I turn back into the room. The doc's talking to me.

"Er . . ." I say.

"That's a great idea," the doc says. "It will give you something to focus on."

Before I can tell him that I'm not taking part in any damn triathlon, let alone one that's called a rehab triathlon, he ushers me backward toward the bed, propelling me with his hands on my shoulders.

"Okay now," he says, pushing me down so I'm sitting on the edge of the bed. "We're just going to take off these bandages and see how we're doing."

We? I raise my eyebrows. I figure he's still got his sight, so I'm not too sure why there's a *we* in this equation. I sigh, though, say nothing, and let him unwrap the bandages.

When he's done I have to blink a few times to get my eyelids to work, they're so unused to the action. They feel gummy, my eyelashes are all glued together. I wait, blinking furiously, expecting, even though I know it's futile, for my vision to miraculously return like it always seems to do in the movies.

Nothing happens. It's like floating in space, light-years from any sun. There are no flickers of light, not even shadows in my peripheral vision. I can't make out a damn thing.

The doc tilts my head backward and makes some humming and hahhing noises as he lifts my eyelids in turn to examine my eyes.

I have blast-related ocular trauma. Basically, the pressure waves from the explosion detached a retina, causing blindness in my right eye, but so far they haven't been able to tell me anything about why I'm blind in my left eye too. They just mumble about blast injuries and contusions.

"Okay," the doc says. "Everything looks good. The retina has reattached. You're healing up well."

"Then why can't I see anything?" I ask, frustrated.

"We're going to need to run some further tests," he answers in that placid noncommittal doctor tone I'm getting used to. "I'm going to make an appointment for you later this week."

I shake my head. More tests.

"The orthopedic surgeon tells me your knee's looking good," he says in a jovial voice.

"Yeah," I answer, unable to match his tone.

"You'll have to take it easy with the triathlon training. Watch that knee. Or use a wheelchair."

A wheelchair? He's got to be joking. I came first out of my entire marine class in the physical training exam. There's no way I'm using a wheelchair for anything. Ever.

I guess he must notice my expression because he pats me on the shoulder. "Okay, Lieutenant, you have a good day now. I'll arrange those tests for you and be in touch."

"Wait," I say as I hear him head for the door. "What about the bandages?"

"Oh, you don't need those on anymore. You're good. It was just to protect the retina from any dirt or dust and the chance of infection, but you're fully healed."

My eyebrows lift and I can't stop the snort. Yeah. Sure I am.

Didi

Thursday has come round.

"This, or this?" I ask Jessa, holding up two dresses, one black and figure-hugging, the other a strappy white cotton sundress.

Jessa gets up from my bed and strolls to my closet. "I think you should wear whatever you feel most comfortable in."

"But he's used to hanging around actresses and beautiful people."

"*You're* beautiful," Jessa says. "And you also have a brain. Most people in Hollywood do not. Believe me."

I pull a face. "But I'm not, you know, *beautiful* beautiful." *Like you*, is what I want to add. Jessa is effortlessly, turn-heads-on-the-street beautiful, and she also has the body of a slightly shorter than average supermodel. I inherited my parents' short genes and my mom's Kardashian curves. And whereas Jessa is beautiful even first thing in the morning without a scrap of makeup on, I require a helping hand from MAC and Bobbi Brown.

"Oh, shut up," Jessa tells me, laughing. "How about this?"

She pulls out a blue, fifties-style halter-necked dress.

"That makes my boobs look massive," I tell her, wrinkling my nose.

She arches an eyebrow and smirks.

"Well, even more massive than normal," I mutter and shove the dress back on the rail. I'd like him to notice more than my boobs. With some guys that seems to be all they focus on. Sometimes I want to yell, *Hello, I do also have a face. And a brain!*

"Go with the sundress, then," Jessa says. "You're only going around to his place, right? You're not going out?"

"No," I mumble, "we're staying in." I hold the dress up and study my reflection in the mirror, sucking in my cheekbones and striking a pose. One of the joys of having two therapists for parents who regularly walk around the house naked is that I learned early on to love and accept my body, Kardashian curves and all. But Zac is a movie star and he's drop-dead gorgeous and used to being around girls who are thinner than a matchstick.

"I don't think it matters what you wear," Jessa tells me with a smirk. "It's not like it's going to be staying on for long." She laughs and flops back down on the bed, picking up the script she's trying to learn for an upcoming audition.

"Hmmm," I say, pulling on the sundress. "I don't know if I'm going to sleep over."

"Why not?" Jessa asks, looking up. "You stayed over last time, didn't you?"

I shrug at her. "I don't know. I just feel like maybe I rushed into it too fast last time around. You know . . . I got caught up in the moment."

I smooth the dress down, thinking back to what my mom said and whether Zac is being genuine. I mean, he is an actor, after all. But then again, Jessa is an actor, and she's genuine. "I think maybe I should make him work for it this time around," I say, frowning at my cleavage. I tug the dress down a little lower, throw back my shoulders and lift my chin, feeling a jolt of nerves.

"Is that your mom's advice?" Jessa teases.

I shrug. "Yes," I admit. "But I think she's right. I mean, look at you and Kit. You waited."

Jessa smiles to herself like she's guarding a secret.

"I don't want a one-night stand again. I want something . . . more romantic. I want to be someone's girlfriend, not someone's bootie call. For once."

Jessa nods at me. She gets it.

"How did you know Kit was the one?" I ask her, flopping onto the bed beside her.

She tosses her script aside and grins at me. "I just did." She stops smiling and a sudden dark shadow passes over her face. "Without him, nothing made sense. I missed him so much I honestly thought I might die from it." She laughs sadly, shaking her head. "God, you remember what I was like."

I nod. I do. I remember it clearly—I remember her sobbing uncontrollably for days after we got the news, having to force her to eat and get out of bed in the morning, the black days that marched on for months, the blank expression on her face like she was lost and didn't know how she would ever find a way out of the darkness.

"And it's not like he completed me or anything," she says now. "I'm not going all Jerry McGuire here, but I missed the me that I was when I was with him. Does that make sense?"

I nod. I remember how quiet and introverted Jessa was and how Kit brought her out of her shell, made her believe in herself.

"It's like he made me a better person," she goes on, "and I didn't know how to be that person without him around." She glances at me. "That's totally cheesy, isn't it?" she says with a grin. She holds up her script. "Oh my God, if acting fails, I could always write scripts for a living."

I laugh too. But then her expression turns serious again. "Kit used to say that I was his north star. It's the one they teach soldiers to navigate by," she explains when I look at her, bemused. Her voice chokes up a little. "He used to say that I was the reason he would make it home."

I clutch my stomach, feeling guilty for laughing. "Oh my God. That is so romantic."

I think about the flowers Zac sent me and bite my lip.

Jessa laughs under her breath, but I catch the flicker of sadness in her eyes. "I think that pretty much sums up what love is, though. It's the person you always want to come back to. I've thought about this a lot, and I don't think home is a place. I think it's a person. And when you find home, the place you feel the safest, the place you go to for shelter and where you can be fully yourself, then you know you're in love, really in love, not just infatuated or head over heels in lust."

Jessa smiles to herself, playing with the heart locket she's wearing, and something twists a little in my gut. I recognize it as jealousy and force it angrily aside. After everything she's been through, it's impossible to be jealous of Jessa, but the fact is I want to experience what she's talking about. I want to be loved like that. I want what my parents have—someone who, after thirty years of marriage, will come home and ravish me in the kitchen while I'm trying to cook spaghetti. I want someone who'll tell me that I'm their north star. Someone who'll look at me and really *see* me. Someone who isn't cynical about love and, most important, someone who won't break my heart.

My first semester of college I started dating a basketball player called Ben who I was convinced was the one. I got all the feels whenever I was around him—clammy hands, pounding heart, weak knees, all the textbook signs—and when he told me he loved me, I believed him and told him I loved him as well. I lost my virginity to him that same night—after he took me on a date to the Olive Garden. And then a week later I walked in on him in his dorm room in bed with another girl. I guess it wasn't love after all.

It took me a year to get over that. I couldn't eat, sleep, or focus for months. After Ben, I dated another guy I met speed-dating, who it turned out just wanted to be friends with benefits, though he really just wanted the benefits.

Then came Zac.

Will things turn out differently with him this time? Can I trust him? He's been linked to a lot of his co-stars in the past, but, as Jessa points out, so has she. You can't believe anything you read in celeb magazines.

I swallow, nervous all of a sudden about tonight, but then, without any warning whatsoever, my thoughts divert to Walker. My hand slips and I manage to scrawl eyeliner across my face. Damn. I grab a tissue and wipe it off. Why did he pop into my head?

I scowl at myself and try again, pulling the edge of my eyelid down. It's because I haven't been able to stop thinking about him all day, that's why. Even when I was sitting in on my dad's sessions and helping out in the art therapy room earlier, my mind kept returning to Walker and what happened last night.

I kept wondering if he was aware of me being in his room, if he wondered what I was doing there, and tried to rehearse what I'd say to him if he asked me about it.

I walked by his room twice today, trying to catch a glimpse of him, but the first time his door was shut—I think the doctor was in with him—and the second time he wasn't there.

I guess I'll see him tomorrow. I'm going in to help plan the Fourth of July party along with José and some of the other staff who've volunteered.

"Didi?"

"Huh?" I turn.

"I was just asking you how it was going at the center?"

"Oh, sorry."

"What were you thinking about? Tonight and Zac?" She's smiling as she says it, teasing me.

I shake my head. "No."

Walker

"Hysterical?"

"Not as in funny," Doctor Monroe explains to me in the level, easy tone he never seems to deviate from. "It's a medical term. An outdated one. Now we use the term 'conversion disorder.'"

I burst out laughing. *Right. Okay.* What he's telling me is madness, plain and simple.

"How do you feel about that?" he asks.

I laugh again, a bitter snort. Is he kidding? "How do you think I feel about that?" I answer.

"Judging by your reaction, I'd say you're struggling to come to terms with it."

"Yeah, you can say that again." What a load of crap. How is it possible that it's just in my head?

"Have you thought any more about recording a journal?" he asks.

That was a therapy idea—that I write down my memories of that day—but I can't see to write, so he suggested recording it instead.

"Yeah," I say.

"And?"

"And no thanks."

There's a pause. I picture him with steepled fingers beneath his chin, watching me carefully through round, frameless glasses. I have no idea what he looks like in reality; I'm just basing him on the images I have in my head of therapists from movies. Maybe with a little Freud thrown in for good measure.

"I'd like you to talk to me about that day," he says now.

I make an effort to keep my face straight and not fidget. I sit in my squishy chair—designed, no doubt, to encourage patients to kick back and relax—with a ramrod straight back. And I say nothing.

I hear him take a long breath in, the reverse of a sigh. "It's been eight weeks now. I think it's time. Especially given the diagnosis."

"What do you want me to say?" I ask. "A bomb went off. People died. The end."

When he answers, it's with the same infinitely patient tone of voice. Does he ever lose it? Has he ever once exploded? Thrown an iPod across a room? How does he stay so calm all the time when he has to deal with patients like me? "It wasn't just people, though," he says. "It was your friends, your colleagues, brothers, the men you were responsible for."

My hands grip the arms of the chair as though I'm waiting for the executioner to throw the switch.

"I think that's the crux of this disorder," he continues. "You blame yourself."

A laugh explodes out of me. This is just psychobabble.

He ignores my laughter and keeps going. "And that's why

I think revisiting the event in your mind, walking through it slowly and with my guidance, will help you see more clearly that you were not responsible, that you did all you could and more. It was a horrific event, a tragedy—but not one you are to blame for. I don't think you're going to see any progress until you confront what happened and find a new way of processing it."

If I could see I would stand up right now and walk out the room, but because I'm blind and don't know what obstacles are between me and the door, or how to get from here back to my room, which is on an entirely different floor, I can't do anything. I just have to sit here and listen as he hands out this crap.

All this stuff he's told me about the conversion disorder or whatever he called it sounds ridiculous. And now he's trying to get me to revisit that day? How the hell is that going to help? If this is how modern therapy works, Jesus, take me back a hundred years and give me electroshock treatment. Lobotomize me.

"We need to help you create a new thought process around the event," he carries on, seemingly oblivious to the grimace on my face and the tightrope tendons in my neck. "We work on it until the memory no longer triggers emotions of anger and guilt."

I take a few deep breaths and let go of the chair arms. I will myself to relax and even try out a smile. There is no way I'm reliving that day or walking through it with him. It's bad enough that I have to do it every night in my sleep. The only way around this, to get him to drop the idea, is to convince him that I'm fine. I need to start playing ball, sounding more positive. I need to channel some Sanchez.

"I'm fine, doc," I say. I try another smile but it feels like an alien action, using muscles that have atrophied from lack of use.

"José says you're still taking sleeping tablets."

"I find it hard to sleep, that's all," I mutter.

"Okay." I hear the dubious note in his voice. "And how's the physical therapy going?" he asks, clearly deciding it's time to move on. At last.

I shrug.

"I hear you're taking part in the triathlon."

I roll my eyes. How the hell has that rumor suddenly become fact around here? "Sanchez is doing it," I tell him.

"Aren't you doing it with him? He said you were doing it together."

"Nope," I say. Damn Sanchez and his big mouth.

"Well, I think you should," he says. I can hear him gathering up his papers. Does this mean this session is over? Halle-fucking-lujah.

"Aha," I say, already wondering if an orderly is waiting for me outside Doctor Monroe's office to take me back to my room or to whichever appointment they've lined up for me next.

"Walker—do you want to get out of here?" Doctor Monroe asks. Finally a trace of impatience has wormed its way into his voice.

I don't say anything. Yes, of course I want to get out of here, though where the hell I'm supposed to go is another question altogether—home to my parents? Yeah, I can just imagine my mom fluttering around me, not knowing what to say or how to treat me, can already hear my dad's stony silence—the waves of disappointment bouncing off him as he's confronted every day with the fact that his son isn't ever going to become a general or head of the army or whatever other shining-bright career goal he had in mind for me.

No. Home is not an option. So what else is left for me? Where do I go? If I take an honorable discharge, then I get a pension, but it's not enough to live on. The thought of what I do next is impossible to wrap my head around. What do I do? What *can* I do? I can't see.

Ten seconds go by and the doc still hasn't said anything. Is he waiting? Oh, for God's sake. I nod. "Yes, I want to get out of here."

"Then you need to start working with me, with the whole team. It's normal to go through a period of adjustment, but now you need to draw on those qualities I know you have in abundance. I've read your military service record. You were top of your graduating class at the Naval Academy. You were the youngest lieutenant in the marines. You've received the Silver Star for gallantry in action. You were on a fast track to being a senior commanding officer."

My stomach muscles contract. My breathing speeds up. Where's he going with this? I don't need a reminder of who I once was or the stellar career path that was ahead of me.

"Your superiors say you never quit, never stood down in the face of danger, that you're a role model to your men and that—here I'm quoting directly from Colonel Kingsley in his letter recommending you for the Silver Star—that you 'personify the finest qualities of a marine.'"

I stare into the void, trying not to blink and to keep my face impassive. If I embodied the finest qualities of a marine, then five men wouldn't be dead. Those words are bullshit—meaningless platitudes some PR assistant picks from a stock list whenever a soldier is wounded or killed in action.

"What are the qualities of a marine?" Doctor Monroe asks.

"Excuse me?" I say, shaking my head in confusion. Why's he asking me that?

"Tell me."

I laugh. *What?*

He doesn't say anything, though, so I sigh loudly and then start to rattle them off. "Courage. Resourcefulness. Leadership. Endurance. Loyalty . . ."

He still doesn't say anything. Okay, okay, I get it. He's telling me to cheer the fuck up. Man up. Stop moping. Show some goddamn endurance and courage. I grit my teeth harder until my molars almost crack under the strain.

"I'm going to set an appointment for you with the occupational therapy team. You need to start becoming more independent. And I think you should increase the time you're spending on physical therapy now your knee and shoulder are healing up."

I don't say a word about the pain in my knee or the fact that I'm not taking the painkillers or the antidepressants he prescribed me.

I hear him scratch a few things down on paper and then close a book and zip up a bag. "Okay, Lieutenant, I'll see you tomorrow," he says. "I want you to think about what I've said about going back over the events of that day."

I hear him stand up and take that as my cue to stand too.

"Do you want some help getting to the door?" he asks.

"No," I say, banging straight into what feels like a coffee table with razor blades for edges. My shin explodes, the pain rocketing up into my kneecap, but I suppress the grunt and shuffle my way toward the door, which I can hear that he's opened for me.

Outside, José is ready to lead me back to my room, and takes my arm like I'm an old man.

The occupational therapist keeps trying to give me a white stick. But from what the doc just told me, I don't need a white stick. What I need is a straitjacket.

It's been a long day; I'm glad it's another one nearly over. I pick up the iPod and listen to the file that Didi put on it that day she sat in silence beside me on the bench. It's a guided meditation, and in the background is the sound of the ocean, waves crashing against a shore. It's the first time I've bothered listening to it, and I wonder whether she chose this particular one deliberately after she heard me talking about sailing. Halfway through it I'm starting to drift off when Sanchez comes charging into the room.

"Yo," he says. "You gotta check out Dodds's painting." There's a pause. "Oh, shit. Sorry. Keep forgetting you're blind. Now you got your bandages off you look normal." Another pause. "Kind of."

What does he mean by that?

"I mean you don't look blind," he clarifies.

I can feel the stiff furrow forming between my eyes.

"You got normal eyeballs and stuff. Like, right now, it's like you're looking at me. You sure you can't see? How many fingers am I holding up?"

I think about holding up one finger—my middle one—in response.

"Huh," I hear him say. "Mad. You really are blind. By the way, did you know you have a full-on beard? You're starting to look like bin Laden."

I hear his uneven steps as he walks to the bed and sits down, and then I hear him unrolling something. "So check this out," he says. "It's too funny. In art therapy, Dodds drew this poster. I got it here. He stuck it up on the wall in the canteen and they tore it down, but I managed to sneak it out the trash. I think I'm going to frame it."

"What is it?" I ask, curious now as to what Dodds might have drawn. I wouldn't have thought of him as an artist, not that I know all that much about him.

"It's a marine with his legs shot off and he's gone and sprayed red oil paint all over it for blood. It's spurting out of the two stumps and he's lying on the ground bleeding out, and"— Sanchez heaves with laughter—"there's a rainbow coming out of his ass. And a unicorn flying in the background. Wait. I think it's flying. I'm not sure if those are wings or not. And maybe it's not a unicorn. Could be a rhino."

Sanchez is now sucking in air and laughing so hard I can barely understand him. "And then he's written above it in the clouds, '*Fuck God's will.*'"

I raise my eyebrows. "Sounds like Dodds's version of Guernica."

"You-what-ica?"

"It's a painting," I explain. "By Picasso. About the horrors of war." I think back to my art history class in school. I always liked art. Another sharp stab, through the gut this time. Will I ever get to look at a painting again?

"Well, I don't know much about art," Sanchez says, "but this don't look much like a Picasso. It is pretty damn horrific, though."

I listen to Sanchez scroll the painting back up. "I got to hide it from Valentina," he says. "Can I keep it in your room?"

"Yeah, sure," I tell him. "But why?"

"Because she'll go ape-shit if she sees it. You can't take the Lord's name in vain around her. Her and the pope, they're, like, tight. She thinks it really is God's will. Even what happened to me. Like God wanted me to lose my leg and an arm so I could get bionic ones instead."

"You believe that too?" I ask him. For all his talk about his wife, I know Sanchez is religious as well. He wears a cross under his uniform, and he was the only one from the unit who ever went to the religious service when we were stationed at Camp Bastion.

"I gotta believe something," Sanchez says, and I hear him crossing to my nightstand and pulling open the drawer.

I muse on that. I guess having faith in a higher power helps. Maybe that's how come he can be so upbeat all the time. But to my mind, if this is God's will, then fuck God. I don't want to believe in him anymore. I'm with Dodds on that one.

"Holy Crackamoli," Sanchez exclaims. "What the hell is this doing in here?"

"What?" I ask.

"What is this—eighty carats or something? It's the size of a baseball. How much did you pay for this?"

He's found Miranda's engagement ring.

"You shouldn't leave this in here," he tells me. "Anyone could just walk in and take it. Hell, I'm tempted myself. Could get myself an island in the Caribbean with this. Maybe a seat on that Virgin Galactic space flight. I always wanted to try out zero gravity."

"It's not worth that much," I tell him. But he's right. I should at least have put it somewhere safe.

"What you going to do with it?" he asks me now.

I shrug. "Sell it, I guess." My first thought after I'd reconciled myself to the fact that Miranda wasn't coming back was to cash it in and buy a boat, but a blind man can't sail, and I guess I'm going to be needing the money seeing how I'm going to be unemployed soon.

"You don't think you guys might work things out?" Sanchez asks.

"I don't know." I turn my head toward the window. When I think of Miranda, it's like recalling someone from the distant past. From another life. The old me—the one in my memories— feels like a character from a movie I once watched, and Miranda's just a supporting role, already fading from memory like a negative left out in the sun. "I doubt it," I clarify.

"Yeah? Well, that's good," Sanchez says, "because Valentina's invited her cousin Angela to the party."

"What party?"

"The Fourth of July party—what do you mean *what* party? We're all supposed to volunteer to help out. I'm gonna be the DJ."

"Have they got Dodds doing the decorations?"

"Ha! You're funny, Lieutenant. But you know what? That's not a bad idea. I might volunteer him. Didi's in charge of the decoration committee. I told her she didn't need to do anything, she just needed to come along. Looking at her would be enough decoration. Swear to God, that girl is so fine, if I weren't already married I would be in there like swimwear."

I shake my head, wincing. "You use a line like that on your wife?"

Sanchez gives a full-on belly laugh. "How else do you think I got her to marry me?"

Didi

"Man, it's good to be home," Zac says, sighing with satisfaction as we stare at the view.

His new house in the Hollywood Hills is a modern affair, all concrete and glass. We're standing in front of the window. LA stretches out beneath us. We could be standing on the bridge of a spaceship staring out at a galaxy of glittering stars.

"How was Vietnam?" I say, turning to face him.

He smiles. "It was okay. Reshoots went well. Like I said, though, it's good to be back." He holds my gaze when he says this last part, and my breath catches in my chest.

I keep having to pinch myself. It's so surreal to be hanging out with someone who's famous. I keep making assumptions about him based on the roles I've seen him play on-screen—a breakout part in a vampire movie in which he played a blood-sucking John Keats, and another part as the young doctor heartthrob in a romcom. I have to keep reminding myself that in real life he probably doesn't know anything about poetry or how to remove a burst appendix.

"What do you think of this painting?" he asks me now,

pointing to an enormous abstract canvas hung on the living-room wall.

We stand in front of it. I know a little about art—I took a history of art class in my freshman year, and my parents collect a little—but I know a lot more about psychology, and my guess is that someone very angry painted it. It's a black canvas with vivid white scratches scored through it—like it's been clawed by a wild beast. It looks like the painting Dodds described to me that he drew in his art therapy class.

"Um," I say, clearing my throat. "What do you think about it?" Oh God, classic therapist tactic—throw the question back at the questioner. I hope he doesn't call me on it like Walker did.

"I'm not sure," Zac says, tapping a finger against his lips. "My interior decorator bought it. She says it's an investment. But I don't know anything about art."

"Well, really, with art, it's not about what it looks like," I say, "so much as the way it makes you feel. Good art should always make you feel something."

Zac tips his head to the side and frowns at the painting. "I feel depressed when I look at it. It's kind of ugly."

I laugh. "You have to have this painting on your wall and look at it every day! If I were you I'd choose something that at least makes you feel happy. Or hopeful. Not one that makes you want to jump out the window." I think for a brief minute about the platitudes on the wall of the rehab center. I guess there's a middle ground.

"Come on," Zac says, turning from the painting and nodding toward the kitchen. "Can I get you a drink?"

He strides to his industrial-size refrigerator and pulls open the door. "I've got three types of water, beer, vodka, champagne, wine . . . My PA does all my grocery shopping for me. She likes to keep me stocked up. What's your poison?"

"Just water, thanks," I say, catching a glimpse of my reflection in the windows, which act like giant mirrors. I tug on my dress. Is it too tight? He keeps staring at my boobs.

Zac looks at me with raised eyebrows and a one-sided smile. "I can't tempt you to a beer or a glass of wine?"

"No," I say, shaking my head. "I have to drive."

He pouts and gives me a look that I've seen him use on-screen, when he was the vampire John Keats trying to seduce the human Fanny Brawne. "No you don't," he says. "You could stay over."

My stomach flips. It's tempting. He's gorgeous, and every time he looks at me my heart goes into arrhythmia. And it's not like we haven't had sex already . . .

But I stand firm on my convictions. I don't want him to get the idea that I'm just there for a quick bootie call whenever he's in town. I want it to be more than that. But then again, if I don't stay over maybe he'll figure I'm not interested. God, it's confusing.

"Let me start with water," I say, buying myself some time.

He gives me a curious, appraising look, then smiles. "Okay, one water coming up."

He brings it over and sits down beside me on the sofa, leaving a few centimeters' gap between us.

"So, how's it going with you?" he asks.

He does this thing of always looking right into your eyes when he speaks to you so it makes you feel as if you're the only person in the room—in the universe, even—and that whatever you're saying is the most important thing that anyone has ever said. It makes me incredibly self-conscious. I wonder if he likes that, though?—enjoys seeing women get flustered when he fixes them with his gaze?—so I determine not to show any sign of anxiety.

"How's your job?" he asks. "You're working, right?"

I frown a little. The last time we had a date I told him all about my summer internship and my PhD. I guess he's forgotten.

"Well, I'm doing my PhD . . ." I remind him.

"Wow." He grins. "You must really like school, huh? I hated it. I was out of there the first chance I got. Acting was all I ever wanted to do."

I nod. "Yeah, I get that. All I've ever wanted to do is be a therapist. Other kids used to play doctors and nurses, and I'd play therapist and patient. I'd try to talk my Barbie dolls off the ledge and diagnose them with anorexia and body dysmorphia."

Zac gives me a quizzical look. I hurry on, embarrassed. "I'm actually doing some work experience over the summer at a center for wounded marines. It's where my dad works."

He nods again. "Wow. That's awesome."

"Yeah," I say. "It's interesting. These guys . . . some of them have the most awful injuries—they've lost arms, legs, some of them are blind, and yet the atmosphere in there is so positive." I shrug. "Mainly. I mean, there are a lot of people with depression and post-traumatic stress disorder too."

Zac nods again, his eyes burrowing into mine.

"There's this one guy who's blind," I go on, feeling a little flutter in my stomach. Why am I bringing up Walker? "You might have seen him on the news a few weeks ago. He was part of that marine unit that got ambushed in Afghanistan. Five people died."

Zac shakes his head. "No. I try not to watch the news. I have Google alerts set up, but that's it."

"Oh. Well, most of his unit was killed, and he was blinded by the explosion but he managed to carry one of his men to safety. It's . . . I don't know . . ." I shrug. "Humbling, I guess. As well as heartbreaking." I think about Walker talking in his sleep, crying out "sorry." That was what he said. Something twists painfully in my gut. "I can't even imagine what that must feel like. So, yeah, I'm learning a lot." I take a sip of water. "It makes you think twice before complaining about the silly things in life, that's for sure."

Zac suddenly sits up straighter, his eyes bright. "You know what?"

"What?"

"You just gave me an idea. My agent's putting me up for this role. I have an audition for it next week. It's about a guy who's in this car accident and ends up paralyzed from the neck down and fighting for his right to assisted suicide." His eyes light up. "It's a total Oscar role."

"What's an Oscar role?" I ask.

"You know—one of those roles you're almost guaranteed to be nominated for an Oscar for. The kind of role where you have to lose fifty pounds and make yourself ugly or play a blind person or someone mentally ill, or, like, in a wheelchair." He grins at me.

I frown.

"Do you think I might be able to come into the center with you one day?" he asks next. "To hang out, and maybe research a little bit for the role? You know, get a feel for what it's really like to be disabled?"

I bite my lip.

"Oh, come on," he says, pouting hopefully. "You'd be doing me the biggest favor. I'd pay you back." His gaze dips to my lips and I feel an answering tightness in my belly.

"Let me ask," I hear myself say.

"Okay," he murmurs, his gaze still fixed on my lips. "Now come here and kiss me."

He curls his hand around my neck and pulls me closer. I draw in a breath and close my eyes, and when his lips touch mine, I feel like I could be starring in a movie. I'm half expecting someone to yell "*Cut!*" but no one does, and we keep on kissing, but I can't fully relax into it. I feel stiff, too self-aware, worrying about whether or not he thinks I'm a good kisser and where this might be leading.

His hands slide down my neck and then lower, running down my sides to my waist and then back up again.

"Has anyone ever told you that you have the most amazing body?" he whispers in my ear.

I laugh under my breath.

"I can't wait to see you naked."

Butterflies swarm in my stomach. He already has, I think to myself. Has he forgotten?

His lips find mine and we kiss for a few more minutes, until, breathing heavily, Zac pulls back and strokes my hair behind one ear.

"Stay the night?" he asks.

He sees me hesitate, and his eyes glimmer with intensity in just the same way as they do on-screen.

"I promise you won't regret it," he murmurs.

Walker

bench-press until my arms burn and the physical therapy guy has to come over and tell me to stop. I'm dripping with sweat but I don't want to stop. I didn't want to come down here, but José pep-talked me into it and Sanchez wouldn't get off my back either. I remembered, too, Doctor Monroe's admonishment yesterday about acting like a marine.

That bugged me. More than I let on at the time. But when I got myself calmed down, I realized it was because I knew he was right. I've been moping around for too long. Sanchez isn't lying around feeling sorry for himself. He's back in the game, setting himself goals, working toward them. In the end, as well as being sick of hanging out all day in my room, it was the taunt about being able to beat me in a physical that got me going. I was always top of the class—no one could ever beat me in endurance training. Now a three-year-old could probably slay me, no trouble. So I keep going, switching to the rowing machine with the help of the physical therapist. He warns me to go gentle on my shoulder and knee, but I tell him it's fine. In truth, I like the burn. It gives me something to focus on.

And I'm also thinking that if I push myself to the edge, maybe tonight I'll sleep right through, no nightmares.

Last night I woke up screaming again, but this time there was no Didi waiting in the dark by my bed to chase the dreams away.

"Hey, Lieutenant."

I don't recognize the voice. "Who's that?" I ask.

"It's me. Dodds."

"Oh, hey," I pant, keeping up my pace on the rowing machine.

"You training for the triathlon?" he asks in a strong Alabama accent.

"Nope," I say.

"Why?" he asks. "You scared Sanchez is going to beat you?"

I slow my pace. "No."

"That's what he says."

"Oh, is that right?" I grit my teeth and push harder, feeling the pain flare hot in my knee as it bends and straightens, bends and straightens.

I should probably give it a rest, but I can't seem to make myself stop.

"I'm thinking I might take part too," he says. "In the wheelchair race."

"Awesome," I say drily, but then I feel a flicker of guilt. "I'm sure you'll ace it, Corporal," I say with more feeling.

"Thanks," he says, and I hear the slight swell of pride in his voice.

I remind myself to make more of an effort. That's another thing the doc's talking-to did—reminded me that I'm an officer. I should be setting an example—it doesn't take much. And there are people in here worse off than me. Dodds has lost both his legs and Sanchez told me that he's got no family. Not that having family necessarily makes that much difference, in my experience, but still, offering him a little support isn't going to hurt me.

I start trying to think of a question to ask him that won't seem awkward or tactless, but my conversational skills seem to have dried up these last few weeks. Before I can think of anything, he speaks up anyway, in a low voice.

"Oh hey, Lieutenant, someone's checking you out."

I tilt my head up. "What?"

"Didi—you know, Doctor Monroe's daughter? She's over by the door. She's staring at you."

I frown and swipe at the sweat pouring down my face. She is? She hasn't been by my room for a few days now. I hate to admit it, but I've been anxious about it, wondering whether it has something to do with her being embarrassed to see me because of the other night. I figured I wouldn't bring it up if she ever did come by, then I got annoyed with myself for thinking about her so much. It's another of the reasons—probably the real reason—I wanted to get out of my room. To take my mind off her. I couldn't concentrate on anything, or even listen to any audio books, because I kept listening for her footstep in the hall.

"She's gone now," Dodds says. "Man, she's hot. I'd get in there if I were you."

I stop rowing and fumble for the towel I thought I'd left on the side. Dodds hands it to me. "She has a boyfriend," I tell him.

"If I was her boyfriend, I don't think I'd be happy about the way she was just looking at you."

I wipe the sweat off my face. What's he saying? He's probably just shit stirring. Maybe Sanchez put him up to it. But . . . I pause for a minute. What if it's true? I shake my head, laughing at myself. No, of course it's not true. Who am I kidding?

I chuck the towel back at Dodds and stand up gingerly, my knee throbbing, out of breath. But as I make my way with the physical therapist's help toward the door, I feel a lightness in my step and in my body that wasn't there before. Whether that's a result of the endorphins flooding my bloodstream from all the exercise or because of what Dodds just told me, I couldn't say.

Didi

walk down the corridor, passing Dodds's room, and note that my heart has started beating extra fast and I'm really nervous. I don't know why. I wasn't this nervous when I was at Zac's, the memory of which still makes me blush.

Walker's door is open and I hesitate a beat, taking a deep breath before walking over, my hand already raised to knock. My arm drops to my side. He's not there. The room's empty. Maybe he's still in the gym. The image of him on the rowing machine flashes suddenly into my mind and I have to shake it away.

"Damn it . . ."

I jump. The door to the en-suite bathroom flies open and Walker appears. He's wearing just a towel wrapped loosely around his waist, and he's holding a razor in one hand. He has shaving foam half covering his beard, and blood is trickling down his neck. My gaze drops from his face to his chest and my mouth falls open.

"Who's there?" he asks.

I drag my eyes from his rock-solid abs with difficulty.

"Um, it's me, Didi," I stammer.

His expression changes, softens. Or maybe I'm imagining it.

"Hey," he says.

It's disconcerting. The bandages are off—I was taken by surprise when I saw him in the gym earlier; I found myself staring at him—and he's looking straight at me as if he can see me.

"You need a hand?" I ask and immediately regret it. I remember what happened the last time I offered to help.

"No," he says, and I nod to myself and start to leave, feeling disappointment welling up and trying to brush it away.

"Actually, yeah," he calls out.

I turn back around.

"I do. Really I need eyes, but I'll take a hand." He frowns. "You still there?"

"Um, yeah," I say, taking a step into the room. "You trying to shave?"

"Yeah," he says, pointing at the blood on his neck. "Trying and failing. I cut myself."

"Here." I step toward him and take the razor from his hand, but then find myself suddenly overwhelmingly flustered. We're standing so close, and he's half naked—I'm assuming fully naked beneath the towel—and his chest fills my vision.

"Um, should we go back in the bathroom?" I finally manage to stammer.

He turns and bumps me with his arm. "Sorry," he says.

"No worries," I mumble and stand aside to let him feel his way into the bathroom.

I stare at his back. Holy shit. I don't think I've ever seen anyone as ripped in my life. He has broad shoulders knotted with muscle, and perfect, smooth, tanned skin. On the back of his right shoulder there's a tattoo of what looks like a sword with some Latin script through it, but I can't read the words from where I am.

"Should I sit? Would that be easier?" he asks when we're in the bathroom.

"Um, yeah," I say. "Why don't you sit on the toilet?"

He does, and now I'm confronted once again with his chest, which, close up, is every bit as solid and defined as his back. The only thing that mars his skin is an angry, raised scar just down from his shoulder. I have to stop myself from reaching out and running my fingers over it, and— I catch sight of myself in the mirror, flushed and with my jaw hanging open, and frown angrily, ramming my mouth shut. Thank God he's blind and can't see me gawking like a schoolgirl.

I distract myself by filling the basin with hot water, and then I take a corner of the towel, wet it, and wipe off the trail of blood down his neck.

"Sorry," I say when his body tenses.

He laughs under his breath. "It's fine. I've had a lot worse than a shaving cut."

Right. Of course.

I spray the shaving foam into my palm, then I kneel down in front of him and start applying the foam to his face, aware that my hands are shaking a little and hoping he doesn't notice. Neither of us says anything. It feels weirdly intimate, and I wonder for a second if this is something I should be doing. I mean, does this breach some patient–doctor boundary? But I'm not his doctor. And he's not technically my patient. I push the thought away. I can't exactly stop now that he's half covered in shaving foam.

Resting back on my haunches to wipe my hands on a towel,

I take the opportunity to study him. His eyes are gray-green and beautiful, framed with the kind of thick black lashes that it takes me three layers of mascara and an eyelash curler to achieve.

I knew he was good-looking—the bandages couldn't hide that fact—but I didn't realize he was this good-looking. It's the eyes that do it, ironically enough. Not just their color, which is striking on its own, but something about the sadness in them. When I look at Walker, I see someone physically strong, fit and capable, but when I look into his eyes, I see someone hurting, someone vulnerable, someone in pain. It gives me a jolt—the sharpness of the contrast—and it makes my heart bruise.

Zac is beautiful—but boyish with it. Walker is the complete opposite. Though they're the same age, twenty-four, you could never, ever call Walker a boy. He's fully, one hundred percent man. He's well over six foot, whereas Zac is about five eight. And though Zac works out, Walker's physique is more than just sculpted, it's like he's hewn from rock. I muse on their differences a little more. Zac is charming and flirtatious, always smiling and easy in conversation, whereas Walker's gruff and silent a lot of the time. But there's a quiet confidence about him that I like. I get the feeling that he's never trying to impress anyone. If anything, he's trying to keep people at a distance.

Why am I comparing the two of them? I shake my head and grimace to myself. Walker's a *patient*. I need to be professional. These thoughts are about as professional as a lap dance.

"Okay," I say, "let's do this." I grasp the razor.

"You done this before?" Walker asks.

I pause with the razor halfway to his throat. I'm a pro at shaving my legs. How much harder can this be? "Um, yeah," I say.

His eyebrow arches, but he lets it lie.

"Hold still," I tell him, taking his chin firmly in one hand. I start slowly shaving his right cheek.

He holds still.

The only sound is the scrape of the razor and the splash of water as I wash off the blade. It requires concentration. But after a while the silence gets to me.

"I saw you in the gym," I say. I'm pretty sure that Dodds caught me staring and said something to him, so I may as well admit to it.

"Yeah," he says. "I figured I should get back into shape."

Get *back* into shape?

"Are you doing the triathlon?"

The edge of his mouth quirks up into a smile but his eyebrows draw together. "Who told you that?"

"No one. I just heard Sanchez say he was doing it. So are you doing it too?"

"Yeah," he says. "I am."

"You are?" I'm surprised, for some reason.

He nods at me.

"That's great. Now hold still." I move to his top lip, trying not to focus on it or on his mouth, though this close it's hard not to.

"How are you getting on with the books?" I ask quickly to distract myself.

"Good," he says, trying not to move his lips. "I'm listening to *Misery*."

"The Stephen King?"

He nods, and I tighten my grip on his jaw and move the razor to his left cheek. He smiles. He has a dimple on this side.

"Did you get to the part where she cripples him to stop him

from leaving?" I wince. "Oh . . . sorry." God, I keep putting my foot in my mouth.

Walker laughs. "No. It's okay. Don't say sorry. I'm so tired of that word."

"Sor—" I clamp my mouth shut before I can finish saying it again. "I'll just shut up," I mumble.

"No, don't do that either."

A half smile, half smirk pulls the edge of his mouth up. I start on his neck, accidentally flicking some shaving foam onto his chest and having to reach for the towel to wipe it up.

He says nothing as I run the towel across his chest trying not to stare. I glance at the scar on his shoulder. It looks like a shrapnel wound. Something tugs harshly on my insides. What are the scars on the inside like? Are they just as bad? And how do you heal those ones when you can't even see them? I guess that's a therapist's job and I should know how, but I don't.

I pick up the razor and start shaving him again.

"Um . . . you know," he says, "it's better if you shave downward."

"What?"

His hand comes up and circles my wrist. He covers my hand with his own and then guides the razor downward. "Like this."

"Oh," I say, swallowing hard.

He still hasn't let go of my hand. I try it myself. "Like this?"

He lets go. "Yeah. Otherwise it causes razor burn."

"Oh, sorry," I say.

He shakes his head as if to say don't apologize.

My heart has started beating triple-time and my hand shakes as I finish off shaving his neck. I need to get a grip. When I'm done, I stand aside and let him wash his face.

"How do I look?" he says, turning to me. There's a sardonic smile on his face.

"Good," I say. *Really* good. "Wait." I snatch the towel from his hand and dab at a fleck of shaving foam by his ear. "There," I say.

His hand comes up to take the towel and our fingers touch and stay there for a beat too long. My breathing hitches, then speeds up. I resist the urge I have to stroke my other hand down his newly-shaved cheek.

There's a look in his eye now—confusion overlaying the sadness. His head cocks slightly to one side. I pull my hand away and just then the bathroom door swings wide open.

"Hello? . . . Oh."

I spin around. My dad is standing in the doorway. He blinks a few times and frowns as he takes in the fact that I'm standing almost pressed up against a half-naked Walker.

"Hey, Dad," I say, turning bright red. "Um, I was just helping Walker, I mean Lieutenant Walker, shave. His beard." *Oh God.*

"I can see that," my dad says, raising his eyebrows and pursing his lips at me. "I just came looking for him because he missed his appointment time."

"Sorry," Walker says. "I didn't know it was that late. José normally comes to get me."

"Um," I mumble. "I'm going to go now. Bye," I say quickly to Walker, and then ease past my dad and rush out the door.

I know from the look on my dad's face as he turns to watch me go that this won't be the end of it.

Walker

I don't say much in Doctor Monroe's session and he doesn't push it, makes no mention about me going over what happened in Helmand. I'm grateful for that but also uncomfortable, aware from the tone he used with Didi that he thinks he walked in on something and that he's not happy about it.

I feel awkward, but then again, what is there to feel awkward about? There's nothing going on. Even without being able to see and pick up on the normal cues, my gut is telling me that all those things I'm feeling—the connection, the hyperawareness when I'm around her, this attraction, if that's even what it is— are one-sided. If she was staring over at me in the gym, it was probably because she was surprised to see me with my bandages off. Dodds was probably overplaying it. She just feels sorry for me. Hell, she's said it two or three times. And she has a boyfriend.

If the girl who supposedly loved me and wanted to spend her life with me—in sickness and in health—was so repulsed by me, why would a girl who never knew me before, and who barely knows me now, ever look twice at me? No. If Didi feels anything for me, then it's just pity.

After the hour's therapy session is up and I'm back in my room, I find I can't stop thinking about her. It's frustrating as hell. I need to find a way to get her out of my mind. I think about going to the gym again. My knee is throbbing, but I could probably go a few more miles on the rowing machine. Maybe I should take the painkiller next time José comes around with it.

"Hey, Lieutenant."

It's Dodds. I hear him bang his wheelchair into the door.

"How you doing?" he asks.

"Good. You?"

I hear him sigh. "Yeah, okay. You shaved."

"Yeah." I run my hand across my jaw. She did a good job.

"You want to come and play poker with Sanchez and me?" he asks.

I give him what I think is an arch look.

"Oh yeah," he says, realizing how stupid the question was. "Well, the game's on the TV," he says. "You can come and watch it. I mean listen to it."

I start to say no thanks, but then I figure what the hell. Anything to take my mind off Didi. And I should really give my knee a rest or I might not be able to work out tomorrow at all.

In Sanchez's room I sit on his bed and listen to the game, though I can barely hear it over the bitching happening between Sanchez and Dodds as they shuffle and deal.

"I'm putting fifty dollars on Walker beating you," I hear Dodds say.

"Nah," says Sanchez, "it don't work like that."

"What do you mean?"

"We're going to be tied together."

"What?"

My ears prick up. What are they talking about?

"Yeah, that's how they do it with these kinds of triathlons. They tie us together for the running and the swimming part."

"Like on a leash? He's, like, your dog?"

"Wait," I say, interrupting. "Hold up. What are you talking about?"

"The triathlon," Sanchez says. "We're entering as a team."

Dodds bursts out laughing. "You're going to be tied to him!"

"I'm your eyes," Sanchez explains. "You're my legs. It's a win-win. We use a tandem bike for the cycle ride. When we swim and run you're tied to me."

Tied to him? For a moment I think about laughing and telling him there's no way I'm taking part, but then I remember that I'm supposed to be setting a positive example. I also recognize that Sanchez needs me as much as I need him, and I know how much this triathlon means to him, so I just nod. I can feel the competitive streak in me stirring to life.

"You better be fast," I say.

"Road Runner's got nothing on me," he answers, laughing. I hear him tossing some coins into a pile. "Figure between the two of us we've got about one and a half functioning bodies. We're gonna win this thing for sure."

"How the hell did I let you talk me into this?" I say, shaking my head.

"He could sell ice to the Eskimos, that's how."

It's Valentina. She bustles into the room and I hear her planting kisses on Sanchez and Dodds before my turn comes. She wraps me up in a hug and I get a waft of eyewatering perfume.

"You know, you can't call them that anymore," Dodds interrupts. "Eskimos. The real name's Inuit."

There's a pause.

"I watched this show on National Geographic," Dodds explains.

"You know what, Dodds?" Sanchez laughs. "You aren't half as dumb as you seem."

"Screw you, Sanchez," Dodds says, but he's laughing under his breath too.

I join in.

"*Amor*," Valentina interrupts, "I just stopped by to bring you boys some food." I hear the sound of plastic containers being snapped open and suddenly the aroma of Mexican food fills the room, making my mouth water. "I have to go."

"Where?" Sanchez asks.

"To the volunteer meeting," Valentina tells him. "I'm helping with the food for the party next week."

"Sweet," says Dodds. "I was thinking we'd just get cold cuts and jello."

"My cousin Angela's coming. She's going to help too."

"What with? Eating all the food?" Sanchez asks.

Valentina says something in Spanish that makes Sanchez mumble something under his breath like a scolded child.

"Okay. I have to run," Valentina announces. She strokes her hand down my cheek. "You look so handsome without the beard," she clucks. "Keep it off. Angela prefers her men clean-shaven."

"Shame she doesn't apply the same philosophy to herself," Sanchez laughs.

There's a pause, then a sharp slap, and Sanchez lets out a yell.

"You say one more word about my cousin and I'm going to tell Doctor Monroe all about that thing you don't want anyone to know about . . ."

"*You wouldn't dare!*" Sanchez shouts, but I hear the fear in his voice.

"Oh, wouldn't I? Just watch me." And with that she leaves. I imagine she probably flounces out the door.

"Damn woman," Sanchez mutters once she's out of earshot.

"Don't say that," Dodds says and I pick up his angry tone. "You got a wife. And she loves you. You know how lucky you are? Jesus. You got way more than the rest of us have got."

Sanchez doesn't say anything in reply. A minute later, though, he mumbles "Fold" and I hear Dodds gathering up the coins.

I get up from the bed and make my way to the door, my hands out in front of me, feeling for the wall. I've counted the steps from here to my own room and if I hug the wall I can manage on my own.

"See you, Lieutenant," Dodds calls to my back.

"Yeah," I say in answer.

I head to my room, leaning against the wall the whole way.

Didi

After the volunteer meeting I head down to the canteen. My dad manages to corner me just as I'm getting in the elevator.

"Hi," he says. "Are you leaving?"

"No," I say, unable to look him in the eye. "I thought I might get started on organizing the decorations for the party and then do some work on my thesis."

"Okay. I'm heading home in half an hour, but how about we get a quick coffee before I go?"

"Sure," I say. *Here it comes.*

We head down to the canteen, which this late in the afternoon is empty. My dad sits down opposite me, setting down two cups of coffee.

"I know what you're going to say," I tell him as I start stirring Sweet'N Low into mine.

"Do you?" my dad asks.

I keep my eyes on the coffee. "Yes. You're thinking that something is going on between me and Walker, *Lieutenant* Walker," I correct myself, "but it isn't. I swear. I was just helping him shave." I risk a glance up. Why is my voice shaking?

My dad squeezes my hand. "Sweetheart, your empathy and your compassion are what are going to make you a great therapist one day, but you need to work on keeping an emotional distance. It won't help him in the long run when you leave. He needs to be independent, not come to rely on you. And there should never be any question of anything else developing."

Anything else? He means anything *romantic*. I'm fairly sure my face is a convincing shade of tomato by now. "I was only helping him shave. You're making this into a much bigger deal than it actually is."

"Lieutenant Walker's a special case."

I frown. "Why?"

"He won't open up about what happened to him."

I raise my eyebrows. That's not uncommon with members of the military. They're taught that showing vulnerability or complaining is a sign of weakness.

"I know," my dad goes on, seeing my expression. "That's not so uncommon, but post-traumatic stress can manifest in various ways, and with him it's manifesting in a really unique way."

Now I'm curious. "What do you mean?"

"Okay." My dad looks at me sternly. "This is between you and me and you need to treat this like a doctor-to-doctor confidence. I'm only telling you so you know exactly why I'm warning you to keep a distance. Whatever Walker seems like on the surface, there's a lot going on underneath."

I frown at him again. Now I'm worried.

"His blindness is psychosomatic," my dad says.

"What?"

"There's no physical reason for it."

I shake my head in confusion. "I know what psychosomatic means. But I don't understand."

"It's a conversion disorder caused by psychological trauma. In the old days they used to call it hysterical blindness."

I sit back in my chair, blinking, trying to process this. "So," I finally say, "he can actually see?"

My dad tips his head to one side. "Yes, but no. There's nothing physically making him blind. It's purely psychological."

"But what's the cure for that?" I ask, still reeling.

My dad shakes his head and pinches the bridge of his nose. "Honestly, there isn't one standard approach. It's not a very well documented condition. Recovery often takes a long time, and even then nothing is certain. He seems to be in denial about the diagnosis as well."

I stare at my coffee for a long while before looking back up. "But you think if he talks about what happened to him, if he processes it and deals with it, then it might go away? He might get his sight back?"

My dad shrugs. "Well, it's the most likely scenario. If he doesn't deal with it, it's only going to manifest in other ways too."

I let out a long breath. I know what else post-traumatic stress can cause—debilitating depression, angry outbursts, inability to control emotions, a change in personality that can lead to marriage breakdowns, affect job prospects, and in some cases lead to suicidal thoughts. It's the single most diagnosed condition among members of the military. In fact, I was thinking of writing my thesis on the subject.

I play with my cup of coffee. Walker's angry and definitely depressed. He doesn't seem to be suicidal, but do I really know about what's going on in his head? What do we ever know about another person? I have a sudden thought.

"You want to get him to talk, right?" I ask my dad.

He nods.

"I think maybe he would open up to me."

My dad shakes his head. "I don't think that's a good idea."

"Why?"

"Because I think he's developing feelings for you that are more than just platonic."

"Why do you say that?" I ask, my voice uneven and my heart starting to thump so loudly I'm sure my dad can hear it.

He arches an eyebrow and smiles at me. "I might be getting on, but I know something about men and women. I know what I saw."

I look down at the tabletop and grip my coffee cup tighter to stop my hands from shaking. How can Walker be attracted to me? He doesn't even know what I look like. My dad's got to be wrong.

"Well, what if I make it clear to him that we're just friends?" I say, looking up.

"Didi, this is what I'm talking about—you can be friendly, but you can't be *friends* with a patient."

"But he isn't my patient." I hear the truculent tone in my voice.

"Semantics," my dad says. "You're here at the center, working as an intern. You need to abide by the same rules as all the staff here. There are very strict guidelines. You know this."

"Okay," I say, looking him firmly in the eye, though it's hard to.

My dad finishes his coffee in one gulp and stands up. "Well, I'd better get going. I have another meeting."

"Okay," I say, and I smile, but inside a million emotions have started to wage war. My dad leaves and I sit there staring at my coffee as it grows cold.

Five hours later, having gotten nowhere either with my thesis or with ideas for decorations for the party, I decide to call it a night. I glance up at the clock in the darkened canteen. It's almost midnight. I close my laptop and walk to the door, hesitating when I get to the elevators. I should leave, go home, get some sleep. But I can't stop thinking about Walker. It was around this time the other night, maybe even earlier, when I walked in on him having a nightmare.

I tell myself I just want to check in on him and that once I know he's okay I'll leave, choosing to ignore the voice in my head that yells at me that I'm being stupid. Before I know it I'm riding the elevator to his floor, my foot tapping, my heart starting to gallop.

What am I doing? I scold myself even as the doors open and I step out. I shouldn't be checking in on him. That's José's job. I should be keeping my distance from him. But I can't stop myself. He's all I've been able to think about since the conversation with my dad.

Can it be true? Does Walker have feelings for me? I can't ignore the buzz in my stomach at the thought that he does, the quickening of my pulse.

The door is ajar so I can see that the light is off in Walker's room. I tiptoe closer and then stop, holding my breath. Walker's asleep, lying on his side, facing me, the sheet thrown off the bed. He's bare-chested, wearing just a pair of gray boxers, I watch him, my heart starting to crash against my ribs. He's mumbling in his sleep, but then he rolls over, away from me, and falls quiet.

I stare at the tattoo on his shoulder, still unable to make out the words.

I hesitate. I could take a step into the room. One step and I'd be able to make out what it says. One step, just to make sure he's okay.

I remember my dad's warning. I think about Zac.

I turn on my heel and walk away.

Walker

've been forced into helping with the setup for the Fourth of July party. Forced by Valentina, who hunted me down like a sniper on the prowl. I'd been hiding out in Dodds's room playing cards, hoping I could avoid the whole thing.

Dodds, like me, was refusing to take part, even in the decorating, but Valentina had us assigned to jobs before we had a chance to even finish our round of cards. And there's no sense in trying to argue with Valentina. Dodds got told to help out in the kitchen making pigs in blankets, and I've been told to help Sanchez in his bid to launch himself on the world as a DJ.

Valentina leads me to the cafeteria, where he's setting up his decks. I'm not sure what help I can be, and I say this to Valentina.

"You got ears, haven't you?" Valentina answers roundly. "So tell him what's appropriate music to play. We're going to have children and generals present. He can't be playing any of that rap music with all the cursing."

She dashes off and I fumble around for a seat until Sanchez pulls one over for me and guides me to it.

"Man, that woman had her way she'd have me playing Lionel

Richie and Bruce Springsteen and nothing else. I'm not even allowed to play Miley Cyrus because she doesn't want any twerking going on."

I sit there while Sanchez busies himself setting up. Within a few minutes he's playing Lil Wayne at deafening volume. It's so loud neither of us hears the interruption.

"Gentlemen?"

Sanchez kills the volume abruptly.

"How are you doing?" It's Doctor Monroe. Immediately my senses are on high alert, wondering if Didi is with him, but straightaway I know she's not and register a dull disappointment.

"Hey, Doc," Sanchez says. "Just setting up for the party."

"I've got a visitor. He's here doing some research. I was wondering if you two might have time for a quick chat with him."

"Sure," says Sanchez.

I say nothing. Research? I'm starting to feel like a caged guinea pig in this place. I try to think of an excuse to escape, but before I can the doc has left and Sanchez is introducing himself.

"And that's Walker," he says, obviously nodding at me.

I lift my chin in a vague greeting and wonder if I should hold out my hand, but I don't. I can't be bothered with niceties. I wonder if he can tell that I'm blind?

"Well, it's great to meet you," the guy says in the overly enthusiastic voice I'm starting to get used to. It's the one people use when they're uncomfortable around me. "I'm Zac."

"So what can we help you with? What are you researching?"

"Well, actually it's for a role I'm auditioning for."

Auditioning for? He's an actor?

"Wow, that's cool, bro," Sanchez says. "What's the role?"

"It's a paraplegic guy who takes on the government for the right to commit suicide."

There's a beat of silence before Sanchez fills it with a forced, "Huh, well, I guess you came to the right place. It's paraplegic central here."

Zac laughs and I grind my teeth. How exactly is that funny?

"What I want to do is find out what it's really like to be in a wheelchair," he goes on. "I want to understand what it's like to know you'll never walk again, never be able to do anything for yourself, never be with a woman."

My stomach tightens into a knot.

"I want to get into the mindset," he continues. "Really go method on this one. I'm thinking of borrowing a wheelchair from the center and using it for a couple of days to help me get more into the role."

There's another beat. Is this guy for real?

"You know, I'm not sure we're the right people to talk to," Sanchez says in the tone of voice he uses with superior officers he can't stand. "And we got to get ready for the party and all."

I feel Zac's eyes rest on me. I turn to face the windows. He's not getting anything from me either.

"Okay, well, maybe I'll, um, go take a look around, see if I can find someone less busy."

"You do that," Sanchez says.

He takes his leave and I hear the door shut behind him.

"He wants to go method?" Sanchez mutters. "I know a few people might help him out with that one. Put him in a wheelchair for real." He starts laughing and a second later Lil Wayne is blasting out of the speaker again.

Didi

I find Zac in the kitchen helping Dodds make pigs in blankets. There's a gaggle of kitchen staff around him, all female, and all of them giggling. One of them is trying to show him how to fold the sausage into the pastry and he's joking around with her, flustering her so much that she drops a sausage on the floor. Another girl is filming the whole thing on her phone and in her excitement shoves Dodds out of the way in his wheelchair, her elbow connecting with his head. She doesn't even apologize.

I see Dodds's face darken as he wheels himself out of the way and into a quiet corner of the kitchen. I go over and join him there.

"Hey," I say.

He grunts a greeting at me, his gaze fixed on Zac, who's putting his arm around yet another girl while she snaps a selfie of them together. I watch for a moment, my gaze settling on Zac's hand, which falls from the girl's shoulder and comes to rest on her hip. I feel a pang of something sharp and unsettling and have to tell myself sternly not to get jealous. It's just part of his job. He's only being friendly.

"Must be nice," Dodds mutters.

"What must be?" I ask, dragging my eyes away from the ongoing selfie snapping.

"Having girls throwing themselves at you all the time."

I don't say anything.

"You think if he was in a wheelchair for real they'd be acting the same way toward him?"

I put my hand on Dodds's shoulder and squeeze. What is there to say to that? We both know the answer is that they'd be ignoring him as much as they ignore Dodds.

Zac turns and sees me and his face lights up. He waves, excuses himself and comes toward me and then, in front of everyone, he kisses me on the lips.

I'm so taken aback that I forget to close my eyes, so I can see all the girls over Zac's shoulder as their jaws hit the ground. Someone raises their phone and takes a photograph and I pull away, but Zac takes my hand and smiles at me, not even appearing to notice that we are now the focus of everyone in the room and that even Dodds is gawking up at us in astonishment.

"Were you looking for me?" Zac asks.

I nod, though the truth is I'd actually been looking for Walker. Ever since the conversation with my dad I've been both avoiding him and unable to stop thinking about him. Even now I'm with Zac my mind keeps flitting to Walker.

"Do you want to come and see the rest of the center?" I ask, wanting suddenly to get away from the glare of the spotlight. "I could show you the physical therapy room if you like?"

Zac nods. "Yeah, maybe we could find somewhere private," he suggests.

I lead the way out of the kitchen, aware of the gossip machine roaring to life behind us, and I have to admit to myself that there's a certain thrill to being with Zac, though the therapist side of me asks why that should be the case. Would I be as excited to be with him if he wasn't famous? Dodds's words linger in my mind. As we leave the kitchen, I notice that Dodds is staring after me with a scowl on his face. Is it disappointment? I glance quickly away and let the door fall shut behind us.

Walker

There you are!"

She's found me. I was hoping that in my Dress Blues and sitting away from the crowd I'd be able to keep a low profile, but Valentina's like a heat-seeking missile.

"Can I get you some food?" she asks, rubbing my arm.

"I'm good, thanks." Truth is I'm starving, but eating in public is hard. I can't see what's on my plate and I always end up dropping food down my front.

"You sure?" Valentina presses.

"Yeah," I say, forcing a smile. "I'm just not hungry."

She pats my cheek. "You're looking thin. Are you not eating?" She tuts. "It's the food here. It's so bad I wouldn't even feed it to my dog."

"It's not so bad. But not as good as yours, for sure."

"Oh, there she is!" Valentina shouts and rushes off.

I sit there alone, listening to the party going on all around me. I'm sitting at one of the tables that they've set up outside on the lawn in front of the lake. I was steered here by José. I'm not sure how many people are here, but it sounds like hundreds. All around me I can hear people chatting and laughing, kids scream-ing and yelling as they tear around—it's setting my nerves on edge. Someone drops a tray of cutlery or something and the sound makes me leap out of my seat, my heart hammering in my throat like it's an animal trying to claw its way out of my body.

Bruce Springsteen wafts across the lawn. I've been wonder-ing where Didi is and whether she'll try to find me. She hasn't talked to me in five whole days. On the third day I asked Dodds if he'd seen her and he said that he had, that she's been sitting in on his therapy sessions and helping with the art therapy classes, so I know she's around, which leads me to believe that she's avoiding me on purpose.

I almost thought about joining an art class, but what am I going to do? Throw paint blindly at a canvas? Mould my feelings out of clay like an angry toddler mushing Play-Doh?

I don't know what I've done, and that's the hardest thing. If I knew, maybe I could put it right. I keep thinking back to the bathroom—to her shaving me. Did her dad tell her off? Say something? I hope not. I don't want her getting into trouble over me.

My beard has grown back again but I haven't wanted to ask José for help. I'm probably getting funny looks, but that's one of the benefits of being blind—you don't have to deal with funny looks. You just get to imagine them instead.

"Noel, this is my cousin Angela."

Oh God. Valentina is back.

"Angela," she says, "this is Lieutenant Walker."

"Noel," I say, standing up and holding out my hand for her to shake. I never use my first name. All my friends call me Walker, so it sounds strange even to my ears.

"You know, he's the one I was telling you about," Valentina says, stressing the *about*. I can picture her elbowing her cousin in the ribs.

"Oh, hi." Angela giggles. Her handshake is clammy and feels a little like a damp puff pastry filled with cream. It's weird the images that spring to mind now I can't see. I picture her having a beard, but that's just because of what Sanchez said and I doubt it's true—I hope to God it's not true.

"Oh my goodness, you're so tall," Angela exclaims.

She says something in Spanish in a whisper to Valentina, something I catch the gist of and which speculates on the size of another part of my anatomy.

"And so handsome. Isn't he handsome?" Valentina says. "He looks even better when he shaves."

I grit my teeth. I know Valentina has good intentions, but the way she's trying to set me up is so obvious it's making me feel as pathetic as hell. I don't need any help being set up. And I don't want to be set up with anyone anyway. And then there's the fact that she's emphasizing what I look like, blatantly trying to compensate for the major blindness detail that's literally staring them in the eye. I smile politely, but it hurts my face. If they knew that it wasn't a physical issue but a mental one causing the blindness, then I wonder if they would still be standing here, if Valentina would be trying to sell me quite so hard. For a second I wonder if I should tell them. That would definitely buy me some alone time.

But I don't want to tell them, or anyone. I figure I'll just have to make small talk for thirty seconds and then I'll make an excuse to leave. But if I do that, I'll have to try to make my way across the lawn without help, which will be like crossing a minefield, what with there being so many kids and people in the way. Damn. I'm trapped.

"Ooooh, there he is!" Valentina suddenly squeals. "Did you see him?"

"See who?" I ask, wincing as she and Angela both start to gasp and shriek loudly enough to split my eardrums.

"Zac Ridgemont! Oh my God, I can't believe he's actually here! I have to go and take a photograph."

She's talking about that actor. He's still here?

"I'll be back in a minute," Valentina says, and she's gone. I pray for a second that Angela has gone with her—that the lure of Zac Ridgemont will be too great—but then I feel someone touch my arm.

"Do you want me to feed you some cake?" It's Angela.

"I'm good, thanks," I say.

"Here, sit down," she says, tugging on my arm.

I sit, heavily, and suppress a loud sigh.

"Here, try the cake. I made it myself. It's my mother's recipe. You like cake?" She doesn't let me answer but keeps on talking. "Well, even if you don't, you'll like this cake." And the next thing I know a heavily-frosted cake is being pressed against my lips.

I take the smallest bite, trying to control the urge I have to push her hand away.

"Mmmm, lovely," I manage to say through gritted teeth, holding up my hand to stop her from forcing more at me.

She dabs at my face with a napkin. "There we go," she says. "Do you want some lemonade?"

"No," I say. "No thanks."

I can feel all my muscles winding up like someone's ratcheting them with a wrench. Jesus, anyone, rescue me.

Angela is still jabbering away—a stream of consciousness that I realize, with relief, I don't need to interrupt. She just needs an audience. A disabled one. I have never wanted my sight back so much in all my life as I do right now, but no one is coming to my aid, and though I will my sight back with every fiber of my being, it doesn't come.

I zone out and instead focus on the last memory I have of Didi helping me shave. It's about the only good memory I have since the bomb went off, and I've run over it so many times in my head it's starting to wear thin.

Didi

Colonel Kingsley is stepping up to the podium to give his speech. I can see his wife, Jessa's mom, standing to one side, smiling up at him proudly.

Zac is beside me, and I'm fully aware that all eyes are on us and not Colonel Kingsley. Even my mom is raising her glass to me across the crowd, her head cocked not so subtly in Zac's direction.

Zac notices and raises his own glass. My mom smiles at him, and even from this distance I can see the blush rise across her cheeks. Even she isn't immune to his charms, I note.

I scan the crowd and spot Walker over at the edge of the lawn. My heart kicks in my chest but my smile falters. He looks like he's trapped with a woman in a kaftanlike flowery dress. She's all over him like a rash, keeps trying to feed him cake, and I can see him nodding politely every now and then, but I can tell from his body language that he's unhappy. His back is ramrod straight, his mouth is drawn into a line, and his nostrils are flaring.

I think about going over there to rescue him. This must be his idea of hell—all these people, all these obstacles, all this noise. At least they thought to cancel the fireworks. What's stopping me from going over there? I sigh. Everything. Nothing. My dad. Zac. The knowledge that if I do I won't be able to stop myself . . . *From what?* I ask myself angrily.

I glance sideways at Zac. I'm standing next to a film star. He's impossibly gorgeous and seems to be completely into me, so why can't I stop thinking about Walker? Am I deliberately trying to sabotage my shot at happiness? At what might turn out to be the real deal?

I study Zac's clean-shaven cheek, the skin as smooth and flawless as a mannequin's, the smile that shows off his perfect white teeth, and then I think of Walker's rough stubble and the slightly sardonic smile that sometimes plays on his lips.

A voice in my head yells at me that I'm crazy, that Zac is the one, that I'm living the dream I've always yearned for. Zac glances my way as if sensing me staring and grins at me. I grin back at him but a bead of sweat is snaking down my spine.

Oh my God.

I want to be with Walker.

I'm drawn to him like a crazed, suicidal moth to a blazing bonfire.

I can't stop my gaze returning to him again and again. A couple of times I catch him turning his head and seemingly scanning the lawn, and my heart shoots into the stratosphere. Is he trying to find me? Can he see? But then disappointment crushes me when his gaze passes over me. Even though I know he's blind.

I'm here, I want to shout. *I'm here.*

More beads of sweat break out, this time on my brow. I swipe at them and give myself a fierce, silent talking-to. I can't walk away from Zac for a guy who's moody and messed-up and a hundred kinds of broken. And a hundred kinds of out of bounds.

That woman is trying to press a glass of something against his lips and my hands twitch. I take a step in his direction and stop myself. I have an overwhelming urge to place myself between them. I've never felt a surge of protectiveness like it before and it takes me completely by surprise. There's a roar in my chest and it's compounded by the applause that's now broken out.

I realize that Colonel Kingsley has stopped talking and everyone is clapping.

Zac takes my arm. "I was wondering if I could take you out to dinner tonight, to say thanks for organizing my visit."

"Oh, um," I say, aware that we're being looked at, that people are nudging each other all around us.

Say yes, you should say yes, the voice inside my head tells me. Only my tongue won't obey.

And then, before I can answer, Valentina has placed herself between us. "I'm sorry," she says, breathless and fanning herself with excitement. "I don't mean to interrupt, but I just love you."

I take a step back to give her some space. It's clear she's not talking to me. In fact, I'm not sure she's even noticed I'm standing here.

Zac gives her a brilliant red-carpet smile. "Thanks," he says.

"Could I just get a picture with you?" Valentina asks. "Do you mind?"

"Not at all," Zac answers.

Valentina rustles through her bag for her phone and I think about taking advantage of the opportunity to edge backward and leave, but before I can, Zac grabs for my hand.

His thumb caresses my hand and Valentina notices and

shoots me a dumbstruck look, her mouth falling open.

Zac drops my hand and turns back to Valentina. "Ready?" he asks, and he throws his arm around her shoulders and, taking her phone from her, takes a photo.

"Thank you, thank you!" Valentina says, scrolling straight through to check it's come out okay. "Oh my God!" She clutches the phone to her chest and gives me another really unsubtle look—widening her eyes in Zac's direction and looking as if she's about to burst.

I shrug awkwardly.

"I'll leave you two to it, then," she says, winking at me. "You have a good day now. Oh, and try the guacamole. I made it."

"I will. You have a great day too," Zac answers, waving at her. He turns back to me and, still grinning, grabs for my hand. He pulls me away from the crowd and instantly, as though a switch has been flicked, his smile vanishes and a hard veneer replaces it. "Come on," he says, and starts pulling me toward the doors to the canteen. "Let's get away from this circus."

It's as if a mask has slipped and I've seen a glimpse of the real Zac. I start to protest, looking over my shoulder at Walker, but then I see that he's now been joined by Dodds and also by Kit's father, the Marine Corps chaplain. That woman in the flowery dress who was trying to force-feed him is still there, but I can see that Dodds is talking to her now.

I guess Walker doesn't need me.

I let Zac lead me back inside.

Walker

Major Ryan, the Marine Corps chaplain, saves me, which if I still believed in God would be in some way poetic.

"You look about ready to dig a tunnel," he whispers in my ear.

Angela is momentarily distracted, talking to Dodds. I think she's telling him all about her dogs.

"God, yes," I answer him. I'm trained well enough to know that when an opportunity arises, you take it. You don't hesitate. Hesitation gets you killed.

I'm on my feet in the next second.

"You're leaving?"

It's Angela. Damn.

"We have gentlemen's business to attend to," the chaps answers for me.

I shrug. If he told her we were heading off for a gay tryst in the bushes, I wouldn't care. In fact, I consider putting it out there anyway, thinking it might deter her from any future advances, but I'm not sure how the chaps would feel if I did that.

"Oh, okay, well, I'll come find you in a bit," Angela says, giving my arm a firm squeeze.

The chaplain threads my arm through his and starts to lead me through the crowd.

"Nice girl," he murmurs. "Maybe a little too keen."

"Thanks," I tell him. "I really appreciate it."

"Where would you like to go?" he asks when we're out of earshot.

My room is what I want to say, but I don't. I'm here now and I want to speak to Didi. Maybe she's inside where all the food and preparation is going on. Maybe she's helping organize the volunteers. Maybe she's standing right in front of me but just doesn't want to talk to me. The thought hurts. More than it should.

"Inside, please," I tell the chaps and he guides me, speaking in a low voice and giving me careful directions about where to put my feet and where there's a step coming up. He's a good guy. I have a feeling he paid me a visit when I first arrived at the center and I may have told him where to stick his Bible. I wish I hadn't now.

"Yo, Lieutenant!" It's Sanchez. I stop. "I saw you got stuck talking to Angela. I am *really* sorry about that. I told Valentina she should stay out of it, that you weren't interested in being fixed up, but she wouldn't listen."

"It's fine," I say.

"You okay if I leave you now?" the chaps asks.

"Yes, thank you, sir," I say.

He clasps my hand and shakes it. "It's an honor, Lieutenant," he says, and out of nowhere a lump forms in my throat that I struggle to swallow away.

"Oh man, you think Dodds is okay?" Sanchez asks.

I can only guess that he's seen Angela trying to force-feed him cake.

"Yeah," Sanchez continues without waiting for me to answer. "I'm sure he's fine." He sounds doubtful.

"Have you seen Didi?" I ask him, throwing the question out there before I can stop myself.

"Nah," he says. "Why?" There's a pause, then he punches me on the arm. "Oh my God! You like her. You dirty dog. You're blushing."

"I am not."

"Yeah, you are, you're blushing like a virgin on her wedding night."

Now I can feel the heat rising up my neck. I glare at Sanchez.

"You totally have the hots for her." He slaps me on the back. "And Lieutenant," he says, "I got to congratulate you on your fine taste in women. Even though you can't see shit, you managed to pick the hottest girl in the building, 'cept for my wife, that is."

"Who's hot? Who are you talking about?"

It's Valentina.

"No one," Sanchez mutters quickly. "Hey, Tina, you seen Didi anywhere? Doctor Monroe's daughter?"

"Yes! I just saw her with Zac Ridgemont."

My gut tightens like someone's thrown a lasso around my waist.

"I think those two are an item," Valentina gushes in a reverent tone. "Did you know? Oh my God, can you even imagine? Dating a movie star! I wonder what he's like in bed. That body . . ."

"He's a dick," Sanchez cuts in fast.

"Don't say that," Valentina yells. "You don't even know him. He was so polite to me just now. Look, he let me take a photo with him."

"He asked Dodds how he goes to the bathroom and José told me he went around shaking everyone's hand in the physical therapy room telling them how 'inspiring' they are."

"That's sweet," Valentina coos.

"No it isn't. Anyone tells me I'm inspiring I'll punch them in the face."

I barely hear the conversation. My brain is still trying to decipher the news. Didi's dating Zac Ridgemont? That's her *kind of* boyfriend? I hear myself laughing out loud.

"What's so funny?" Valentina asks.

I shake my head. "Nothing."

What's funny is that she's dating a movie star and that I thought maybe, possibly, there was a chance that . . . I can't even finish the thought. Angela made me feel pathetic earlier, but now I feel I've reached a whole new level of pathetic I never knew existed. I laugh some more. That's why Didi hasn't been to see me in five days. She must have figured out I was into her like some panting stray dog and felt embarrassed about it. I'm so fucking stupid. I spin on my heel, trying to get my bearings.

"Where you going?" Sanchez asks.

"To my room," I mumble.

"That's the wrong way," he says.

"Why are you going?" Valentina chimes in. She takes my arm. "Stay! Did you try my guacamole yet?"

I can feel my face burning, the laughter gathering in my chest, bubbling up my throat—hysterical laughter, bitter-tasting. I shake her off.

"I need to take some pain meds," I say. Lying. I'm lying. I just want them off my back.

"Let him go," Sanchez tells her. "I'll walk you back if you like," he says to me.

"I'm fine," I say, feeling the laughter ebb and swell then disappear, tamped down all of a sudden by a growl of rage that's trying to burst free—pent-up anger and frustration triggered by shame.

"Okay," Sanchez backs off.

I concentrate on orienting myself, though my head feels like it's about to burst and I'm finding it hard to focus on my surroundings. The noises around me seem to be amplified and the smells too—it's as if the smoke of the grill and the eye-watering stink of onions is turning into the acrid smolder of gunpowder and the stench of burning skin. The doors are open to the lawn and I can hear the chink of glassware and loud conversation blasting from my right, which means if I walk straight ahead I should get to the doors to the hallway that leads to the elevators. I'll just find the wall and follow it.

I hear Valentina and Sanchez arguing in loud whispers, probably about letting me go unaccompanied, and I imagine Sanchez telling Valentina that I have the hots for Didi.

Embarrassment propels me even faster toward the doors. At least toward where I hope the doors are. I smack a table, sending something smashing to the floor, but I keep going. I bang into someone and mumble an apology and finally, hands out in front of me like a real blind man, I find the wall and follow it until I'm out in the hallway.

I yank on my collar to loosen it—it's so hot I could choke—and then, on shaking legs and with a hand against the wall, I keep walking.

Didi

Zac pulls me into a room—I think one of the art therapy rooms. It's dark, but when I fumble for the light switch he stops me, takes my hand, and pulls me close.

"Hey," he whispers, his arms looping around my waist.

I freeze.

He ducks his head, pulling me toward him with his hands, and his lips find mine. His hands start tracing my body and he groans.

I kiss him back for a few seconds, but then I pull away. I can't. I can't stop imagining it's Walker kissing me.

Zac is giving me a curious half smile through the dark, wondering why I've pulled away.

I look at him. "I'm sorry," I say.

"What?" Zac asks, sounding confused. "What for?"

"I don't think I can do this."

He glances around at the room. "Yeah, maybe it's not the best place for it. Maybe we should go back to my place." He leans forward and kisses me again, but I duck out of his arms.

He pulls back with a shocked expression on his face and I

realize that he's probably never been rejected by a woman before. That, in turn, makes me wonder how many women he's been with.

"What are we even doing?" I ask him.

He gives me a strange look and shakes his head. "What do you mean?"

"What is this?" I say, gesturing between him and me.

Zac sighs and, stepping forward runs the flats of his hands up my arms. "I don't really know what I want," he murmurs, "but I do know that I like you. I like hanging out with you and I'd like to get to know you better." He gives me that look, the one that's designed to make girls dissolve into puddles, and I feel the muscles in my legs start to come loose, my will start to weaken.

"But, you know, I think the whole exclusivity thing isn't something I'm wanting to do right now," he says. "We're both really young."

I nod, staring down at my feet. Yeah, we are. And maybe that would work if I was a different person, but I'm not. I want the guy I'm with to be fully, one hundred percent with me, and not even looking at other women, let alone sleeping with them. I glance back up at Zac feeling resolved. He doesn't know it, but he's just made it much easier to walk away.

"I don't think that works for me," I tell him. "So, I guess we should maybe say good-bye."

He raises his eyebrows. "No one's ever broken up with me in real life," he says. Then he nods, still smiling. "There's a first time for everything, I guess."

"I should go," I say.

"Okay." He sticks his hands in his pockets and rocks on the

balls of his feet, looking like a little boy. My resolve is given another boost.

I reach for the door handle. "Bye, Zac."

When I walk out into the hallway, I come to a sudden halt. As if the universe has planted him there, Walker is right in front of me, heading toward the elevators, one palm pressed to the wall to help guide him there.

"Walker?" I say.

He stops and slowly turns around. In his uniform he looks altogether different—older, professional, almost a stranger.

"It's Didi," I say, but I can tell that he already knows it's me.

His face is tight, his jaw tensed, and the pain and hurt flashing in his eyes makes me draw breath. What's happened? Was it that girl? I clench my fists thinking about what I'll do or say to her if I find out she's hurt him in any way.

"Oh, hey," Walker says and tries to give me a smile, but it doesn't work. A muscle in his jaw pulses. Is he angry? At me? Because I've been avoiding him?

"Where are you going?" I ask and step toward him. Why is he so upset? I want to put my hand on his arm but I get a very clear sense that he's not looking for sympathy or comfort right now.

"I'm just . . . going back to my room," he says, gesturing toward the elevator.

"Oh," I say. I think about it for half a second. "You want me to come with you?"

"No," he says quickly, angrily. "I can manage."

"I didn't mean did you need help, I meant do you want me to come with you and . . . hang out?"

One of his eyebrows shoots up. "I'm good, thanks," he says

brusquely. His beard has grown back. I want to run my hand down his cheek. I want to take his hand. I have to stop myself.

"Didi?"

Oh crap. It's Zac. I turn around.

"Hi," I say.

Zac glances at Walker. I can feel the heat rush to my cheeks. "Um, this is Walker," I say, because what else is there to do but introduce them?

"Hi," Zac says, holding out his hand for Walker to shake. "We met earlier, I think."

The scowl on Walker's face intensifies. His mouth purses. I look at Zac, who's staring at Walker confused, wondering why he isn't shaking his hand and why he's staring off somewhere over his head into the middle distance.

"Walker's visually impaired," I say quietly, feeling myself cringe as I do. He must hate me having to explain it. And I'm right. I can see Walker's nostrils flare, the color rise in his face.

"Oh, right," Zac says, dropping his hand like it's been burned. "Sorry, man."

Walker smiles tightly. "It's fine. I'm just going. You two have fun." He turns away again, his hand going out to the wall.

"Wait," I say. "I'm coming with you." I turn quickly back to Zac. "Bye."

"Yeah, okay," he says, shooting a look at Walker, who's now halfway down the hallway. "I just wanted to ask if you could say thanks to your dad for me. I'm going to sneak out so I don't have to run the gauntlet of all those middle-aged women."

"Okay," I say.

I watch him walk away, wondering about what I've just done, but when I do a scan of what I'm feeling, there's no regret.

I turn and run after Walker, catching him at the elevator, where he's jabbing at every button repeatedly.

"Hey," I say. "Hold up."

He stops punching the buttons. For a moment we both stand there in awkward silence waiting for the elevator to arrive.

"Don't you want to go with him?" Walker asks me suddenly.

I glance at him. "No. Why?" I ask.

"No reason," he mumbles.

The elevator doors slide open.

We both step inside without a word.

"I thought you guys were . . . a couple," Walker suddenly blurts as the doors slide shut.

Oh. I open my mouth to speak but nothing comes out. Could that be why he's acting so weird? The thought makes me break into a smile.

"No," I say. "I mean, we were sort of seeing each other, but I just broke up with him."

The scowl drops off Walker's face and surprise takes over. He turns to look my way—or at least to face me. "You did?"

"Yeah."

He turns back to face the elevator doors. For five seconds we both just stand there, and when I glance at him I see he's trying as hard as I am to hide a smile.

Walker

We walk along the hallway to my room, neither of us talking. I'm having to concentrate on remembering what obstacles are where so I can avoid them. I don't want a white stick, but this groping around and having to hold on to the wall isn't working so well. I must look like an idiot. Didi doesn't say anything, though.

Is she looking at me? Can she see the smile I'm trying to hide? I tell myself it doesn't mean anything that she broke up with Zac. But I can't completely snuff out the spark of hope that's ignited inside my chest. Hope for what, I'm not sure. Why this girl? Why now? What am I expecting? I have to keep asking these questions. I barely know Didi. I don't even know what she looks like, but it's there—undeniably there—some kind of connection. Even now, as we walk along in silence, I'm so aware of her that my nerve endings feel like they're being stroked with a feather. I'm so finely tuned to her that I can hear her footsteps from twenty feet away. I can hear it in her voice when she's smiling. I can sense it when she enters a room full of people. I can even pick up on the smallest variation in her mood. Right now I can tell she's buzzing slightly, though whether she's nervous or happy I can't quite tell.

When we get to my room, I push the door open and stand aside to let her through. She brushes against me and I get a sense of her height—she comes up to my shoulder—as well as a hit of whatever perfume it is she's wearing, the one that reminds me of long summer days spent out on the water. I hear her walk toward the windows and open one. The sounds of the party drift up and into the room.

"Poor Dodds," Didi says under her breath.

I walk toward the sound of her voice. She must be looking down on the people below us. "Has Angela still got him cornered?"

"Is that her name?" Didi asks.

"Yeah, it's Valentina's cousin. She was trying to set me up with her."

"She was? Oh." There's a clear note of disappointment in her voice that fans my spark of hope into an ember.

"Yeah," I say. "She's not really my type, though."

"How do you know if she's not your type?" Didi asks. "She might look like a supermodel."

I smile. "Even if she does look like a supermodel, I'm still not into her. And, just so you know, I'm not that superficial." I stop. Maybe that's not true. Maybe I used to be. Maybe all sighted people are to a degree. "I never used to think I judged people on their looks," I say, shrugging, "but I think we all do, if we're honest. One benefit of this"—I gesture at my eyes—"is that now I guess I'm learning to judge people by their actions and their words instead."

Didi laughs under her breath. "Yeah, we should all do more of that."

She walks away from the window. I stand there, unsure where

156

to go or what to do, even where to "look." The atmosphere is thick with unspoken words—at least on my part. I miss being near her and have to fight my inclination to follow her over to the bed, where I can hear she's sat down.

I lean instead against the windowsill and cross my arms over my chest. I'm hot in my uniform and want to take off the jacket. I make do with taking off my hat. Self-conscious, I run my hand through my hair, which is getting almost as long as my beard.

"You look very *Officer and a Gentleman*," Didi remarks.

"Is that your favorite movie?" I ask. She never did tell me what it was.

"No," she says, and I hear the smile in her voice, the one that makes me strive that bit harder to say something funny.

She mumbles something.

"What?" I ask.

"It's *Avatar*. Don't laugh!" she warns, but she's laughing herself so I join in.

"*Avatar*? Seriously? The blue alien movie?"

"Yes."

"The one that's basically a didactic, cliché-ridden lesson in how humans are losing their connection to nature and destroying the planet?"

"Yes, that would be the one."

I shake my head.

"So what is your favorite movie, then?" she asks me, laughing.

"*The Shawshank Redemption*," I answer.

"I've never seen it," she says. "Isn't that the prison one?"

"Yeah," I say. "You should watch it some time."

"What's it about?"

"It's about this guy who gets locked up for a crime he didn't commit and after years and years he manages to escape. And then, at the end, you see him on the beach somewhere in Mexico. He made it. And he's got a boat and he's happy. And . . ." I shrug. "He's free."

"You just ruined the ending for me, thanks."

"Oh, sorry. Well, at least it has a happy ending. I bet you like those." I wince. That came out wrong. "Um," I say hastily, "I mean, I'm guessing you like your stories to have happy endings."

Didi laughs. "You guessed right. *Love Story* just about killed me. And *The Fault in Our Stars*. I cried so hard in both those movies I almost burst a blood vessel."

"Is therapy a good career move for you, then?" I ask. "Are there ever any happy endings?"

"Yes, of course there are. All the time," Didi says. "The patient has got to want it, though. And work with the therapist."

I nod to myself. Touché.

"And they've got to be positive about the future."

I can't stop the snort.

"Don't you ever think about the future?" she asks.

"Nope." What I don't want to tell her is that it's hard enough to get through each day without having to think about tomorrow as well. Isn't there something to be said for living in the moment? Tomorrow might not even come. But I don't think Didi would want to hear these kind of thoughts. I think she's the kind of girl who likes to plan for old age.

"So I finished that other book," I say, wanting to steer the conversation away from the direction it's going in. "The sex and relationships one."

"Oh yeah?" she says.

"It was interesting. Your mom wrote it, right?"

"Yeah," says Didi. "She's a sexpert." She laughs, but I pick up on the slight tinge of embarrassment when she says it.

"She's smart. It was well written." I pause. "What was it she said? 'Attraction plus obstacle in the way equals—'"

"'The ultimate erotic encounter,'" Didi finishes for me, and there's an edge to her voice, a slight breathlessness that wasn't there a moment ago.

"Yeah. That's it," I say.

It was a quote that stood out for me among all the others. Can't think why.

"It's what all good romance stories are built on," Didi jokes, but there's a jangle of nerves beneath her laughter.

"Yeah," I say, then, "So, you like Justin Bieber, huh?"

"Oh God, you found it." Her voice is muffled and I assume she's buried her head in her hands.

I laugh. "Yeah. I was thinking that could be a problem."

"What kind of a problem?" Didi asks, curious.

"An obstacle to us . . ." I pause, weighing my next words carefully. "Being friends." I put an inflection on *friends*.

"Oh."

Shit. I was hoping for more than an *oh*. I don't know how to take that *oh*. Maybe I played my hand too soon. Maybe I misread the situation—the tension between us.

"I . . . ," Didi stammers.

I shake my head, embarrassed. "Sorry. I didn't mean—"

"No," she interrupts, "I do totally want to be friends." Is that an emphasis on the word friends? "It's just—"

I force a smile. "I get it. Don't worry. It's cool."

I hear her get up from the bed and then suddenly she's right beside me.

"Walker. I do want to be friends," she says so quietly it's almost a whisper.

I hold my breath.

"I really, really want to be *friends*," she says, and now her voice really is a whisper and that really was an inflection. The back of her hand brushes mine, just the lightest of touches, but it sends an electric jolt through me.

Everything beyond us goes still. Even the noise outside the window fades. All I'm aware of is Didi and how close she is and what she's just said and the feeling inside my chest—an easing of the metal bands that have been wrapped around my ribs for the last two months.

I let out the breath I'm holding. But then I register that there was something off about her tone. She didn't sound happy. And she moves her hand and steps away from me.

"But I can't be friends with you, Walker."

I shake my head, not sure I've understood. "Why?" Is it because I'm blind? Because I'm a fucked-up disabled vet with no prospects?

"Because I *work* here. There are rules around these things. You know, patient–doctor boundaries. It could damage my career. I could get thrown off my college course."

"Oh." Shit. I hadn't thought of that. I've got to say I'm relieved it's not for the reasons I thought, but that doesn't make me feel much better. "I'm sorry," I mumble, turning away again so she can't see the disappointment that must be flaring across my face.

"Walker," she says, and the way she says my name feels so like a caress I close my eyes on reflex. "I wish it wasn't the case."

"Didi, it's fine," I say, and suddenly I find I have to put as much distance as I can between us because she's standing so close I can't concentrate. I take three or four steps until I get to the bed. My head is reeling, and now she's not so near to me I wonder if I imagined the longing in her voice and the brush of her hand against mine. Was she implying that she wanted more than to be friends, or did I misread things? Either way it doesn't sound like it makes much difference.

"I get it," I say. "This is your life we're talking about. You don't want to screw it up. You've worked so hard to get this far." I can't seem to make myself sound enthusiastic.

"Yeah," Didi answers, and she doesn't sound any more enthusiastic than me.

"So," I say, sitting down on the bed. "Does this mean we don't get to hang out anymore?"

"No," she says carefully. "We just have to agree to keep things professional."

I consider her choice of words. That suggests that she thinks there's a danger of not keeping things professional. I can't stop a smile taking over my face.

"Is that a problem?" she asks.

I kill the smile and shake my head. "No." I hesitate. "We can keep things professional."

"Just until you're out of here, and then . . ." She stops.

"Then?" I ask.

"Then, um . . . we can go on a date . . ."

"Well, I'd better hurry up and get the hell better," I say, laughing, but inside I'm wondering how the hell that's ever going to be possible. It's not like I have a cold. How do I get better? Here she is thinking of the future and planning for it, and I'm struggling to get through every single goddamn second.

But Didi starts laughing too, and the sound fills me up with lightness and my vision seems to lighten around the edges as though someone's lifted the edge of a blanket.

Didi

t's an impossible line to walk, and I feel myself teetering every time I see him. I know he's aware of me whenever I'm in the same room as him because straightaway his head snaps up and he looks over in my direction, his gaze always landing either on me or not far away from me. It's a little unnerving, and at the same time it stirs a flutter in the pit of my belly that's getting harder and harder to ignore.

We've fallen into a routine where I drop by every afternoon for an hour. We chat, him sitting on the bed, me in the chair, and it feels like there's an electric fence between us and that with every minute that passes the voltage steadily increases. I stare at his mouth when he talks, imagining what it would be like to kiss him, and have to force the thought away over and over again.

I'm desperate for him to open up and talk about that day—the day of the explosion—but I haven't pushed him. He steers away from the past and never mentions the future; in fact, all we seem to talk about are books, movies, and current affairs. We don't talk about our lives—that would be pushing it into friend territory.

He's clearly trying to stick to the terms of our agreement to keep things aboveboard, and something has shifted in his attitude—even my dad has remarked on it. He's more focused, happier even. His scowl has vanished, and I have to stop myself from smiling when I think that I might be part of the reason. He's working out with Sanchez for several hours a day, either in the pool or in the gym, and sometimes I'll take a deliberate detour so I can look in through the windows and watch them, or rather watch Walker, and then I have to give myself an angry talking-to because I feel like a voyeur.

As I head down to the art therapy room before my hour with Walker, I notice the bounce in my step. I can't stop smiling, either. The only thing that slightly takes the edge off is a worry that maybe the chemistry we have might disappear if he gets his sight back. But that's blotted out by the bigger worry of what will happen if he doesn't get his sight back.

An enormous crashing sound from the room I'm passing brings me to a sudden halt. It's followed by an angry bellow and the sound of glass splintering. I push open the door to one of the therapy rooms and have to duck my head as a mug filled with paintbrushes soars past me and smashes into the doorframe.

I glance up and see that Dodds is the one doing the yelling. He's in his wheelchair, his face ablaze with fury, and he's grabbing anything in sight and throwing it. Paint splatters the walls. A torn-up canvas hangs off an easel. Jars of dirty paint water have been upended over the floor and now he's reaching for the pots of paint and is throwing them like grenades at the art-therapy teacher—a woman in her sixties—who's holding up her arms to shield herself. One of the auxiliary staff—a guy in scrubs—is trying to get close to Dodds, but he's so angry, so filled with rage and lashing out so hard that it's like trying to get close to a spewing volcano. The guy is now having to dodge oil-paint tubes that Dodds is chucking at him.

I'm completely frozen, not sure what to do or how to help, but then two orderlies rush past me and into the room. They approach Dodds from two sides as if he's a rabid dog and I hear myself yell at them to stop, but too late. They've grabbed his arms and are restraining him, which only enrages him even further, and he starts thrashing wildly with his arms. I can see they're trying to be as gentle as they can be—one is talking calmly in Dodds's ear, but Dodds is beyond listening. It's as if he's possessed. His neck muscles are as rigid as steel cables and his eyes are popping out of their sockets.

He jabs at one of the orderlies with his elbow and there's a struggle which ends abruptly when his wheelchair overturns and he's is thrown out of it, crashing facedown on the ground.

I run into the room, my legs finally ungluing themselves, and throw myself down on the floor beside him. One of the orderlies is still standing and the other is bending down, reaching for Dodds, trying to help turn him over, and I push him off.

"Leave him," I hiss.

He's lying facedown and I'm caught momentarily by the disorienting sight of his legless torso, his pant legs pinned up under him. He pushes himself up onto his hands and then collapses down onto one side as though the anger has drained from him and he's entirely spent. He starts sobbing.

I put my hand on his arm. "It's okay," I say. "It's okay."

He curls toward me, his arms coming up over his face, his

sobbing getting louder. I don't know what to do. I look up and the orderlies are watching me as if they're waiting for me to give them an order.

I stroke Dodds's hair, feeling the wormlike scar beneath his scalp. My heart aches for him. How can a person be so broken and ever be put back together again?

"Shhh," I say, and slowly, slowly, the sobs wracking Dodds's body start to ease.

He says something, hiccups it through his tears.

"What?" I say, bending closer.

"I don't want to do this anymore," he whispers, his eyes screwed shut, his fists clenched.

My hand, stroking his hair, stills.

Behind me I can hear the orderlies talking in whispers and the door opening, and then my dad is suddenly beside me, crouched down by Dodds.

"Hi there, Corporal," he says. "Let's get you sitting up."

The orderlies move to help my dad hoist Dodds to a sitting position and I back away, but not before my dad has caught my eye and nodded at me.

"We'll take it from here," he tells me.

I watch from the doorway as Dodds is lifted, listless and still curled in on himself, into his wheelchair, and I watch my dad kneel beside him and talk to him quietly for a moment before he stands up and nods at the orderly, who then wheels him out the room.

"What happened?" my dad asks once they're gone.

I shake my head.

"He just lost it," the art-therapy teacher interrupts. She's pale and seems a little shaken still. She picks up one of the upended jars and sets it on a table. "He's been in here a lot lately. I thought he was doing well. I was encouraging him to explore what was triggering his anger."

"Well, that worked," I mutter to myself.

"But what triggered this particular episode?" my dad asked. "Did he say anything? What was he painting at the time? Anything?"

The woman gestures at the ripped canvas on the easel and my dad crosses over to it and holds up the torn pieces. It's another painting like the one Dodds's did of a soldier with no legs lying in what looks like a flame-ringed minefield. Or possibly it's hell. Body parts and broken bodies are scattered everywhere. I flinch backward. My dad frowns.

The other orderly speaks up. "He just came from an appointment with his prosthetist."

My dad turns to him.

"I think he was told he can't get any legs fitted yet. His stumps haven't shrunk enough."

My dad nods. "Okay," he says. "I'm going to go and find his doctor. I'll see you in a while," he says to me.

I stay to help the art therapist clear up the room.

"Does it work?" I say to her after a few minutes.

"What?" she asks.

"Art therapy?" I say, nodding at the canvas. It doesn't seem to have worked.

"Better out than in," she says with a shrug.

I muse on that.

She sighs and starts unpinning the canvas. "In my view, anger manifests either by turning inward and becoming depression, or outwardly, like we just witnessed. The idea is that through art you can help transform that anger into something else . . ." She trails off.

I nod. There's so much anger in this place. Even though the platitudes and the smiles of staff and patients are designed to hide it, it's there constantly, pulsing like a death knell beneath the surface. I think of Walker and how angry he was when I first met him—and how depressed. Has that anger gone anywhere? He's using exercise and sport to help transform it, I guess, but what happens when you finish the race? You can't keep running, literally and metaphorically, for the rest of your life. One day it surely has to catch up with you.

Walker

H ey."

It's Didi at the door. She sounds tired, sad. "What's up?" I ask, sitting up straighter in bed.

"Nothing," she says after a little pause. She's lying, but I don't push it. "You want some company?" she asks.

"Sure," I say.

She has no idea how much I crave her company, how when she's not with me I'm counting down the minutes until the next time I hear her voice. My whole day is built around these afternoon visits.

"What are you watching?" she asks.

"Fox News," I say, grimacing. "It's the only channel I can get."

"What?" she asks, stepping into the room.

Closer. Come closer. I take a deep breath. This enforced state of propriety is hard to handle. I'm trying my hardest to keep things friendly but not too friendly, though my thoughts have overstepped the mark a hundred times already, leaped beyond the friend zone and into the X-rated zone. I can't seem to stop them.

"I can't change the channel."

Next thing I hear her beside the bed and she's taking the remote from my hand. Her arm brushes mine. I force my hand to stay where it is, though I'm imagining stroking my fingertips down the inside of her elbow all the way to her wrist, imagining, wondering how soft the skin is.

"Hmmm," she says. "I think the remote's broken."

I hear her walk out of the room. She's back less than a minute later. "I swapped it for the one in Dodds's room."

"Does he know?"

"He's asleep. I think they sedated him."

"Why?" I ask.

"He had a kind of breakdown in the art room."

"Shit," I say.

"Yeah. I wish there was something we could do for him. He needs visitors. Is there anyone from his unit, anyone he was friends with that I could call?"

I shake my head. "They're all deployed overseas."

She exhales loudly.

"Oh, look," Didi says suddenly.

"What?"

"*The Shawshank Redemption* is on tonight."

"What time?" I ask.

"Nine p.m."

"Want to watch it with me?"

"Um . . ."

Shit. Overstepped the line. It's so easy to do because it's so damn blurry. "Sorry," I say quickly.

"Yeah, okay," she says. "It's a date."

"A non-date," I clarify.

"I'll bring popcorn." She's smiling, I can tell.

Didi

Around eight thirty I peer into Dodds's room to see how he's doing. He's awake and lying on his back, staring at the ceiling.

I knock on his door. "Hey," I say.

He looks my way briefly then goes back to staring at the ceiling.

"Can I come in?" I ask.

He shrugs.

I walk into the room trying not to notice the sheets drawn flat against the mattress where his legs should be. He heaves up onto his elbows and wriggles himself into a sitting position, wincing as he does.

"Are you okay?" I ask.

He gives me a flat-eyed stare. "It hurts," he says. "It's like where my legs should be I can still feel them and it fucking hurts. All the time."

I nod. He's describing phantom limb syndrome. "Is there anything they can give you?"

He shakes his head bitterly. "I'm on more drugs than a fucking junkie. I'm taking so many pills I don't even know what half of them are for anymore."

I don't know what to say. I wanted to speak to my dad but I didn't get the chance, and now he's gone away for a few nights to a conference. I glance around the room, spotting the photograph on his nightstand of the blond girl. Dodds really needs a visitor. I wonder who she is and why she doesn't visit.

"You feel like watching *The Shawshank Redemption*?" I ask him.

He shrugs. "Okay," he says.

"Great," I say. "It starts at nine. We're watching in Walker's room."

I turn to go but then remember something. "I brought you something," I say, suddenly having second thoughts about the wisdom of it, but now it's too late to back down and he's looking at me expectantly.

"Um, it's this," I say, handing him a booklet I got from the employment counselor.

"What is it?" he asks, turning it over.

"It's a book about possible career routes."

He doesn't say anything and I cringe inwardly. Stupid idea. This is not what he wants to be thinking about. I just thought it might help give him something to focus on or think about other than unicorns with blasphemous phrases coming out their butts.

He nods and flicks through the pages, then looks up at me and smiles. "Thanks," he says.

Is he being genuine? It's hard to tell. "I know it's probably the last thing you want to think about, but—"

"No," he says. "It's good." He holds up the book. "I'll be sure to read it."

"Okay," I say. "Um, I guess I'll see you later."

When I walk out of the room I bump straight into Sanchez and Valentina. Valentina throws her arms around me, and after she's done hugging me she pulls back and holds me by the tops of my arms. "So tell me all about that gorgeous boyfriend of yours! Is it true? Are you really dating Zac Ridgemont? Oh my God!"

She's practically bouncing off the walls with excitement. Behind her Sanchez rolls his eyes.

"No, I'm not dating him," I say. "We broke up."

"Oh," says Valentina, giving me a sympathetic look. She pats my arm.

"I broke up with him," I clarify, to Valentina's openmouthed astonishment.

"You did?" asks Sanchez, grinning ear to ear.

"Yeah," I say, feeling my face starting to get hot. Does Sanchez know anything about Walker and me? No, he can't. There's nothing to know.

"That's great," Sanchez says, still grinning. "Does Walker know?"

Valentina elbows him in the ribs and he lets out a yelp. Oh God, he does know.

"Hey," I say, trying to change the subject, "I've been meaning to ask, do you know how we can get some visitors for Dodds?"

"Leave it to me," Valentina says with a knowing smile. "I'll organize something."

I think about arguing with her—what if she invites her cousin Angela? That might make things worse, not better—I can only imagine the artwork that a visit from her might inspire in him. But what can I say?

"Okay," I say and make to move off. "Oh, by the way, we're

watching *The Shawshank Redemption* in a little while. You want to watch with us?"

"Who's us?" Sanchez asks.

"Walker," I say and catch his answering smirk. "And Dodds," I add quickly.

"Nah, we're good," he says. "You have fun, though." He winks at me and I can hear him and Valentina talking in loud whispers as they walk off.

Walker's door is ajar, and when I nudge it open I catch him stripping off a T-shirt and rummaging through his drawer for a new one. One glimpse of his body and my legs turn to jello. Oh God. What was I thinking agreeing to this? Thank God I invited Dodds along, otherwise it would feel way too much like a date.

I'm glad too that I went home earlier and changed into sweatpants and a T-shirt so I don't feel like I'm dressed up. I have to say it's one of the benefits of Walker not being able to see—I no longer care so much what I'm wearing or what I look like and it's a huge relief.

He turns as he pulls on his T-shirt and freezes as if he's sensed me standing there, watching him.

"Hi," I say.

"Hey," he answers, and my stomach flutters when I hear the softness in his voice. I only hear it when he speaks to me. With everyone else he's either polite and distant or just plain gruff. "I'm not sure what time it is," he says, pulling the T-shirt on over his head.

"It's nearly nine," I tell him. "Am I too early?"

He shakes his head, trying to hide his smile. "No. Come on in. Where do you want to sit? I tried to make the bed."

I glance around. There's the bed, which he has indeed tried

hard to make, and then there's a chair over by the window.

"I invited Dodds," I tell him, trying to work out where the wheelchair will fit.

Disappointment flares across Walker's face but he quickly tamps it down. "Great," he says.

He's a terrible liar but it makes me smile all the same.

"Oh. Hello."

I turn around. A woman in white scrubs is standing behind me. I've never seen her before.

"Hi," I say.

"Are you Lieutenant Walker's girlfriend?" she asks with a warm smile.

"Er . . ." I say, wondering who she is.

"That's great," she cuts in before I can answer. "You stay as long as you like," she tells me, patting me on the arm. "There are no visiting hours."

"I know," I say, then, glancing over her shoulder, ask, "Where's José?"

"I don't know," she says, shrugging. "I'm just agency staff. They needed cover for the night shift." She smiles. "I'd better just go and get started on the paperwork." She bustles off and I turn to look at Walker, who's scratching behind one ear and wearing an amused smile on his face.

"So," I say. "I brought popcorn." Before I can think about what I'm doing, I cross to the bed and sit on the edge. The butterflies in my stomach erupt into a frenzied dance.

Walker is staring right at me and it's slightly disconcerting because it seems like he can see me. He seems to be contemplating something, but then he gives a small shrug and walks toward the bed, feeling for the edge with his hands. He sits down on the other side of me and I put the popcorn between us as a barrier—not a very substantial barrier but one I feel is necessary, because every other barrier appears to have already collapsed. Or rather, been nuked into oblivion.

I can't stop staring at Walker's arms. And his lips. And his eyes. In fact, I just can't stop staring at him full stop, and the thoughts I'm having are in no way professional. I keep wondering what it would be like to be held by him, to be kissed by him. I keep thinking about the bed we're on and what it would feel like to lie down next to him, and then I start thinking about what it would be like to lie *beneath* him and feel his weight on top of me, pressing me down, and . . . I need to stop this train of thought. Thank God, right at that moment, Dodds arrives, the whir of his wheelchair interrupting my not-so-pure train of thought.

"Hi," I say extra loudly, leaping off the bed as though I'm on fire.

"Hey," Dodds says, barely making eye contact with either of us. He steers into the room and parks himself just in front of the bed.

I switch on the TV, feeling flustered even though nothing has happened, and when I sit back down, leaning against the headboard, and Walker follows suit on his side of the bed, I cannot focus on the movie. At all. For the first fifteen minutes all I can think about is Walker stretched out beside me and his bare arm lying just inches from mine. He can't see the movie, and I wonder if he's listening to it or if, like me, he's distracted. When I glance over at him I can see he's still wearing that small smile, which can't be anything to do with the film because when I do focus on it for a brief second, it doesn't seem either amusing or happy.

"Popcorn?" I ask, nudging the bowl in Walker's direction. He takes some and then I get up and give the bowl to Dodds, who takes not just a handful but the whole bowl.

I return to the bed empty-handed, barrierless. When I sit down, Walker moves an inch over on his side as though making room for me. I feel my resolve weakening. I think about how nice it would be to rest my head on his shoulder.

No, I tell myself firmly, *stop it*.

For the next hour I barely notice what's happening on-screen because all I'm aware of is the pulsing electricity that's building between Walker and me. I feel like if either of us moved an inch a spark would ignite out of thin air. His hand rests on the bed barely half an inch from mine. It wouldn't take much to brush his hand or his arm with my fingertips, but I hold back.

Before the end of the movie, just at the scene when the old man who's been released from prison after serving forty years kills himself, Dodds drops the popcorn bowl to the ground and starts wheeling himself out of the room. I jump off the bed.

"Dodds, where are you going?"

"I've had enough," he says, jerking his head toward the television. "I'm going to bed."

"Okay," I say, resting my hand on his shoulder. "Night."

He nods and then he's gone.

I turn back and see that Walker is half-sitting, half standing, with a frown on his face. "You want to keep watching?" he asks.

"Yeah," I say, though that's not strictly true. I'm not watching the movie at all.

I sit back down beside him. Walker swings his legs up onto the bed, and I swing mine up too, and this time we are touching, just the edges of our knees. Both of us could move, but neither of us does. There's just this tiny bit of contact, and it's enough to set me alight. My whole body starts to thrum.

Every time I turn my head to look at him, he smiles as if he can see me doing it. When I notice, I start doing it more to see if I can catch him out, but he smiles every time.

"How do you know?" I ask him.

"Know what?"

"Know when I'm looking at you."

He shrugs. "I just sense it." He pauses. "I can always sense you. Where you are in a room, what your mood is, when you're looking at me. Sometimes I guess at what you're thinking or doing."

"You do?"

He nods.

My heart is beating like a wild thing, bouncing around in my chest. I glance at his forearm and have to stop myself from stroking my hand down it. Then I glance up at his lips. "What am I thinking right now?" I whisper.

He turns his head to face me. His eyes look smoky gray in the light from the television. "I'd like to think you're thinking about what it would be like if we kissed. Because that's all I'm thinking about."

I draw in a breath and hold it.

He carries on staring at me, his lips slightly parted in a smile. Shit. I've never wanted to kiss anyone so much in my life.

"Am I right?" he asks.

"Yes," I whisper in a croaky voice.

He turns back to face the television. I let out my breath slowly. I turn back to the television too, but all I can think about is what he just said. His hand nudges closer across the bed. I move my own hand to meet his. Our fingertips brush—that's all. But it feels like I've just leaped across a line, smashing every last boundary that lay in the way.

Walker

It's not enough, but I'll take it. I want to slide my hand over hers. I want to do a whole lot more besides, most of it involving stroking my fingertips over every inch of her naked body, but I make do with this, our fingers barely touching, completely thrown by how this tiny bit of contact is holding every ounce of my attention.

I can't focus on anything but Didi—the fact that she's so close I can smell her shampoo, feel her breathing, yet so far away she's unreachable. If only she really was my girlfriend, as that nurse thought, then there'd be nothing holding either of us back. If there were no barriers, I wonder what we'd be doing right now. I try not to think about it because I know in a minute I'm going to have to stand up.

When the movie's over, Didi gets up off the bed. Disappointment rushes at me that it's time for her to leave, but then she surprises me by switching off the TV and lying back down beside me. I'd been getting ready to get up, but now I sink back down against the cushions, wondering, waiting. My heart rate speeds up. I can't tell what she's thinking and it's as frustrating as hell. I decide to wait it out.

"Do you ever think about what you're going to do when you get out of here?" she asks.

"You mean besides go on a date with you?" I answer.

"No," she says a little timidly. "I mean where you'll live, what you might do?"

I shake my head. "What about you?" I ask, not wanting to focus on me. "You got plans?"

She takes a deep breath, let's it out in a rush. "Get my PhD, start my own practice, buy a place in LA, somewhere near the water . . ."

"You've got it all mapped out."

I can tell I've said the wrong thing, that she's tensed up. "I used to," I say quickly, "map things out, I mean. But now . . . I don't know. Now I know how meaningless it all is, how it can all be ripped away in an instant, I just don't see the point in it."

There's a long silence, but it's one of the things I'm getting used to between us. It's not uncomfortable but actually, weirdly, comforting.

"How's the training going for the triathlon?" Didi asks after a while.

"Not bad," I say. "Being tied to Sanchez isn't exactly my idea of a good time, though."

"Is it the being tied to someone you object to, or being tied to Sanchez?" she asks with a laugh.

I smile. "Well, you know, I'm down with a little bondage now and again. I would just rather it wasn't with Sanchez."

Didi laughs. I want to take that laugh and bottle it so I can pull it out and listen to it when she's not there.

"Bondage, huh?" she asks.

"Yeah," I say, wondering where I'm taking this conversation. It's suddenly veering into territory that feels uncertain, and not being able to see her expression, I'm worried about saying the wrong thing. "You know, nothing too S&M," I add in a joking tone. I don't know why I've just made a joke like that. It's not as if I've ever done it before. Miranda would probably have broken up with me for suggesting it.

"No paddles and whips, then?" Didi asks, laughing.

"No," I say. "But tying someone up and blindfolding them? I could be down with that."

"Oh?" There's a hitch in her voice.

"Yeah," I say, feeling the buzz between us suddenly increase a notch. "I can state with some expertise on the matter that blindness has one very clear benefit."

"What?"

I pause, enjoying the slight breathlessness in her voice. "It heightens all your other senses."

She swallows. I hear it. And then I hear her lips part.

"Touch, taste, hearing, smell," I continue.

"Right," Didi whispers.

Another pause.

"Walker?" she says, after a beat.

"Yeah?"

She hesitates. "I need to go home."

"Oh." Shit. Did I take it too far? I can feel the disappointment flooding onto my face. Suddenly her hand is against my cheek.

"I *need* to go home," she says, "because I'm scared that if I don't leave right now, then I'm never going to be able to leave at all."

"Oh," I say, and I have to fight hard to keep my arms by my

sides and not pull her against me. She has no idea how much I want to hold her, trace her face and her lips with my fingertips, how much I want to get to know her in every single possible way.

"Good night," she says.

I make to get up off the bed to see her to the door, but she pushes me back down. "No, don't get up," she whispers and then I feel her leaning over me, the soft sweep of her hair brushing my face. I have to hold my breath, clutch the covers to stop myself reaching for her. She kisses me softly on the cheek. Then she hovers over me, and I can sense her just an inch away from me, her breath warm against my lips. I hear her breathing quicken. Is she going to kiss me? It's torture not knowing what's coming, not being in control—having to relinquish the power to her. I can't make a move because I can't see what I'm doing, and that's not a position I've ever been in before. With Miranda and every other girl I've always made the first move. Having said that, I don't think I've ever been so turned on, either. My own breathing has ratcheted up. My hands are gripping the sheets.

After a long, torturous moment, Didi gets up and crosses the room.

"Sleep well," she says before she shuts the door.

I lie there, heart racing, trying to steady my breathing but getting nowhere. Sleep? I don't think I'm going to be sleeping anytime soon.

Didi

The next day I'm walking around like I have ants in my pants. I'm so on edge, so distracted by the internal battle waging in my head, that I can't concentrate on anything.

"What's with you?" José says when I have to ask him three times to remind me what patient I'm supposed to be observing at what time.

"Nothing," I say.

He shoots me a suspicious look.

The elevator doors open and I step out. "I'm just going to check in on Dodds," I say, trying not to stare over my shoulder at Walker's room. "How's he doing today?"

"Not talking," says José, shaking his head grimly. "He had a visitor, though. Some cousin of Valentina's."

I grimace. Oh God, is that who she rustled up? I walk quickly to Dodds's room and knock. He's alone, sitting in his wheelchair, staring blankly out the window.

"Hi," I say.

He doesn't turn his head. I step into the room and walk toward him. I open my mouth to ask how he is but then shut it again. I can imagine that's the last question he wants to be asked. He's probably sick of it.

"Can I do anything?" I ask.

A faint smile flickers on his lips before being snuffed out. He shakes his head.

"Did you have a visitor?"

He gives a dismissive shrug. I frown. Where's Angela?

I glance at the photograph on his nightstand. "What about her?" I ask, wandering over and picking it up. "Can I call her for you? Do you think she'd like to visit?"

He frowns at me. "No, just leave it. Leave me alone."

I put the photograph down. "Okay," I say, noticing as I walk away from the nightstand that the brochure I gave him yesterday on careers is in the trash can.

I pause by the door, glancing back at him over my shoulder. How do you do it, I want to know? How do you keep an emotional distance from people? I'm really not sure I'm cut out to be a psychologist, and the doubt that's been niggling at me for the last few weeks is increasing in volume. It's no longer niggling, it's harassing me. What if, after all this study and all this dreaming, it turns out I'm not suited to the job?

Just outside Walker's room I hear voices, or rather one voice—a woman's—and pull up sharply. I peer through the crack in the door and see Walker pressed up against the foot of the bed while Valentina's cousin Angela talks at him ten to the dozen. She's wearing another of those flowery kaftan dresses and her bosom, which rivals my own for size, is torpedoing him. She's in danger of knocking him backward onto the bed.

I burst into the room. "Hi," I say loudly.

Angela turns around, her sentence trailing off.

"Are you ready for your appointment, Lieutenant?" I ask.

I see the question start to form on Walker's lips, the frown of confusion, then a second later realization dawns and his expression clears. "Oh yeah, my appointment." He nods vigorously. "I'm so ready for that. Let's do it."

"Okay, great," I say, stepping into the room.

"What appointment is that?" Angela asks, frowning at me. "Are you a doctor?"

"Um," I say. I'm so bad at lying.

"Yeah, she's my doctor," Walker cuts in.

"Yeah. I'm his doctor," I repeat, nodding. "I'm here to . . ." I blank.

"Change my dressing," Walker finishes for me.

"What dressing?" Angela asks, looking him over.

"On my . . ."

"Knee. His knee," I blurt.

"Your knee?" Angela asks, scrunching up her face.

"Yeah. Surgery," Walker explains, pointing at his knee. "I had surgery. Busted my kneecap."

Angela pouts, one hand flying to her chest. "Oh, you poor thing. Shall I wait for you to be done?"

"No," Walker answers quickly.

"It's going to take a while," I add. "After I've changed the dressing I have to give him a thorough . . . physical exam."

Walker's eyebrows shoot up and he gives me a smirk. "Oh," says Angela. "Okay. Well, I'll come by later."

"Why don't you go see Callum?" I ask, even though I regret it the instant it's out of my mouth.

"Callum?" she frowns.

"Dodds? The guy in the room next door."

"The guy with no legs?"

"Yes."

Her nose wrinkles. "I'm not sure. I don't think he really wants a visitor. He's kind of"—she lowers her voice—"weird."

I grit my teeth. Any sympathy I might have had for her just went entirely out the window.

"Well," I say, stepping to one side and motioning to the door. "I'm sure you're busy."

She takes the hint and, turning back to Walker, squeezes his arm. "Bye," she says. "I'll drop by later."

"Bye," he answers with a fixed smile on his face. He really is the worst at pretending, and for that I'm stupidly glad.

Angela leaves, shooting me a suspicious look as she goes. I'm wearing jeans and a blouse and I definitely don't look like a doctor.

"Oh my God," Walker says, collapsing onto the bed once she's gone and I've shut the door behind her. "Thank you. I wanted to pull the emergency cord in my room but I couldn't find it."

I laugh. "It's okay. I don't mind you owing me."

"Chalk it up. Let's start keeping count."

"Count?" I ask.

"Yeah. Then when I get out of this place and we can finally go on a date, I'll start paying you back all I owe you."

I take another step toward him. "How?" I ask.

A smile lifts the edge of his mouth. "In ways you cannot even imagine."

My stomach gives way again as if the floor's collapsed beneath my feet. "I don't know," I manage to say. "I have a pretty good imagination."

He pulls a face and shakes his head. "No," he says. "Your imagination will need a reboot after this."

He isn't even touching me and I'm as breathless as if we'd just spent half an hour making out. "Oh," I whisper.

We're standing just inches apart now, and I can see he's breathing as fast as me. Neither of us says anything.

"Didi?" he asks.

"Yes?"

He bites his lip and frowns. "Can I—?" He stops and frowns.

"What?" I ask.

He lifts his hand and I freeze, not sure what he's going to do, but then, very lightly, with just his fingertips, he starts tracing my face. First my cheekbones then my brow, then stroking along my jawbone, his touch so gentle that I feel like I'm made of glass. He traces his fingers down my nose, over my eyebrows, strokes his fingertips over my eyelashes, and finally runs his thumb over my lips.

I haven't breathed the whole time he's been touching me, but I start almost hyperventilating when he strokes my lips with his thumb.

"You're beautiful," he says, finally taking my face in both his hands.

"Thanks," I say, my voice shaking.

His thumb presses against my lips again. My resolve is one thin iota away from vanishing completely.

Walker

f in our heart we still cling to anger or anxiety or possessions—anything at all—then we cannot be free."

I hit the pause button on the meditation that Didi has put on the iPod. Sometimes she's as subtle as a sledgehammer. I know she's trying to get me to open up about what happened, but the closer I get to her the less I want to tell her the truth—about what happened in Helmand. I can't bear the thought of what she'll think if she knows the truth.

The elevator doors open at the end of the hallway and my ears prick up. It's Didi. I can tell first by the sound of her heels clicking on the tiles, and then from her laugh when she greets José. I smile at the sound of it. She doesn't come straight to me. I hear her stop in with Dodds and chat to him for a few minutes, but I can tell by the lack of response on his part that it's a one-way conversation. I went through the same thing earlier with him.

A minute later there's a gentle knock on my door.

"Hey, Miss Monroe," I say.

"How do you always know it's me?" she asks, and I hear the

happiness in her voice, a slipstream of bubbles beneath the surface.

I shrug. "I'm blind, not deaf."

She laughs.

"But even if you tiptoed like a ninja I'd still be able to sense you."

"I remember, you told me. You always know how I'm feeling or where I'm standing in a room. That's quite a party trick."

"It only works with you."

"Okay, so what am I feeling now, then?" she asks. "And where am I standing?"

"Well, the second part's easy. You're over by the window. It's where you always stand. I'm thinking it's because you like to keep the table between us because you can't trust yourself." I grin, hoping I'm right.

From the sharp breath she draws in I'm guessing I am. "And you're happy this morning, but underneath it there's a little sadness. No, maybe not sadness, maybe . . . frustration? Conflict?" I'm guessing this. It's actually how *I* feel. But there is a slight breathlessness to her voice and I know I'm not imagining the electric buzz passing between us.

"You guessed right," she says quietly. "You'd make a good therapist. You have really great intuition."

Not that great, I think to myself. If my intuition had been better, five people wouldn't be dead now. And just like that my mood swerves into darkness.

"You still haven't shaved," Didi comments.

I shrug, running a hand over my chin, forcing a smile. "Figured I might see if the Seals were recruiting."

"Did you ever think of becoming a Navy Seal?" she asks,

and I hear her putting her bag down on the chair and coming toward me.

I shrug. "Yeah. But my dad pushed me toward the marines. He was a marine, so, you know . . ."

"I thought he worked in military intelligence."

"He does now, but he made colonel in the marines. I think he's pretty disappointed that I'm no longer following in his footsteps."

"And are you?"

I frown. "What?"

"Are you disappointed? Is that what you wanted? Before, you said that you never thought about becoming a marine when you were growing up, but that when your brother dropped out of school you kind of ended up following the path set for him."

"Um . . ." I pause and sit down on the bed. "I guess. I mean, I love it. Loved it." My fingers are twisting the sheet into knots. "At least, I thought I did. But—" I break off. "I thought I loved a lot of things. Turns out I was wrong."

Didi sits down beside me. Her thigh brushes mine and for a second that's all I can focus on, the heat of it, the pressure. It's a welcome distraction from the images that are starting to flicker at the edge of my memory.

"What would you have done otherwise?" Didi asks. "If you hadn't become a marine?"

"I don't know. I wanted to do something using my hands."

Didi laughs under her breath and I grin in response, the dark thoughts vanishing. I can guess what she's thinking. I elbow her lightly in the ribs. "I'm good with my hands. Woodwork, metalwork, engines . . . other things too."

She takes a deep breath.

"At the Naval Academy, my degree was in naval architecture. I had this idea that I'd one day design boats, build my own."

"Really?" asks Didi, sounding surprised.

I nod. "My grandpa had this old boat he used to take us out on when we were kids. Nothing fancy. Wood hull, only twenty foot, but big enough. It was so beautiful. I think it's still moored somewhere up the coast here. He sold it just before he died." I smile to myself, recalling all the times my brother Isaac and I went out on the water with our grandpa, every summer spent learning how to sail until our hands were calloused and our skin so tanned and our hair so long and bleached so blond that our own mother didn't recognize us.

"That was where I was happiest," I tell Didi, and I realize as I say it that it's true. I was happier as a kid learning to sail than I've ever been before or since. Even Miranda didn't make me as happy.

"Out there it's just you and the water, and nothing else really matters. It's the closest you can get to freedom. To being in the present."

I can feel Didi nodding beside me.

"It's just this immensity," I go on. "Out there, away from land, you realize how small you are in comparison. How insignificant."

As soon as I say the word insignificant, the image of the boot—the foot still in it, the bone sheered clean through—slams into my mind. The laces were tied in a double bow. Who did it belong to?

"You're not insignificant," Didi says quietly, almost as if she's picked up on the shift in my thoughts.

I turn my head toward her, momentarily confused and disoriented. Why did I think of that and why now?

Suddenly I feel her hand against my cheek, her fingers sliding against my jaw, stroking the stubble. "Do you want me to shave you?" she murmurs softly.

"Huh?"

"Do you want me to shave your beard?"

I nod, my mind still struggling to erase the picture of the boot.

Didi's hand moves, brushes through my hair. My body releases a sigh at her touch. For a split second I imagine myself pulling her onto my lap, imagine feeling the weight of her pressing on top of me, imagine burying my lips in her hair, losing myself in her, trying to forget everything. But the fact that I'd be using her to try to black out the memories makes me hold back. She deserves more than that. She deserves more than me.

"Come on," she says, standing up. She takes my hand and pulls me to my feet, then leads me through to the bathroom. She shuts the door to give us more room and sits me down on the toilet seat. I hear her start to fill the basin with water.

I close my eyes. I'm still distracted—I can't shake the image of the boot—but when Didi starts dabbing shaving foam onto my face and neck I find that my focus immediately switches to her. She works better than any drug or antidepressant at lifting me out of the dark.

Her touch is gentle but sure—surer than it was last time. She stands close, so close that I have to spread my legs so she can stand between them. At one point she kneels, and I'd be lying if I said I wasn't having to force myself to think about my old sergeant major yelling at me during drills to try to rein in my body's immediate reaction.

Her hand rests on my shoulder while she shaves my cheek,

and I have to check myself again because now I'm imagining her holding onto my shoulders, gripping them tight while I make love to her.

"Why are you smiling?" she suddenly asks me.

"No reason," I answer, trying to wipe the grin off my face. "Why are *you* smiling?" I ask her, because I can tell she is.

"No reason," she answers back, still smiling.

When she's done, she stands up and dabs at my face with a warm towel to wipe off the remains of the shaving foam, then tosses the towel aside.

"There you go. That's better," she says, pressing her hand to my face. She rests it there, and without thinking I press my own hand over hers and hold it in place. Didi takes a long breath in. I turn my head so that her palm rests against my lips and kiss it. She doesn't pull away.

Fuck. I know this isn't what we agreed, but I think we crossed the line a while ago, and right now my brain might be wiring messages at me to stop but they're not making it through.

Didi's free hand slowly slides through my hair, sending a shiver down my spine. I drop her palm and take hold of her hips, drawing her closer and hearing a sharp intake of breath in response. Her hand falls to my shoulder, squeezes it tight, and I hear her murmur something. I think it's my name.

I stroke my hands over the curve of her hips, loving the feel of them through her jeans, realizing simultaneously that she's more petite than I imagined but curvier too, and the combination is a total turn-on. I have to fight the urge I have to explore the rest of her. I make do with stroking my thumbs over her hip bones and following the dip of her waist. She's breathing faster now, matching my own heartbeat.

I press my lips to the flat of her stomach through her blouse. I'm content to stay like this, breathing deep, trying to control the rising heat in my body, but Didi wraps her arms around my shoulders and pushes her hips closer against me, and all my efforts to keep control fly out the window.

I lift the edge of her shirt, running my fingertips along the top of her jeans, feeling her skin—soft, smooth as silk— contract into a tight shiver. I follow my fingers with a trail of kisses and Didi lets out a small moan that takes my imagination to another level.

I tip back my head, trying to catch my breath, though I keep my hands on her hips, holding her in place, not wanting her to move away. I'm not ready to let her go. I'd be happy to stay like this for the rest of the day, in fact, but Didi suddenly shifts away from me. She's backing off, and disappointment makes my shoulders slump, but the next thing I know she's thrown her leg over mine and is lowering herself down onto my lap. Holy shit. She has to be feeling how turned on I am. There's no disguising it now.

I wrap my arms around her waist, enjoying the weight of her, the feel of her, after so long just imagining it. My imagination failed. The real thing is infinitely better. I trace my fingers up her spine through her clothes. Her back arches in response and she lets out another groan, this one louder, and pushes closer against me. I wonder if she has any idea what she's doing to me, and then wonder briefly what the hell will happen if her dad walks in again. We need to stop, but honestly my willpower is shot to pieces.

My lips are level with her collarbone and I can't resist kissing her, tasting her skin. She smells of coconut and spice and something else too, not her normal perfume, but whatever it is it makes me want to pick her up and carry her over to the bed. It makes me want to strip her naked and inhale every inch of her. Fuck. I reach her shoulder and Didi dips her head. Her hair is tied back so it doesn't tickle me, but her breath does, hot and feathery against my neck. I tense. Is she going to kiss me? Her cheek rests briefly against mine and I close my eyes and find myself holding her tight, like a man clinging to a buoy in a storm-swept ocean. She's keeping me afloat. How do I let her go after this?

"Walker?" she murmurs into my ear, her voice shaky and uneven.

"Mmmm," I answer.

"I think I need to kiss you. Sooner rather than later."

I nod. "Yeah." My body's as taut as a guitar string.

Didi takes a big breath in and pulls away from me. I wait, on edge. She takes my face in her hands. She's the one in control again.

I wait, but the kiss doesn't come and for a second I'm confused, but then I realize that she's doing it deliberately. She's taking her time, teasing me, enjoying the way my breathing is hitching and my fingers have tightened around her hips.

I hear her lips part, can feel the heat of her, know she's barely millimeters from me, and it's pure torture, but it's also the sweetest torture I've ever known. And then, after however many seconds it is, she finally presses her lips against mine, and any doubt that we might not fit, that we might not have chemistry, evaporates. Instantly I let go of her hips and take her face between my hands, hungry for more, tasting her, kissing her until she's breathless, until she's begging for more, until every thought and image in my head is erased for good. She responds as hungrily, her fingertips running along my jaw, her legs wrapping around my waist.

I knew from when I traced her face with my fingers that her lips were perfect—soft, heart-shaped, the bottom one slightly fuller than the top—but kissing her makes me appreciate them in a whole new way. She opens her mouth to me and I start to explore her with my tongue, and what started off as a gentle, almost tentative first kiss becomes a hungry, almost desperate attack. It's as if all the pent-up energy of the last few weeks is tumbling out, and now that we're finally touching, have done away with those flimsy, half-hearted barriers that separated us, we're struggling to catch up. We could be up against the clock for how we're acting.

Didi's hands wander unhesitatingly over my stomach and chest, though on top of my T-shirt, and so I do the same, letting her set the pace and following her lead. I keep my hands above her clothes, though I'm burning to stroke more of her bare skin.

But it can wait. For now, this is enough. Having her in my arms, finally kissing her. It's more than enough, more than I expected, and definitely more than I deserve.

And then there's a bang on the door and both of us jump apart as if we've been electrocuted. Didi is off my lap in the next second.

"Noel?"

My head is still spinning from that kiss, and it takes me two or three seconds to come back to the present and figure out that it's Angela calling my name from the other side of the door. What the—

"Noel?" she calls again.

"Um, yeah?" I say, aware that my voice is hoarse and unsteady. My whole body is actually shaking, now I focus on it. Blood roars in my head, adrenaline rips through my body. I can still feel Didi's lips against mine, can still feel the perfect weight of her in my lap.

"I just wondered if you'd like to try some of my *tres leches* cake? I made it especially for you."

I close my eyes and shake my head, trying to get a handle on my breathing. It sounds like I've just run a five-minute mile. "I'm actually kind of busy," I say, grimacing to myself. There's no way I can go outside in my present state. Angela might take it as a sign and offer me more than just her cake.

"Oh," she says, sounding disappointed. "Well, I can wait!"

"No," I say quickly. "I'm going to be a while."

I grimace again. What will she think I'm doing in here? Actually, I don't really care what she thinks I'm doing. Let her think I'm waxing my privates. Whatever gets her out the door so I can turn my attention back to Didi, who has taken my hand and is squeezing it hard.

I caress her palm with my thumb, trying to reassure her, because I can sense she's in a panic and now I'm mad that Angela has ruined the moment. We could still be kissing.

"Oh," says Angela, sounding disappointed. "Well, if you're sure."

"Yep, I'm sure," I shout through the door. "I'm taking a shower. Thanks, though."

"I'll just leave it on the side in your room, then, and I'll come back later."

"Okay," I say, my attention already back on Didi. I tug her toward me and my hands start exploring her stomach again, her thighs and her ass, which is probably the nicest ass I've ever come across. God, I could spend all day exploring her body with my hands, another whole day doing the same with my lips. I wish we could just lock ourselves in this room for a week, her dad and everyone else in the center be damned.

We listen to Angela leave the room, closing the door behind her, and Didi lets out a long exhalation. "That was close," she whispers.

I stand up and pull Didi toward me. She has to go up on tiptoe and I have to bend my head to kiss her, but we fit, perfectly.

She pulls away within seconds, though. "I have to go, Walker," she says, and I hear the note of anxiety in her voice. Immediately I become anxious too. Does she regret what's just happened? Is she having second thoughts already?

"Okay," I manage to say.

Her hand lingers on my cheek once more, just for a second, before she turns to the door. I hear her open it and my arms fall to my sides.

"Bye," she says, and then she darts back and quickly presses her lips to mine.

Didi

I'm still shaking when I walk out of the bathroom. I take a few deep breaths, smooth down my hair and press my fingers to my lips, which, like every other part of me, throb with heat. I'm in danger of weaving into a wall, my legs are so weak, and my heart is beating so erratically that I can feel it leaping around in my chest like a ping-pong ball.

When Zac kissed me, my brain wouldn't shut up, posing questions about technique and worrying about whether he thought I was a good kisser. With Walker there was no thought whatsoever—my brain switched off completely. It was the most intense kiss, the best kiss, of my life. In fact, my brain still feels woozy and discombobulated. Electric shocks still resonate through my body in little jolts triggered by the memory of his hands exploring my body.

I open the door to the hallway, certain that if anyone sees me right now they'll know without a shadow of a doubt what I've been up to. Guilt sends a new shock of heat to my face, which must already be flushed red. What did I just do?

"Oh, hello."

I come to an abrupt halt. Angela is standing right in front of me.

"Hi," I say in an extra bright voice. Why is she hovering right outside Walker's door?

Angela tips her head quizzically at me and then over my shoulder at the door to Walker's room through which I've just walked. I swallow.

A question furrows her brow. The frown clears as understanding seeps its way in. She narrows her eyes at me. "Aren't you his doctor?"

"Um . . ." I say.

"Didi's interning here for the summer."

I turn around. José has walked up behind me, holding a tray of meds.

"But she was just in the bathroom with Walker," Angela starts explaining to him.

My eyes go wide. Oh God. Now I'm in trouble.

"Didi was helping Lieutenant Walker shave," José says. "He won't let any of us do it. Girl's got mad shaving skills."

Angela's mouth drops open. She shuts it. I force myself to smile at her while darting a glance in José's direction. How did he know I was doing that?

He winks at me. My mouth falls open.

"Right," says Angela. "Well, I'm going to pay a visit to Jesús."

José smiles at her and she bustles off, but not before shooting a curious glance over her shoulder at me.

I stand there, biting my lip, too nervous to look at José. He leans in close.

"Don't worry," he whispers. "I won't say a word. You guys want to hook up, that's fine with me."

I turn to him. "Really? You don't think it crosses some kind of professional line?"

He shrugs. "Look, you're not his doc." He grins now. "And whatever you're doing, it sure as hell is working. He isn't throwing yogurt at anyone anymore and the dude's finally smiling. I even caught him singing in the shower the other day."

"Really?" I ask.

"Yeah. Sounded like Justin Bieber."

"How long have you known?" I ask, shaking my head at him. I thought we were so good at hiding it.

José rolls his eyes at me. "Didi," he laughs, "pretty much the entire hospital barring your dad knows that you and Lieutenant Walker have been making googly eyes at each other. There's even a little sweepstake running in the canteen on how long it will take you guys to finally get it together."

My mouth falls open. "Are you serious?"

He nods, grinning, but suddenly his expression becomes serious. "Yeah. I think Sanchez might be the winner. Just don't, you know, break his fucking heart, okay? That really wouldn't be what he needs right now. What any of us needs."

I nod, suddenly feeling more sober. José is right. Up until this moment I hadn't fully absorbed the ramifications of being in a relationship with Walker—if that's what this even is—but the mention of his heart being broken makes me realize that whatever's happening between us isn't just physical. Hearts are involved. My heart, at least, and from what José is saying, Walker's too.

The last thing I want to do is break any more of him.

Walker

W here are we going?" I ask.

"It's a surprise," Didi answers.

She leads me out of the building. I think we might be heading to our bench or to the lake, perhaps, but she takes us left down the path toward the parking lot. I'm holding on to her elbow. In spite of the fact that most of the center seems to know about Didi and me, when we're with people we put up a front of propriety. Behind closed doors, however . . . well, I'm not holding on to her elbow.

During this last week, pretty much every afternoon José has turned a blind eye as we shut the door to my room and undertake what Didi has termed a "physical exam." I'm happy to submit to this kind of physical exam. It beats the one I get from my orthopedic surgeon.

Things have stayed aboveboard—to a degree. We've kissed. A lot. And I know every curve and contour of her body . . . through her clothes. We've agreed that we'll take things slowly until I'm out of the hospital. If she's trying to dangle a carrot, it's working. I've been hitting the gym every day for four or five hours, mainly because I need to find an outlet for all the pent-up energy in my body, and partly because I'm trying to convince the docs to sign me off. I figure that if they see me getting fit in my body, they might not focus so much on what's going on in my head.

What I'm not telling anyone is that the nightmares are still happening. Only José knows. I think I'm even managing to convince Doctor Monroe that I'm recovering because he hasn't spoken again about going back over the event or recording a diary. However, he's pushing me to attend art therapy classes. I hear they're starting to work for Dodds, who spends a lot of his time down there in the art studio, but it's just not my thing. The only therapy I need is Didi, though if I'm completely honest there's a part of me—a small, hissing voice in my head—that whispers to me in the darkness, questioning the justness of what I'm doing. It's the same voice that questions the fairness of me being happy every time I think of Didi and feel an answering fluttering in my chest. *What right do I have?* I try to quiet the voice, but it's refusing to go away. Then there are the possible ramifications for Didi and her career.

"Here," Didi says, stopping.

I hear the sound of a car door opening.

"We're going off the base?" I ask her, surprised.

"Yes," she answers. "I got permission, don't worry."

I get into the car and she shuts the door behind me and gets in on the driver's side.

I'm not used to being a passenger. Miranda never drove; I drove her. My dad used to joke that I was her chauffeur. The roles are constantly flipping with Didi, and I find I quite like it. To a degree. I still hate the feeling of helplessness that comes from being blind, but Didi never makes me feel helpless, and when we're making out I'm able to flip the tables a lot, something she seems to enjoy too.

I wind down the windows as Didi drives, breathing in the ocean. God, I've missed this, missed the feeling of freedom that being in a car brings. I hope we're in for a long drive.

Didi puts the radio on, and for a moment, with my eyes closed and my head turned toward the sun, it feels as if we're a normal couple heading to the beach and I'm not a patient on day release from a mental hospital.

I wonder for the millionth time whether I should tell Didi about the theory that my blindness is psychosomatic, but I've left it so long now I wonder if she'll consider it a lie. I'm scared, too, of her reaction. I don't want to ruin today. But then again, the voice in my head pipes up, maybe it's only fair if I do have my day ruined. And I don't want to live with the lie any longer. Before I can stop myself, I open my mouth.

"Didi," I say.

She turns down the radio. "Yeah?"

"I need to tell you something."

She doesn't say anything. Shit. I think about making something up, but I have to tell her. I can't back down now. "The whole blindness thing. It's, um . . . it's not physical," I say. "It's in my head."

She doesn't speak, but I feel the car start to slow as if she's taken her foot off the accelerator. "I know," she finally says.

I turn to face her. She what?

"My dad told me."

"He did?"

"Yeah. He thought it would help for me to know. Don't be mad."

I don't know what to think, but I do know that I feel relieved, not mad. If anything, she should be mad at me. "I'm sorry I didn't tell you."

"It's okay. I understand," she says, putting her hand on my thigh.

I press my head back into the headrest and let the knowledge that she knew, and didn't think worse of me for it, settle.

"You're going to get your sight back," she tells me, and the certainty in her voice buoys me for a moment. Until she lifts her hand away. I don't know how to tell her that it's never going to happen.

Didi

As I make the turn into the parking lot I feel a flurry of butterflies. I hope this is the right thing and that Walker won't be mad at me. As I spot an empty space and turn into it, I catch sight of someone walking toward us and almost drive straight into the curb in shock. It's like seeing Walker's identical twin.

I switch off the engine and get out the car, telling Walker to stay put for a second.

"Hi," I say, as Isaac, Walker's brother, walks toward me.

It's only now he's right in front of me that I see the differences. He's thinner than Walker, less built up, with longer, disheveled hair, and he's an inch or two shorter. But he's every bit as good-looking.

"You must be Didi," he says to me, smiling, holding out a hand.

I shake it. They have the same smile. The same dimple. Different-colored eyes, though. "Hi," I say, still marveling at the similarities.

"Isaac?"

I turn. Walker has gotten himself out of the car and is facing in our direction, frowning in confusion.

I watch Isaac reel back in shock as he takes in Walker, whose gaze is not quite hitting us but landing somewhere over my shoulder. Isaac gathers himself. "Hey, bro," he says with a forced joviality and walks around the car toward him.

Walker scowls. Is he angry? I watch on tenterhooks. Maybe this wasn't such a good idea after all. Walker said the two of them no longer talked, but the fact is I think he needs his brother. He needs someone besides me and the other workers at the center. Though watching the two of them now, I'm wondering if I've overstepped the mark. Isaac hesitates for a moment, then walks forward and throws his arms around his brother, pulling him into a hug that makes my throat tighten. For a few seconds Walker's arms stay rigid at his sides, but then he softens, the frown vanishes, and he hugs his brother back with a fierceness that takes me by surprise and makes me think of all the times he's held me the same way.

However Walker might appear on the outside—tough, brooding, distant—I know him well enough now to know that he needs this. He needs this contact with people, this connection. Sometimes it feels like he's holding on to me as if I'm an anchor keeping him from being swept out to sea, and I know, watching him with Isaac now, that bringing them together was absolutely the right thing to do. Maybe between the two of us we can find a way to help him.

When I found Isaac on Facebook and contacted him, all I knew was that he and Walker hadn't talked in a few years. Walker was vague about the details. I saw from his Facebook page that Isaac lived in Miami, and when I mentioned his name to my mom she said she'd heard of him, that he's quite a well-known artist.

Looking at the two of them embracing, Isaac holding Walker by the tops of his arms and studying him hard before pulling him back in for a second hug, I see the Walker that could have been if he hadn't gone into the marines.

Isaac is wearing skinny jeans rolled up at the ankle and a tight-fitting T-shirt. He's a hipsterish version of Walker; I have to suppress a smile at the thought of Walker strolling through Brooklyn talking artisan beers or indie record labels. We've already joked about his beard making him look less like Osama bin Laden and more like a hipster, a joke that made him even more keen for me to shave him every day. Though possibly it wasn't just the fear of looking that way that motivated him, but what tends to happen after I've finished shaving him.

"I don't get it," Walker says now, turning his head in roughly my direction.

"We're taking you out on Grandpa's boat," Isaac says.

"His boat?"

"Yeah," Isaac says. "I bought it a few years ago."

Walker shakes his head. "You did?"

"Yeah. Just before he died."

Walker frowns.

"I was going to have someone sail it around to Miami, but never got round to it," Isaac explains. "Then this girlfriend of yours got in touch with me out of the blue last week and we hatched this plan."

Walker's eyebrow shoots up. Was it the word *girlfriend*? I didn't call myself that—I just introduced myself to Isaac as Walker's friend—but when Walker doesn't say anything to set him straight, I feel a rush.

"I can't sail," Walker says, gesturing at his eyes. "In case you hadn't noticed, I'm blind."

"Bullshit. You could sail blindfolded even when we were kids. And besides, Didi and I are going with you. We'll do all the hard stuff."

"Um," I say, raising my hand, "just so you know, I've never sailed before."

Isaac raises his eyebrows at the both of us. "You make me fly all the way out here and then you both make excuses? I don't think so. I've spent the last day getting the boat ready. Let's go."

I walk around the car and let Walker take my arm, noticing the little glances Isaac keeps throwing our way. He's rattled by seeing his brother like this, and I can tell that Walker is uneasy too, thrown by Isaac's presence and self-conscious about being blind.

"Are you okay?" I ask under my breath as we make our way down the jetty.

He nods, but a muscle by his eye twitches.

I take in the super yachts on either side of us and am relieved when we get to the end of the jetty and find a much more modest, yet no less impressive, wooden-hulled boat. It's freshly varnished and looks well loved.

"Chiara?" I ask, reading the name written on the glossy painted side.

"Our grandmother's name," Isaac explains, jumping on board and holding out a hand for me. I take it and let him pull me onto the narrow deck.

He does the same for Walker, who steps on board carefully, feeling for the railing which Isaac helps him find.

We both sit down, Walker by the steering stick thing, and

me trying to stay out of the way of Isaac who's leaping all over the boat doing stuff with ropes.

"Our grandfather met our grandmother in Italy during the war," he explains. "He was a GI, stationed over there in '44. She was a translator for the Allied forces."

Isaac throws me a life jacket and then passes one to Walker. I fumble with mine, and Walker, even though he's blind, deftly finds the nylon straps and helps me tighten them.

"He said he fell in love with her the minute he heard her voice, and then he fell in love with her all over again when he saw her." He laughs. "She was pretty hot stuff, Grandma. But she was also married."

"Oh," I say, frowning at him, confused.

"After the war," Walker carries on, picking up the story where Isaac's left off, "Grandpa came back home, but he couldn't get her out of his head. He only had her name—no address—but he went back to Italy on a mission to find her. It took him two months to track her down. She was living in Rome, working for the Red Cross, helping refugees find their families."

"But what about her husband?" I ask as Isaac unties us from the jetty and gives an instruction to Walker, who takes the rope Isaac tosses into his lap and starts wrapping it around a metal hook.

"He had died at the end of the war, somewhere on the Russian front. She was a widow."

"Happily for us," says Walker, "or we wouldn't be here right now."

"They got married, moved back to America, and lived happily ever after," Isaac says with a grin. "He said that she was the only good thing that came out of that war."

"That's so romantic," I say as Isaac jumps down into the boat and starts the engine, steering us expertly out through the rows of boats toward the harbor entrance.

"Didi's a closet romantic," Walker laughs. "Actually, not so closet."

I poke him in the ribs and he grins at me before turning his head toward the breeze and closing his eyes. I smile as I watch him.

"They were married forty years, had five kids, our dad was the youngest," Isaac goes on. "After Grandma died he gave up the ghost. There was nothing physically wrong with him, but he died in his sleep six months later. Doc said it was a broken heart."

"That's so sad."

"That's the way it goes. Us Walkers, when we fall, we fall hard." He winks at me then nods at the rope by my side. "Okay, you ready to sail?" he asks.

"Uh . . ."

"If you're going to be part of this family, you need to learn to sail. That's the deal."

Part of the family? I glance at Walker. His eyes are still closed and he's still smiling into the sun. I stand up.

"Okay," I say. "What do I have to do?"

Walker

can hear Didi and Isaac talking, and the sound of their voices over the whip of the wind lulls me into a feeling as close to peace as I've experienced since that day.

I close my eyes and feel the sun on my face and taste the salt spray on my lips. I didn't realize how much I missed this, how much I was craving it, and to tell the truth I'm finding it hard to process everything—the feel of the hull cutting with speed through the waves, the snap of the sail when Isaac turns us against the wind, the sound of the gulls calling far above us. It's all I can do to sit still, legs dangling over the side, arms thrown over the rail, and just absorb it. This is exactly what I needed and I didn't even know it. I thought I'd never be able to sail again and I'd been forcing myself not to think about it, yet here I am, thanks to Didi.

The only downside to today is not being able to join in, though Isaac let me steer once we were out in open water. Now it's Didi's turn at the helm. A part of me is jealous that my brother's the one getting to teach her, but I tamp it down. She did this for me. Somehow she found Isaac and plotted all this, and the thought astounds me. Miranda would never have done anything like this. Miranda didn't even like boats. She used to moan about her hair going all frizzy with the salt air and getting seasick.

"Woah!" Didi yelps and suddenly comes crashing into me where I'm sitting at the prow of the boat. I put my arms out to catch her and she collapses down at my side, throwing her arm around my shoulders to steady herself.

"Careful," I say. "I don't want you going overboard."

"This is amazing," she says, leaning into me and kissing me on the cheek.

I nod, pulling her closer.

"Are you happy?" she asks.

I nod again. But the mention of happiness causes a stabbing feeling in my gut, like someone's taken a piece of jagged glass and twisted it sharply into my side. The images of the boot, the twisted, smoking piece of shrapnel, Sanchez's face streaked with blood, the flicker and blaze. It's like a reflex action. Every time I think I might be happy, every time I let that spark of hope and possibility take hold inside me, the darkness comes along and snuffs it out, the screams in my head clamor louder and more insistently to be heard. It's a sneak attack by my conscience, which keeps questioning my right to be happy, my right to enjoy moments like this one—face to the sun, girl at my side, laughter in my ear—when others are denied them.

"Where are you?"

"Huh?" I turn to face Didi.

"You went somewhere. I can tell by your expression."

I force a smile. Nothing passes her by. "I'm here. Right here. With you," I tell her.

She doesn't buy it, but her hand squeezes mine and she rests her head on my shoulder. I kiss the top of her head.

"Why won't you talk to me? I wish you'd let me in."

I frown. She sighs.

"So you don't mind me calling Isaac and arranging this?"

I shake my head, my lips still pressed to her hair. "No."

"Because I know you guys fell out, so I wasn't sure if it was the right thing to do," she says.

I don't answer her.

"He told me that he'd been wanting to visit you, but hadn't known if you wanted him to. He said you hadn't returned any of his calls."

"I haven't returned anyone's calls," I say. "My phone isn't switched on."

"What happened between you guys?" Didi asks. "You seem to get on so well."

I turn my face into the wind. Where to begin?

"It probably sounds stupid," I say with a sigh, because, truth be told, so much time has gone by that the details are fuzzy even to me now.

"I want to hear it anyway," Didi says, brushing her hand through my hair.

I shrug. "He got kicked out of school, like I told you. He had a massive blowout with my dad and left home. We didn't hear from him for a couple of years. I was so mad at him. He was my older brother. We did everything together, and then—just like that—he was gone, leaving me to deal with the fallout."

"He told me. You know, I think he feels really bad about it."

"Yeah?" I ask, frowning. Why can't he tell me that himself?

"So what happened?" Didi asks.

"One day he just showed up. I was in my senior year of high school, was due to start at the Naval Academy in the fall. He'd found out about it and came back to stage what I guess he thought was some kind of intervention. He turned up to my high-school graduation ceremony and told me I didn't need to do it, that I could come live with him in Florida, go to college there."

"Why did he do that?"

I shrug. "Because I guess he felt like the fate he'd avoided had been dumped on me and that I was being pressured into it by my dad. Anyway, we argued. He left. I went to the Academy. We didn't really speak after that. You know, different paths, different ideas . . . back then, anyway."

"But that's okay. I mean, to have different ideas. You don't need to fall out over it."

What I haven't told Didi is that Isaac turned up high as a kite to my graduation, walked onto the stage where the principal was giving his speech, grabbed the mic and gave his own speech, in which he called me a coward, accused me of falling for establishment propaganda and of throwing my life away for a cause I couldn't possibly believe in, and then to top it all called Miranda a stuck-up East Coast princess and my dad Stalin. When the principal and another teacher tried to wrestle the microphone from him, he took a wild swing at them and ended up falling off the stage and landing in the lap of the principal's wife.

Remembering it now, I actually smile to myself. At the time I was mortified, as were my parents. All it did was make me even more determined not to let them down. Having one son embarrass them was enough. So his plan to rescue me backfired somewhat.

With the benefit of hindsight I can see that Isaac was only doing what he thought was best.

"I like him," Didi says, nestling her head on my shoulder.

I laugh under my breath. Miranda hated him. She thought he was a loser because he wasn't following the socio-economic pathway laid out for our peers, by which she meant he wasn't going to Harvard Law or doing an MBA.

"He reminds me of you," Didi says.

I raise an eyebrow. "Not too much, I hope."

Suddenly a bolt of fear punches me right in the solar plexus. What if she sees Isaac as a nonfaulty version of me?

Didi leans in closer and I feel her lips press just below my jaw. "There's only one Walker boy I want," she whispers into my ear.

As always, she's seen right through my fears and insecurities and addressed them without making me feel like an idiot. I turn my head and she kisses me, tugging on my bottom lip. Her words ring in my head. She wants me. She can't possibly know how much I want her too.

"Hey, you two lovebirds, stop canoodling. I need my first mate," Isaac yells, interrupting us.

"That's me!" Didi says, jumping to her feet. I support her as she wobbles. She still hasn't found her sea legs.

I listen as Isaac gives her instructions on what to do with the boom, and as Didi follows them I smile to myself. We're at sea. And I have my brother and my girlfriend alongside me. And for this one moment there's no past digging its claws into my back, there's no future slamming its doors in my face, there's just this.

Freedom.

Didi

Isaac takes in the center with the same expression I've seen on Walker when José comes to tell him he has a psych appointment with my dad. His nostrils quiver and his lips purse. They really are uncannily alike, though Isaac is much quicker to smile and has a more frenetic, unbottled energy to him. I can't help but wonder if Walker used to be the same, before what happened happened. Or was Walker always the quieter more thoughtful one of the two?

In the lobby Isaac pauses to read the platitude posters and there's no disguising the look of distaste on his face. The look transforms into one of shock when he sees two marines come through the door, both on crutches, both missing legs.

"Shit," Isaac murmurs under his breath as they pass us by.

"This way," I say quickly and lead him toward the elevators.

When we're in the elevator, Isaac turns to read the poster stuck to the elevator door showing a marine summiting a mountain. The original slogan was "*Nothing is impossible,*" but someone—that someone probably being Dodds—has added the line, "*Except growing a new pair of legs.*"

Isaac turns to Walker. "So how long do you have to be in here for?" he asks.

"I don't know." Walker shrugs.

As soon as we got back here Walker's mood deflated. He was as happy as I've ever seen him on the boat, and stupidly I thought that maybe it would last, that it would be enough to finally lift him out of the lingering depression he's been in. I wanted him to have a sense of what was possible. But now that we're back it's as if the blanket's been pulled down even more firmly over his head. He's barely responsive, not returning my squeeze when I take his hand, no longer smiling.

"Hopefully it'll be just a few more weeks," I say brightly, willing him to smile at me.

"And then?" Isaac asks.

Walker shrugs again. "And then I don't know. I haven't given it much thought."

We get out of the elevator and start walking toward Walker's room. He lets go of my elbow. He knows how many steps to take along this hallway and where to turn into his room, and I know he likes to feel independent, but even so I feel a tug that he's let go of me, as if he's pushing me away.

"You going back to Mom and Dad's?" Isaac asks as we enter Walker's room.

Walker shakes his head. "Not if I can help it."

"Yeah, I don't blame you." He pauses, studying Walker for a moment. "You know, you're welcome to come stay with me."

I look from one to the other. Walker looks momentarily phased. He starts to talk, but Isaac cuts in.

"Only if you want to. I have space. I'd love to have you. Until you figure out what you want to do, that is . . ." He looks awkward. It's there unspoken, hanging in the air. What is Walker going to do next?

Walker runs a hand through his hair. "Thanks. Yeah, I need to think about it." He turns away to face the window.

"I guess you want to stay near Didi," Isaac says.

Walker nods, but it's a vague nod and he's frowning into the middle distance. I watch him closely, holding my breath. We haven't spoken about this, but it has crossed my mind. What if he decides to go back to his parents? Would we keep things up long distance?

"Yo!"

I turn around. Sanchez is standing in the doorway. He's wearing shorts and his prosthetic is proudly on display. I see Isaac's gaze fall to it immediately.

"Where you all been at?" Sanchez asks.

"We went sailing," I tell him.

Sanchez does a double take. "You went sailing? What? There I am in the gym, my triathlon buddy, and you're out sailing?" Sanchez suddenly notices Isaac standing in the room. He walks toward him and holds out his hand. "Hey," he says. "I'm Jesús. You gotta be Lieutenant Walker's brother."

Isaac shakes his hand, looking bemused. "Yeah, how'd you know?"

"You two look like twins." Sanchez glances my way. "Better keep him out of the way of Angela." He smirks. "She'll think all her Christmases have come at once."

Isaac shakes his head, confused. "Who's Angela?"

"Just some girl who's got the hots for Walker over there," Sanchez tells him, then slaps him on the shoulder. "You do realize who your brother is, don't you? As well as being the resident man candy and uber player at the center, that is?"

Isaac seems to be struggling to keep up with Sanchez's divergent train of thought. "Um, no? Not sure I do."

Sanchez's expression falls serious. "Your brother is the reason I'm still standing here today. On one leg as that may be. But better one leg than dead, as my wife keeps on telling anyone who'll listen."

Isaac shoots a look at Walker, who's standing now with his back to us, staring out of the window. I want to go to him and put my arm around him, but I can't. Not here, in front of people. Anyway, I can tell he wants to be left alone, that he hates being reminded of that day.

"This guy," Sanchez goes on, nodding at Walker, "isn't just your brother. He's mine. There's nothing I wouldn't do for this man." He slaps Isaac on the back again. "You take care of him, okay?"

My throat is all twisted up. It's hard to swallow. Even Isaac seems moved by Sanchez's admission.

"So," Sanchez says, switching tack all over again. "What do you do? You're not a military man, that I can tell," he says, glancing at Isaac's skinny jeans and long hair with bemusement.

"I'm an artist," Isaac tells him.

Sanchez's face lights up. "Like, for real?"

Isaac nods.

"Awesome. You gotta come see this," he says, and starts tugging on Isaac's arm, pulling him toward the door.

"Where are we going?" Isaac asks.

"To the art room. I want to show you something." Sanchez looks over his shoulder. "You guys come too. You'll want to see this."

I glance at Walker, who hasn't moved. "You coming?" I ask.

He shakes his head.

I walk over to him and put my hands on his shoulder blades and briefly rest my cheek against his back. I wish there was a way inside that heart of his, a way to find the wounds in there and heal them.

"I'll be back soon," I tell him.

I feel him nod.

I walk away toward the door, but then turn back. "Walker?" I say.

He turns to face me.

"I . . ." I stop. "Nothing," I say. "I just had a good time today."

I swallow, cheeks burning, and walk out the door. What had I been about to say? That I loved him? No. That's ridiculous. Yet there it is, the word still hanging on the tip of my tongue. I do love him. And the discovery is startling. It's crept up on me, yet now I turn and face it I realize it was there all along, like my own shadow.

"Didi, hurry up!" Sanchez yells at me. He's holding the elevator doors.

I glance back over my shoulder. Walker is still standing looking in my direction. There's the smallest frown line between his eyes.

I think back to what he said a few weeks ago about not being a romantic, how he was cynical about love. How on earth would he react if I told him I was in love with him? I almost laugh at myself. He'd probably think I should be the one locked up in this place, not him.

"Not bad. Not bad at all," Isaac says, nodding thoughtfully. He tips his head to one side. "It's raw, but he has got talent."

Sanchez pulls a face as though he can't quite believe what he's hearing. "Seriously?"

Isaac nods and goes back to considering Dodds's paintings, which cover most of one wall of the art studio. He's moved on since his unicorn blasphemy phase and his technique has definitely improved. I can tell that the picture I'm staring at is of a Care Bear.

"It's a fascinating portrayal of war," Isaac says, nodding. "He's taken the original medium of the platitude poster and turned it on its head. And there's a beauty and a truth to these paintings, an authenticity that some artists strive their whole lives to achieve."

Sanchez's face is now scrunched up fully. He stares at Isaac as if he's punking him. "You what?"

Just then a whirring noise catches our attention. I turn around. Dodds has wheeled into the art room. He looks at us staring at his paintings and stops dead. With his sagging cheek it looks like he's pulling a face at us.

"This is Callum Dodds. He's the painter," I say, introducing him. "This is Isaac, Walker's brother," I tell Dodds.

"He's an artist," Sanchez butts in. "He says you got authenticity, Dodds. You hear that? You're going to be the next Picasso. This"—he gestures at the nearest painting—of a dove with a bloodied stump in its talons flying against a sunset—"is your Guerniwhatica."

Isaac laughs. He shakes Dodds's hand. "These are great," he says. "Didi says you've had no training."

Dodds stares at him with as much suspicion as if Isaac had just told him he could grow him a new pair of legs.

"I'm serious," says Isaac. "You've got real talent."

Dodds still continues to stare at Isaac as though he's talking a foreign language he doesn't understand.

"Shit. Good thing I saved that first picture you painted, hey, Dodds? Wonder what that'll be worth one day? What do you think?" Sanchez looks at Isaac hopefully.

Isaac shrugs. "I couldn't say. Let me take some photographs and speak to my agent. There's a big market right now for anything authentic. Story is everything." He nods at the paintings and smiles at Dodds. "This stuff is potent."

Dodds is still staring at him blankly. I put a hand on his shoulder and smile at him encouragingly. "He's right," I say.

"There are people who want this on their walls?" Dodds finally asks. "You're shitting me." He looks at me. "He's shitting me, right?"

We all look at Isaac.

"No, I'm not shitting you. There are people who want to buy paintings like this."

I think about the painting on Zac's wall. It must have cost thousands. We all stare silently at the array of artwork. Who'd have thought Dodds might be the next big name in art?

After a moment Sanchez shakes his head and tuts loudly. "There we are, stuck with these images in our heads, do anything to erase them, and there are people who want to see this shit on their walls." He looks over at Dodds. "No offense, Dodds."

Dodds shakes his head too. "Shit don't make sense to me neither."

Walker

miss Isaac once he's gone. As he left he pulled me into a hug and whispered "sorry" in my ear. I could hear the emotion in his voice.

I know he thinks that I took his place, that I ended up here because of his actions, but that isn't the truth. I wanted to be a marine. I took the path willingly. I just don't want to be one anymore. I can't be one anymore. Not because I'm blind, but because back on that road in Helmand I stopped believing. I stopped believing in God. I stopped believing in significance. I stopped believing in a war on terror. I stopped believing in myself as a hero, in what we were doing as heroic. How can horror on that scale be a price anyone is willing to pay, for anything?

"Okay, you all set?" Valentina calls through the door.

I come out the bathroom. I hear her draw in a loud breath. "Oh my God, you look so handsome I could eat you."

"Leave that to Didi," Sanchez cuts in.

I rub a hand over my neck, feeling self-conscious. I'm wearing a pair of pants and a shirt that Valentina bought for me. I have no idea what I look like—I could be dressed like Liberace.

The pants could have pink seams down the sides. The shirt could be bright pink. I just have to trust her. And Sanchez isn't laughing, so that has to mean something.

"So," says Valentina, "it's all set up. José and all the staff are in on it, so no one will disturb you."

"You dirty dog," Sanchez ribs, nudging me in the elbow. "You better get some tonight after all the shit we gone through organizing this."

Valentina slaps him. "Honestly, why do you always have to lower the tone? They're having a romantic date, that's all. Who said anything about them sleeping together?"

"You got protection, bro? You want me to leave some condoms by the bed?"

Another slap. "Why do you even have condoms?" Valentina shrieks. "I thought you said you wanted to try for another baby?"

"No," I interrupt, having to raise my voice to be heard. "I'm good. We're not going to . . . we're just having dinner."

"See," Valentina says triumphantly, squeezing my arm. "Noel knows how to be romantic. He knows that a woman needs to be wooed. It's not all about the physical side of things. You could learn a thing or two from this man, Jesús. And from Doctor Monroe."

Sanchez mutters something under his breath.

"Right, come on, she's going to be here soon," Valentina says, and I hear her bustling Sanchez toward the door. "Tell her happy birthday from us!" she calls.

I nod.

Suddenly Sanchez is back, whispering in my ear. "So listen, we got another sweepstake running. I won six hundred bucks last time, this time the pot's over a thousand dollars."

I cock my head in his direction. I know that the center had a sweepstake running on Didi and I getting together, but I have no idea what this one is about. Maybe how long it takes before Didi's father finds out about us. Not that I want anyone to win that particular one.

"This one is on whether you get her into bed or not tonight."

I pull a face at Sanchez. Seriously? I have no plans to try to seduce Didi tonight. It's not exactly the most romantic of places for our first time. *Here, come try out my hospital bed. Let me tie you to the IV drip stand, and, hey, try to keep it down in case your father interrupts us . . .*

Sanchez leans in and whispers conspiratorially in my ear. "I had my money on three times before morning, so, you know . . . if you want to split the winnings . . ."

"Sanchez," I say, slapping him on the shoulder and pushing him toward the door, "if I slept with Didi ten times by morning, you'd be the very last person I would tell. In fact, I wouldn't tell anyone, because that stuff is between Didi and me."

"Sure, I get it . . ." Sanchez says. "It's private. But what's a little truth between brothers?"

"Sanchez, you're lucky I'm blind, because otherwise you'd be having to explain to Valentina why having a third kid would now be impossible."

Sanchez sucks in a breath. "Ouch. Okay. Right. I got you, Lieutenant. No more sex talk."

"Jesús!" Valentina yells.

"Gotta go. You have fun," Sanchez calls. "And try to make it three, not ten."

I sit on the edge of my bed and wait for Didi to arrive. She's due at eight. I told her I wanted to watch a movie with her, but the truth is I've spent the last week organizing a date night to rival all date nights. Once I found out it was Didi's birthday and mentioned it to Valentina, there was no looking back. If Colonel Kingsley ever retires, then I think Valentina could run for his job and do it standing on her head. The woman could organize an army better than Napoleon. I didn't have to do much at all, other than submit to Valentina measuring my inside leg for new pants.

The only difficulty was making sure that Didi's father was out of the building, and Valentina managed to handle that one by inviting him and Didi's mom for dinner with her and Sanchez, ostensibly as a thank you.

I fumble in my pocket for the present—something I also had Valentina help me buy. It's a silver bracelet. I know Didi likes wearing jewelry as she's often wearing necklaces, rings, and bracelets, though recently she's only been wearing earrings. I hope she likes it. The only other jewelry I've ever bought for a girl is sitting in my top drawer, so I hope this doesn't end up the same way.

The elevator doors ping and I stand up, listening for Didi's familiar footstep. There it is. She's wearing heels. I smile to myself, trying to picture what she's wearing. Twenty paces and she's at my door.

"Hi," I say.

"Hi," she says back. There's a smile in her voice and the warmth in it wraps around me. God, even just hearing her voice makes me feel like I'm standing in the sun on the deck of a boat. She comes toward me. "Where's José?" she asks. "It's so quiet tonight. I didn't see anyone when I came in."

I shrug, smiling to myself. José has made himself scarce too.

"Wait," Didi says, stopping. "Why do you look like you're about to shoot an aftershave commercial?"

I smile. "Happy Birthday. I'm taking you on a date."

"What?" she asks. "I thought we were watching a movie."

"No movie tonight," I tell her. "I have something else planned."

She steps toward me and I take a deep breath as I smell her perfume. I run my hands down her arms. They're bare, toned, soft to the touch. She loops her arms around my neck and reaches up to kiss me. I let my fingers smooth a path down her spine. She's wearing a silk dress. The zipper teases me. How easy it would be to slide it down and let it drop to the floor. I wish like hell I could see her, tonight of all nights. I want to drink her in.

I dip my head and kiss her neck. "God, you smell so good," I tell her.

She squirms—I've discovered a few of these spots around her body where when I kiss her she practically vibrates. I've spent a lot of time thinking about how much I'd like to pin her down and take my time kissing all those places.

"And you look so good," Didi answers. "Where did you get the clothes? I've not seen them before."

"Valentina."

"She bought them for you? Just for tonight?"

"Yeah," I say, feeling a little embarrassed. "I wanted to do something special."

Didi pushes her body up against mine, and for a moment I think about letting myself tumble back against the bed, pulling her down with me and forgetting all about the dinner waiting downstairs. I take a deep breath instead and reach for her hand.

"Come on," I say, "I don't want to get started on dessert before we've even had our starter."

Didi

"Wow," I say, pausing in the doorway to the pool. "You did this?"

"Well, no," Walker says. "That would have required Helen Keller skills that I don't possess. I just told Valentina what I had in mind, and she did it. What does it look like?"

I stare at the candlelit table just in front of us and the tea lights shimmering all around the pool's edge. Somehow Valentina has turned the very unromantic rehab pool into a den of romance. She's even strung little Christmas lights in the shape of stars all around the sign signaling the pool's depth, and scattered rose petals around the table to spell out our initials. I wonder if she's embellished Walker's suggestions or whether that was his idea.

"Didi?" Walker prompts, sounding worried.

"It's perfect," I say, tears welling up. He's remembered what I said about my idea of a romantic date being on a beach under the stars. It's not quite what I envisaged, but this is way better. I whack him suddenly on the arm. "You said you weren't romantic! You big liar."

Walker's lips purse. He looks uncomfortable. "It's Valentina's doing. And besides, it's not what I'd call exotic," he says, grimacing.

I squeeze his arm. "It's perfect," I whisper. "I can't believe you did all this . . . Oh," I say, suddenly noticing the painting on the wall over by the showers.

"What?" Walker says anxiously.

"Did Valentina get any help with the decorating?"

"What do you mean?"

"It looks like Dodds might have had a hand in it."

"Oh shit, what did he paint?"

I tip my head to one side and study the painting, which is sitting on an easel to one side of the table. "It's a love heart."

"Oh," says Walker. "Okay. That sounds like a departure. Maybe he's expanding his oeuvre."

"I don't think so. It's exploding."

"Oh."

"But there are no body parts. So that's something."

"Is the iPod set up?" Walker asks.

"Yes," I say, heading toward it where it sits on a little side table.

I hit play. Justin Bieber starts to pump out of speakers arranged in the corner.

"Ha-ha," I say.

Walker grins at me. "Hit shuffle."

I do, and some mellow jazz comes on instead. "We're going to start your jazz education tonight," he tells me.

"Oh really," I say, pulling out a chair and guiding Walker toward it.

"But first, dinner."

I lift the lid on my plate and see that there's a platter of sushi in front of me. "Oh my God," I say. "Sushi! You remembered!"

"Of course," he says.

"Is there champagne?" Walker asks.

"There is," I say, spotting it in a wine bucket at my foot. "Do you want to open it?"

I hand it to him and watch him unwrap the foil and pop the cork. The noise makes me glance over my shoulder. What if someone walks in and finds us in here?

"Are you sure we're okay to be in here?" I ask.

Walker grins, and, feeling carefully for the glasses on the table, starts to pour the champagne. "Yeah, I paid off the orderlies. And besides, there's a sweepstake going. It's in their best interests to leave us alone."

"A sweepstake?" I ask.

Walker nods.

I grimace. "I don't want to know the details, do I?"

Walker shakes his head and hands me a glass. We clink.

"To the future," I say.

Walker says nothing in reply and I frown. I want him to start thinking of the future. I want him to start thinking of a future with me in it, but so far there's no prompting him to go there. He shuts down every time I mention it.

I set my glass down and reach across the table to take his hand, deciding not to push it tonight of all nights. "So," I ask instead, "what do we have to do to win this sweepstake?"

Walker wouldn't tell me any details, but I can guess it involves us sleeping together, a fact that becomes even more obvious when we get back to his room after our five-course dinner and I spot the three foil packages prominently displayed on his nightstand.

"Um, Walker?" I say, suddenly nervous. I had thought we'd agreed to no sex until he was out of here, and though it wouldn't take much to convince me to break that rule—in fact, it would probably take him just saying my name or loosening the top button on his shirt—I'm not sure a hospital bed is the most romantic place for our first time.

"Yeah?" he murmurs, stroking his hand down my arm. My resolve is gone, just like that.

"Do you want to . . ." I stop, not sure how to spell it out to him.

"What?" he asks.

"What's the plan now?" I fudge.

"Well," he says, bending to kiss my neck. "I thought maybe we could have dessert."

"Didn't we just have that?" I say, referring to the chocolate cake we just ate down by the pool.

Walker kisses my jaw and I lose my train of thought, closing my eyes as the champagne in my bloodstream starts to fizz. I press myself against him and feel something hard against my hip bone.

I pull back. "Are you happy to see me?" I ask, laughing, "or is that a long, oblong box in your pocket?"

"Oh shit," he says. "I forgot. Here." He rummages in his pocket and pulls out a neatly wrapped package. "Your birthday present."

"You got me a present?" I ask in amazement. "I thought this whole night was my present. You didn't need to get me anything."

"Open it," he says, smiling.

I do. It's a box. A jewelry box. Inside I find a delicate silver bracelet. I lift it out and see that there are two small charms dangling off it. One's a boat. The other's a tiny Buddha.

"Do you like it?" he asks, looking at me with such intense worry on his face it hurts to see it.

"Yes," I say, nodding, my voice husky. No one has ever bought me jewelry before. But more than that, more than the romance of it, he's actually thought about what it signifies. The boat represents our day on the water. The Buddha is a reference to the meditations I put on the iPod for him.

"It's beautiful," I say, wrapping it around my wrist and doing up the catch.

Then I put my arms around his neck. He shuffles his feet apart so I'm standing between them. "Thank you," I say, kissing him on the lips.

"You're welcome," he murmurs as his lips brush against mine.

"You know, you call me romantic," I say, "but actually I think you're the closet romantic in this relationship."

I brush his hair off his forehead and study him, my heart feeling overwhelmingly full, so full it's almost in danger of exploding like the one in Dodds's painting.

"Let's be clear. I am not a romantic and I'm not in the closet about anything. I just want you to know what you mean to me. How grateful I am," Walker tells me.

I look into his eyes. There's a tiny flicker of anxiety in them still, a flicker of that deep-down buried hurt, and all I want to do is find a way to excavate it and get rid of it completely.

I run my hands down his arms, thread my fingers through his. "I think you need to show me," I whisper.

"Show you what?" Walker murmurs back.

"How much I mean to you."

I glance at the nightstand. There's a part of me that wonders whether giving someone like Walker my heart is a wise thing to do. He might not mean to break it, but the future is so uncertain. And though he's getting better, he's still not fixed. He might never be. I've seen the damage that the kind of trauma he's been through can wreak on a relationship, and I know full well what I could be walking into. Sometimes Walker frustrates me beyond measure—when he won't talk, when he sinks into his dark place and I can't find a way to him—but still I can't keep away. If my dad found out what we were doing, he'd kill me. I'd be kicked off my course, too, and for good reason. But all those arguments are meaningless in the face of my huge wanting for him.

I want him. I don't care what stands in the way. I'd sacrifice it all. If I'm going to get my heart broken, then at least it will be by someone who was worth giving my heart to, not someone who sees only the top layer of me and who isn't interested in what lies beneath.

Walker is biting his lip. "Didi," he says. "I don't think we should sleep together."

"Oh," I say, glancing at the nightstand again. "But you have, uh, condoms, on the nightstand. I thought . . ."

Walker turns his head as though he can see. "What? Oh man, that was Sanchez . . ."

"He put them there?" I say, finally catching on. "Oh."

He catches my hand. "Believe me, there's nothing I want more. Nothing. At this moment, I wouldn't even trade getting my sight back."

It's my turn to bite my lip.

"But not here," he continues, gesturing at the room. "Not in this room. Not when anyone could walk in and there's a bet on and when your job is on the line. I want it to be . . . better than this."

"Okay," I say, trying to hide my disappointment.

"I want to be able to see you. I want to look in your eyes the first time I make love to you."

My stomach flips. No one has ever said those words to me before. No one has ever told me they want to make love to me. It's always been about sex. I am biting my lip so hard I can almost taste blood. *But what if you never get your sight back?* I want to ask.

"Having said that," he goes on with a small smile, "there are other ways I can show you how much you mean to me."

"There are?" I ask.

He nods and stands up. My legs are suddenly boneless. I tip my head back. One of the things I love most about Walker is his height, how when he puts his arms around me I feel completely safe and protected.

He takes my face in his hands and his thumbs caress my jaw and my lips. I close my eyes. My breathing speeds up.

"I want to touch you," Walker says in a low voice.

"Mmmm," is all I manage to murmur in response.

"All over."

My body starts to tingle as his thumbs draw a line down my neck toward my collarbone.

"Starting with my hands," he whispers into my ear. He kisses the spot just beneath my ear that makes my toes curl. I have to hold on to his shoulders to steady myself. "And then my mouth," he murmurs in a low voice that sends a shudder right thought me. "And then my tongue."

There's a sharp tightening in my stomach, butterflies being

let loose, starting to riot. Walker's hands slide up my back, making it arch in response. He hasn't even started yet and I'm already one hundred percent under his control. He could do anything he wanted to me right now.

"Are you okay with that?" he asks.

"Ye-e-s," I stammer.

"Good," he says. And his fingers locate the zipper of my dress and slowly start to ease it down.

I hold my breath, fire racing through my veins. When he's done with the zipper he just as slowly traces his hand up my bare spine. I draw in a breath. It's the first real skin-to-skin contact we've had, and little jolts of electricity have started to spark down my limbs. The tiny hairs on the back of my neck stand on end. He reaches my shoulders and hooks his thumbs through the sleeves of my dress and slides it off, pausing to kiss his way along my collarbone.

My dress drops to the ground and I'm standing in just my underwear. Walker's hands fall to my waist, resting on the curve of my hips. His expression is serious and I can't stop myself from reaching for his face.

"Are you okay?" I ask, suddenly worried that he isn't liking what he's finding.

He smiles and takes my hand to kiss the palm. "Yeah," he says. "I'm just trying to savor you, take my time. It's taking monumental amounts of willpower that I'm not sure I possess."

I smile and start unbuttoning his shirt. He frowns. "Wait," he starts to say, "this is supposed to be about you—" but he silences himself abruptly when I slide my hand beneath his shirt and press it against his chest.

He shuts his eyes and his jaw tenses as I move my fingers

over the solid lines of his stomach. His skin is warm, soft, perfect. Is this how he feels when he touches me? Almost frantically I start tearing at the rest of the buttons on his shirt, desperate to finally be properly skin to skin with him, to feel myself pressed against him.

Walker helps, pulling the shirt off over his head, and I take a deep breath and step back so I can fully appreciate him. He doesn't let me for long—his hands reach for me and he pulls me against him, his hands exploring my waist, my stomach, smoothing up my back until they come to my bra. He pauses and I press closer against him and he expertly undoes my bra one-handed. It joins my dress on the floor and I stand there and watch the darkening desire on his face as his hands move to cup my breasts.

He dips his head and takes my nipple into his mouth, drawing on it softly at first, and when I grip his shoulders and let out a gasp, harder. His free hand pulls my leg up against his hip, strokes behind the knee. I'm breathing so hard I have pins and needles in my arms and legs.

He kisses me, deeply, and the pins and needles magnify. Lights start to flash behind my eyes. Walker suddenly takes my hands and turns me around so I'm facing the bed and he's behind me, pressing against my back. I want to ask what he's doing, but then he starts to kiss down my spine, his hands stroking across my stomach, outlining my ribs. He's so gentle it hurts, makes me push my hips back and into him, makes me impatient for more. I reach behind and pull him against me, wanting to feel him.

I hear his low-throated laugh in response. He catches my wrists and pulls them in front of me, pinning them to my stomach with one hand. With his other he keeps caressing me, slowly, torturously slowly, until every nerve ending in my body feels like it's being licked by flames.

The whole time he lays kisses across my back, the tops of my shoulders, my neck. When his hands reach the waistband of my underwear, I'm so on edge that I let out a moan. He pauses and I bite my lip to stop from begging him. He has me exactly where he wants me.

"I haven't even used my tongue yet," he whispers in my ear, and I let out another moan before I can stop myself.

His hand slides briefly inside my underwear and then out again as if he's decided to slow things down. I try to get control of my breathing. Walker releases me and turns me around again so we're facing each other.

"You're so beautiful," he says, kissing me.

"You can't even see me."

"I don't need to."

I run my fingers over the ridges of his stomach again, as hungry for him as he seems to be for me. When my hands find his belt I start to undo it, but he catches my hand and pulls it away, shaking his head with a smile.

I frown.

"Not yet. I think we should slow things down because I have a lot more exploring to do, and I want to take my time. Okay?" he asks.

"Yes," I croak.

He nudges me backward onto the bed and stands between my legs. I take him in. "You're beautiful," I murmur. "So beautiful."

My words are stolen from me by his lips. "You can't call a marine beautiful. There's a law against that," he jokes, still with his lips against mine.

"But you are," I say.

His jaw tenses. "Shhhh," he says. "Lie back."

I lie down on the bed, looking up at him standing over me. With a smile on his face he hooks his thumbs into my underwear and pulls them down. I lift my hips to help him, and next thing I know I'm lying naked on the bed. Walker takes a deep breath in, as though steadying himself, and then comes and lies down next to me.

I curl toward him and he pulls me closer, kissing the top of my head.

"So I'm completely naked and you're wearing pants still, how is that fair?" I ask.

He considers this for a moment. "Okay," he says and gets up off the bed. I watch him undo his pants and drop them.

Holy shit.

He climbs back on the bed beside me and we start to kiss. I can feel how hard he is, but every time my hand wanders lower he catches it and brings it back up to his chest. His hand, however, is circling lower and lower, even as he kisses me. Finally he reaches my thighs and gently pushes them apart. He's propped on one elbow and I'm lying on my back.

His fingertips stroke the inside of my thigh, teasingly soft, and he keeps it up until my back is arching off the bed. He must be able to hear how ragged my breathing is.

Just when I'm on the verge of begging him, his fingers are there and then sliding inside me. He murmurs something, his lips against my neck, but I don't hear what. I can't hear. I can't think. There's just this feeling that takes over, wipes my mind clean, blood surging, electrifying.

"You're so wet," he murmurs into my ear.

I arch again as he presses into me, building up rhythm, stroking his thumb over me.

My nails bite into his arm. He stops.

My eyes flash open, heavy-lidded, drugged.

He's smiling. "Not yet. I still want to taste you."

I grab a pillow and bury my head in it to smother my frustrated groans. I can hear him laughing.

I toss the pillow aside and reach for him again, but he snatches my wrist once more and pins me down on the bed. "Ah-ah-ah," he says, with a smile that turns serious. "I want to be in control tonight. Let me."

I stare up at him, into the dark gray of his eyes, hooded in the low light but shining. He's driving me slowly insane but I see that relinquishing control to him is what he wants, or even needs, so I give in.

I relax, and he senses it and lets go of my wrist to start kissing his way down my body. By the time he makes it to my stomach, I'm so on the verge that when his tongue starts to circle where his fingers left off, I lose control completely. Walker pins me to the bed with his hand on my stomach and doesn't let up, his fingers joining in, until I'm gasping, my fingers twisting through his hair.

He keeps me on the verge, I don't know how, but sensing every time I'm close and slowing down, and it could be minutes later or it could be hours, but when he finally lets me fall over the edge, it's not so much a fall but a tumble that goes on for what feels like infinity and leaves me lying there afterward breathless and shaking and close to tears.

Walker lies down beside me and pulls me into his arms. I lie there, unable to talk, surges of electricity making my muscles twitch. I curl tighter, almost into a ball, and Walker wraps himself around me, stroking my hair, and now the tears do come and I don't know why and I don't want him to know that I'm crying because I feel stupid.

"Hey," he says, propping himself up on one arm. "Are you crying?"

"No," I mumble. "Yes."

"Why?" he asks, anxiety rich in his voice.

I roll to face him. "Just because," I say. "I didn't know that's what it could be like. I thought people were exaggerating."

A grin splits Walker's face. "I'm not finished with you yet," he says, bending to kiss me again.

Walker

S o, did I win the bet?" Sanchez asks, storming into my room before they've even brought breakfast round. I sit up. What the hell time is it?

"Shit," Sanchez says. "I guess not."

I hear him walk around to the nightstand and pick up the condoms. "Unless she brought her own?" Sanchez asks. When I don't answer he sits down on the bed and whispers, "So did you get to third base at least? Come on, I want details. Everyone's waiting."

I don't answer. I can't hide my smile, though, as memories from last night rise to the fore. Fuck, that was a good night.

"Oh man, you dirty dog, you did get some!"

"A gentleman never talks," I say, getting off the bed and making my way to the bathroom.

"Come on, it's me, Sanchez. We're like bros, you gotta tell me. Dodds said he heard a lot of noise coming from here last night. I'm guessing you two weren't playing Scrabble."

"Monopoly," I tell him, shutting the bathroom door behind me. It doesn't fully mute Sanchez who I can hear still peppering questions my way. Didi only left a couple of hours ago. I should be tired—I've only had about an hour's sleep—but I'm not. I'm fully awake. And I think I need a cold shower. I'm still buzzing, and the memories are now racing through my mind on play-back. I can smell Didi on my skin, can still taste her on my tongue.

"You up for some pool time?" Sanchez hollers through the door. "Or are you all spent after last night?"

"Give me five minutes," I yell back. Maybe ten, I think to myself. I think I want to relive last night again, on my own, in the shower.

"Okay, I'll see you down there," he says.

I don't make it to the pool. I make it to the doorway where I bump straight into José.

"You got an appointment down with occupational," he tells me.

I sigh and roll my head backward.

"Come on, let's get going," he chides. "I've spent all morning clearing up petals from the pool, and now I'm running late."

Oh shit. I forgot about the clearing-up part. I was too distracted last night.

"You have fun last night?" José asks as we walk to the elevator.

"Yeah," I say. "Thanks for your help."

"You're a lucky guy," José answers. "She's a catch. If her mother's anything to go by, Didi's going places."

I fall silent as we get into the elevator, and by the time we make it to the occupational therapy room my good mood has evaporated. I don't even know why for certain, but José's words echo around my head, sticking there like a burr. Didi's going places, he said. And I'm going exactly nowhere. That's the crux of it. She has this bright future ahead of her. She wants to move to LA, for Chrissake. My future involves learning how to use a white stick and probably moving in with my brother, because it's not like any other options are cropping up. I've got no job, no prospects. How can I tie a girl like Didi down? I'd be crippling her.

"So, Lieutenant Walker, how we doing today?" the occupational therapist asks in a bantering tone. "How was last night?"

I arch my eyebrows. Is there anyone in this place who doesn't know about last night?

"Right," he says hastily, seeing my reaction, "let's get you set up. Are you ready to start practicing with a stick? I know you're resistant, but the sooner you learn, the sooner you'll be out of here. I also have some information here about seeing-eye dogs."

I grit my teeth. Welcome to the future.

Didi

"How's Lieutenant Walker?" my mom asks as I drive her into the center in the morning.

I glance her way, panic-stricken, my gut clenching. Does she know? Has she somehow read something on my face? Did I say his name without realizing it?

"Um, he's . . . fine. I think." My mind flits back to last night, to Walker kissing me. My skin still tingles from his touch almost twelve hours later. Every time I think back to last night my stomach flips over on itself.

"How are you finding it?"

"What?" I ask, alarmed.

"Keeping an emotional distance. From the patients."

I swallow and focus on driving. "Um . . . it has its challenges," I say.

"All relationships do. Some more than others. But particularly doctor–patient ones."

What are we talking about here? I cast another glance in her direction. She's putting lipstick on, holding a compact mirror in one hand. She pauses and looks across at me. "That's a lovely bracelet. Is it new?"

Oh shit. I forgot to take it off. "Um, yeah, Jessa gave it to me for my birthday."

I stare straight ahead at the road. I'm the worst liar, and my mom is trained in reading body language. I can feel the heat rising up my neck. Last time I lied to her I was fifteen and told her I had absolutely no idea what had happened to the peach schnapps in the living room cabinet when I knew full well I'd just regurgitated most of it into the toilet.

"Did you have a good time with her last night?" she asks.

The heat scores across my face. I told her and my dad that I was going out with Jessa to celebrate my birthday. Which technically means that the last time I lied to her was last night and not when I was fifteen. "Um, yeah, it was fun," I say. Images of Walker pinning me to the bed are graffitied on my mind.

"What's that?" my mom suddenly exclaims, snapping her compact shut. "Is that"—she leans toward me across the handbrake—"a hicky?"

My hand flies to my neck. "What? No!" Oh God. Is it?

My mom arches a thinly plucked eyebrow at me. "Bernadette Monroe," she says.

I cringe at the use of my full name.

"I know a hicky when I see one." She smiles wickedly and I almost veer across a lane. "Just so long as you're having fun and no one is going to get hurt," she says.

Does she know?

"Are you in control?" she asks.

Once again I think back to Walker holding me down last night and taking the lead. "Um . . ." I say, frowning.

"Because I don't want you to get hurt," my mom says, zipping up her makeup bag.

I indicate and pull into the base, my heart hammering. She

knows. Has she told my dad? Or am I being paranoid? Maybe she doesn't know a thing. If this was a game of poker I'd tell myself to hold my cards close to my chest until I knew the other player's hand, so I say nothing.

We get out of the car. My mom walks around to my side and slips her arm through mine. We start walking toward the entrance of the center. I'm still rattled and trying desperately not to show it.

"It's a lot to take on, Didi," my mom says gently as we approach the door. "Go into this with your eyes open."

I almost trip over. I turn to look at her.

"One of you has to," she says before patting my arm and walking off.

I mull over my mom's words all day. She knows, but why isn't she telling me off? I know she doesn't believe in interfering, and she's never judgmental about other people's choices, but her reaction is so tame compared with the reprimand from my dad.

I'm so distracted that I blunder straight into the art therapy teacher by the elevators.

"Did you hear?" she says, eyes bright as I help her collect the paint tubes she's dropped.

Oh God, I think to myself as we straighten up, does she know too? Are there any secrets in this place?

"About Callum."

Dodds? I shake my head perplexed.

"Some fancy art gallery in Palm Beach wants to represent him!"

"Really?" I ask.

She nods, beaming happily.

"Wow."

"It was Lieutenant Walker's brother that arranged it. I've been on the phone to him this morning."

"Dodds must be so happy," I say.

"I was just on my way to find him to let him know."

I go with her, eager to see Dodds's face when he hears the news. We find him in his room staring out the window. His breakfast tray sits untouched on the table beside him.

"Hi!" the art teacher says.

Dodds looks over his shoulder blankly, then goes back to staring out the window. He doesn't say hi.

"I have news," the teacher says, bustling forward.

Dodds turns around again, still stony-faced. Undeterred, the teacher proceeds to tell him about the exhibition and slowly Dodds's blank expression gives way to a frown, and then, once she's finished talking, to utter bemusement.

"For real?" he asks, looking at me for confirmation that she's not joking.

We both nod. The teacher nods so hard it looks like her head is about to fall off. I think she's seeing Dodds as her protégé and her excitement is contagious. At least to me. Dodds, however, appears to be immune.

"So can I tell them yes?" she asks, clapping her hands together. "That you're happy for them to represent you?"

The half of his face that works scrunches up. I'm not sure he fully understands what she's talking about.

"It means they'll sell your work on your behalf and take a small cut of the sales price," I explain.

Dodds nods thoughtfully, then shrugs. "Sure. I guess. Why not?"

The teacher beams some more and hurries past me, probably to make the call to Isaac.

"Congratulations," I say to Dodds.

Dodds gives me a tight smile in response.

"I guess you don't need that brochure about careers anymore then," I laugh. "I mean, now that you're going to be a famous artist."

He gives a bitter snort and turns back to the window. "Yeah."

I frown at his back. He isn't as happy as I thought he would be.

"Are you okay?" I ask.

"Sure," he says. "Why wouldn't I be?"

Is he being sarcastic? His empty pant legs seem to taunt me. I think about saying something more, trying to gauge what his real thoughts are, but it's clear he's not wanting to talk. I turn to leave. I'm due to see a patient with my dad anyway.

"Hey, Didi?"

I turn back. Dodds is wheeling himself over to his nightstand. He roots through the drawer and then wheels himself over to me. "Here," he says, handing me his pack of playing cards. They're military issue ones, the ones we played poker with a few weeks ago. They have the faces of wanted Afghan and Iraqi terror suspects on them. "These are for you," he says.

I frown at the cards. "Um, thanks," I say, not sure what to make of the gift.

"Think of it as a late birthday present," he explains, giving me a wry smile. "They're my lucky cards." He pulls a face. "Well, they were until you beat me with them. Figure you should have 'em now."

"Thanks," I say, looking him in the eye. "You know, I really hope your paintings do well."

He nods. "Yeah. Maybe I could, I don't know, donate some of the money to, like, charity or something." His face reddens. "You know, if they actually sell."

I smile.

"Didi?"

I turn around. José is standing in the hallway holding a huge bunch of red roses. He raises his eyebrows at me over the top of them. "These just arrived for you," he smirks.

My heart lifts and a smile bursts on my face.

I take the proffered flowers from José, glancing at Walker's half-open door and grinning.

"There's no card," José tells me, "but no guessing who they're from." He tips his head toward Walker's room. "On the outside he's a tough marine, on the inside he's a marshmallow," José calls to my back as I head toward Walker's room.

I knock and push the door open. Walker's sitting on the bed, scowling toward the window, and I stop abruptly, struck immediately by the powerful storm front in the room. Something's up.

"Hi," I stammer, my heart starting to thud heavily.

Walker turns his head slowly toward me. Gone is the look of longing, the glint of desire I saw in his eyes last night. Gone too is the lightness I've seen in him over the last few weeks. He looks just like he did the very first time I met him: glowering, unapproachable, completely untouchable. My heart drops.

"Thanks for the flowers," I hear myself say. "You didn't need to—"

"I didn't," Walker cuts in.

"What?"

"They're not from me." He stares at me stonily.

I look down at the flowers, realization dawning. They're the exact same flowers I received before, even down to the black silk ribbon binding them and the name of the florist written on it in gold font.

They're from Zac.

Walker

What are the chances I'm going to get my sight back?" I ask Doctor Monroe before I've even sat down in his squishy chair.

There's a pregnant pause and then he speaks. "That's up to you, Lieutenant. There's nothing more I can do. You have to confront the trauma head-on if there's to be any hope of lifting the blindness."

Frustration bites at me. "But I just want to move on," I growl at him.

He replies very quietly, as if countering my outburst. "Sometimes we can't move on until we've looked back and dealt with the past."

I scowl, my fists punching the chair. "I can't."

"I think you can."

Now I'm angry. Why doesn't he get it? "I can't!" I yell. "You don't understand! I think about it all the time already. I can't get away from it. It doesn't matter how much I confront it, how much I look back, it doesn't get me anywhere. There is no way of dealing with it."

"There is." Doctor Monroe answers in that ever-calm voice of his. "It's called forgiving yourself."

I laugh, short and sharp. It comes out like a whip cracking against bare skin.

"If you can't do that, Lieutenant—"

"Don't call me that," I snap. "I'm not a lieutenant anymore. I've applied for a discharge. I'm going to be a civilian soon enough—call me by my name. My real name."

"Is that what you want? Because you know you can stay in the military. There are options."

"A desk job?" I scoff. "What am I going to do? Learn to read Braille?" I laugh again, this time even more bitterly. I shake my head at him. "I don't want to stay in the marines. I'm not a marine anymore."

"I thought it was once a marine, always a marine. Isn't that what they say?"

"Not in this case," I shoot back.

All those qualities he made me list off during that session we had are all just lies, adjectives they use to make us believe we're better, stronger, more capable than other people. They're lies they tell kids like Dodds who don't have any other options and nothing better to believe in, and idiots like me who should know better. But now I've seen the truth, faced it in a way none of the PR people who make up those adjectives ever will. We're as weak and vulnerable as everyone else.

And what I know is this: there's no honor in dying on a dusty road in a foreign land for a cause you don't even understand, screaming for your mother who's ten thousand miles away as you bleed out, begging for someone to save you. There's no peace to be had in knowing you're fighting for something bigger than you, there's just horror when you come to realize in that moment—that infinite time-stretching moment—how insignificant you really are, how, in a blinding flash, you can be reduced to nothing but ash and bone and a boot lying tipped on its side.

And that cancels everything out.

All that bullshit they spout about heroism . . . they tack a silver star to my shoulder and think that's all it will take to make me feel better, to erase the memories? Five people dead and a silver star is my reward. My punishment.

"And then?"

I realize the doc is talking to me. Waiting on an answer.

And then . . . nothing. And then . . . nothing will ever be the same again.

"And then I don't know," I say because he's still waiting on an answer. "I might go stay with my brother."

As soon as I say it I know I'm talking out of my ass. I can't stay with Isaac. What am I going to do? Tag along with him to glittering art openings? The blind brother who can't even make small talk about the art on display? I just want to hole up and hide. I want to hole up and hide with Didi. His daughter. Because in bed with her, holding her in my arms, is the closest to peace I've come since that day, the closest I think I'll ever come. Last night was the first night I've had with no nightmares.

But I can't tell him that. I can just picture his expression if I did—his glasses fogging up with fury. Yeah, a mental patient probably isn't too high on the list of potential suitors for his daughter. And how can I run away and hide with her—with a girl who has a *bright future*? A future I'd be holding her back from. I can't do that to her.

"Well, I'm glad you've started thinking about the future," Doctor Monroe says, "even if you're reticent in thinking about the past."

Yes, I have started to think about the future. And it's becoming more and more apparent that my future points one way and hers points another.

Didi

decide to wait for Walker in his room. I tried explaining to him about the roses, that Zac wasn't in the picture anymore, that I had no idea why he'd sent them, but he didn't seem to want to hear it. He became as deaf as he's blind, I couldn't get a response out of him, and then José came to take him to an appointment with my dad and he left without a word—so add mute to the equation too.

My mom's speech this morning rattles around my head. Maybe she's right. Maybe I should have thought twice about getting involved with him, with someone who can't, even after all this time, trust me enough to tell me what's going on in his head, who refuses to open up to me.

I sit staring at the roses, then I get up and walk into the hall-way, looking for a garbage can. Sanchez walks past as I drop the bouquet into the cleaning trolley.

"Hey," he says in alarm. "What are you doing?" He retrieves the roses. "Why you throwing them away?"

"They're from Zac."

Sanchez frowns at them, then starts dusting them off. "If you don't want them, I'll give them to Valentina."

I shrug. She's welcome to them.

"What's up?" he asks, noticing my gloomy face.

I tell him about Walker's reaction to the flowers, about my explanations, about his impenetrable silence, his refusal to talk. About my worry that I've taken on more than I can deal with. That maybe I should be dating a normal guy. Straightforward, romantic, easy. Like Zac. Maybe leave Walker behind. It looks like that's what he wants, after all.

"You serious?" he asks when I'm done.

I nod.

"Dude, this is just how relationships go. You can't quit every time it gets rough. You know what your mom says? She says that relationships go through ups and downs and it's how you act during the down parts that matters most."

I fold my arms over my chest. I do not need my mom's words thrown in my face at this moment, but Sanchez ignores me. He's on a roll.

"I know you like your romance, but that's just surface shit. That ain't what matters deep down." He waves the roses in my face. "Anyone can buy you roses—don't let these distract you. This guy Zac, you think this means anything to him?" Sanchez shakes his head. "He could afford to send you diamonds, probably. In fact, his PA or whatever you call them probably sent you these. I don't think Zac Ridgemont was on the phone to Interflora this morning."

Sanchez has a point. Zac did tell me that his PA does all his online shopping and orders his groceries. He seemed inordinately proud of the fact he no longer had to go to the supermarket like the rest of us mortals.

"Sure," Sanchez goes on, hitting his stride, "Walker's a grumpy fucking bastard most of the time, but he's also the most stand-up guy I've ever known. You didn't know him before." He shakes his head and sighs. "He's the real deal, Didi. You aren't going to find a more loyal guy, a more selfless guy, no matter how hard you look. And he might be a grumpy bastard on occasion, and he might not buy you flowers, but he did buy you sushi. And a bracelet with, you know, dangly things on it. That shit's gotta count for something."

I sink down into a plastic chair by the nurse's station. Sanchez sits down beside me.

"But it shouldn't be this hard," I mumble, thinking of the constant ups and downs with Walker, the way he keeps shutting me out, letting me in, shutting me out. I'm exhausted by it. It's like being stuck in a revolving doorway. I just want to get through to the lobby or walk back out onto the street. I can't keep up with the round-and-round. It's making me dizzy.

"Didi," Sanchez says, shaking his head softly. "Open your eyes and look around you." His words echo my mother's and make me wince. "Life isn't a fucking fairy tale. You've seen the reality. You're surrounded by fucking reality."

I lower my head. With his sniper's ability, he's managed to hit a major nerve.

"It is a fairy tale for some people," I mutter under my breath.

Sanchez bursts out laughing. "For who? Show me one person for who life is a fairy tale and I'll show you a very good line in bullshit."

"My parents. They never argue."

"Yeah, well, that's just freakish. Valentina and I argue all the time. Don't mean I don't love her. Man, I adore that woman, even when she's busting my balls over something stupid like who ate all the guacamole or who let the kids stay up late and watch a horror movie."

I laugh. Maybe he's right. Maybe holding my parents up as the paradigm for a perfect relationship is stupid.

"But he keeps pushing me away," I argue weakly.

"Don't let him," Sanchez says in a fierce tone that makes me flinch. "Don't walk away. Don't do that to him. No matter how far he pushes you. The last thing he needs is you walking away."

Sanchez pats me on the shoulder and gets up. "And I'm not just saying that 'cause I got money riding on you two lasting until at least Christmas."

My mouth falls open.

"Just joking with you!" he grins.

I watch him head back to his room, roses in hand, and my gaze lands on a poster on the wall by the elevator.

"*If at first you don't succeed, try, try again,*" this one says.

Someone—no guesses as to whom—has taken a magic marker and scratched through the last three words, scrawling instead the words, "*Give the fuck up.*"

I slump back in my chair.

Walker

haven't heard from her for five days. José passes on a message from her that she's had to go to LA for something to do with school, a conference or something, but I wonder if that's a lie, if she's really meeting up with Zac.

I don't know how we got from the night of her birthday to here, and I wrack my brains, playing over that last conversation in my room. I was mad about the roses, but only because I was already worked up about the future. The roses were just the icing on the cake. Zac's got everything, can give her everything, and the plain fact is, I can't. So maybe she is with him in LA. Isn't that what I want? For her to be happy? And doesn't it make things easier if she's decided to break things off with me?

But that doesn't mean I can stop thinking about her. Or about the night of her birthday. She's imprinted into my memory, a bruise that refuses to fade but that just keeps getting darker.

"You get back to sleep last night?" José asks, walking into the room.

I shake my head and listen to him settle the breakfast tray on the table.

The nightmares have been getting worse. Maybe there's a link to Didi being gone. Maybe not. In the daytime my head's all over the place, thoughts landing like flies, bothering me until I shake them off and they flit away, only to land in the same place a few seconds later. Mainly they're thoughts about Didi—more memories than thoughts, really . . . the curve of her body pressed against mine, the sunshine sound of her laugh, the softer sound of her moaning when I made her come. I try not to dwell on that last one, but it occupies a lot of my waking moments until I interrupt it by thinking back over every conversation we've ever had.

But at night my thoughts aren't about Didi. They return to that day. The day of the incident. The nightmares jolt me out of sleep and then I'm awake for the rest of the night, heart racing like I've taken a handful of amphetamines, the images on the backs of my eyelids flickering past like Dodds's paintings come to life.

"You want me to talk to the doc and get you some different meds prescribed?" José asks.

I shake my head. José still thinks I'm taking the cocktail of colorful pills he pours into my hand each morning and night.

"You want me to shave you?"

I shake my head. I barely have the energy to get out of bed. I hear José sigh loudly and leave the room, and I lie down and close my eyes, trying to switch off the plasma screen on the back of my eyelids.

"Yo, Lieutenant."

I don't stir. It's Sanchez. If I pretend I'm sleeping maybe he'll go away.

"You got to get out of bed, bro. This moping around like a

girl who's been ditched at the altar? It's not working for you." He walks into the room and settles himself on the end of the bed. "You know, this one time Valentina didn't speak to me for nearly a month. I can't even remember why—I think maybe I forgot our anniversary or something—but my point is that she got over it. You just got to talk it out." He pats my leg. "And then make love to her. Like, plenty of times. Like maybe three times at least, before next Sunday."

I ignore him. I don't want to talk things out. I want things to be over.

He exhales loudly.

I'm glad he's going to lose that damn sweepstake.

"If you keep it up, I'm going to have to invite Angela to pay you a visit, see if she can *raise* your spirits." He chuckles. "I'm sure she'd love the opportunity to do that."

My eyes flash open. I scowl in his direction.

Sanchez stands up. "So you going to get up? Triathlon's in two days. We still got a chance of winning this thing."

I stare resolutely toward the ceiling.

"Or, you know," says Sanchez in a sing-song voice, "there's always Angela."

I swing my legs off the bed.

"Atta boy!"

Didi

S o have you decided what you're going to do?" Jessa asks, setting a cup of coffee down in front of me.

I shake my head and stare out of the window at the ocean, which only serves to remind me of Walker. Everything, in fact, reminds me of Walker. The other day in a bookstore I saw a signed copy of *Misery* and thought of him. In the paper I saw a photograph of the Brazilian soccer team and thought of Walker and his dream to sail to South America. Jessa bought me sushi. I thought of Walker. I saw a stuffed seal toy in a shop. I thought of Walker. I watched *An Officer and a Gentleman*. I thought of Walker. Every time I look in the mirror I think of Walker.

Six days since I last spoke to him and my skin still burns from where his hands traced patterns over my stomach and thighs. When I lie in bed and close my eyes, I can still feel the aftershocks from his touch, small electrical pulses like signal fires being lit along my neural pathways.

I miss him. I miss him like phantom limb syndrome. It hurts. I keep expecting him to be there. I've been so used to being with him, seeing him every day, and now I feel lost, at sea, completely disoriented without him. All the time I thought I was the one holding him in place, anchoring him, keeping him from being pulled into his dark place, he was doing something similar for me and I didn't realize it.

"Are you going to go?" Jessa asks, sitting down beside me and drawing her knees to her chest.

"I don't know."

"Where's this triathlon happening?"

"Monterey."

"I think you should go," Jessa says. "See him. See how you feel when you do."

"I know how I'll feel when I see him." How I always feel. As if I've been hit with a cloud-wrapped sledgehammer, as if my heart is shattering in my chest from the impact.

"I'm scared," I admit to Jessa. "I mean, things are never going to be easy with someone like Walker, are they?" I don't say anything more, but I'm thinking of Jessa's father, whose battle with post-traumatic stress disorder has caused absolute chaos in her family. Things are better now, but the things Jessa and her mother went through . . . is that what I want for myself? Not that Walker is that bad, but the potential is there, especially as he refuses to confront his issues. "Maybe I should just walk away completely."

"Is that even possible?" she asks. "Can you just leave?"

I sigh. "I think my mom was right. I should have gone into it with my eyes open wider. Dad tried to warn me that getting involved with a marine, and a wounded one at that, was a dumb idea."

"Not always so dumb," Jessa comments, sipping her coffee. "Look, Didi—you don't get to choose who you fall in love with."

"Who said I was in love with him?" I counter.

She raises her eyebrows at me. "You've been staying with me for six days and you haven't talked about anything but Walker. You've barely eaten. You're not sleeping. I'd say that sounds like love."

"That doesn't sound like love. That sounds like depression."

Jessa smirks at me and I avoid her eye. She's right, though. I am in love with him. Totally. It's just that admitting it out loud isn't something I want to do. What's the point?

"Talk to him," Jessa says. "Tell him how you feel. Isn't that what you therapists are always preaching? Talk. Get things out in the open. Here you are accusing him of not talking to you or opening up, and you're doing the exact same thing to him. The only way you can have a relationship with someone is if you're honest."

She puts her coffee cup down and takes my hand.

"Didi, speaking from experience, when someone's pushing you away the hardest, that's often when they need you the most."

I remember what José said to me about not hurting Walker, and Sanchez warning me not to walk away, too. I didn't listen to them. But then again, Walker hasn't tried to call me these last few days either. He obviously doesn't want to see me or hear from me.

Jessa's looking at me expectantly. I stare back at her, at a loss for words. I don't know what to do.

Walker

José drives Sanchez, me, and a couple of other guys to Monterey where the triathlon is taking place. It's been a week now and still no word from Didi. I guess I shouldn't be surprised. Not after pushing her away like I did.

The hurt has calcified now. I've buried myself in a coffin, thrown acres of dirt on top of myself, closed everyone out. I don't feel anything anymore. It makes things easier.

I'm aware Sanchez is talking to me, but the words are like further fistfuls of dirt. I stare into the darkness as the others exclaim over the views all the way along the coast road.

"We're here. Lieutenant, wake up."

Sanchez prods me to my feet and helps me down off the bus. I'm finally using the stick they gave me, still getting used to it, and I take Sanchez's arm as he guides me into the hotel, where I stand waiting to be assigned a room. The race is in the morning. I just want to go to bed.

"Lieutenant," Sanchez says, "I would share a room with you and all, but Valentina's coming later tonight and, you know, we haven't had much privacy to, you know, get jiggy-jiggy these last couple of months."

I wave him off. "It's cool."

"I want to show her what I can do with my bionic hand."

I wince.

"Here's your key," he says. "I'll show you to your room. Help you get set up. It's next door to ours."

I stand up and take his elbow. We take two steps and then he stops. I trip into him.

"Shit," he says.

"What?" I say, but as soon as I say it I know. I can smell her, feel her, sense her.

"Hi," Didi says.

My body starts to hum like a tuning fork. "Hi," I say. What the hell is she doing here?

"Can we talk?" she says.

Sanchez, remarkably, for once stays silent. He pats me on the arm and I hear him walk away.

"I'm sorry," Didi says in a rush. "I just needed some time."

I nod. "Me too. I'm sorry." Calcification. A hardening of the heart.

"Those roses didn't mean anything."

I nod. She takes a step nearer and my senses burst into hyperdrive. My fingers twitch and I have to fight the urge to reach for her.

"I don't want him," she says quietly. "You know I don't want Zac. I want you."

Her hand slides into mine, gently, tentatively. Her palm feels warm.

But something makes me pull my hand away and take a step backward. I bang into something, a table. Something heavy falls to the floor and I hear Didi bend and pick it up, then put it back on the table. We're still in the damn lobby. Anyone could be watching us.

"Didi, I can't see," I say, gesturing at my eyes. "I can't do anything. I can't drive. I can't make a cup of fucking coffee. I can't shave. I can't even dress myself properly. I put antiseptic cream on my toothbrush the other day."

She doesn't say anything. Is everyone watching us? I don't care.

"You deserve someone who'll take care of you," I say desperately. "Protect you, look after you."

"And there I was thinking we lived in the twenty-first century," Didi answers. She laughs under her breath. "I don't need a guy to do all those things. I can take care of myself."

It's my turn to laugh. "You're lying. You do want those things. I know you. You're a romantic. You want someone like Zac who'll send you flowers and take you out to dinner and open doors for you and whisk you off to Paris for the weekend. You want the knight on the white horse. You want a lobster. Someone who believes in all that stuff. And I can't be that person. I can't give you those things. I can't whisk you anywhere. I can't even walk in a straight line."

"Why are you doing this?" Didi asks.

"What?"

"Pushing me away."

"I'm not. I'm just laying it on the line. What are you going to do? Give up your studies to take care of me?"

"No!" she exclaims. "As far as I was aware you don't need taking care of. You're perfectly capable, or you will be soon enough. And you won't be blind forever. In fact, if you actually tried to open up to me instead of constantly shutting me out, then maybe you wouldn't be blind by now." She stops, takes a deep breath as though to calm herself. "But if I did want to take care of you, why would you want to stop me?" She pauses and takes another step closer. "That's what people do when they love someone—they take care of them."

She takes my hand again. It takes me a second to register what she's said, what she means. I'm thrown for a split second, reeling. And then I recover. I snatch my hand away.

"You don't know what you're saying," I tell her.

"Walker . . ." she says, a pleading note in her voice I've never heard before. She sounds close to tears.

"Didi," I say, shutting my senses down, closing my ears to the note in her voice, "let's just call this a day. You and me, it was never going to work. We can't have a future." *I don't have a future* is what I really want to say to her.

"How would you know?" she exclaims. "You refuse to even think about the future."

"And that's all you ever do," I shoot back.

I sense her pull back.

"You're always talking about when I get out of here, when I can see . . . well, I hate to break it to you, but it doesn't look like I'm going to get my sight back, whatever anyone says."

"Then . . ." She hesitates.

I butt in. "Then nothing. Just go." I hold up my hand as a good-bye and move away from her. I have to. I can't allow myself to ruin her life.

I can feel the pain thrumming off her. It's like a knife through my own ribs. But I don't look back, even though there's a voice screaming in my head.

Please stay. Please don't go.

* * *

There's a knock on my door an hour later. Immediately hope springs up in me that it's Didi, that she hasn't listened to me, that she's stayed. But why should she?

I know even before I heft myself off the bed and fumble my way to the door that it's not her. It's Sanchez. And he's with Dodds. Dodds isn't competing in the race, but José figured it would do him good to get out of the center for a couple of days.

I hear Dodds wheel himself into my room. "Hey," he says.

"Hey," I answer. I'm not in the mood for this. Why are they here?

"How you doing?" Sanchez asks. "I saw Didi leaving."

I turn away so they can't see my face. Shit.

"You two didn't make up, then?" Sanchez asks.

"Is this about the sweepstake?" I ask. "Because I'm not in the mood."

"Nah," he says, sounding offended.

"Did you break up with her?" Dodds asks.

"We weren't exactly a couple," I tell him.

"You know, Lieutenant, you're one lucky bastard," Dodds suddenly explodes. "Girl like that wants you, what right have you got to turn it down?"

"Excuse me?" I say.

"The rest of us should be so lucky," Dodds goes on angrily, his hands tapping the wheels of his chair manically. "It's all fucking meaningless. All those goddamn posters in the center—all of them are bullshit—but there's just this one makes sense to me. It says that love will see us through."

Sanchez smirks.

"Yeah, I know, sounds like a Celine Dion song, but you know

what? It's true. Connection. That's what it's about. I ain't got nobody. Nobody gives a damn about me."

"Dodds, that's not true," Sanchez argues.

"It is true," Dodds says without a trace of self-pity. "And that's okay. I'm used to that. Figure I'm not meant to have anyone, not in this lifetime, anyway. But you, you been given this thing, this chance, with someone like Didi, for Chrissake, and you're giving it up. And why? Because you're 'scared of the future.'" His voice has taken on a mocking tone.

I stare down at the ground, his words hitting raw flesh and nerve like shrapnel.

"At least you got a future, unlike some of us," he tells me.

"Dodds, you're talking weird," Sanchez says, trying to make light of it.

"I'm just saying," he growls in answer.

I hear the whir of his wheelchair, the door being yanked open. "Fuck you," he says as a parting shot. "You know, fuck you. You don't know how good you got it." And then he slams the door.

There's a moment or two of silence. Then Sanchez opens his mouth.

"Well, that sure told you."

Didi

told him I loved him. I'm a total idiot. I lie facedown on the bed and try not to imagine what Walker is doing on the other side of the wall. My immediate plan was to leave and drive back to LA, but it was getting late and I was crying too hard, and then Sanchez found me in my car and made me come back inside. He gave me his and Valentina's room and they upgraded to a suite.

So here I am. For the night, at least.

A dozen times I've got up off the bed and thought about going and knocking on Walker's door, but when I finally made it out of my room, I heard him and Sanchez and Dodds all talking and didn't want to interrupt.

My eyes land on the clock. It's 11.27 p.m. Is he sleeping? Or is he lying awake like me? I roll onto my side and bury my head under a pillow, but it does nothing to muffle the yell that suddenly comes from Walker's room.

I throw the pillow aside and sit up. It comes again. A yell, as if he's fighting off an attacker. My pulse is firing, my heart hammering. I get off the bed. A broken sob makes its way through the wall, and that's enough to get my legs moving. I rush out into the hallway, forgetting that I'm only wearing an old T-shirt.

I try Walker's door. It's locked. Shit. I try knocking, but he doesn't hear me. I glance up and down the darkened hallway. I could run to the lobby and ask for a key, but it turns out I don't have to because José pops his head out of a room farther down the hallway.

He sees me and comes jogging toward me. "Walker?" he asks.

"I think he's having a nightmare."

José has a spare key and he unlocks the door. Then he stands back.

"I think maybe you should handle this one," he says.

I start to protest, but then another cry twists my attention back into the room. I step inside and José pulls the door shut behind me.

The TV is on mute, the light throwing blue shadows over the bed. Walker is naked but for a pair of boxers. The sheets are tangled around his legs in knots and he's thrashing on the bed, his face contorted as if he's being tortured. Tears stream down his cheeks.

I sit down beside him and put my hand on his shoulder. He tenses and then jerks wildly, throwing my arm off. He growls something unintelligible, but undeterred, I wrap my arms around him and lie down behind him, holding him, stroking his hair back from his face.

"It's okay," I whisper in his ear. "It's okay. I'm here. I've got you."

He lets out a wracking sob and then his hand closes around my wrist, grips it tight. A man sinking in quicksand grabbing for a branch. It hurts, but I ignore it.

"Shhh," I whisper. "It's okay. You're okay."

He mumbles something.

I lean closer to make out the words. "What?"

"Please don't go. Please stay."

I close my eyes, my arms tightening around him. "I'm not going anywhere," I reassure him. *Ever.* The word rises unbidden in my mind.

His hold on my arm doesn't loosen, but the rest of his body slowly starts to relax. I kiss his shoulder, making out for the first time the words that are inked there. *A posse ad esse.*

My Latin is rusty, but I think it means "from possibility to actuality" or "reality," or something like that. I muse on the words. There's so much possibility here, between us, *in* us. What's it going to take to turn that into something real?

After ten minutes Walker's breathing has settled to something approaching normal, and his grip on my arm has eased, though he hasn't let go.

I prop myself up on my free arm. "Talk to me," I whisper through the darkness.

He doesn't respond, but I know he's awake because I can see his eyes glimmering, reflecting the light from the television.

"Walker," I say, stroking his arm. "Tell me about the dream."

Again there's no response, and I'm about to give up and lie back down when finally he starts talking, his voice low, raw-edged. I have to struggle to make out the words.

"I left them."

"What?" I say.

Walker's shoulders start to shake. "I left Bailey," he chokes out. "And Lutter. They were my men. I left them behind."

Understanding blazes through me. I squeeze Walker tighter, holding on to him as hard as he's holding on to me. He's started crying, quietly, burying his head in the pillow.

"It wasn't your fault," I tell him. "There was nothing you could do."

He shakes his head angrily, then turns his face so I hear the next words clearly.

"You don't get it. They were still alive. I left them to die," he says. "There's no getting away from that."

Walker

Jonas glancing over his shoulder, looking at me for reassurance. Me yelling at him to stay frosty.

My breathing's shallow, my attention focused on the surrounding countryside. There's silence all around, grave-like silence, rent only by the cry of a bird of prey. Something's not right. I can sense it. Something about the car and the way it's sitting on the side of the road. Sunlight glints off the windshield and for a moment I'm blinded, both by the light and by the realization of what it means.

I open my mouth to yell out, but Harrison has reached the car and my command is obliterated by the roar of an AK-47. Bullets start to pock the car. The windshield shatters. We're under attack. My men hit the ground, dive for cover—Sanders behind a rock, Sanchez and Lutter behind the car.

I start firing back, lying flat on the ground, bullets whipping past my shoulder, smacking into the dirt all around me. It's an ambush. I call in our position. Yell for backup.

Beside me Harrison goes down, pitching face-first into the dirt. Bailey—loudmouthed, nineteen years old—is lying in the center of the road, clutching his leg, screaming a high-pitched scream that cuts out in the next second as a bullet slices through his windpipe.

I ignore the dancing bullets and sprint toward him, lace my arm beneath his shoulders and drag him back, off the road, down into a ditch. His eyes roll in his head, big with fear, bright with pain. He makes a choking, gurgling sound and blood foams over his lips. My hands are hot with it, slick with it. I fumble for the tourniquet on my belt.

Taylor, the unit medic, is at my side. He jabs a morphine shot into Bailey's thigh and snatches the tourniquet from my hand. I roll onto my stomach, poke my head above the ditch, and do a head count.

Sanchez and Lutter are still sheltering behind the car, taking turns to spot and return fire. Sanders, barely concealed behind a boulder, makes a mad dash for it, out into the open, before throwing himself down in the dirt beside Sanchez. He's opting to ride out the ambush with them, behind the solid wall of metal.

The car. They're trying to get us all to shelter behind the car.

I stand up, my knee jolts out, a hot eruption of pain behind my kneecap. "Sanchez!" I holler. "Get back!"

Sanchez looks in my direction.

"The car!" I yell.

I see the flare of understanding cross his face, and then it's gone, obliterated by a wall of white light that opens up the sky, rips apart the earth beneath my feet, and sends me hurtling headfirst into an abyss . . .

. . . And then I hit the ground like a meteor crash-landing to earth. My ears ring. My heart's a clanging bell. I can't stand up straight. I veer sideways like a drunk, stagger, fall, stand, stagger again, blinking through a haze of dust, my ears singing, ringing. I'm in the center of a sandstorm. Where am I? And then the swirling clouds part almost biblically, and on the ground in front of me I spy a boot. I stare at it for a moment, confused. What's a boot doing in the middle of the road? And what's that inside it? That white stick surrounded by stringy red meat. It looks like an uncooked leg of lamb.

My eyes blot and blur as the boot pulls in and out of focus. It's a foot. Inside the boot. I career in a spastic circle. My gun. It's in my hands. I don't remember taking aim, but I have. But I can't see to shoot and I weave wildly, jerking the rifle this way and that. I still can't hear anything beyond the alarm going off in my head. Are we under attack still? Where is everyone? Where are the others? Automatically I fumble for my radio and scream for a CASEVAC. We need helicopter support. Medics. I hear a crackle, a response. Alpha Whisky Tango. What the fuck does it mean?

"Sanchez?" I yell, but my voice sounds like it's coming from an underwater cave and my throat feels as if it's been stripped with paint thinner.

My eyes fall on Taylor, the medic, down in the ditch not three feet from where I'm standing. I collapse beside him in relief, calling his name, and that's when I see his helmet's been blown off and a piece of metal from the car has embedded itself into his skull like a Halloween knife. He's dead. His eyes stare at me sightless, already filmy.

I can't compute. I stare back at him and the world starts spinning around me, the edges of it slamming into my sides, forcing the air out of my lungs, and blackness begins to roll around the edges until I hear a whimper and realize that Taylor's fallen on top of Bailey. I roll Taylor aside, trying to ignore the thud as his body rolls down the sloping hillside and smacks into a rock, and I discover Bailey, his face ashen, the tourniquet around his throat a red rag, ghoulish against the white of his dust-coated skin. His hands paw pathetically at it as though it's a hangman's noose he wants to loosen.

I take it all in with a madman's sense of horror and a dead man's numbness. This isn't happening.

Bailey's staring up at the sky, trying to breathe, but the air is rattling like loose change through the hole in his trachea. I bend down beside him, grab for his hand before he manages to pull off the tourniquet, but his palm slips from mine, slimy with blood and gritty with dirt.

"It's okay, help's on its way," I tell him, but he doesn't seem to hear.

I look up, cast around desperately. Where are the others? I called it in. Where's the help?

"Sanchez?" I yell. "Lutter?" Smoke scours my eyes. All I can make out is the iridescent glow of the flames shooting out of the car. And that's when I remember where Sanchez and Lutter and Sanders were sheltering before we got lit up.

I move toward the fire, throwing up an arm to protect my face from the heat. I'm aware of a jack hammer slamming into my knee and a white-hot poker jabbing at my shoulder, but the searing heat of the fire cancels it all out.

Terror cancels it all out.

"Harrison!" I shout, and then I see, through the choking black smoke, lying amid the wreckage of the car, a body, or at least what looks like a body.

I drop to my knees and cover my mouth to stop the smoke from filling it and start crawling toward it. The car is burning fiercely. If the engine's full of gas then it's going to explode any second, but I keep going. My hand closes around a leg, maybe, or a torso perhaps—something wet, something mulchy. I pull my hand away. My eyes are streaming—I can't see. The contents of my stomach are halfway up my throat, filling my mouth. I fumble again on the ground.

My fingers make out a hand, trace up an arm. They sink into mud. Not mud. Warm. A face. Half a face. Sanders. Not Sanders. I reel backward onto my haunches. Flames lick my back. Acid creeps up my throat.

A murmur. A voice. Alive. Someone's alive. I crawl to a mound a few feet away. It's Sanchez. His helmet is half off. His face is black with grime, smeared with blood. I grab him by the shirt. *Alive. Be alive.* His eyes roll back in his head then forward.

"My leg," he says through gritted teeth. "I can't feel my leg."

I glance down. There is no leg. There's just shredded uniform and a fragment of bone poking out of the fabric and lakes of blood. So much blood. I thought I was kneeling in oil that had leaked from the car.

Sanchez hacks, his lungs filled with smoke, and the effort makes his eyes roll further back in his head. I force my arm under his shoulder and drag him a few feet away from the car, then I tear his tourniquet off his belt and wrap it around his thigh. When I'm done I bend once more to heave him over my shoulders. We need to get away before the car goes up. Sanders. Forget Sanders.

Sanchez, face black with grime and sweat, grabs my shirt in

his fist. "Lutter," he hisses before he falls back with a grunt to the ground.

Shit. I turn around and scour the area around the car, and then I spot a body a few feet away, lying half in and half out of the ditch. I glance at Sanchez, then drag him a few more feet from the car, praying it's far enough if it blows, and the whole time I'm thinking of Bailey and how I need to get back to him and move him and how the fuck am I going to move him *and* Sanchez? And what about Lutter? Don't think of the others. Don't think of the dead. And where's the helicopter? Where's the Cobra? Where the fuck is the CASEVAC team?

My leg won't work properly, keeps twisting the wrong way, but I ignore it and limp over to the ditch. Lutter is lying there on his side, half his body buried beneath a hunk of twisted metal. I throw myself down beside him. He's alive, breathing, but there's blood trickling down his temple.

Instinct has kicked in, has taken over. The rest of my brain is in chaos, cannot put it all together, but there's a quiet, isolated part of me—the part that was trained especially for this one moment—that clicks on like a pilot light. Methodically, pushing everything else to the side, I start checking Lutter for injuries. I need to free him, see what the damage is, but when I heave my weight onto the still smoldering engine block that's pinning him to the ground, it won't budge. Lutter lets out a groan.

"Get Sanchez," he hisses at me, his mouth tight with pain.

I glance over at Sanchez, ten feet away. And then past him to where I left Bailey, lying in the ditch. And then I remember Jonas. Jonas? Shit. Where is he?

A bullet slams into the dirt by my foot. I duck. They're still out there. I swing my rifle into my hands and take aim, but through the wafting black smoke there's nothing to aim at. No clear shot.

That's my cover, I realize. The smoke. I shoulder my rifle and glance between Lutter, Sanchez, and Bailey. Time stands still. Choose. Choose. Choose. I can only carry one. The decision is made by the cold, rational part of my brain that's taken over.

Take Sanchez. Bailey's as good as dead.

Another bullet ricochets off a rock an inch from my foot.

Lutter's alive and might survive until help can get here. I can't free him on my own. Sanchez is bleeding out. But there's a chance he might live. A small chance, yes, but if I leave him he'll die for sure.

Decision made, just like that, sentencing Bailey to death like I'm playing a round of poker for bottle caps. I crouch low and dart back over to Sanchez.

"My leg?" he mumbles when I reach him. "What's happened to my leg?"

I ignore him, and I ignore too the other part of my brain that has started to stir, that has begun to question the decision I've just made. There's no time.

I throw Sanchez's arm over my shoulder, heft him across my back and stand, wobbling dangerously as my knee buckles and my shoulder explodes. Pain lights me up from the inside.

I make it ten meters, and then, as I stumble under the weight of Sanchez, the car explodes at our backs, searing the shirt off my back, and the roar fills my ears, hollows out my head, obliterating everything and sending me hurtling into the ditch.

I lie there, buried beneath Sanchez.

And then, air scorching in my lungs, I force myself to my

knees, to standing, and I start to move, still carrying Sanchez across my back. And the smoke is so dense I'm walking blind.

The smoke doesn't clear. I can't see where I'm going. All I can see are Lutter, Bailey, Jonas, Taylor, Sanders.

The boot.

Didi

He stops talking, and silence as deep as an ocean fills the room. I don't know what to say. I don't know how to rescue him from this. He lies still on his side, facing away from me, and I stare down at him, dazed by what he's told me, horrified.

That he's been living with this, not telling anyone, makes my heart feel too big for my chest. How can he blame himself for not saving them?

"Walker," I say, kissing his bare shoulder. "Look at me."

He makes a snorting sound.

"Just roll over," I tell him. "Face me."

I pull him around so he's lying on his back. He stares upward, toward the ceiling.

"Walker," I say, stroking his cheek. God I've missed touching him, being close to him. "If you had been in Lutter's place, or Bailey's, and they were in yours, what would you have told them? Would you have wanted them to save you, or would you have told them to save Sanchez?"

His brow creases.

"You made a decision, a decision no one should ever have to make. And you made the right one."

"How can you say that?" he hisses.

"Because you saved Sanchez. You couldn't have saved Bailey. No one could. And Lutter? He told you to save Sanchez. And he was trapped. You couldn't have freed him on your own. You know this. Deep down. You did all you could do."

Walker's jaw tightens. He squeezes his eyes shut.

I stroke his brow. "Walker. You have to stop blaming yourself. They didn't die because of you."

"But I—"

"No," I interrupt, pressing my finger to his lips. "You saved a life, Walker. Miraculously. You salvaged one piece of good from what could have been a complete tragedy."

"Lutter had a family. A wife and kids."

"And so does Sanchez."

"And Bailey?" he asks. "He'll never have those things."

"Because someone on a road in Afghanistan shot him."

Walker's hands make fists in the sheets. I unclench one of them and force my fingers between his. "Walker, the best thing you can do is honor them, live your life for them. If it was the other way around, you would never want them to blame themselves for your death, would you?"

"You sound like a therapist," Walker mutters.

"No," I say, "I sound like someone who loves you."

He winces.

"And wants you to forgive yourself, even though you've got nothing to forgive yourself for. You've done nothing wrong."

He shakes his head. My heart bounds around my chest.

"Why do you say that?"

"Because it's true. And because if you don't forgive yourself, then you're never going to be able to move on."

"No. I mean why do you say that you love me?" He turns his head in my direction, still frowning.

"Because I do," I stammer. "I love you, Noel Walker— everything about you, even when you scowl at me like you're doing right now. I love you even though you're grumpy and try to shut me out all the time. I love you even though you do your damnedest to push me away. I love all the parts of you—the broken parts that you try to hide most of all."

"Why?" he whispers, his throat hoarse.

I stroke my fingertips down his arm. "Because you act tough but you're not. On the inside you're as soft as a marshmallow," I tell him, quoting José. "And you act like a cynic, but you're not. You're a closet romantic. Don't deny it."

His nostrils flare. I lay my hand against his cheek.

"And you might be blind, but you see me."

He turns his head sharply toward me. I run my fingertips over his eyelids. "You see me better than anyone. I've never felt so comfortable, so at home, with anyone in my life before."

He still hasn't said anything, and my brain starts to tell me that maybe I should shut up, that this probably isn't the right time for a declaration of love, but I can't make myself stop talking.

"And you say we don't have a future, Walker, but that's a lie. We do have a future. The future's what you make it."

I cannot believe I just ended that declaration of love with a quote from a platitude poster. I wince.

"Did you just say that I see you?" Walker asks, cocking an eyebrow at me.

"Um, yeah," I mumble.

"Are you quoting lines at me from *Avatar*?"

"Um, maybe."

He bursts out laughing, and the sound is so startling, so wonderful, that I burst out laughing too. And then his hands are in my hair and he's pulling me down toward him and his lips find mine and it feels like everything might be stitching back together.

"I'm sorry," Walker says, pulling away.

"Why? What for?" I ask, the stitches coming undone. Is he about to shut down again?

"For pushing you away, for not opening up sooner."

"It's okay," I murmur. "Just don't do it again."

"I won't." He drops a kiss on my lips. "And Didi?" he says.

My eyes flash open.

"I do see you."

Heat washes up and down my body in waves. His hands stoke the heat further as he strokes up my bare legs. I pull him closer, my hands running over his chest. We've not yet been fully skin to skin, and Walker reads my mind. He pulls me to sitting and then lifts off my T-shirt, tossing it to the floor before wrapping me in his arms and pulling me back down onto the bed. We lie facing each other, my skin burning and prickling with goosebumps like I've got a fever as Walker starts to trace every single inch of me, lightly, using just his fingertips, like a blind man reading Braille.

I do the same to him, drinking him in, every line, every contour, from the flat of his hip bone to the scored ridges of stomach muscles to the tight knots in his shoulders. My fingers outline the raised scar there and then I kiss it, wishing I could kiss it away, erase it, just like I wish I could erase all the scars on the inside too. He draws in a breath, holds it, and then when he finally lets it go he rolls me over onto my back and pins me there, looking down at me. His eyes are clouded, dark, and he looks like he's being held behind a fence, awaiting a starting whistle.

I grip his hips and pull him down so all his weight is on me.

"Didi—" he starts to say and tries to lift off me.

I cling to him, refusing to let him go. "I want you," I tell him.

"I want you too," he says, "but . . ."

I remember his stupid rule about not wanting to make love until he got his sight back. "You just told me you see me," I whisper.

He hovers above me, carrying his weight on his arms, and I watch the internal battle wage behind his eyes. I help it along by arching my hips and pressing myself against him.

It works. He groans and sweeps me into his arms, and in one swift movement rolls me so I'm lying on my side, one thigh flung over his hip.

He kisses me, hungrily, his tongue searching my mouth, until the room is spinning and I can feel flames licking their way up my legs. When his hand brushes my stomach, I jump because I'm so on edge. His fingers slide into my underwear and I arch again, my hips rising off the bed on reflex. With his free hand he keeps me pinned in place, and my breathing comes so hard and so fast my lips start to tingle.

He bites gently on my bottom one and pushes into me with his fingers, his thumb circling on the outside. I let out a gasp. How does he know exactly how to touch me? I reach for him and feel the shudder pass through his body. It's good to know he isn't as in control as he pretends. I press harder and he lets out a groan, and then, in the next moment it becomes frantic, desperate. Our hands get tangled as we pull each other's underwear off and then his fingers are exploring again, and his tongue, and he has me. He owns me. I've never wanted anyone or anything as much as I do Walker, right now, in this moment.

Within seconds I'm on the edge, but he stops, expertly reading my body, pulling me back gently. Frustrated, I wriggle from his grip and push him backward onto the bed so he's lying flat. When he tries to protest, I put my finger to his lips. He gives up and relaxes into the bed, and then I take my turn exploring him, tasting him. His fingers bite into my thighs as I inch lower down his body, his stomach muscles tensing hard.

I kiss all the way down his body, taunting him the way he taunted me, until finally, with a growl, he throws me off him, rolls me over and pins me back down on the bed, nudging my legs open with his knee. I'm so aching for him that when he pauses, his chest against mine, his lips hovering just above mine, I hear myself whimper.

"What?" I ask. *Please don't stop.*

"Do you have . . . ?" he asks.

Oh God. I forgot about that. My body sags into the bed, frustration almost making me cry. Fallen at the last fence. I turn my head and see something on the nightstand and grin.

"I think Sanchez thought ahead, though," I tell him.

"What?"

I reach for a condom. Walker takes it from me and rips open the packet. When he's done, he hovers over me, looking down. His fingers caress my face, my lips. And then he's inside me, pushing into me gently, slowly, so slowly.

He kisses my neck, my face, my lips as he pulls out and then pushes into me again, still gently, but faster. I wrap my legs around his waist to pull him in further, my fingernails digging into his back.

Spurred on, Walker drives into me harder, though his touch stays gentle, his hands caressing me.

I can't speak, can't keep track of my thoughts, except for one—that this is how it's meant to be. This is what all those movies and books are hinting at. But even they don't come close. It was just sex before, but this is more, this is way more than just sex.

I can feel myself coming apart, and Walker can feel it too because he shifts his weight so he's pressing into me in a way that makes me cry out, stars bursting on the back of my eyelids. His fingers slide through mine, squeeze.

When I come, Walker does too, his body shuddering against mine. He collapses down on top of me and I hold him, both of us shaking, breathing so hard we can't catch our breath.

We're filmed in sweat, and the sheets are tangled at our feet. I don't want him to pull out. I just want to lie like this, holding him, being held by him.

Walker rolls off me and pulls me against his chest, holding me like he's never going to let me go. I close my eyes. I feel like I'm floating. I can't stop smiling, and then it becomes a laugh that ripples through me.

"What are you laughing about?" he asks.

"I made it into the eleven percent," I say, thinking of the statistic in my mom's book.

Walker

"Dude, come on, you can tell me. I promise I won't say a word."

I try to keep my face stony, but I can feel the cracks starting to appear.

"I saw Didi come out of your room this morning," Sanchez says, nudging me in the ribs.

If I could get away from him I would, but we're tied together. The race is about to start—we're lined up on the beach in a crowd of jostling people. Sanchez tells me there are about two hundred and fifty of us.

"So, you going to tell me all you did was talk and watch TV?"

"No," I say. "I'm not going to tell you anything."

"You're walking funny," he says.

I laugh.

"Ahhh! You did get some. I knew it," he shouts, pulling me into a headlock. "That's my man. Finally. Jesus, took you two long enough."

I ignore him and try to listen out for the starter whistle. When we hear it, Sanchez and I are supposed to dive in off the jetty we're on, and then we have to swim twice around a buoy, about a mile and a half in open ocean, before we make our way to the beach. Once there, we strip out of our wet suits, climb onto our tandem bike and pedal forty clicks to the second point, where we ditch the bike and have to run twelve clicks more. I'm pumped up, primed, blood roaring in my ears, but that's nothing to do with the race—it's all to do with Didi.

Even thinking about her now makes me grin. She's waiting on the beach for us with Valentina, and knowing she's there, that she's not going anywhere and will be waiting at the very end to see me home, is all the incentive I need to win this thing. I hate to admit it, but Doc Monroe was right. Talking it through, reliving it with Didi, did help. I saw it through her eyes, saw that what I thought was a choice, wasn't. I did the only thing I could do. For the first time in months I woke up without feeling the boulder-weight of guilt resting on my shoulders. I felt light. Free.

"You know the Brazilian soccer coach won't let the team have sex for a week before the race," Sanchez says, "so I hope I haven't destroyed our chances of winning today by leaving those condoms by the bed."

"You haven't," I answer, crouching low, ready to make the dive. The waves slap the side of the wooden pontoon. I've had Sanchez describe everything as best he can: the height of the waves, the distance and direction of the buoy, the strength of the tide, and we've practiced enough in the pool that we're fluid when we swim. Sanchez says if we don't do well in the triathlon, he's going to enter us in a synchronized swimming contest. So far we've only practiced in a pool with no current and no waves and without fifty other guys—the size of our heat—pushing and shoving around us, chopping up the water. Then there's the cold. My blood might still be pumping furiously around my body, but the second I hit that water I know I'm going to feel it like a machine-gun round to the chest.

"Ready?" Sanchez asks, and I feel him crouch into a dive pose beside me.

I nod.

The whistle blows.

We dive.

Hitting the surface is like hitting a steel wall at full speed. The cold slams into me, bites savagely through the rubber of the wet suit, and when I break the surface I gasp for air, my lungs shrinking. And then I feel the tug on the rope attaching me to Sanchez and I kick hard and start to move my arms. Within seconds I'm powering through the waves, building a steady rhythm, letting Sanchez take the lead, trying to block out the cold and just keep moving. Someone kicks me, an arm connects with my head, but I dig harder, snatch breaths from between icy waves, until we're finally clear of the crowd and I can tell we're getting ahead.

But then, without warning, after about half a mile, the rope between Sanchez and me slackens. I veer to the left, thinking I'm about to plough into him, but before I can take a second stroke I'm dragged under. I kick, smack my heel into something hard, break the surface, grab a mouthful of air, but then I'm sucked under again. Head bursting, water rocketing up my nose, I fight my way back to the surface, but something keeps pulling me down.

My brain scrambles to make sense. What's happening? Sanchez. Sanchez is pulling me down. I kick hard, harder, burst through the surface waves one more time, snatch down a lungful of air and then dive, grabbing for the rope, hauling it through my hands until my fingers snag on the belt attached to Sanchez's waist. He's facedown, sinking fast, pulling me down with him like a lead weight.

I try to grab him, but my hands are numb and he slips from my grasp. I lunge for him again, grab the collar of his wet suit and then kick up, kick out, let out all the air from my lungs to propel me upward toward the light.

I burst through the waves, coughing, spluttering, gasping, drawing in oxygen, kicking as hard as I can to try to stay afloat as my arms hold on to Sanchez, whose head is lolling back against my shoulder. His eyes are open. Waves slam into us, over us, into Sanchez's open mouth.

My eyes are open. I register that I can see—that the world is a spinning kaleidoscope of color—as I simultaneously register that Sanchez isn't breathing. I roll instinctively onto my back, slide my arm beneath his arms, and start swimming toward the shore, tugging him with me.

Another swimmer—I'm not sure who—grabs hold of Sanchez's other side and helps me. Panic propels me faster. The shore's still one hundred and fifty feet away and I can see it, see the people crowded there, can hear the roar of people yelling over the sound of the waves thrashing. It feels as if we'll never make it, that it isn't getting any nearer, but then my heel smacks a rock.

We hit the shore and I stagger to my knees. The other person, not a guy but a girl in a wet suit, helps me drag Sanchez into the shallows and I collapse down beside him. I can hear people yelling in my ear, can sense people crowding in, but I shut them out. I'm already covering Sanchez's mouth with my own, breathing into him, for him, pumping his chest. Breathe, pump for five, breathe, pump for five, breathe.

And there's more screaming, loud, piercing my eardrums. I block that out too. Focus. Breathe. Pump. Breathe.

Nothing. Sanchez is turning a ghostly shade of blue. Water trickles out the side of his mouth in between my breaths.

"Come on," I yell, putting all my weight onto his chest. "Breathe!" I yell at him.

"*Jesús!*"

It's Valentina. She's clawing at him. And there's someone trying to drag her back. How long has it been? How long were we under? How long have I been doing this? I'm vaguely aware that I'm beginning to tire, that my muscles are starting to shake, from the cold, from the swim, but I can't give up now.

The color has drained entirely from Sanchez's face. There's no pulse. No heartbeat.

Someone pulls me by the shoulder, tries to haul me back, but I shove them hard and keep forcing air into Sanchez's lungs, keep pounding on his chest, massaging his heart. He can't be dead. I won't let him fucking die. Not after all this.

"Walker." It's José's voice. He drags me back again, this time using all his strength, and I must be weaker than I thought, more spent, because I tumble backward onto my haunches.

"Let them take over," José tells me, wrapping his arm around my chest to stop me throwing myself forward again toward Sanchez.

I finally notice the men in green overalls who've bent down beside Sanchez. Paramedics. They've already taken over from where I left off—they're pumping his chest, fixing an oxygen mask over his face.

I stare in horror as Valentina sobs over him, rocking back and forth. The crowd has fallen silent. The only sounds are one paramedic counting breaths and barking orders to the other, and the waves slapping the shore.

And then another couple of paramedics appear with a stretcher, and without breaking count, without letting up on the heart massage, they heft Sanchez onto the stretcher and start to carry him at a jog up the beach toward the flashing lights of an ambulance. Everyone follows, José with his arm around a wailing Valentina.

"Walker."

I glance up. There's a girl in front of me. Dark-haired, full-mouthed. I know her. I'd know her anywhere.

Didi collapses in front of me, her jeans soaking through in the waves.

"Walker," she says again, her hand against my cheek.

I blink, fall forward, and she catches me.

Didi

Walker sits slumped on the plastic hospital seat, leaning forward, elbows on his knees. He's wearing his wet suit still, but it's peeled to his waist and someone's given him one of those foil blankets to keep him warm. It's wrapped loosely around his bare shoulders. I stop in front of him and rest my hand on his back. He looks up. Our eyes connect and my breath leaves my body like I've been punched in the stomach. He can see me. I can't get used to the fact.

I sink to my knees in front of him. There are around thirty people in the waiting room and Valentina's quiet crying has silenced us all. I take Walker's hands—they're still freezing—and squeeze them tight, trying to warm them. His gaze has dropped to the ground. I know what he's thinking. He's thinking that he failed to save Sanchez, that it's his fault. Again. I can see it in his eyes—shuttered and dark—in the lock of his jaw.

And I can't let him go there. I won't. Not again.

I take his face in my hands and force him to look up at me. He scans my face as though looking for something there, as though he's still trying to reconcile my voice and my touch—which are so familiar—to the stranger he's now seeing in front of him. Am I what he expected? What he pictured? What does it matter right now.

"Stay with me," I whisper to him.

He bites his bottom lip hard, a shadow darkening his face. I want to brush it away but I know there's no way of doing so. If Sanchez dies, I don't know how there will be any saving Walker.

I put my arms around his neck and pull him close. His body tenses. He doesn't respond, but all of a sudden he grabs for me, his arms locking around my waist, his head burrowing into my neck, and he clings to me like I'm the life raft keeping him afloat.

We stay like that for minutes on end, maybe half an hour, and with every passing second I know that the chances of Sanchez making it are fading. We should have heard something by now. And I start to wonder what will happen when they bring the news, how I'll keep Walker afloat. And what about Valentina?

A commotion by the door makes me raise my head. I pry myself out of Walker's tight embrace and glance over.

A doctor in scrubs is standing there. "Mrs. Sanchez?" he asks, looking around the crowded waiting area.

Valentina makes a sound, a sobbing hiccup, and steps forward, her face tear-stained and swollen. José is with her and she clutches his arm. And there's Dodds too, in his wheelchair, sitting over by the door. Everyone is staring at the doctor, fearful and desperate, poised on the knife-edge.

The doctor steps toward her and puts his hand on Valentina's arm. Her face crumples.

"He's alive."

There's a collective inhalation of air. Valentina's face blanks. "What?" she chokes.

"He's alive," the doctor repeats with a smile.

She shakes her head. Tears go flying. "I don't understand."

"You can see him if you'd like."

She clutches onto the doctor's arm and then covers her face with her hands and starts sobbing, as all around her people begin to pull out phones and laugh and slap each other on the back.

"Did you hear that?" I say to Walker.

He's staring after the doctor, his mouth open. He turns back to me slowly and nods.

"You saved him," I say.

Walker's shoulders heave. His eyes are filled with tears.

"And you can see," I say, wiping at my own eyes because I'm now crying too.

Walker smiles. "I can see you," he says.

I laugh through a film of tears and he pulls me toward him and kisses me.

Walker

Didi drives us back to the base. I sit beside her, my hand on her leg, drinking in the view through the open window: ocean, sky, trees. Were colors always this bright? Did I ever notice before the way light splashes diamonds on water or the way the sky is a pixellated mass of a million different blues? I feel drunk taking it all in. This must be what religious people feel when they talk about a spiritual awakening, this feeling of absolute wonder as I study the world as if it's the very first time I'm seeing it, which in a way it is. How, why, did I take it for granted before?

But even with everything there is to absorb outside the car, it isn't long before my gaze lands back on Didi.

I can't stop staring at her, can't believe that this girl—who's more stunning than I could ever have imagined—wants to be with me, chose me, a fucked-up, moody, disabled soldier who did his utmost to push her out of his life. What was I thinking? A dark mass of curls tumbles to her shoulders, and I reach over and run my hand through them, tucking a strand behind her ear so I can see her face better.

Those lips, the strong dark line of her eyebrows, the narrow point of her chin. I thought I had a pretty good idea of what she looked like from having traced her face and body with my hands so thoroughly, but what I didn't, couldn't possibly have known was how luminous she is, how flawless.

She looks across at me now, a tiny frown forming between her eyes—which are chlorine blue—and chews on her bottom lip. She's worried that I'm going to change my mind now I've seen her, that I'm disappointed.

I grin. Can't help myself.

"What?" she says, her eyes returning to the road.

"Nothing," I say.

"Am I what you imagined?" she asks, tentative, nervous.

"Didi, my imagination needs a reboot."

She laughs, the sound lighting me up inside like it always has done, but this time even more, because now there's no lead weight on my chest crushing it out of existence. There's not a single chance of this light being snuffed out. Ever.

"I still can't believe Sanchez almost died," Didi says, a hitch in her voice.

My throat is still rasped dry from the salt water. A vivid memory of the cold, like needles being stabbed into my eyes and ears, the feeling of being dragged into the depths, down into the obliterating darkness, fills my senses and I have to suppress a shudder. Didi reaches over and puts her hand on my leg. It's jumping up and down. Her touch stills me.

"If you hadn't been tied together . . ." she says.

I nod. She doesn't need to finish that sentence. The doc said that the shock of the cold water and a pre-existing heart condition no one knew about sent Sanchez into cardiac arrhythmia and then into full-on cardiac arrest. He basically had a heart attack in the water. And if we'd been further out to sea, if we hadn't dragged him to shore and started CPR when we did, he'd be dead. I did save him. For a second time. And that has to be significant.

Didi

Dodds and José make it back to the center at the same time as us. We all cram into the elevator. Dodds is silent, but José is talking about Sanchez having more lives than a cat and telling Walker that he deserves a second silver star, something that makes a frown stalk across Walker's face.

When we step out of the elevator, José dashes off to do something and Dodds trundles his way to his room. He stops halfway down the hallway and looks back at us. "Hey, Walker—you got a second?"

Walker looks at Dodds and then at me. "Can it wait until the morning?" he asks.

Dodds nods. "Sure."

"See you tomorrow," I call.

He wheels off and I turn to Walker, twining my fingers through his. "So," I say. "I guess I should go home?"

As soon as I say it I realize that home isn't where my parents are any longer. It's right here. With Walker.

Walker leans against the doorjamb and stares at me. I can't get over the way he looks at me, or the smile that plays on his lips when he does. He hasn't taken his eyes off me since we got in the car, and even though he's barely touched me I feel like he's been stroking me all over with his hands. My body is vibrating.

He considers me for a moment, and I realize that he hasn't, that I've noticed, looked anywhere but at my face.

"Or," he murmurs, his voice low, his eyes glimmering, "you could stay."

I swallow, my heart rate starting to accelerate.

"Because now that I can finally see you, I'm not sure I'm ready to let you out of my sight for a while." He pauses. "Possibly not ever, in fact."

I bite back the smile.

The center is quiet. It's past ten at night. I could stay.

"I can live with that," I say, stepping closer so there's less than a breath of space between us.

Walker catches my hand and pulls me into his room, kicking the door shut with his heel. Now he can see, I'm meeting a whole new side to Walker—a more confident, self-assured side, a lighter side. Without taking his eyes off me, he pulls me near, his hands falling to my hips. He holds my gaze as he lifts my arms and then peels off my shirt.

I start to protest, think about asking him to turn off the light, but the look in his eyes, the pure, red-hot desire, silences me.

He strips me slowly naked, and I stand there, not saying a word as he steps back and finally lets his gaze run up and down the length of me. He takes a deep breath and shakes his head as though in wonder. I feel self-conscious, but then . . . not. When he looks at me I feel like I'm the most precious thing he's ever seen.

He lifts his head and looks me straight in the eyes, and then he reaches for me and I'm already moving toward him.

Walker

I'm inside her, staring into her eyes as I move, slowly, carefully, enjoying every sensation. Her eyes are dilated, wide, unfocused. Her other hand is clenched in mine, squeezing hard.

Finally, I realize that all those other times I thought I was making love were just sex. This is what they mean by making love. It's a revelation as startling as sight. Last night when we slept together, it was hungry, desperate, amazing, but this is something else altogether.

Because I've memorized every inch of her body with my fingers, I know exactly where to touch her, exactly how to touch her, to make her moan, to make her fingernails score tracks down my back.

I can sense now that she's close, and just the thought of that takes me to the brink as well. But I want to play it out, I want to make this last. I don't want this to be over, so I pull out, smiling to myself as she lets out a cry of frustration.

I kiss her neck, nudging her chin aside, and start kissing down her body, eyes open, watching the goosebumps spread across her skin. I taste her, sliding my fingers into the warmth of her, and she cries out again. I could keep on like this, but I'm not sure I can hold on. I want her too much. I want to be inside her again. I push her legs wider apart and listen to her breathing start to speed up. Her fingers knit into my hair, and when she opens her eyes and looks at me I push into her again.

I pull out and push in again, harder. She cries out again. I stop and wait for her to open her eyes and look into mine. I push into her one more time, and this time she comes, and I feel it surge through her in a wave that stretches out and floods over me and I come too, still staring into her eyes.

My arms shake. My whole body starts to shake. Unable to hold myself up any longer, I collapse down on top of her.

Didi

The door flies open just as Walker collapses down on top of me.

"What the hell?"

Oh my God. Walker is off me in a flash and I'm left scrabbling for the sheet.

"I can explain," Walker says.

I scramble to sit up, pulling the sheet around me. Walker's naked, standing in front of me, blocking me from view, but my dad sees me anyway.

"Didi?" he says, shaking his head in utter shock and dismay.

I can't speak. He looks at me, disgusted. And then I realize that there's something beyond disgust on his face, there's grief. As if he's witnessed a tragedy.

"Get up," he says wearily. "Get dressed."

I glance at Walker. He looks at me. There's apology and more on his face. Everything is crashing down around me—my job, my career. I'm in so much trouble. But then I become aware of people stampeding past in the corridor—orderlies—and I see José leaning against the wall outside, pale and shaking.

"What's going on?" I hear myself ask. "What's happening?"

"It's Dodds," my dad says, walking out the room.

My heart palpitating, Walker and I exit his room twenty seconds later, still pulling on our clothes. Gathered around us are center staff talking in low whispers. We barely get a sideways glance despite our half-naked, tousled appearance.

I grab José, who is still leaning against the wall.

"What's happened? Is Dodds okay?" I ask.

He shakes his head, unable to look me in the eye.

I turn to look toward Dodds's room. What's going on? I glance at Walker, but he's looking as bewildered as me, blinking at the people gathered around the door.

And then Walker moves off, toward the room. I follow him. José calls after us, but we don't listen. At the doorway Walker stops abruptly. I run into the back of him. He spins around, catches me, encloses me in his arms and tries to push me backward and out the way.

"Don't look," he says, but it's too late. I've already caught a glimpse of Dodds. But it's not Dodds. It can't be. It's some sick wax replica. It can't possibly be anything human. Walker hauls me backward, pulls me out of the way, my head buried in his shoulder. It was a half-body, a bloated, purple face, a black tongue protruding between blue lips.

The floor disappears beneath my feet. It's there one moment and gone the next. My knees buckle. Walker catches me.

Walker

It's nearly time. I need to get dressed. Shave. Pack. Moving, though, is like dragging myself through wet mud. I still can't wrap my head around the fact that Dodds is dead. I keep listening out for the whir of his wheelchair, expecting at any moment to hear it banging into my door. His face keeps flashing like a broken neon sign onto the back of my eyelids, bursting like a firework—and it's the last image of him, not him alive but dead, his face a grotesque fright mask. That's not how I want to remember him, but no matter what I do, I can't seem to replace that image with another.

I could have stopped him. If I hadn't been so self-absorbed, so focused on Didi, I would have seen something was up, I would have given him some time, we would have talked things through, maybe played some poker. He would have won, gone to bed smiling. He wouldn't have shut his door on us, tied his belt to the handle and hanged himself.

Someone knocks on my door. I turn around.

"Are you nearly ready, Lieutenant?" asks the overweight, hassled-looking woman that's replaced José.

I nod and go back to staring out the window at the calm expanse of lake. José is on administrative leave. He should have been on post when it happened, but he wasn't. I think he was giving Didi and me space, which only serves to double my feelings of guilt.

And then there's Didi. She's been told to stay away. I can't get any details beyond that as there's no José to ask and Doctor Monroe has been busy, wrapped up in the paperwork that erupts when a patient, *your* patient no less, commits suicide.

I've tried calling her, but her phone isn't switched on and I don't have an e-mail address for her. I tried Facebook, but she won't accept my friend request. Does she blame herself? Or me? Is that why she hasn't called me? I don't know what's going on. Nothing makes sense. The world has turned inside out.

Finally I force my legs to move toward the bathroom. The funeral is in an hour. I need to be there. Ashamed as I am, it's the very least I can do. I step into the shower, letting the hot water needle my eyes.

When the hot water fails to wash away my guilt, I switch it to cold—as cold as I can take it—but that just reminds me of sinking beneath the waves with Sanchez. I step out of the shower, shaking, adrenaline pumping in fits and starts. Sanchez is going to be okay, I tell myself. He's alive. I saved one person. I saved him.

I failed so many others.

Why am I still alive?

I wrap a towel around my waist and walk on unsteady legs into my room.

My bag is packed on the bed. I've been discharged. I'm leaving today. I still don't know where I'm going. My parents want me to come home, my brother is still urging me to come stay with him. Colonel Kingsley is encouraging me to re-enlist. The only place I want to go to, the only person I want to see, the only person I want to be with, is Didi, but I have no idea where she is or what she's thinking.

I scan the room, the place I've lived in for three months. On the nightstand sits Didi's iPod and beside it a photograph. It's an old one of Miranda. The one I used to keep in my wallet. She's standing in her garden in Hyannis the day we got engaged. It was found in Dodds's room. I'm not sure how he got hold of it or what it meant to him. A couple of orderlies said he told them that it was his girlfriend, and the thought that he had to invent a girlfriend and that the photograph was among his only possessions sends another stab of pain through me. His words come back to me—his anger at what we take for granted.

The elevator doors ping as I'm heading to the closet to get my uniform out, knowing it's the last time I'll ever wear it. I pause my hand on the hanger, my ears pricking, on alert for a familiar footstep, wanting, hoping, praying that it's her.

It isn't. It is a woman, though. I can hear her heels clicking mercilessly as she strides my way. Must be a doctor. The footsteps stop at my door. I turn around.

"Hi, Noel."

I have to blink a few times to make sure I'm not seeing things.

"Miranda?"

My ex-girlfriend smiles at me, her eyes tearing up.

"What are you doing here?" I ask, shaking my head in bewilderment.

"I heard you were being discharged."

There's a long moment while we just look at each other and I take in her cool, sleek beauty. For a half second my heart does a leap before slamming back into my chest with the heaviness of an axe smashing into rock. I shake my head at her and let out a bitter laugh. "Or you heard that I got my sight back?"

Her face contorts, a frown creasing her forehead. "Noel, that's not fair." She takes a step toward me. "Your mom called me," she says. "I'm sorry. I should have called you, but I wanted to surprise you."

She reaches out and takes my hand. I'm still in so much shock that I don't react, don't move to shake it off. My mind is reeling, trying to filter through all my conflicting reactions, trying to weigh up what the right response is: anger, rage, laughter, mockery, coldness, forgiveness?

"I should never have walked out like that," she continues. "I regretted it the minute I got on the plane. I'm sorry," she says, her voice breaking.

I cock an eyebrow. She's had ten weeks, longer, to act on that regret and put things right. She didn't even call me to see how I was doing. Not just as a lover but as a friend she failed me.

"I'm so sorry," she says, stroking my palm and looking up at me with hang-dog eyes. "I was going to call. It was just so hard . . . you know? I didn't know if I could give you what you needed. I was going to call you . . ."

I pull my hand from hers, laughing. "Sure you were."

She places her palm against my cheek and the action jars me because she's not Didi and her touch is alien to me—wrong. I don't want Miranda touching me. I jerk my head away and her hand falls instead to my chest.

She presses herself closer, her hips brushing mine. Her perfume's cloying. It makes my eyes water.

"Noel," she murmurs, "I missed you. I came to get you, to bring you home. I want us to try again. Now that you're not going off on deployment, it'll be so much easier. We can be together. We can get married, just like we planned."

She gives me a smile, her fingers twining in mine.

"Isn't that what you want?"

Didi

Married?"

Walker's head flies up. He sees me standing in the doorway and I watch his eyes widen like a cartoon character's and his mouth drop open.

It takes everything I've got to stay there in the doorway and not run away.

The girl—I know her, somehow; there's something familiar about her—turns too. She's blond, slim, so beautiful she looks airbrushed. A little frown of puzzlement mars her perfect face. "Hi," she says.

"Who are you?" I hear myself ask, my voice sounding husky and unfamiliar to my own ears.

"I'm Noel's fiancée," she says with a smile that makes my insides churn.

"Fiancée?" I repeat. My eyes flash to Walker.

He's wearing just a towel wrapped around his waist and the girl's hand is still resting on his chest. What were they just doing? I blink again, trying to clear my vision, but she's still there when I open my eyes, still with her hand resting on his chest as if she owns him. Oh my God, he's engaged. It takes a few seconds to sink in but then it all becomes clear. Startlingly clear. That's why he was pushing me away the whole time.

I'm such an idiot. He was using me. He had a girlfriend. I'm such a fool. My chest feels as if it's being carved open, a sob starts to build, and all I know is that I can't let it out. I clamp my lips together and bite my tongue.

"Didi."

Walker steps around the girl and moves toward me. I stumble backward into the hallway, away from him. I don't want him near me, touching me. I haven't seen him or spoken to him for three days, and for those three days all I wanted was to touch him, see him, hold him, and now, suddenly, I can't stand the thought of being anywhere near him.

Walker stops in his tracks, his face twisting up as if he's in pain. "Please, just listen," he pleads.

"To what?" I ask. "To you trying to explain to me why you lied? Was it just a joke to you? Another sweepstake bet? How much did you win?"

Is that why he didn't return my calls? I left messages with the person who'd taken over for José, asking for Walker to call me on the landline, but he didn't. Probably because he's been busy with his fiancée.

"What?" he asks, shaking his head. "You know—"

"I know nothing," I say, tears choking my throat closed, "except that I'm an idiot and I should have listened to my parents. They were right all along. I should never have gotten involved with you. What a mistake."

"Didi," Walker says and takes another step toward me, his arms outstretched.

"Who is she?" Walker's fiancée demands, glaring at Walker before turning to me with a sneer.

"I'm nobody," I tell her, still walking backward. I spin on my heel and head back to the elevators, tears blinding me. There are footsteps behind me and I swipe angrily at my face. Walker catches me by the arm and pulls me around to face him.

"Didi," he says, his tone desperate. "It's not what you think."

I snatch my arm from his grip. "Oh really?" I ask. I can't stop the tears from falling. "I lost my internship because of you, Walker. I'm probably going to be pulled up in front of the ethics committee. Everything I ever worked for I threw away for you. For nothing."

His hand falls to his side.

"You were so busy trying to get into my underwear that you didn't even spare a second thought for Dodds when he was trying to talk to you. I hope that's on your conscience too."

All the blood drains from Walker's face and I know immediately that I've overstepped the line. I didn't mean to say that. Walker staggers back a step and a dagger slices through my ribs. I want to take it back. Turn back the clock. I want to take it *all* back. It's not his fault about Dodds. It's mine. It's all of our faults. But it's too late to take anything back. Too late to make any difference.

That girl—his fiancée—has walked up behind him and has put her hands on his shoulders, is steering him backward toward his room. And he's letting her. But he stares at me the whole time like a drowning man slipping slowly beneath the waves.

Walker

I don't know how I make it through the funeral. It's all a blur. The chaplain speaks at length, but I don't hear the words. All I'm aware of is the grave yawning in front of me and the deeper yawning hole opening up inside me, threatening to swallow me whole, bury me deep.

Miranda is standing next to me. I think she thinks she's playing the part of the dutiful wife. I told her I didn't want her to come, but she refused to hear me and I was in such shock I couldn't argue with her. She swipes at tears and I almost turn and growl something at her. She didn't even damn well know Dodds, would never even have glanced his way if she'd passed him on the street, but I don't have the strength. I barely have the strength to stand, to keep breathing.

Everything takes on a dreamlike quality. Nothing feels real anymore. Dodds dying, lying right there in front of me in a coffin draped with a flag, Sanchez here for the funeral, still pale, holding the hand of a sobbing Valentina. He catches my eye across the top of the coffin and gives me a grim smile of greeting that I ignore, pretending not to have seen it. That part is easy at least.

I notice José is here too, hovering at the edge of the crowd, his eyes downcast, his shoulders heaving. My stomach twists at the sight. I know exactly what he's going through right now, the weight of guilt piling onto him like an avalanche.

I become aware of an itch at the back of my neck. Heat spreads out, scratches a path down my spine. I turn. Didi is standing a little way behind me. She's with a woman. Her mother, I'm guessing, from the similarities between them and the Medusa-look her mother gives me. Didi refuses to look at me but I see the tears tracking down her cheeks, the tremble in her bottom lip. What must she be thinking? Why am I standing here with Miranda? Why am I not doing anything to fix this? I turn back around to face the coffin, my vision blurring all of a sudden. Maybe I should try again after the funeral to speak to her.

Or maybe not.

Miranda dabs again at her eyes. I wrench my arm from her hold. She glares acid up at me. I'm ruining her performance.

I feel nothing. That's the problem. I'm tumbling headfirst back into that abyss, the one Didi hauled me out of, and there's a part of me—most of me, not just a part—that wants to hit the bottom. Finally. I failed five men. I had just managed to drag myself over the precipice with Didi's help, was starting to imagine a way forward and back into the light, but now I've failed someone else. And this time there's no forgiveness, no redemption. Giving up Didi seems like the only thing I can do. The right thing to do.

A sacrifice. Atonement. A way to right the wrongs, make it all balance out. The thing I want most. The thing I deserve least. If I give it up and walk away now, will it count?

Some time later, after the volley of gunshots and the lowering of the coffin and the folding of the flag, which gets given to Colonel Kingsley in lieu of the fact Dodds has no family and nobody to take it, everyone scatters between the gravestones that poke like rows of milk teeth between the grass.

"Come on," Miranda says, pulling on my sleeve. "Let's go home."

I don't move. I stand there instead, staring at the coffin and the gaping depths of the grave.

Didi

The hallway echoes with my footsteps—a hollow sound that matches my heartbeat. The ward is dark but for the emergency exit lights on the far door and the soft glow of a reading lamp at the empty nurse's station.

I walk past Dodds's room and my step falters. The door is ajar, the bed stripped bare. I stop and stare at it. The ground tips beneath me, and the world upends briefly before righting itself once again. I lean against the wall, breathing hard, staring at the plastic-covered mattress. How can he be dead?

My brain can't compute. Everything hurts so much. It's as if my ribs have been ripped open and my insides are being torn out and shredded in front of me. I can't stop screaming. Though no noise makes it past my lips.

He's dead. And it's my fault.

If we hadn't been so wrapped up in ourselves . . . if we had stopped to actually look at him, we would have seen the signs. They were so obvious, even a freshman psychology student could have spotted them. His depression, his mood swings, the way he started giving his things away. He gave me the playing cards. He gave Sanchez his lucky lighter.

Suddenly I remember the night we watched *The Shawshank Redemption*. He left just after the scene where the old man hangs himself. I falter and have to lean against the wall to steady myself. Vomit rushes up my throat and fills my mouth. I gave him the idea. For a moment I think I might collapse.

I should have known. I should have guessed. *It's nobody's fault*—that's what my mom and dad have been telling me over and over. Dodds wanted to die. It wasn't a cry for help. He wanted out. One way or another he would have found a way to do it. But is that true? Can I believe it?

A sob bursts up my throat as I push open the door to Walker's room. It's as empty as Dodds's room—the bed stripped bare, the closet door hanging open. I can't believe he's gone, and I have to lean against the wall again, shuddering as I try to breathe through the pain. I stumble toward the nightstand, trying to ignore the assault of images that rush at me—of the first time I ever saw Walker, sitting on the bed stabbing at the yogurt pot, or one of the last times I saw him, standing in the doorway, staring after me as my dad led me away sobbing, following the stretcher bearing Dodds's body.

I kneel down by the bed and reach beneath it, searching for my phone. I lost it that same night, and after racking my memory I'm fairly sure the last place I had it was here. I find it wedged down behind the back of the nightstand and pull it back. It's dead. I stare at it, wondering if Walker tried to call me during those three days we didn't see each other, or if he was too busy with his fiancée.

A noise startles me and I spin around. I get to my feet and walk out into the hallway. It's empty, no one in sight. But then I hear it again—a low sobbing noise, like someone is crying and trying to muffle the sound.

I take a few steps down the hall and notice a light seeping out from beneath Sanchez's door. I draw in a breath.

There's another noise. A moaning sound.

Heart thrumming, I push open the door.

What I see is this: skin, a solid wall of muscle. Then I see her, her head thrown back in abandon, her lips parted and her eyes squeezed shut as though in pain. His hands are on her hips, gripping them tight, possessively, and she's straddling him, her arms around his neck, hands knotted in his hair.

For a moment I can't reconcile what it is I'm seeing, and then, when the pieces finally fit together, I stumble backward in shock, banging into the door.

They start at the noise and her eyes flash open. She sees me. He turns to look over his shoulder. I stare at him, mouth open. He stares back at me, his expression as horrified as mine.

I turn and run.

Nothing is certain.

Everything can change in a heartbeat.

Walker

Didi,
I'm sorry. I'm so sorry.
I miss you.
I think about you all the time. Every second of every day.
I love you.
I —

I scrunch up the paper and toss it onto the floor. This is so damn hard. It was never this hard to speak to her in person. I wish I could sit with her now in silence and feel my way to the right words.

Thinking about her makes my throat tighten up, my chest constrict. I fucked up. How do I make it right? Is it too late?

My mom knocks on my bedroom door just as I'm writing her name on a clean sheet of paper.

"You've got a visitor," she says, eyeing the snowballs of scrunched-up paper littering the floor.

My heart leaps. "Who?" I ask. I haven't been in touch with any of my friends since I got back, and none of them have been in touch with me either, so no one knows I'm back.

"A Major Ryan?" my mother says. "He said you know him."

The chaps? What's he doing here?

I swing my legs off the bed, feeling foggy and light-headed as I sit up. I've not been sleeping and my head is all over the place. My mom purses her lips at the sight of me. I haven't shaved in four days and my clothes are rumpled. I spend most of the time just lying on my bed staring at the ceiling.

"What does he want?" I ask, rubbing my face to try to wake up a little.

"I don't know," my mother answers, tight-lipped. "Why don't you come and find out. He's in the front room. I'm just making him tea. I expect you down in five minutes." She looks me over. "And straighten up before you show your face, darling."

I shake my head at her departing back. I'm twenty-four and she makes me feel like I'm four. I have to get out of here—but go where? Do what? Even a trip to the bathroom these days requires as much energy as climbing Mount Everest. I'm back to square one. I'm not sure why I got on the plane and came back here. That's a lie. I do know why I got on the plane and came back here. It was because there were no other choices, and at that point Miranda could have told me we were getting on a plane to Kabul and I would have gone, I was in such a deep daze. I should never have walked away, though, should never have left Didi. And now it's too late.

Ten minutes later, having changed my shirt but not shaved, I enter the front room. The chaps is standing over by the window, and he turns and smiles when I walk in, his eyes crinkling.

"Lieutenant," he says, walking toward me.

"Walker," I reply.

He nods and sets his teacup down. He holds out his hand and I shake it.

"I'm sorry for the unannounced visit. I hope you don't mind."

I shake my head. "What are you doing in this neck of the woods?"

"Oh, I had some meetings close by," he says. "Thought I'd drop in and see how you were doing."

I raise my eyebrows. Meetings nearby? Really? More likely someone put him up to it. It crosses my mind that as a man of God he really shouldn't be lying, but I let it go because, strange as it is to admit it, it's good to see him.

"So how are you doing?" he asks, looking me straight in the eye.

I look away, unable to hold his gaze. "Yeah, okay," I mumble.

He doesn't say anything and I sink down onto the sofa.

"You know," he says after a beat, "I've been where you are, Walker." I look up. He sits down opposite me. "I know what it's like to feel like you've failed a friend."

I bite back my response because the look in his eye quiets me, tells me he does know. There's pain there, buried deep.

"I didn't just fail him," I hear myself say in response. "I failed others." I stare down at the carpet, squeezing my hands together tightly. "So many others." It feels as if a knife blade is wedged in my throat and I'm having to push my words past it.

"Sounds to me like you're shouldering a lot of responsibility for other people's choices."

I mull on that. It reminds me of what Didi said to me not even a week ago. Maybe they're both right. A small piece of my brain recognizes that by shouldering the guilt and blame I'm paralyzing myself as surely as taking a knife and cutting my own hamstrings. The problem is that I'm trapped under the weight of it all once more, and there's no Didi this time to help pull me to the surface and back into the light.

"Do you believe in God?" I ask suddenly, looking up. I catch the chaps' bemused expression and it strikes me what I've just asked. I laugh under my breath. "Stupid question. Of course you do. I didn't mean that."

"Are you going to ask me *how* I can believe in God? Given what I've seen, and the pain and suffering there is in the world?"

I nod. That was the general idea, yes.

He nods thoughtfully back at me. "I get asked that a lot. There are times when I doubt, times when I wonder what God can possibly be thinking, why he asks us to suffer so much." He spreads his palms wide. "What's the point of all this pain? What does it achieve?"

I stare at him, expecting him to follow through, but he doesn't. I wonder if he's just asking rhetorically, but then he continues. "You know, the Buddha taught that life is suffering. It's one of the four noble truths."

I shoot him a semi-amused glance. "Aren't you Christian?"

He laughs. "Yes, but I think the Buddha had it right on a lot of things." He nods his head again and sighs. "The truth is, I think, that we suffer when we expect things to go a certain way, when we resist the way things actually are. If we let go and learn to live every day as it comes, to accept the present moment as it is, then I think we can find happiness. Or at least we can put a moratorium on the suffering."

"That sounds pretty Buddhist to me."

He smiles. "Christianity teaches that suffering opens you up to grace and helps you appreciate the goodness in the world." He pauses, frowning, before going on. "I guess in the same the way you probably appreciate your sight a whole lot more now, having been blind for a time."

I mull on that, thinking about how right he is. When I got my sight back, I saw the world in a completely different way—colors became bigger, became brighter. For a brief stretch, in the hours before Dodds died, I was transfixed by things I'd never noticed before—the scattering diamonds of light hitting water, the million different blues above me, the variations of color in just a strand of Didi's hair.

"Loss makes you appreciate the little things more," the chaps goes on.

I think of Didi—her laugh, her touch—and feel the familiar tearing sensation in my chest as if my heart's being ripped apart.

"You think there's some big master plan?" I ask, taking a deep breath to try to ease the pain.

He nods. "Yes, I like to think so. I mean, I reckon we're here for a reason. I believe God has a plan for each of us."

Some damn plan, I think to myself. The chaps sees my expression, the cynical flare of my nostrils, and smiles sadly. "You see what happened to your men and to Dodds as your fault," he says, "but it isn't."

"Well, whose fault is it, then? God's?"

"It's no one's fault. It just is. You're struggling to find a reason for it all, to understand it, but there is no reason and you'll never be able to understand it. So the only course of action, I would counsel, is acceptance of what is."

I stare at him sullenly.

"You saved Sanchez. Twice." He smiles. "You might not think of yourself as a hero, but you are."

A hero?

"You are," he repeats. "Not just for putting yourself on the line every single day out there and for risking your life to save your men, not just for saving Sanchez's life twice, either, but for enduring all that and still keeping on going."

He stands up, and I do too, out of habit—I have to stop myself from saluting. He puts his hand on my shoulder.

"And you will get through this. I have absolute faith in that."

Didi

Zac kisses my shoulder and climbs out of bed. I watch him stroll to the bathroom and immediately I think of Walker. I can't stop myself from comparing the two of them. And the comparisons aren't good. Zac turns on the shower and shuts the bathroom door.

I roll onto my back and stare at the ceiling, pulling the sheets tight around me. What am I doing here? It's been five days since the funeral and instead of getting better, the wound's starting to feel infected, suppurating. I keep seeing Walker with that girl. My face burns as I think of all the things he said to me, all the lines he fed me about *seeing* me. What bullshit. I'm such an idiot. He never told me that he loved me. That should have been a sign right there that he wasn't serious, that he was just playing me.

I hate him. I still love him. I hate him. And I can't stop thinking about him. Or Dodds. I still can't believe he's dead. It still doesn't feel real. None of it does. It's like a never-ending nightmare. At night I start awake, heart pounding, seeing Dodds's face swollen purple. His tongue lolling out.

I reach over to the bedside table and slide my hand into my

purse, pulling out the letter. It's creased and stained I've read it so often—I have it almost memorized; but I can't stop myself from scouring it again for clues. What could I have done differently?

Didi,

Thanks for being a friend. I know you're the kind of person who'll try to figure out what you could have done to stop me, but you couldn't have done anything. No one could have.

Life's not all rainbows and unicorns, but I hope it is for you. If anyone deserves it you do.

Become a doc. Marry Walker. Be happy.

Callum

My phone buzzes. I reach for it: it's my mom. I switch it off. I don't want to talk to her. I don't want to talk to anyone, in fact. Being with Zac is easy because he doesn't ask questions.

And how would I even be able to start telling him, or anyone? I'm still reeling from the shock and can barely admit it to myself. My own mother. And José. All Zac knows is that I've had a falling out with my mom and I don't want to go home.

The image of them having sex is seared into my brain. After everything she's always preached to me about honesty and trust being the bedrock of a relationship, after believing that her and my dad were the paragon of a happy marriage . . . I feel sick to my stomach.

After I walked in on them in Sanchez's room, I ran to my car and just drove. I was planning on going to Jessa's, but halfway to LA I remembered she was away filming, so instead I ended up driving to Zac's. If I stop to examine it, probably the motivation was a giant *screw you* to Walker, for leaving with Miranda without saying a word to me, for lying to me all along, for not being there when I needed him.

But it hasn't worked. Falling into bed with Zac hasn't made me feel in any way better. It's made me feel worse, because every time Zac touches me all I can do is think about Walker and how much better it was with him.

Zac comes out of the bathroom a few minutes later wearing a towel wrapped around his waist. "So," he says, sitting down on the edge of the bed and resting his hand on my leg. "This is becoming a regular thing, you staying over."

"Yeah," I say, sitting up. "I'm sorry. I can—"

"No," he says, interrupting me. "I like it. Stay as long as you need."

"Oh," I say. "Thanks. I mean, right now just having a place to crash is great." My eyes start to fill with tears. I'm like a busted, leaking fire hydrant. "Until I figure out what to do with my life."

I swallow the lump in my throat. I don't know what's happening with my internship or my PhD. I want to talk to my dad, but I can't bring myself to call him. I don't know what to do, whether to tell him about my mom or not, and I'm embarrassed to face him after what he walked in on.

So I'm doing the only thing I can do—avoiding him and everyone else into the bargain.

Walker

"She's a beauty."

I turn around and see Isaac strolling down the jetty toward me. He pulls his sunglasses off and grins at the thirty-foot sailboat I'm standing beside before turning to me. "Didi?" he asks.

I shrug and look away, glad I'm wearing sunglasses.

"She know you named a boat after her?"

I shake my head. Isaac knows I haven't spoken to her. "I don't think she'd be that impressed," I tell him. "Her boyfriend probably has a luxury yacht moored in San Tropez that he whisks her off to on the weekends."

"I doubt he's named it after her, though," he says, one eyebrow lifting in a sardonic smirk.

Whatever. I hop on deck and Isaac follows suit. I probably shouldn't have named the boat Didi. It was a whim. I was thinking of my grandpa calling his boat Chiara, but now, every time I see the name, picked out in glossy white against the hull, I feel as if a fishing hook is snagging in my gut. Eight weeks and still the pain shows no sign of abating. I heard from Sanchez, who heard it from Valentina, that Didi is back dating that actor Zac Ridgemont. I found that out the day after I named the boat after her. The day after I finally sent her the letter it had taken me weeks to write. I drank an entire bottle of whisky that night. Every day since, I've tried not to think about her, tried instead to focus on the present, just like the chaplain, or the Buddha, or both of them, ordered.

I open the cooler and hand Isaac a cold beer, and we settle on deck, looking out over the masts and rigging at the open ocean ahead of us glinting chlorine blue. *Aegean* blue, I revise. Miami could be a whole lot worse, that's for sure. And on the upside, it sure beats Afghanistan.

"I'm thinking of taking her out on a maiden voyage down to the Keys," I tell Isaac, running my hand over the side of the boat. It's amazing what a three-carat diamond translates into in boat terms. It covered the down payment, and my retirement and injury pay covered the rest.

"So long as you're back next week for the exhibition," Isaac says, taking a swig of his beer.

"Yeah, I wouldn't miss it," I tell him. I wouldn't miss it for anything.

"How's the job going?" he asks.

I smile. "Actually, it's going pretty well."

I got a job working as a boat builder, fixing up old boats, and putting my degree to use working with a design team on building new ones to contract. It's my dream job. No chance of anyone dying on my watch or of stepping on an IED, which is a bonus. My dad is still pissed. He set up a meeting with an old army buddy and lined up a job for me working for a military defense company, one that supplies guns and bullets to the army as well as to countless insurgencies around the world, but I told him

I wasn't interested, that I'd had a lifetime of bullets and war. He told me it was far more profitable than boats. He's probably right, but I guess it's all about how you define profitable.

"You spoken to Mom?" Isaac asks, interrupting my thoughts.

I shake my head. "Nah, every time I call she wants to know why Miranda and I haven't set a date for the wedding. She's in denial about us breaking up."

Isaac throws back his head and laughs.

"I told her if I married Miranda we'd have to rewrite the wedding vows to take out the part about in sickness and in health."

"You're better off without her," Isaac says. "I still can't believe you dated her as long as you did. Girl was psycho."

I laugh to myself. My dad said the same thing. It's amazing to me now that I ever saw anything in a girl like Miranda. How I could ever have thought that was love.

After the chaplain paid his visit, I thought for a long time about what he'd said about suffering and about living. I thought, too, a lot about Dodds in his coffin, in his grave. And what I decided was that either I could follow him down there into the darkness—end up dead myself, or as good as—or I could do what the chaps told me to do: fix my eyes on the present, accept what is, and live each day as best I can.

So while every day still has its challenges, and while loss has wrapped its iron bands around my chest again, I'm learning to live with it. There's work to do, amends to be made. A life to live in lieu of all the lives lost.

I'm staying busy, trying every day to keep my head above the surface. Being by the water helps.

"Smile," Isaac says suddenly, and snaps a picture on his iPhone, then chinks his beer bottle against mine.

Didi

It's like being in the heart of a riot. Zac grips my hand and tugs me along behind him, past Rayban-wearing security guards and a woman in a ballgown clutching a clipboard, and what sounds like a stadium of screaming teenage girls.

On television premieres always look so glamorous, but in reality it's like being an animal at the zoo with people poking sharpened sticks through the bars. It's breathtakingly terrifying.

"Smile," Zac whispers under his breath as he pulls us to a stop in front of a bristling forest of microphones and cameras.

I force a smile, blinking in the dazzling glare of lights. I try to remember what Jessa told me about how to stand so I look good on camera. I'm wearing so much makeup I feel like a clown, but Zac's makeup person said it was necessary so I didn't look washed out in the photographs.

"Is this your girlfriend, Zac?" someone in the press pen shouts out, louder than the others.

I hear Zac laugh and then deflect the question by answering another about his role in the movie. He runs a hand self-consciously through his hair, styled just so. His other arm comes around my waist, helpfully anchoring me, because my legs have started to shake.

"What are you wearing?"

Zac turns to me and nods encouragingly. Oh. They're asking me. I snap to. "Um, a dress," I mumble.

Laughter. I can't see who's laughing, though, as everyone is cast in shadow, thanks to the floodlights.

"Who's the designer?"

Zac's assistant steps in with the answer.

"Relax," whispers Zac. "You look beautiful. Let's go," he says to me under his breath. "The movie's about to start." He waves at the photographers and starts walking back along the red carpet to the theater entrance, past giant posters of himself.

We take our seats in the front row, and Zac pulls my hand into his. His palm is clammy. He's nervous. He turns and smiles at me, and I feel a twinge in my heart. A Walker-twinge as I've started to call them. I brush it aside. I'm with Zac now. And Walker's with the girl I thought was Dodds's girlfriend. I figured out that's where I knew her from—the photograph Dodds had on his nightstand. He must have taken it. It was literally staring me in the face, and I never realized. I wonder if Sanchez and Dodds and José knew all along and were laughing behind my back.

It's been two months since I saw Walker. I've made my Facebook account private. I had to after it became public that I was dating Zac. There are a lot of crazy people out there with no filter and no boundaries.

School started back up, so I've been throwing myself into that. In a hugely ironic turn, we've been studying repressed emotions.

I still haven't been back to the center, or spoken to my mom or dad, though they're both peppering my phone daily with calls and texts. I texted them both back to tell them that I'm busy and need some time to work through my feelings, and since then they've been respecting my need for space.

My mom wants to meet me to explain, but I'm not ready to hear her explanations, and while my dad never reported what happened with Walker and me so I'm still officially a PhD student, I'm still too embarrassed to face him. I know I have to soon, though. Jessa won't let up about it. But the truth is, I've needed the time to process what happened to Dodds, and my role in his death. I have some inkling of what Walker was feeling now when he struggled to forgive himself over Lutter and Bailey.

The movie has started, and I try to push all those thoughts away and focus on the screen, though seeing Zac wearing a soldier's uniform makes me think about Walker. I spend the whole movie wrapped up in thoughts about him, wondering what he's doing at this moment, thinking about him and Miranda. Are they married yet? Are they on honeymoon? Is he happy? I hate myself for thinking about him, for not being able to let him go, for torturing myself with my memories.

I glance over at Zac. Why don't I feel the same way about him that I do about Walker? Why am I still in love with someone who doesn't love me, who never loved me? I scream silently at myself in frustration. Zac is my future now. I link my fingers through his and squeeze, and he squeezes back.

When the credits roll, Zac leans over and kisses me on the cheek.

"What did you think?" he asks.

"You were amazing," I say, forcing a smile, praying he doesn't start asking me questions about the plot because I have no idea what the movie was about.

We walk out into the lobby to smatterings of applause and more flashlights going off. My phone buzzes. Thinking it must me my mom again, I ignore it, but Zac is busy signing autographs so I pull it out of my handbag and decide to check it. Maybe it's time I did speak to my mom.

It's not from my mom. It's from Isaac Walker. A message. I open it.

There's a photograph attached.

Walker

The gallery is bursting at the seams, people tumbling out through the doors and gathering in knots on the street. There are a few people in uniform, art dealers, art students, friends of Isaac's, even a few celebrity faces.

As I make my way through the crowd to the bar, someone grabs me from behind. I turn around and am swept straight into a hug that's more like an attack. I'm about to drown in cleavage when I'm dragged back to the surface.

"Tina, let the guy breathe."

I laugh, happy to see Sanchez and Valentina, dressed as if they're walking the red carpet at the Oscars. I wasn't sure they'd be able to make it. Sanchez nods at me, and then before I can do anything he pulls me into a bear hug to rival his wife's. We slap each other on the back and then, holding each other by the tops of the arms, we just grin and nod at one another like long-lost brothers.

"The Lord put you on this earth for a reason," Valentina tells me, her eyes filling with tears and her hand seizing my arm in a vise-like grip. "That's twice now you've saved my husband."

She pats her rounded stomach. "We're naming this baby after you, I've told Jesús. He wanted Ronaldo after some soccer player, but I said, no, we're calling this baby Noel."

"What if it's a girl?" I joke.

"Then we'll call her Noelle."

I laugh and kiss her on the cheek.

"I was thinking Ronalda had a better ring to it," Sanchez mutters, "but you know, you did save my life, twice. And Ronaldo has only won the World Cup, so no contest."

Isaac weaves his way through the crowd just then. I introduce him to Valentina, who immediately lets go of Sanchez's arm, brushes her hair over her shoulder and flutters her eyelashes.

"Why didn't you tell me you had a brother?" she asks, whacking me on the arm. "And so handsome, too." She beams at Isaac. "You got a girlfriend?"

"Not currently," Isaac answers warily.

Valentina takes his arm. "You know something? You'd be perfect for my cousin Angela . . ."

Sanchez rolls his eyes at me. "So how you doing?" he asks as Valentina starts selling the benefits of Angela to my brother as if she's a real estate agent and Angela's a prize pad in Malibu.

I nod and shrug at the same time. "You?" I ask to deflect the question.

He nods and shrugs too. "Yeah, you know how it is. Hard to adapt."

I don't think he's talking about the prosthetic leg. Adapting to civilian life is challenging. I'm still waking at dawn every morning, though the nightmares are infrequent now, and I'm still struggling without a strict daily regimen. The job and the boat help, and I'm still training hard, thinking also of taking part in a triathlon in the spring.

"I got a job," Sanchez says, his face lighting up. "Get this. I'm training to be a prosthetist. You know, learning how to make and fit limbs."

"That's great," I say.

"Yeah, well," he says with a shrug, "third baby on the way. Little Noelle needs her daddy to put food on the table."

I nod.

"So you seen Didi?" he asks.

I knew the question was coming, but it still hurts, flays off a layer of skin. I shake my head.

"You guys . . ." He shakes his head forlornly. "I had you down to last the distance. What happened? Why didn't you make up?"

I shrug, not wanting to go there because the explanation makes no sense to me and I can't bear to hear myself scramble for the words.

Thankfully, before Sanchez can press me for details, I spot two familiar gray heads over the crowd and make my excuses. I wend my way over to my parents, who are standing by the door looking like two straight hellfire-and-damnation Christians who've wandered accidentally into a transgender S&M conference. My dad is staring at the art student cohort who are occupying the bar area like a Fox News pundit surveying a room full of liberal women's rights activists, and my mom's eyes are popping as she takes in the array of art on the walls.

I greet them both. My dad is clearly here under duress, as can be judged by my mom's iron grip on his arm and the fact that he's still wearing his jacket, even though it's at least seventy degrees inside and he's already worked up a sweat.

"What is this?" my dad asks, pointing at the nearest of Dodds's paintings. "Some kind of anti-war propaganda? Was he high on meth when he painted it or something?"

I wince, hoping that the art teacher isn't within hearing distance. I heard her earlier discussing the anti-war sentiment of the paintings with a member of the media.

"It's lovely, darling," my mom intercedes, though her eyes tell a different story. She looks like she's surveying a scene from *Dante's Inferno* . . . which actually isn't too far from the truth. "Is that a unicorn?" she queries, frowning.

I nod, hoping she doesn't ask what's coming out of its rear end.

"What a show!" she exclaims. "Did you organize it all yourself?"

"With Isaac, yeah," I say.

My dad's head springs up at his wayward offspring's name. He covers it swiftly and jerks his head at the paintings. "Who'd want this on their wall?" He leans in closer. "Anyone actually buy this stuff?"

"Actually, I think you'll find we've already sold eight paintings and the evening hasn't even gotten started."

It's the art teacher, Valerie. She's overheard and has inserted herself into the conversation. She pushes her glasses up her nose and introduces herself to my parents. I take the chance to extricate myself, not wanting to be witness to the conversation I can imagine is about to happen. I head over to the podium where I take the mic and clear my throat. I've been dreading this part. I might as well get it over with.

When I look up, the room has fallen mostly silent, except

for a faint hum of chatter at the back and the happy clink of glasses. Shit. There are a lot of people. I take a deep breath, spying the chaplain over in the corner. I nod a greeting to him and he raises his glass and smiles at me.

Here goes nothing.

"I didn't have enough time for Dodds when he was alive," I begin. "I think that happens a lot. We get so absorbed in our own lives, in our own inner turmoil, that we forget sometimes to look up and see others, to notice what's going on right in front of our faces."

The room has fallen completely silent. My mouth is so dry it feels as if I've swallowed a mouthful of dust.

"I've failed a lot of people in my life," I say, daring a glance at the audience and seeing a lot of furrowed brows. "I wish I could reverse time. If I could, I'd go back and change a lot of things. For one, I'd be a better friend to Dodds." I rock back on my heels and stare down at the ground. Was I even a friend to him at all? "But, the thing is," I continue, "we can't go back." My voice starts to crack. "That's life's greatest punishment. We can't go back and right the wrongs, fix the mistakes, undo the tragedies, change our minds, make different decisions, unbreak hearts, take back words. All you can do is own your mistakes, forgive yourself, and keep on living."

I take another deep breath.

"Dodds told me once that the future's what you make it. And so it is." I glance up at the ceiling. "If you're up there, Dodds, looking down on us now, I hope you're drinking a Bud and laughing, and I hope you're happy. I'm sorry." I choke down the meteor-size lump in my throat and quickly survey the crowd, who are studying me, a lot of them with their heads tipped to one side. There's pity in some eyes, sorrow in others.

"One other thing he said . . ." I pause. "Actually, he yelled it . . ." A smattering of laughter. "He told me that life was meaningless. For a time, I also believed that—that we were insignificant nothings floating through space, that there was no rhyme or reason to anything. That life was just suffering. But what Dodds went on to say was that the only thing that wasn't meaningless was love. That that connection was all we had as human beings, and that when we found it, when we were lucky enough to experience love—to love and be loved in return—we shouldn't squander it."

Tears film my eyes. I stare down at the floor. I can't fucking cry now. Not up here, not in front of hundreds of people, but my throat has closed up. I can't seem to get the words out.

I don't need to. Isaac jumps onto the stage beside me. He wraps his arm around my shoulder and takes the mic.

"And all proceeds from the paintings will be going to the Veterans' Association, as per Dodds's wishes," he shouts. "So get your wallets out, people, and spend, spend, spend!"

There's a swell of applause that carries me off the stage.

"You okay?" Isaac asks as he ushers me down and toward the back of the gallery.

I nod.

"Nice speech," he tells me, then comes to a sudden halt.

"Hi, son."

My dad is blocking our path.

"Hi," Isaac answers. He didn't know that I'd invited our parents, and now he throws an *I'm going to kill you later* look my way.

My dad casts about wildly, his eyes refusing to land on either of us. Isaac looks about ready to bolt. I step back, angling myself behind him just in case he does try to do a runner.

"Your mother wanted to come," my dad blurts.

Isaac expels air through his nose.

"This is impressive," my dad says in a salvage attempt, nodding his head at the gallery.

Isaac narrows his eyes.

"This one of yours?" my dad asks now, jerking his head at a painting on the wall. It depicts a field turning from brown to green, like a time-lapse painting. An orange sun burns neon above it. It's Isaac's latest painting, on sale for a cool twenty thousand dollars.

Isaac nods warily. The last time dad commented on his art was when he was seventeen and dad told him one of his charcoal paintings looked like it had been drawn by a toddler with physical and mental delay.

"Not bad," my dad remarks.

That's the highest praise Isaac or I have ever heard from him, and I can tell by the way Isaac shoots a sideways glance at me that he's wondering if Dad's been occupied by an alien from *Invasion of the Body Snatchers*.

"I wouldn't mind having that on my wall," Dad muses. "Not sure about this other stuff, though," he mutters, tipping his head conspiratorially toward us and jerking his head at Dodds's paintings.

I suppress a laugh. Isaac's painting is an ironic statement about genetically modified crops and the corporatization of government. The tangerine sun is a riff on a global GMO company's logo. Neither Isaac nor I are about to explain that to my dad, though.

Then I feel that burning sensation at the back of my neck. The hairs on my arms stand on end and all my attention switches instantly away from Isaac and my dad.

I turn around.

And she's there. Standing in the doorway, scanning the room, looking for someone. I wait, motionless, until her gaze lands on me.

Didi

He walks toward me, which is good because seeing him again has caused temporary paralysis of all my limbs and my breathing. He keeps his eyes fixed on me as he forces a way through the crowd, and I'm struck all over again by the heart-jarring feeling of being seen by him. And though he's still too far away from me to hear him speak, he doesn't need to because the look on his face tells me everything I need to know. I can read the surprise and the joy and the sorrow and the pain and the fear better than if he'd spoken out loud.

He stops in front of me. "Hi," he says.

For a moment I worry I've lost my voice. I'd forgotten what being close to him does to my breathing, to my heart rate. My legs feel hollow. The whole world fades out and it's just Walker and me, and I'm oblivious to the people pushing past us. The roar of the crowd matches the roar of the blood in my ears.

"Hi," I finally manage to say.

His eyes haven't left my face. "What are you doing here?" he asks, and for one horrible moment I wonder if maybe I've made a mistake. Maybe he doesn't want me here. Maybe she's here. I glance over his shoulder, scanning for a blond head. There are several.

"Um . . ." I stammer. "Isaac invited me." What I don't say is that he sent me a photograph of Walker sitting on a boat. A boat bearing my name. What I also don't say is that I walked out of a premiere, went back to Zac's, packed my bag and went straight to the airport, still wearing a dress that cost more than my annual college tuition. But Walker's now frowning at me and I'm wondering if maybe it wasn't some kind of hoax. "And I couldn't miss this . . . Dodds's big show," I say with a false laugh.

My face is burning. Oh God, how do I get out of this? I cast about for a lifeline and spot Sanchez and Valentina. Maybe I could go and talk to them.

"I'm glad you're here," Walker says.

My eyes fly back to his face. His eyes are storm-gray. There's no light in them. I can't read him like I used to.

"He would have been glad."

It takes me a moment to realize he's referring to Dodds.

"I heard your speech," I tell him.

"You did?"

I nod. "It was beautiful."

Walker nods back, his gaze grazing the ground. He shoves his hands deep into his pockets and rocks backward on his heels. He can't even stand to look at me.

"So you've moved here to Miami?" I ask.

He looks up at me through his lashes. "Yeah. I'm working in a boat yard."

I can't stop the smile. "That's awesome."

His face lights up with a smile too, and my heart twangs as

if someone's pulled a cord. My own smile fades. Did Miranda move with him? But if so, why did he call the boat Didi?

"What about you?" he asks now, and a frown furrows his forehead. "Did you . . . ?"

I shake my head, blood rushing to my face and other places as the images of our last night together—of us making love in his bed—scream through my head like a freight train.

"Um, no, it's okay. I'm back at college. My dad didn't report me. I guess he figured that having a daughter who'd still be talking to him and not living at home for the rest of her life because she was unemployable was a better option than reporting me to the ethics committee. I still have my internship for next summer. Though with a strict warning that I'm not to sleep with any more patients."

Walker winces. I stare at my feet. That probably wasn't the best thing to say. Now I can't look at him.

"That's good. That's great," Walker says. "I'm pleased."

I glance up and he looks awkwardly away, scratching behind his ear. He's acting as if he'd rather be anywhere than standing here with me. We always used to be good with silence, but now it feels prickly and uncomfortable.

"So," I start to say, trying to think of a way to get out of this, to leave without appearing rude or like I care. I want to get out of here with my dignity intact.

"Did you get my letter?" Walker cuts in.

My head flies up. "What letter?"

"I sent it to the center. I didn't have an address for you." He runs a hand through his hair. "I, uh . . . wanted to explain, give you my number in case you wanted to get in touch . . . but I guess . . ."

"I didn't get it. I haven't been back to the center." I pause. "What did you want to explain?"

He shakes his head. "It doesn't matter now."

"Oh." I look away, glance at the door. I need to go.

"So how's Zac?" Walker asks.

Oh. I turn back around. He knows. I wonder how. Embarrassed, I shrug. Walker's eyebrow shoots up. He nods thoughtfully, but his jaw is tensed, pulsing. He's angry. *How's Miranda?* I almost shoot back.

"Right," he says, glancing over his shoulder again. "Well . . . I should probably mingle . . ."

My insides roil. *No, don't go!* I want to yell. I want to reach for him. In fact, standing here an inch away from him and not being able to touch him gives me an idea of what prisoners must feel when they stare through iron bars at blue sky.

"Sure." I manage to squeeze the word out through a closed-up throat.

"It's good seeing you again, Didi." He gives me a terse smile and then turns and starts walking away.

"We broke up."

Walker turns back around to face me.

"Zac and I." I close my eyes, scrunch them shut. "We weren't really together. I just . . . I was mad. And I needed somewhere to go."

I open my eyes. Walker is studying me with—indifference?

"How are the wedding plans?" I blurt. "Did you set the date yet?"

Walker's lips edge up into a half smile. My face starts to flame. Why am I asking? I don't want to hear it.

"There is no wedding, Didi."

"What?"

"Miranda was my ex, emphasis on the *ex*. She broke up with me straight after I got injured."

"What?" I ask, dumbfounded.

Walker shrugs. "It was the best thing that could ever have happened to me."

"But—" I start to ask.

"She found out I got my sight back and wanted to pick up where things left off."

My mouth falls open. She did *what*? Walker nods, seeing my expression.

"Yeah, I told her I wasn't interested, that things were over, and then you walked in."

"Oh," I manage to say. "It just . . . it looked . . ."

"I know how it looked. I tried to explain. You didn't want to hear. And I don't blame you," he adds quickly.

"But you left," I say quietly. "You went with her."

"I was discharged. I was a mess. Dodds, the whole thing with you, knowing I'd screwed up your life. I tried calling you, but you wouldn't answer. I left messages and you didn't respond."

"I lost my phone," I say.

He looks surprised.

"And I left a note with José. Or rather, I left it at the desk for him, but I guess . . . maybe he never got it?" He frowns. "I thought that if you wanted to call me, you would call me. But you didn't. I was going to try again a few weeks ago . . . but then I found out you were dating that Zac guy."

Oh my God. The cogs turn. This whole thing has been one big chain of miscommunication from end to end.

"So . . . then . . ." I can't stop hope flaring hot in my chest.

Walker takes a step closer. I stop breathing.

"Didi," he says, and the way he says it is a caress, a whisper of fingers across my skin. My stomach flutters in response. His eyes flit over my face, taking me in, and though his jaw is still pulsing, I see the storm front in his eyes lift a little. But then he shakes his head, softly and a little sadly. "I'm sorry," he says. "I can't give you what you want."

The hope fizzles out, my stomach turns to lead. "What are you talking about? What do you mean?"

"The love you want," he answers simply.

I draw in a breath that feels like a punch to the solar plexus. What's he saying? I don't understand. He doesn't love me. Didn't love me? Ever?

"I—"

"*Didi!*"

I turn around in a daze. My parents are right behind me, looking at me with expressions of ecstatic surprise on their faces.

"Hi," I stammer.

"What are you . . . ?" my mom asks.

I turn back around, my head spinning, but Walker is gone, heading through the crowd toward the back of the gallery. My shoulders slump.

"Didi?" my mom says. She pulls me around, and the next thing I know I'm in her arms and she's hugging me and I cling to her, having to suppress a sob, and I register my dad has his arm around my shoulder too and that we're blocking the doorway, and then I remember why I'm not talking to my parents and reel backward out of my mom's arms.

"What's the matter?" she asks. "Oh, it's so good to see you. Are you okay? Are you doing okay? We've been so worried."

"We wanted to respect your need for space," my dad explains, "but you could have called and let us know you were coming to Miami. We could have caught the same flight."

I look at my mom. They came together? Has she told my dad? Does he know about José?

"He knows," my mom says as though she's read my mind. "He's always known. That's what I was trying to tell you. I guess you haven't been listening to your messages?"

I look at my dad. He gives me a tight smile and a tense shrug. I look back at my mom. "I don't get it."

My mom bites her bottom lip. "Shall we move inside and get a drink, find somewhere to talk?"

I look between her and my dad. My dad smiles at me, puts his hand on my shoulder, and starts steering me to the bar. "Come on," he says.

"We all make mistakes," my dad says five minutes later when, wine glasses in hand, we stand in a quietish corner. "It's how you learn from them that matters. You never burned down a kitchen again, did you?"

"You've forgiven her?" I ask him in amazement, ignoring his reference to my childhood arson and glancing at my mom, who frowns at me.

"We were on a break, Didi."

"A *break*?"

"Yes. We'd decided we needed some time apart to assess how we felt about each other."

"And?" I ask.

"And after some reflection, we've decided we want to stay married and work our issues out."

"But . . . but . . ." I shake my head. I can't comprehend what she's saying. "What do you mean *issues*?"

My mother smiles again. "A lot of relationships flounder when the kids go off to college. It's normal. Your father and I were going through a bad patch."

"A bad patch?" I ask, still stunned.

"Yes, a bad patch. We do have them. All couples do."

"No," I say, shaking my head angrily. "You two don't. This whole time I've been thinking you have a perfect relationship . . ." They can't possibly know what this means to me. It's like discovering that I'm the daughter of the Goblin King or that I've been living in *The Truman Show*. "Why didn't you tell me?"

"Because they were our problems to sort out," my mom explains, stroking my cheek. "And we didn't want to involve you."

"It was a stupid thing to do," my father cuts in. "We see that now. We should have been open and honest with you. We just didn't want you to be anxious or upset."

I shake my head. I can't believe they lied to me about something so huge. "You're therapists! You should know how to parent better," I hiss.

My mom nods. "I'm a sex therapist, not a parenting expert, but yes, you're right. We made a mistake. I'm sorry."

"So you still love each other?" I ask skeptically.

"Yes, of course we love each other," my dad explains. "We just have some work to do. All relationships take work. The biggest lie is thinking that they don't."

My mom takes my dad's hand and squeezes it, and they look at each other all dewy-eyed, and for a moment I'm fifteen again, wanting to make hurling noises, but I can't because my heart is too heavy in my chest. There's no room for laughter.

"And what about you?" my mom asks, nodding her head over my shoulder at Walker. "Did you two sort things out? Aren't you dating Zac now?"

"I . . ." I shake my head, tears stinging my eyes.

"For what it's worth," my dad says with a slight wince, "though I may have seen a little more of Walker than I'd ever have wanted to, I like him. You two obviously have a connection."

"Obviously not, actually," I answer.

I blink furiously to stop the tears from coming. I don't want to cry here and I don't want to have to explain to my parents what's just happened, because then I really will cry and I might not be able to stop. I'll save it until we're back at the hotel. I'm hoping I can crash their room, because I never booked one. I had a fantasy that I'd get here and Walker would sweep me into his arms and carry me off to the boat he named after me. Hah. How stupid am I?

"Um," I say. "I just need to go to the bathroom." I'll lock myself in a stall until I calm down or until everyone has left. Everyone being Walker. It's the only way through this.

My mom tilts her head at me. "Do you want me to come with you?"

"No, it's okay," I tell her.

She nods, clearly not buying my attempt at a smile. "Okay," she says, "we'll take a look at the art while you're gone. I quite like that one over there." She points at the exploding love heart. I recognize it from my date with Walker. If only I'd known it was prophetic back then.

I stumble toward the bathroom sign, head down, trying to

bash my way through a sea of pointed elbows and ear-splitting art speak. I don't notice him until he's standing right in front of me and I almost crash into him.

I look up. Walker's scowling down at me. "I didn't get to finish," he tells me, blocking my path with his body.

I shake my head at him. I don't want to hear any more. I need to get into the bathroom and lock myself in a stall. I can't bear being this near to him.

"I can't give you the kind of love you want," he goes on.

Yeah, I got that the first time, my expression tells him. I try to step around him.

"You want a lobster. You want guarantees," he goes on, side-stepping me and blocking my path again. "You want a fairy tale."

I stare at him, breathing hard, angry now.

"And fairy tales don't exist," he tells me, shaking his head sadly.

Have he and Sanchez been exchanging philosophies on love?

Walker takes a step closer, and the static charge between us roars to life. His hand brushes the back of mine, taking me by surprise, muting my anger.

"But this does," he says in a low voice that makes the hairs on the back of my neck stand on end. He gestures at the inch of space separating us. "What's between us . . . this exists. It's real. It's not always perfect, and I can't promise you it won't sometimes go wrong, like it just did, or that we'll last forever. I don't think I'm ever going to be able to plan for the future, and I know you want that. I've seen too much, witnessed too much, to be able to put stock in the future anymore. But what I can promise you is that every single moment of the present I'll be with you. And I know this—that what we have means some-thing. It's significant. It's not 'I can't live without you' love. It's 'I don't *want* to live without you' love."

I can't stop myself. The tears start to fall.

Seeing me cry, Walker's face falls. His hand comes up. He brushes away a tear with his thumb.

"Didi," he murmurs, his voice as gentle as his touch. "Just because the fairy tale doesn't exist doesn't mean the happily-ever-after doesn't either."

I stare into his eyes and see the softening in them, the dark clouds parting.

"I see you," he tells me, his hands already holding my face, his thumbs stroking my jaw. He takes his time, his eyes locked on mine, until the very last moment before he kisses me.

I don't hear the clapping at first because I've fallen so hard into that kiss that my body is reacting like a power station being switched on for the first time. Walker pulls away first, and that's when I hear it. I open my eyes and turn around and find the whole gallery has formed a circle around us and is clap-ping and whooping, led of course by Sanchez and Valentina, who's wiping away tears.

"So romantic," she mouths at me, clutching a hand to her heart.

I grin at them, and see my parents with their arms wrapped around each other laughing too. And then I see Isaac, smiling grimly, walk over to Sanchez while checking his wristwatch.

"Pay up!" Sanchez hollers, slapping Isaac on the back.

Walker puts his arm around my shoulders and laughs, a belly laugh, a new laugh I've never heard from him before.

Isaac shakes his head, still smiling, and takes a thick wedge of cash out of his wallet while Valentina looks on disapprovingly. He hands it to Sanchez, who waves it in our direction, grinning like a clown on crack.

"What was the bet?" Walker calls.

"That you two would get it on before midnight. Isaac here thought it might take a couple of days. But I know what a charmer you are underneath all that manly gruffness."

I look at the clock. It's two minutes to midnight.

"You better kiss her quick before she turns into a pumpkin," Sanchez jokes.

Walker turns to me. "I better," he says.

Acknowledgments

Catherine, Venetia, and Eloise at Pan Macmillan. And Naomi Clark for designing the cover.

Juliet Van Oss for copyediting, and Lorraine Green for proofreading.

Amanda, my agent, for the coffees, lunches, notes, and brilliantly endless support. You are the best!

My family for taking on the heroic task of childcare so I could skip off to Goa and write this on the beach. I don't know what I would do without you!

Becky Wicks, writing lobster, brilliant friend, and superstar ally.

John for always believing in *a posse ad esse*.

Best friends.

Buried secrets.

And a romance that can't be denied . . .

RUN AWAY WITH ME

MILA GRAY

Read on for a sneak peek of Mila Gray's next novel, *Run Away with Me*.

Prologue

The woods are dark as a grave. Not a sliver of moonlight breaks through the firs and alders. The dank, loamy smell of wet leaves and earth fills my lungs and I draw it in deep as though I have been holding my breath underwater for the last twenty-four hours and have finally broken the surface.

I break into a run, stumbling over buried roots, ignoring the branches that whip my arms and face, ignoring the cold that slaps my cheeks and makes them sting, ignoring the damp that has soaked through my shoes and socks and jeans.

As I run I can hear his voice echoing through the trees. He's chasing me, gaining on me. I run faster. I need to make it to the tree house. I'll be safe there.

"Em!" He calls my name again. This time closer. "Em!"

It sounds like he's right beside me.

I push on, sprinting now, desperate to escape him, but I can't because his voice is in my head and there's no running from it.

Fighting through a moat of ferns, I make it into the clearing, dart toward the tree house, and start scrambling up the ladder. A hand grabs my foot; another hand grabs my thigh. I yelp, kick out, almost fall, but manage somehow to keep climbing.

Dragging myself onto the landing, I lean over the ledge to look down. There's no one there. I'm imagining it all. It's not real. It's not real. It's only in my head.

I dig my fingers into the wooden boards I'm lying on—like it's the deck of a storm tossed ship—and I hold on tight, until my breathing finally returns to normal and my heart rate begins to slow.

"Em?"

I jolt upright, scanning the forest floor, my heart bashing wildly against my ribs. There's no one there. Scrunching my eyes shut, I curl into a ball and press my hands over my ears.

"Shut up, shut up!" I scream at his voice in my head.

My skin prickles as if worms are crawling all over my body, leaving dirty, slimy trails in their wake. Another nest of worms writhes in my stomach. Why? Why? Why me? a voice mumbles over and over again, but there's never any answer. I must have done something wrong. That's the only thing I know.

Exhausted from crying and shivering from the cold, I finally open my eyes. My gaze lands on a half-empty packet of marshmallows. Have the Walshes been here? Or Jake?

A rustle in the undergrowth makes me jerk around in fright. Automatically, I cower backward into the shadows, holding my breath.

Is it my parents come looking for me?

Is it Jake?

Or . . . is it him?

Emerson

With my eyes closed and my face turned toward the sun, it's easy to pretend I'm somewhere else, like an island in the Caribbean, and not one in the Pacific Northwest. Though it's at least twenty degrees too cold for the pretense to last longer than a moment.

I stand there, hearing the water lapping the shore, trying to summon some images of my other life—the alternate version, that is. The one I planned for and imagined for years. The one where I get to escape from here—from this island that's turned into my very own version of Alcatraz, only with higher walls and not even the slightest chance for escape.

When the images won't come I give up and open my eyes. The kayak still lies in the sand in front of me like a beached red whale. Sighing, I reach for it. And that's when I hear a voice behind me.

"Need some help with that?"

I spin around.

It takes a couple of seconds for my brain to confirm that it's actually him. That it's actually Jake McCallister standing in front of me and not a hallucination. My heart does this fierce smash and rebound against my ribs as though it's been violently woken from hibernation. I draw in a breath so big it feels like my lungs might explode, as if all that air is filling a vacuum and I'll never be able to let it out again.

I hate this feeling. Hate the way the adrenaline floods my bloodstream and tears sting my eyes. Hate the way my body reacts in a thousand contradictory ways at the sight of him, as though someone has plugged me into the wrong socket and fried all my synapses.

I have an impulse to throw myself at him, but I'm not sure if it's because I want to hug him or beat the living crap out of him. I drop the kayak, my hands fisting automatically at my sides.

I watch the smile on his lips fade when he notices the set of my jaw. His expression started off wary, but now I see him swallow and press his lips together, something he always does when he's nervous.

I take note of that and at the same time notice a dozen other tiny, insignificant, monumental details about this new old Jake. I see the faded white scar on his chin—the one I gave him—and the new scar cutting across his eyebrow. Then there's his height—we were always the same height, but now he's tall . . . much taller than me. His dark brown hair is the same, though—unruly, untamed, falling in his eyes. He's looking at me with the same mix of uncertainty that he looked at me the very last time I saw him.

I glance away, down at the sand. My whole body is shaking, and I can't seem to get it under control.

"Em?" I hear him say.

My head flies up before I can stop it. No one calls me that anymore. His voice is deeper, mellower. The inflection, though, when he says my name is still just the same . . . and instantly something inside me starts coming undone. Jake always used to say my name like it belonged to him, and only him.

I grind my teeth, steeling myself, and grab for the kayak and paddle, realizing only then that I'm wearing just my wet bikini, which I've stripped to my waist. The arms are flapping freely against my legs and my bikini top is gritty with sand and sweat. My hair is plastered to my head, clinging in wet strands to my neck. Great. Just great. So many times I've imagined what I would look like, what I would say, how I would act if I ever met Jake McCallister again, and the universe does this to me.

Without looking at him, I start dragging the kayak up the beach, the blood pounding in my temples almost drowning out his renewed offer of help.

I push on past him, but as I do the end of my paddle smacks him hard in the stomach. He grunts and stumbles back a few steps, hands pressed to his abs. I trudge up the beach, suppressing a smile, feeling his eyes burning into my back.

As I shove the kayak into its rack and ram the chain through the loop to lock it up, I'm aware of him watching me, the same way he used to watch his opponents on the ice, trying to figure out their play. Well, good luck with that, I think to myself. There's no way he's playing me.

I don't know what Jake's doing back in Bainbridge after all these years, but I do know that I am not going to let him ruin my life for a second time.

Jake

Shit. That went well.

I watch Em slam the padlock shut on the rack of kayaks and then shoulder open the door to the store. It slams behind her, rattling the glass, and I wince, rubbing my stomach where Em hit me with the paddle. Was that deliberate? No. If it were deliberate, she would have smacked me around the head with it.

I want to move. I want to follow her. But I don't. I head down to the water instead and stand staring out across the bay. What was I thinking? Coming here. Turning up out of the blue. What did I expect? For her to be happy to see me? Yeah. I laugh ruefully to myself. I guess that's what I had hoped for, deep down, but not what I had expected. I always knew it wasn't going to be that easy.

Damn. I reach for the oar she left by the shore and pick it up, still feeling a little winded.

So much time I've spent thinking about what her reaction would be to me, and I never once stopped to think about what my reaction would be to her.

But there it is. All those years between us are a chasm that probably can't be bridged. And there's a mountain of lies and pain and hurt that might be impossible to climb. But the fact remains that Emerson Lowe is still the only girl who's ever taken my breath away.

Emerson

'm shaking so hard I can't get my wet suit off. After a few attempts, I lean forward over the sink and take in a few deep breaths. Why is he here? What does he want?

There's a knock on the door, and I startle.

"You okay in there?" Toby yells.

"Fine. I'm fine," I tell him, glancing up and seeing my reflection in the mirror. I'm lying. I'm so far from fine. I look like I've seen a ghost. Which in a way I have.

"Okay," Toby says, and I can hear the deep note of skepticism in his voice. "Does it have anything to do with that hottie you were just talking to on the beach?"

"No," I say too fast, too loudly.

I hear a chuckle from Toby. "Did he want a seal-watching tour of the harbor? Because, you know, I'd be more than happy to oblige if you're too busy."

I roll my eyes and start trying to peel off my wet suit again. "No," I shout through the door. "He was just lost. Wanted some directions."

I am not going into details with Toby. He's about the only person on the whole island who doesn't know anything about my past, and that's the way I plan on keeping it.

"I'm going to take a shower," I say, wrestling off my wet suit.

Jake

The store is pretty much how I remember it. Walking over the threshold feels a bit like taking a ride in the Delorean and hurtling back ten years into the past.

Em's family has owned this place since before she was born. Her parents used to be in business with my uncle, though now it's just them who run it. Em and I used to hang out here a lot when we were kids. I glance at the counter, where the Chupa Chup stand still sits like a balding porcupine. Her dad would turn a blind eye to our shoplifting every time we came in.

I smile despite myself and look around, feeling a jolt of nostalgia and a wave of sadness wash over me. It's as if I can sense the ghost of my ten-year-old self in here chasing Em into the stockroom waving a fistful of seaweed in my hand, can hear the echoes of her screams, our laughter.

Kayaks are propped against the far wall, and I notice that now the store is also renting and selling paddleboards, skateboards, and even skates. I walk over to the rack of Rollerblades and smile. I wonder if she still plays ice hockey? Emerson Lowe was the fiercest player on the Bainbridge Eagles team. She could have played at the state, maybe even the national level. It's just one of the many questions I want to ask her. Along with Can you ever forgive me?

Even the smell in here is familiar—board wax and musty, damp wet suits. I close my eyes for a moment and take a deep breath. Other memories flash through my mind, things I haven't thought about in years: Em's mom yelling at us when we took a kayak into the bay and almost got pulled out to sea, an argument over who got the last cola-flavored Chupa Chup that left me with the scar on my chin.

"Can I help you?"

I turn around. There's a guy in a LOWE KAYAKING CO. T-shirt standing in front of me. He's about my age, maybe a little older. Midtwenties at most. Tall, blond, athletic. I try to place him but I can't. His name tag says Toby, and I don't remember any Tobys at school with us. Maybe he's not from around here. I've been gone seven years; who knows who's moved here in that time?

"You want to try those on?" he asks.

I frown and then realize I'm running my hand over a pair of skates. "No," I say. "I'm good. I was just looking for Em." As soon as I say it, I regret it. What am I doing? I should walk away, regroup, figure out a better approach.

Toby's eyebrow lifts and a sudden thought strikes me. What if this guy's her boyfriend? I've often wondered whether Emerson was dating anyone. I had heard rumors a couple of years back but had dismissed them, not wanting to think about it. I stopped asking people for news about her when it became too painful to hear the answers.

The guy crosses his arms over his chest and tips his head toward the storeroom door. "She'll be out in a minute," he says.

I nod and start flicking idly through a rack of T-shirts, glancing surreptitiously over my shoulder at the storeroom. Should I just leave? Why am I still here?

"You on vacation?" Toby asks.

"Yeah, kind of," I mumble. "Actually, I used to live here."

"So you know Emerson, then?" he asks.

"Yeah," I admit, nodding. "Since she was born."

He appraises me with narrowed eyes and I think I see a sudden flicker of recognition cross his face. He opens his mouth to ask me another question, but I quickly sidestep him and head toward the storeroom. I'll knock, walk in there, and get everything out into the open.

"Wait, I'm not sure . . . ," Toby calls after me.

Emerson

The door flies open just as I'm stripping out of my bikini and stepping into the shower. I let out a scream.

"Shit. Sorry. Sorry." Jake turns away, spinning on his heel, flustered.

I grab for my towel. "Get out!" I yell.

"I thought it was the storeroom. It used to be the storeroom," he says through scrunched-up eyes, searching for the door handle. Behind him I can see Toby with his jaw on the floor.

"Get out!" I shout again, kicking the door shut in their faces.

I turn off the shower and sink to the floor, wedging my back firmly against the door. There's silence on the other side of it. Is he waiting for me to come out? If he is, he's going to be waiting a long time. I'm not leaving here until he's gone. If that means staying in here until next Tuesday, I will.

I lean my head back and close my eyes. Instantly, and annoyingly, Jake's face flashes in front of me. Not this new Jake. But the Jake he was back then. The Jake who was, once upon a time, my best friend.

After a while—God knows how long—there's a timid knock

on the door. My eyes fly open. I'm still sitting on the floor of the bathroom in my sandy bikini.

"Emerson?"

It's Toby. I slump back with relief. At least I think it's relief. "Yes?" I ask tentatively.

"You can come out now. He's gone."

I take that in and then laugh bitterly under my breath. Of course Jake's gone. That's his MO. He gives you the surprise of your life, tips your world upside down, and then disappears without explanation.